To Q
Who met Caitlin Priest on
screen earlier than almost anyone
else!

THE GOOD GIRLS
SEASON FOUR OF RILEY PARRA

Geonn Cannon

Supposed Crimes LLC • Matthews, North Carolina

All Rights Reserved
Copyright © 2012, 2021 Geonn Cannon

Published in the United States.

ISBN: 978-1-944591-95-3

www.supposedcrimes.com

This book is typeset in Goudy Old Style.

TABLE OF CONTENTS

THE PROBLEM WITH SAINTS

Ten weeks after the war ended, the reinforcements arrived.

Though the war was officially undeclared, and most people hadn't noticed it as it was waged in their front yards, they still noticed when it ended. The sun seemed to penetrate deeper into the shadows and the night didn't seem quite so dark. There was a sense of hopefulness that was simply present one day without warning. Even people in No Man's Land were friendlier and more ready to smile.

For those who'd been aware of the war, they could pinpoint the exact moment the tonal atmosphere of the city changed. It happened the day Gail Finney, the champion for evil, plummeted to her death from an elevated train platform. Her mentor, a demon called Gremory, had also been destroyed. Marchosias, the demon who ruled over the blighted city, lost both his champion and his most trusted lieutenant in one fell swoop.

Detective Riley Parra, Gail Finney's counterpart on the side of the angels, chose to allow Marchosias to choose a new champion and continue the war. Following that decision was one of the most peculiar months in the city's history. People went about their lives, babies were born and old people died. But when pressed for details about what occurred during that period, people only gave vague and noncommittal answers.

Only a handful of people knew the truth. After Gail Finney's death, Riley ended the war between good and evil at a great personal cost. She gave up her partner, the love of her life, in exchange for peace. When the cost became too much to bear, Marchosias offered to shift reality. He rewrote a single moment, allowed Riley to say yes instead of no, and the entire world changed.

For the most part, things remained the same. People went about their lives under an unseen détente rather than true peace. It wasn't a seismic shift, but it was enough to make people a little uneasy. Memories weren't to be trusted, and everything just seemed slightly off-center. One newspaper article compared it to "feeling like Monday when it's really Wednesday." Some younger people compared it to how they felt while playing hooky.

Eventually the feeling faded, and people put aside the unusual feelings. No one expected an explanation for why they felt so odd about those first five weeks; they simply took it as one of life's oddities and carried on. Ten full weeks passed without Marchosias enlisting a new champion for evil. Ten weeks of quiet, if not true peace.

It was this silence that drew the Good Girls to the city.

They arrived at night, their pristine white gowns just long enough to cover their feet but not so much that they dragged on the pavement. Three of them walked together down McKinley Avenue, one slightly in the lead of the other two. Their hoods were down to reveal the wavy black hair of the leader, and the shorter red and blonde curls of her handmaidens. The leader stopped at the corner and turned to speak to her companions.

Before she could say anything, her attention was grabbed by movement further down the street. The four youths had been following them for blocks, but now they seemed ready to make their move. The blonde handmaiden glanced at her mistress.

"Are you certain, Aissa?" the Mother whispered.

"It is my duty, Paladin."

The Mother cupped Aissa's cheek, then gathered the redheaded handmaiden under her arm and stepped off the street. Aissa turned and walked toward the four men, who spread out and moved to surround her. Aissa was smaller than even the runt of their group, her cherubic face framed by dirty blonde curls. Her eyebrows were thick and dark, and her eyes were pale green underneath them. She loosened the string at her collar, loosening her hood as she addressed the boy who seemed to be the leader of their group.

"Leave us be."

The boy couldn't have been more than twenty, but he carried

himself like someone twice his age. Considering what he'd probably experienced on the streets of No Man's Land, he might as well have been that old. He stopped and looked at his friends, then smiled at her.

"You think we're going to just leave you alone because you asked us nicely?"

"It's my fervent hope that you will."

One of the boys to her right snickered and the leader stepped closer. "Yeah? Well, maybe we can compromise. You give us what we want, and we won't be forced to take it."

"We have no money."

He leaned in, and the smell of his smoke drifted into her face. She wrinkled her nose in distaste. "We aren't talking about money, darling." His gaze lowered to her chest. He reached out and tugged on the material of her robe so he could better see the curve of her breasts. "Yeah, I think you got plenty to keep me satisfied."

"What's your name?"

One of the kids laughed. "She wants to know what to yell out, Lukey."

"Lukey?" Aissa said. "I presume it's Luke?"

The leader chuckled and dipped his chin. "At your service, pretty lady."

"I'm sorry, Luke."

His lips moved to form the words "for what," but before he could speak, his windpipe was crushed by a sharp jab from the side of Aissa's left hand. As he gagged she twisted, pulling up her gown just enough to free her right leg for a kick. The boy rushing her from behind slammed into her foot. Her knee bent and she pushed away, sending him toppling. She stepped back, pressing against Luke as the two boys to her left and right collided in the space she had just occupied. Aissa reached over her head, grabbed Luke's ears, and dropped into a crouch as she pulled him forward. Her back provided the fulcrum, and he hit the pavement in front of her with enough force to make him cough up blood.

One boy produced a knife. Aissa clamped her hand around his wrist and flicked it backward. The bones snapped and the boy went down to his knees with a cry of pain. Aissa took his knife and threw it. She heard the grunt of the boy who received its blade, but she didn't turn to see which of them it was.

She released the broken wrist of the boy with the knife and pushed him away from her. He rolled onto his stomach and scrambled to his feet before he ran away with his arm cradled to his stomach. The last member of the gang, injured only by his collision with his friend, tried to run but Aissa swept her leg under his feet and he fell forward onto the pavement. He was sobbing when she hauled him back up.

"Your kind should get accustomed to seeing us around. The Good Girls are not to be assaulted or otherwise molested by your kind. Am I understood?"

"The Good...?"

"Us, child." Aissa didn't turn at the sound of her Mother's voice, and her grip on the hoodlum didn't relax. "Those in our order are not to be disturbed. You will know us by our manner and the style of our dress. Can you be entrusted with this message, or shall we wait for someone with a bit more sense?"

The kid swallowed hard and nodded. "Yeah. I'll spread the word."

"Run," Paladin said. Aissa let him go, and the kid stumbled before he got his feet back under him. As eager as he was to put distance between himself and the seemingly crazy women, he was quickly swallowed by shadows. Aissa looked over her shoulder in time to see her Sister slipping the bloody knife into the chest of the second gang member. Her actions were different from Aissa's; what she was doing was a mercy.

Aissa smoothed the material of her gown over her stomach in an attempt to still the shaking in her hands, her head bowed so she didn't have to meet the Mother's gaze until she was ready. Finally, the Mother touched her cheek and Aissa looked up at her.

"You know what must happen now."

A tear rolled down Aissa's cheek. "Yes."

The redhead joined them on the sidewalk. Her hands were bloody from dispatching the gang members. She looked at the Mother, who nodded. Aissa watched as the blood was smeared on the previously unmarred white material of her gown. A sob caught in her throat and she pushed it back down before it could break free. Once her Sister's hands were as clean as they could get without soap and water, the Mother loosened the tie at Aissa's throat, while the Sister removed her belt.

Aissa lifted her arms, and the robe was pulled from her. She was left with just a thin cilice undershirt with wooden buttons that ran down the center of her chest and baggy trousers. The Mother folded the soiled robe so that the blood was on the inside so it wouldn't drip or mar her own gown. She stroked Aissa's hair and tucked the curls behind her ear.

"You were very brave tonight, Daughter."

"Brave," her Sister said. "Fearless in the face of the cause." She cupped Aissa's face and lightly kissed her lips. The Mother did the same. Aissa was now crying openly but silently.

The Mother said, "You have one final task to perform for the Girls."

Aissa nodded. "I will do it immediately."

"Farewell, Aissa."

Aissa's sister squeezed her hand as the Mother guided her away. Aissa crossed her arms over her chest as she watched them go. The glaring white of their gowns kept them visible much longer than otherwise possible, but soon even they had faded. Aissa allowed herself a single vocal sob, then brought her arms up to brush the tears off her cheeks with her wrists. Alone, feeling completely naked, she curled her toes in her shapeless shoes and began to walk. Her tears dried as she walked, her mind focused on what she had to do now.

The task she was faced with was an enormous honor, and she wouldn't let it be overshadowed by the fact she had just been evicted from the only family she had ever known in order to deliver a message.

"Someone is knocking on your door."

Riley shifted in bed, her lips twisting unattractively against the shoulder of Gillian's nightshirt. Their legs were tangled under the blankets, and Riley was barely awake, but she could hear the polite but insistent knocking on the apartment's front door.

"Wuzzit mahdoor?"

Gillian, who was just as exhausted but had been awake a few seconds longer, was more coherent. She slid her left hand under her right arm and stroked Riley's arm where it was draped over her. "It's your door right now because people don't come to the medical examiner with emergencies. They have the decency to call when they want me to look at a dead body."

"'m sleeping with my wife," Riley murmured, burrowing her face into Gillian's hair.

"Okay. Then I'll go answer the door in the middle of the night. Wish me luck, hope it's not a criminal."

"Criminals don't knock."

Gillian kicked away the blankets, but Riley stopped her.

"Don't even think about it." She sat up and kept her hand on Gillian's shoulder until she was sure she wouldn't try to get up.

Gillian pulled the blanket up over her stomach. "It's probably just Priest or Kenzie."

"Probably." Riley took her gun out of the nightstand. "Stay here just in case."

She didn't bother dressing before she left the bedroom. Dressed in panties and a tank top, her hair a mess, she figured she could get off a few rounds before they were able to attack. She left the light off and stood to the side of the peephole as the unexpected guest knocked again. There was a light in the hallway, and she could see the shadows of the person's feet standing dead-center in front of the door.

"Who is it?"

"Detective Riley Parra? My name is Aissa Good. It has fallen unto my lot to inform you of a new power that has arrived in your town. As the champion for good, you must be told of our presence."

Riley considered for a moment before she relaxed. "Are you armed?"

"I've been trained in lethal combat, so I am always armed. But on my honor, I would never hurt you or your loved ones."

Riley kept her gun at her side as she stepped away from the wall. She turned the locks and opened the door wide enough to see the girl. She looked young, somewhere in her mid-twenties at a guess. She wore an outfit thin and skimpy enough to count as pajamas, if that, and her bottom lip was trembling from the cold. Riley put aside any remaining concerns and stepped back. She turned on the overhead light and called for Gillian to bring a robe.

The front door opened into the living room, and Riley pointed the girl toward the couch. "What did you say your name was? Ee-sa?"

"Aye-sah. Aissa Good. But you can call me Aissa."

Gillian came out of the bedroom in her robe, carrying two others. She handed one to Riley and offered the other to their new arrival.

"This is Aissa," Riley said. "She has information about a new power in town."

"Oh, God. Did Marchosias pick someone?"

"No, not yet." Aissa twisted and looked over the back of the couch to the kitchen. "May I have something to drink?"

Gillian nodded. "Water or juice?"

"I would appreciate a glass of ice water if it's not inconvenient."

"Ice water." She smirked at Riley as she started toward the kitchen. "I think I can manage that."

Riley remained standing, her arms crossed as Gillian went into the kitchen. "So what is this power I need to be warned about?"

"Not warned. They're on your side. First, however, you may wish to call your constables." She furrowed her brow and considered the word before she corrected herself. "Policemen. There are two dead bodies awaiting discovery on McKinley Avenue. It would be best if you were the investigating officer."

Gillian glanced at Riley as she came back with the water. "Here you are."

"Thank you, Dr. Hunt. It's an honor to be in your home, and I apologize for disturbing your slumber."

"It's okay." She smoothed her hands over her robe. "Why should Riley be the one to investigate these murders?"

Aissa drank half the glass and then touched a finger to her lips. "This is very cold."

"It's from the fridge. Is that okay?"

"It's marvelous. Just unexpected." She passed her tongue over her lips and looked at Riley. "I wish for you to investigate because I am responsible. I killed them."

Riley cleared her throat. "So this new power that's in town... it's you?"

Aissa averted her gaze. "I was part of it, yes. But I have been exiled. My hands were sullied by the deaths, and I was no longer pure in their eyes. I am no longer part of the Family. But because of that, I am free to come and speak to you. We are the Good Girls. Our fellowship was founded to aide those chosen as the champion for good whenever possible. We have been praying for you since you received your tattoo."

"Nice to know I'm not the only one." Gillian touched Riley's shoulder, her hand sliding back to cover the tattoo currently hidden by Riley's robe.

Aissa smiled. "We felt when your prayers were added to our own, Dr. Hunt. They were powerful... equal to the prayers of ten Sisters."

Riley smiled at Gillian. "Only ten?"

"With the fall of Gail Finney and Marchosias' unprecedented delay in choosing a replacement, we had the ability to do something we've never before had the opportunity to do. A group of us have traveled from our enclave to bring our prayers directly to the source. We will stand at the front lines between the city of light and what you call No Man's Land and pray. Given enough time, I feel we can push back the limits until the tide retreats."

Gillian moved to the armchair and lowered herself gently into it. "Can you do that? Push back No Man's Land like that?"

Aissa nodded. "It won't be easy. And if Gail Finney had a replacement, she could simply counter our attacks with prayers of her own. Detective Parra is standing alone for the moment. The balance of power can be dramatically shifted before the war begins anew."

"And the demons will just let you do this?" Riley didn't quite share Gillian's wide-eyed wonder, but she had hope. "You'll be in terrible danger."

Aissa smiled. "When our Family is not praying, we are in training. We are well aware that the war against demons will often require some physical confrontation. And with that, I am forced to remind you of my predicament. Should one of your fellow homicide detectives find the bodies I left behind, they will waste much time fruitlessly searching for the killer. I wish to surrender myself to you to protect their resources."

Riley coughed into her hand and glanced at Gillian. "That's fine, but you'll have to surrender yourself to my partner. If you know Gillian, you must know~"

"Zerachiel, Caitlin Priest. Yes." Her brow was furrowed. "Why can't you take the case?"

"Because I'm not exactly a homicide detective anymore."

Aissa's eyes widened and she looked at Riley's gun. "What? You are still a police officer, aren't you?"

"Yeah. In the traffic division."

"That's not possible."

Riley smiled without humor. "That's what I told my boss. Apparently it's definitely possible. Probable, even."

Aissa seemed shattered by this news. "H-how?"

"Punishment. How much do you know about the way the war ended?"

"More than most, I think."

Riley sat on the arm of Gillian's chair. Gillian slid forward and put her arm around Riley's waist. "When Gail Finney died, Marchosias offered me the choice of ending the war or allowing him to pick a new champion so the war could continue. If I chose to end the war, it meant I would have to sacrifice the thing I loved more than anything else in the world." Her finger began toying with the ring on her left hand. "I thought it was win-win. The war would be over, and Gillian would be safe. So I said yes. I lived without her for five weeks. I nearly lobotomized myself to keep the pain away. Eventually, I couldn't stand it anymore and Marchosias made me an offer. He let me change my answer, and the war... started up again."

"For the love of a woman."

Aissa's tone was unreadable, but Riley assumed she disapproved. Her gaze could have broken glass. "I made the right decision."

Aissa nodded. "Yes. You did. You chose love, Detective Parra. That can never be the wrong choice." She took another drink of her water and then put the glass on the coffee table. "But how does that affect your job?"

"Marchosias just sort of wrote over reality. He couldn't change things too much without rewriting a history in which people had memories of things they never did. He had to stick as close to the real world as possible. After I ended the war, I left town in an attempt to get Gillian out of my mind. In the revised version, I just... skipped town. I didn't show up to work for five weeks. No notice, no anything. My boss was pissed off. I'm lucky to still have my badge. But she decided to reassign me to Traffic for six months as punishment. It could have been a lot worse."

"I suppose." Aissa pressed her palms together and laced her fingers together. After what seemed like a moment of intense thought, she nodded once and sat up straighter. "I still wish to surrender myself to you, and only you. Please, call Caitlin Priest and inform her of the bodies on McKinley Avenue. I will tell her how to find them."

Riley looked at Gillian, who nodded. "Go."

"All right. What the hell? It'll be more fun that writing parking citations all day." She stood up. "I'll get dressed and then call Priest."

She went into the bedroom and turned on the bedside lamp, sitting on her side of the bed for a moment as she considered what Aissa had told her. She looked at her gun, set it on the nightstand, and picked up her phone to dial Priest's number.

The bedroom was aglow. The windows were equipped with special blackout shades to prevent the neighbors from complaining as they had in the past. Pale golden light seeped under the closed bedroom door, illuminating everything so brightly and from every direction so there wasn't opportunity for a shadow. The orb of light was centered over the bed, a small and shifting sun that spun slowly on its axis before tilting to a different angle. It hovered, rising slowly before it moved back toward the bed.

The phone rang.

First an arm appeared and then, as if being birthed from the light itself, a body took shape. Caitlin Priest flattened her palms against the mattress, eyes screwed tightly shut against the now-fading light. She dropped onto her hands and knees, her rear end in the air as Sariel pulled away from and out of her. Their human forms were drenched with sweat, and the muscles of Priest's arms and legs twitched and throbbed as she struggled to catch her breath.

Sariel tucked her knees against her chest as Priest stretched out on her stomach beside her. She pushed her bangs back off her forehead, the sweat making the hair stick up at odd angles, and she groped for the phone. She wet her lips but her voice was still strangled as she answered the call.

"Hello... Riley." She propped herself up on her elbows. "Yes. I was making love to Sariel." A crease appeared between her eyebrows. "Then why did you ask if you were interrupting anyth~ Oh. I'm sorry." She reached out with her free hand and stroked Sariel's bare back. "What do you need? Yes, I know it. I'll be there as soon as possible." She flipped the phone closed and shifted on the mattress. She covered Sariel's body with her own and their skin began to glow.

"You have to leave," Sariel said.

"Yes." Priest's wings appeared, furled against her body. Sariel rolled over and extended her own wings. The light they produced was enough to read by. "We'll continue this when I get home?"

Sariel nodded and lightly kissed Priest's lips. Their light grew, and Priest extended her wings to wrap around both of them.

She decided five minutes later would still count for 'as soon as possible.'

Riley was waiting on the corner when Priest arrived at the crime scene. She noticed that Priest's hair was wet, and the top button of her shirt was undone. She wasn't wearing a vest or tie, and Riley smiled at the angel's relatively disheveled appearance. "Sorry to yank you out of bed, Cait."

"I wasn't in bed. I mean... I... told you I was."

Riley raised an eyebrow and motioned toward the bodies. They walked over together. "You okay?"

Priest shuddered and nodded. "Yes. I'm not certain I'm cut out for a true relationship. It's exhausting."

"Well, stick with it. The end results are worth the trouble." They arrived at the bodies. "Gillian went in to get an assistant, and she'll be here shortly in an official capacity. For now, we get to look at a couple of gang members who were taken apart by a little girl."

The bodies were piled together in the darkness of an alley. Priest took out her flashlight and shined it onto them. She saw a knife sticking out of one's chest, and the other seemed to have been taken out by brute force.

"How little was this girl?"

"Bigger than she seemed, apparently. What do you know about the Good Girls?"

Priest spun to face Riley. "How do you know about the Good Girls?"

Riley had spotted one while waiting for Priest to arrive. She stepped into the street and pointed to a neighboring roof. A woman in a white robe was standing near the edge, her face obscured by a hood pulled low over her eyes. Her hands were folded in prayer. Priest's eyes widened at the sight of her.

"So are they on our side?"

"Very much so. Riley, if one of them did this, then she's been exiled. She's wandering the city, alone and frightened~"

"She's safe. She showed up at our apartment this morning. She said it was her duty to inform me that they were here."

Priest relaxed. "Of course."

"Before this place is crawling with cops, why don't you tell me what you know?"

Priest sighed and began to pace. "In the sixteenth century, a woman and her three daughters traveled to a remote outpost in the Himalayas. No one knows where exactly, not even angels. They built a modest home and began to pray for the champions of the world. Over the years, the daughters would go out into the world and recruit more acolytes. Women began to volunteer, praying until one of the Good Girls came to retrieve them."

"Wait. How do the Good Girls know about the women praying for them? If angels don't know where the Good Girls are, how~"

"I don't know, Riley. But I know they take vows of chastity and poverty, they fast and give themselves wholly over to their cause.

The Good Girls are the closest to being divine that a mortal can hope to be."

Riley took Priest's flashlight and shined it onto the bodies. "So how did Mother Teresa manage to do that?"

"The correct term, if it was a younger girl, would be Daughter or Sister Teresa. The Good Girls train for the possibility of being sent out into the world. If one of them sullies herself through violence, she is exiled from the Family."

"How big is the Family?" Riley answered her own question. "You don't know."

"It's large enough to have sects. There was the Grand-Mother, and her original Daughters acted as her inner circle. When the original women who founded the Good Girls died, they were replaced by their Daughters. Each member of the inner circle commands her own sect, and each sect is made up of soldiers who refer to each other as Sister." She looked at the woman on the roof again. "And now they are here. I wonder how many of them have come."

"Right now, all I'm concerned about is the one sleeping on our couch." She turned as she was caught in the headlights of the OCME van. She waved to the driver and stepped to one side as the van rolled to a stop. Gillian climbed out, wearing her horn-rimmed glasses instead of contacts. She nodded hello to Priest and smiled at Riley.

Riley said, "You were right. I did have the decency to call."

Gillian laughed. "And I thank you kindly. Point me to the bodies, please?"

Riley escorted her to the bodies. "Priest called it in to Lieutenant Briggs. I'll go in with her and explain the Good Girl situation."

"Good luck with that."

"Yeah. How was Aissa?"

"Sleeping when I left. She was out as soon as she hit the pillow." She glanced over her shoulder to make sure Priest was hanging back. "How long do you think she'll be staying?"

"Jealous?"

Gillian scoffed. "No, just making sure we didn't get Priest to move out just to replace her with another nun in the guest room."

Riley chuckled and rubbed Gillian's arm. "I don't think she'll be sticking around long. I don't know where exactly she'll go, but... I didn't see her as the houseguest type." She looked at the bodies.

"What do you think?"

Gillian pointed at the knife in the first boy's chest. "I'd say this one was stabbed." She looked closer. "Hm."

"Was that an interesting 'hm'?"

She used her pinkie to indicate the wound. "The knife entered his body with some force, then it looks as if it was taken out and put back in carefully."

Riley wrinkled her nose. "Why?"

"I'm assuming he was killed first, and then the knife was used to dispatch the other boy." She looked back at Riley. "That girl sitting on our couch saying 'please' and 'thank you' did this to them?"

"Maybe please and thank you didn't work out here in No Man's Land. Be glad you were quick with her water." Gillian smiled and Riley bent down to kiss the top of her head. "I'll see you at the morgue."

"Who says we're not romantic?" She waved goodbye, and Riley stepped aside to let Gillian's assistant take her place. She met up with Priest and they walked back to their cars. "You want to be in the office when I talk to Briggs about all this? You could help fill in some of the blanks on the Good Girls."

"Of course. I'll call Sariel and make sure she knows about their presence as well."

Riley nodded.

"Are you going to be okay? Have you even seen Lieutenant Briggs since she sent you to traffic?"

"Nope. I'm not expecting a happy reunion, either."

Lieutenant Zoe Briggs looked like she was operating on no sleep at all. Her hair was sloppy, she wore no makeup, and instead of a business suit she was dressed in an Academy sweatshirt and jeans. When Riley was finished speaking, Briggs sighed and lowered herself into her seat. She rubbed her eyes and then sagged backward in her seat.

"Nicely done, Detective Parra."

Riley glanced at Priest. "Ma'am?"

"The way you managed to summarize your activities at this... *very* early hour... without once using the phrase 'murderous religious cult.' That is what we're dealing with here, right? When they're not praying, they're training to use their bodies as deadly weapons. Within an hour of arriving in town, we have two dead bodies attributed to them. What else would you call them?"

"Soldiers," Priest said.

Riley coughed into her fist. "Not helping."

Briggs raised an eyebrow and then looked at Priest. "A certain element in No Man's Land is going to see these Good Girls as targets no matter what message they put out. People are going to see apparently defenseless women standing on street corners, and they'll do what they do when they think a woman is defenseless. If their skills aren't what you claim, then they'll be killed. But if these women really are killing machines, we'll still end up with a dead body or two on our hands. And their presence is really supposed to make our lives easier?"

"Well..."

"And Detective Parra... you were involved because the bodies were found on the street, is that it? That's traffic's interest in this case?"

Riley clenched her jaw. "The girl came to me. I handed it over to Priest, but I thought~"

Briggs cut Riley off with a wave of her hand. "Heaven. Angels. Champion. It's always the same excuse with you, Riley, so why don't you save it? Priest, step outside, please."

Priest glanced at Riley.

"Don't look at her for permission. I am your superior officer and I've asked you to step outside my office."

"Sorry, boss." Priest left.

Riley raised her eyebrows once they were alone. "Wow. You are really not a morning person."

"Save it, Riley. How have you enjoyed traffic?"

"It sucks."

"Five months to go. And when that's done, I can make a request to have it made permanent. They're always undermanned, so they'll be happy to have you. Or I could reassign you to homicide right now, tonight, and let you work this case with Priest."

Riley shrugged. "That would be great, boss."

"In exchange for you forgetting my ties to the Hyde family. You've held it over my head long enough. I think I've been more than fair, but now the ball is in my court. You want back in, it's going to cost you. If not... I'd rather have you in traffic where I don't have to deal with you anymore. Make your decision."

"What's going on?"

Briggs winced and looked away. "Make your decision, Detective

Parra."

"You know my answer, boss. I'll tell Priest she has her partner back." She went to the door and stopped with her hand on the knob. "And I'll be here. Right out there. When you're ready to talk about whatever... prompted this."

Briggs turned away and pretended to go through the files behind her desk. "Get out of my office, Riley."

Riley left and found Priest leaning against the wall next to the door. She straightened. "What happened? Why is Briggs acting so peculiar?"

"That's a problem for another day. Right now, I'm back."

"You're back? Permanently?"

Riley nodded. "Yep. I had a little bit of knowledge that finally paid dividends. Gillian won't have anything for us yet, so let's go home. I'll introduce you to Aissa."

The girl was swaddled in blankets on the couch, leaving only the top of her head visible. Riley left the overhead light off and turned on the lamp. "Aissa?"

She immediately came awake, sitting up and shrugging both shoulders to free her arms. She looked at Riley, twisted to address the other person in the room, and relaxed only when she recognized they were unarmed. Her gaze lingered on Priest. "Who is this?"

"I'm Caitlin Priest~"

"The angel Zerachiel." Aissa freed herself from the blankets and stood with fluid grace that made it hard to believe she had just been asleep. She dropped to one knee and bowed her head. "It's an honor to be in your presence."

"Um. Okay." She glanced at Riley, waiting for Aissa to stand. When she stayed down, she said, "Please stand up."

Aissa did as she was told and smoothed down the blouse of the pajamas she'd borrowed from Gillian. It was just slightly too big for her, but it was baggy enough that her hands were swallowed by the sleeves. She looked at Riley. "Did you find the bodies?"

"Yeah. And I'm back in homicide."

"So I can officially surrender myself to your custody."

Riley nodded. "Right. Are you prepared for what's going to happen?"

Aissa glanced at Priest. "What's going to happen?"

"You'll confess what you did, and you'll claim self-defense. Considering the neighborhood you were in and the record I'm sure those boys have, there won't be any doubt you're telling the truth. We'll have to hold you until Gillian reaches her determination, but I don't think any judge will deny you were acting to protect yourself. It won't go to trial."

"But I'll have to spend time in prison."

"You'll be held at the station. It's jail, which is different than prison. You'll be safe." Her cell phone buzzed and Riley checked the message. "It's Gillian. She has something."

Priest said, "That was quick."

"I guess having the killer in your apartment borrowing your pajamas saves a bit of time. Aissa, you should get dressed. Gillian might have some smaller outfits that won't look so baggy on you. Go into the back and get dressed, and we'll go downtown together."

Aissa nodded and left the room. Riley watched her go and turned to Priest. "So what happens to her now?"

"You know the law better than I do."

"No, she'll be fine. No judge in this town, no matter how corrupt, will send a girl like that to prison for killing two gangbangers in No Man's Land. It'll be self-defense no matter what Gillian finds. I meant what happens a couple days from now when she's out of jail? I'm assuming the Good Girls won't just let her back in."

Priest shook her head. "No. Once she's been tarnished by inflicting violence to another person, she won't be welcome. She accepts that sacrifice; it's how they're brought up. She acted to save her Sisters, and she would do it again given the same opportunity. But she can never go back."

"So that's it? She's spent her entire life in this cult, and now she just gets turned out into the cold? How is she supposed to survive?"

"She'll find a way. The Good Girls are trained to protect themselves against adversity. Aissa knew this was a possibility when she left the safety of their enclave. She and the others who came with her will have prepared for this situation."

Riley sighed. "It just seems wrong that they would turn their backs on her. This Family is all she has. All she knows is prayer. What is a saint supposed to do when she's kicked out of her religion? Freelance prayer?"

Aissa returned in a T-shirt that still looked a size too big and a pair of Gillian's jeans with the cuffs rolled up. She held up her hands. "Should I be handcuffed? I was told criminals~"

"No, I don't think that'll be necessary." Riley turned off the lamp and put her hand on Aissa's shoulder. "Come on. Priest and I will be with you as much as we can throughout this whole thing. We'll get you through it without too much trauma."

"Thank you."

"No problem."

Riley guided Aissa out of the apartment and tried not to let on that she was more concerned about was going to happen to Aissa after the case was officially closed.

Gillian presented her initial findings to Briggs and Riley at the same time. The knife had several prints on it, including those of one victim. The handle of the weapon was inscribed with the initials of the boy who had ended up with it in his chest. Priest had run the names from their wallets through the system and discovered they all had lengthy records for assault, vandalism and robbery. Briggs asked to speak with Aissa alone, and Riley returned to her desk in the homicide squad room like a student returning after spring break.

She opened the drawers to make sure nothing had gone missing, threw away some snack foods that had fossilized in her absence, and leaned back in her chair. In traffic, her desk had faced a wall. Homicide had a much better view. She could see the day beginning outside, the day shift of detectives just starting to make their way in. The light coming through the windows was almost blinding, and Riley's internal clock was completely askew.

Priest put a cup of coffee down next to her and squeezed Riley's hand before she continued to her own desk. "It's good to see you back there, Riley."

"It's good to be back." She glanced toward Briggs' office. "I can't help thinking there's something I could do for her. Something I'm *supposed* to do. I mean, she's only in this situation because of me. And she dedicated her entire life to praying for me."

Priest shook her head. "That's not exactly true."

"You said the Good Girls~"

"Yes. They pray for the champion. Aissa is approximately twenty-five? So for the first years of her fellowship, she prayed for Christine Lee."

"Oh. Well, the point stands. For the past couple of years, she's been off in the Alps somewhere~"

"The Himalayas."

"~praying for me. I feel I owe it to her." The door to Briggs' office opened and Aissa came out with the lieutenant behind her.

Riley and Priest stood up. "Well?"

Briggs sighed. "The district attorney was up early, so we managed to get her on the phone. After reading the ME's report, she has decided not to pursue charges against Ms. Good."

Priest smiled. "That's great."

Aissa nodded and smiled tightly. "I'm fortunate things have gone so well for me. I feared the worst."

"There is the question of where you'll go now," Riley said. "Did your Mother or Sisters make any arrangements for places to live while they're in town? I mean, they have to sleep sometime."

"When they aren't praying, they find homeless shelters or bed down in alleys with the others protecting them." She looked between Priest, Riley and Briggs without settling on any of them in particular. "But if you're intending to force them into taking me back, please. Don't. It's not what I want. I knew what I was doing when I confronted those boys. I don't want back in. Had one of my Sisters been the one to fight and kill, I would not want her back in the Family. It's our way, Detective Parra. Don't feel that this is a wrong that needs to be corrected."

Riley stood up. "Well, I'm not going to just put you on the street with twenty bucks and cross my fingers." She looked at Briggs. "Am I free to take her?"

"Yes. Ms. Good, don't leave the city just in case there are any loose ends we need to tie up or if the families of the boys make a stink. But otherwise, you're free to go."

"Thank you, Lieutenant Briggs, for all of your help."

Briggs rolled her shoulders uncomfortably and looked at Riley. "Detective Parra. I apologize for being... brusque this morning."

"It's fine."

Briggs nodded sharply. "I appreciate it, but it's not." She looked at Priest, then Aissa. "I'm going home to change and maybe get an extra hour of sleep. Riley, you should do the same. You did good work today, and it's barely even breakfast. Welcome back."

Riley watched Briggs walk away, trying to sort out the lieutenant's mood swings. Sleep deprivation could be partially to blame but she felt it went deeper than that. She seemed weighed down by something.

"Riley?" She looked at Priest. "Were you, um~"

"Right. Come on, Aissa. There are some people I want to introduce you to."

They walked downstairs to the garage, and Riley waited until

Aissa was buckled in before she started the car.

The streets were more alive than an hour ago, with people heading to work or breakfast meetings. The sidewalks were crowded and the sun had found a niche between two buildings to shine down on the street as Riley turned north. Aissa folded her hands in her lap and watched the city pass out the window. She seemed hypnotized by the sun shining off the glass, and the scores of people on the street. Some of the larger vehicles they passed seemed to frighten her, and when they were stuck in traffic she would focus on the bells and whistles of the car.

"Have you ever been in a city like this before?"

Aissa nodded. "Paris. And I spent some time in Prague. They were different... we were in New York City for a day between flights, on our way here. I'm more accustomed to the small village near our home." She bit her lip and looked down at her hands.

"Realizing you'll never see it again?" Aissa nodded and Riley sighed. "This is a shitty way for them to repay you. You know that, right?"

"Repay me?" Aissa looked up. "I did what was necessary to protect my Family. Their safety is reward enough for me."

Riley shrugged. "So you sacrifice your entire life to save them, and they just wave and say adios? I'm sorry, but to me, that sounds epically cold."

"You don't understand our ways. There are always new members being welcomed into the Family. And by occasionally releasing some of the older members, we can spread our beliefs to the world at large. If we all stayed within the walls of our sanctuary, what good can we do? We would merely be preaching to the converted."

"But won't you miss your Mother and Sisters?"

Aissa smiled. "Very much so. And they will miss me. But such is life."

Riley decided she wasn't going to make much headway, so she stopped fighting. Priest's mention of Christine Lee reminded Riley of her own late-night encounter with a police officer. She had been a lot younger than Aissa, but Aissa was more naive than Riley had ever been. She considered that long-ago night when her life had been put on a different course, and her mind started putting together the pieces as she drove to their destination.

When they arrived at Morton Avenue, Riley parked across the street from the homeless shelter. "This place is run by Eddie

Cashion. He's an old friend of mine, and he's one of the good ones. You can trust me on that. I know he needs a hand around here, and if you're willing to do some work in exchange for a place to stay, he'll be happy to have you."

Aissa was looking at the homeless shelter with wide-eyed hope. "I could help people?"

"Yes. But it's also a safe place where you can learn the real dangers that exist here. You're in No Man's Land right now. You need to fully and realistically understand what that means. Eddie will do his part to educate you on that score while making sure no one hurts you."

"Thank you, Detective Parra." She smiled brightly. "I can't wait to get started."

Riley held up a finger. "There's one more thing I want you to think about..."

Aissa settled back in the seat and listened as Riley explained her other plan. As she spoke, Aissa's eyes widened and she slowly began to smile.

"I'm not going to take your answer right now. I'll let you see what life is like outside of the nunnery, and then I'll come back with an answer. I have to prepare some stuff myself, so it'll work out well. I'll see you here next Thursday. Deal?"

Aissa nodded eagerly. "Deal."

"Good. If you want to quit before the week is up, you know where to find me. I'll figure out something safer for you." She held out her hand, and Aissa clasped it with her own. "See you Thursday. If not before."

Aissa got out of the car and Riley watched her hurry across the street. She would wait to see if Eddie wanted to speak with her, and to make sure he was willing to take Aissa under his wing. As she waited she took out her cell phone and dialed Priest's number.

There were a couple of things she wanted to check on before she made an official commitment to her other plan of action.

A week later, Aissa arrived at Riley and Gillian's apartment just as dinner was ready. Aissa was more relaxed and calmer than on her first night in the city, and she wore clothes that actually fit her, culled from the donation bin at the shelter. She smiled when Riley answered the door, and she nodded once. "Yes. The answer is yes. I spent the entire week justifying my saying no, and it never sounded right. So yes, yes, thank you, yes."

Riley chuckled and stepped back. "Then come in. We'll eat first and then figure out what to do next."

Gillian greeted Aissa with a hug. The night before, she had confessed that she considered Aissa some sort of relative. They finally settled on 'younger cousin.' Priest arrived a few minutes after dinner had been served. They didn't talk about the reason they had all gathered, and used it as an excuse to get to know Aissa before they got down to business. Riley and Priest went into the living room with Aissa, while Gillian pointedly remained in the kitchen to do the dishes. She had told Riley the day before she didn't want to witness what was going to happen.

Two of the dining room chairs had been moved into the living room, with the coffee table moved out of the way. Riley had borrowed the necessary equipment from another person in the building, but Priest insisted Riley had to do the work herself. Riley and Aissa sat facing each other and Riley smoothed her hands over the thighs of her pants.

"I didn't have much of a choice, when I was sitting where you are. So I want to make sure you know what you're getting into."

Aissa smiled. "I spent my entire childhood being told of past champions. I looked up to them, and I thought they were the most amazing people in the world. But I also know what hardships they face." She looked toward the kitchen. "I know how difficult it can be on the ones they love. I've spent a week in No Man's Land, and I've seen how bad things are. I'm aware I probably haven't seen the worst of it. But if all my training hasn't been to become a Mother or a Paladin, then perhaps it can be put to use as a champion. At least I'll be connected to my Family, and I'll know they're praying for me."

Riley looked at Priest, who nodded. "Okay. Then, uh, all that's left is to give you the tattoo. Priest will mark it, and... you'll be my successor."

Aissa beamed. Riley remembered lying in Christine Lee's bed, post-coital and drowsy, when she'd felt her lover's soft touch on her back. *I'd like to tattoo you, Riley.* Christine died before she was able to tell Riley the whole story. She wasn't going to let the same thing happen to her successor.

Aissa took a folded piece of paper out of her pocket and held it out. Her fingers were shaking as Riley took it from her and looked at the painstakingly drawn image. At first she thought it was an oval with a pi symbol rising from the bottom curve, but then she recognized it as two Gs facing each other. She smiled. "Good Girls."

"Yes. Is that okay?"

"I think it's perfect. Just, um... turn around on the seat and lower your shirt off your shoulders."

Aissa turned and straddled the back of the chair. She unbuttoned her shirt just enough to get it off her shoulders, and she flipped her hair forward to expose the back of her neck. Riley had spent the week getting accustomed to the tattoo needle gun, practicing on deli meat until she felt confident she wouldn't screw it up. She had tattooed Gillian without any preparation and that had turned out beautifully. But she was still worried about doing something wrong. She cleared her throat and touched the back of Aissa's neck. "Here?"

"Yes, please," Aissa said softly.

Riley used a marker to sketch the design onto Aissa's freckled skin, which she would then follow with the needle. She kept her hand steady as she traced the narrow lines. When it was done and she couldn't delay any more, she glanced at Priest, and then wet her lips. "Okay. Here goes nothing." She slid forward to the edge of her seat and carefully touched the needle to Aissa's flesh.

The only sound in the apartment was the buzz of the needle and the water running in the kitchen. Riley slowly traced the curves of the G, carefully etched the line of the conjoined letters, and then leaned back to examine her work. "Cait? What do you think?"

Priest nodded. "It looks beautiful. Aissa, are you ready?"

"Yes."

Priest touched two fingers to the design and the ink flared red for a moment. Riley felt a corresponding buzz in her own tattoo, but resisted the urge to reach back and touch it through her shirt.

"It's done," Priest said. "When the time comes, Aissa will become the new champion for good."

Aissa had crossed her arms over the back of the chair and she put her head down. Her shoulders rose and fell as she sobbed quietly, and Priest touched her shoulder.

"Are you okay?"

"I'm... honored. Thank you."

Riley put aside the equipment and rubbed her hands together. They felt numb and, now that the delicate work was done, the nerves were taking the opportunity to tremble.

Aissa pulled her shirt back up and looked at Riley. "If the time comes, I will gladly serve as the champion for this city. But I sincerely hope I don't have to do anything for a very, very long time."

"Hear, hear," Priest said.

"From your lips to... well, I guess Priest's ears." She squeezed Aissa's hand. "I'm going to be here for you. If you need help, if you just need someone to talk to, I'll be around."

Aissa nodded. "Thank you."

"Do you need a ride back to the shelter?"

"No, uh... Caitlin said she would drive me back." They stood, and Aissa wrapped her arms around Riley. "Thank you, Riley. You don't know how much this means to me."

"It's, uh... no problem. Cait?"

Priest smiled. "We should probably get on the road. I'll see you tomorrow, Riley."

Riley nodded and escorted them to the door. Once they were gone, she went to the kitchen. "We're alone. Do you want to yell at me?"

Gillian turned. "No. I'm not mad." She faced the sink again and Riley joined her. Gillian took one step to the right and began to rinse as Riley washed. "I'm scared. You just elected the person who will take over for you when you die."

"Yeah. How do you think I feel?" She put her hand on top of Gillian's, the soap and water forming a seal between them. "But it's not courting disaster any more than when we get life insurance. We're just making sure the bases are covered. If the worst does happen, I don't want to leave the city unprotected. I don't want to die knowing that you're vulnerable to whatever Marchosias decides to do just because I hadn't picked someone to follow in my footsteps. Gail Finney hesitated, and now we have a chance to turn the tide. So I'm not taking any chances."

"I know. But having this little ritual... makes it real." She turned to face Riley, twisting her wrist so their fingers were laced together. "And what about Christine Lee? She died because she gave up her protection for you. When she gave you the tattoo, it made hers was less effective and the demons killed her. Now you've got yours spread across three people, if you include the one you gave me in Georgia and..."

"Sh." Riley kissed her. "I talked to Priest about all of that. The tattoo I gave to Aissa is just a placeholder. Priest sealed it so that it's not drawing anything away from mine. It doesn't actually protect her, but she won't need extra protection if the demons don't know who she is. The power will only be taken away from my tattoo if... i-if I don't need it anymore."

"Right." Gillian sighed and rested her forehead against Riley's. After a moment, she spoke again. "Riley, do you remember the day we got married, when we locked ourselves in the apartment and had our own private honeymoon?"

Riley smiled. "Vividly."

"Do you remember when we talked about fantasy destinations? Where we would go if we had the time and money wasn't an object. And you knew that when I said 'Paris,' I meant that I wanted to think about maybe one day going there. I didn't want to start packing right that minute and head to the airport. I just wanted to put the idea in your head so... maybe one day."

"Right. Yeah."

"So keep that in mind when I say this." She touched Riley's chin and made eye contact. "I want to find out if you can retire."

"What?"

"You have your successor now. I'm not saying I want you to walk away tomorrow. But I'd like to know that there's a way out that doesn't involve you being in a box. I want to know we might have a chance for a regular, peaceful life when all of this is over. I don't think that's too much to ask, is it?"

"Of course not." Riley took Gillian in her arms. "I'll talk to Priest and see what she knows about the pension plan."

Gillian laughed and held her hands out behind Riley's back.

"Why aren't you hugging me?"

"My hands are wet."

Riley scoffed. "Clothes can be dried. Hold me."

Gillian put her hands on Riley's back and pulled her close.

Two squad cars were blocking traffic at either end of the street, their red and blue lights flashing on the buildings on either side. Riley slowed and held her badge up to the officer directing traffic and he waved her through. "I'm not giving you my two weeks notice." Priest took Riley's question about giving up her position as champion the wrong way, and Riley spent most of the drive convincing her it was eighty percent hypothetical. "Like my job as a cop. I'm not planning to quit any time soon, and I'd fight tooth and nail if they tried to take it away tomorrow. But I still like knowing I have a retirement fund."

Priest nodded, finally comprehending what Riley was talking about. "Okay. But to answer your question, I don't really know.

You're the first champion I've ever known personally. I know Christine Lee was killed, and the majority of the champions die... very young."

"You're making me feel very good here, Priest." She parked at the edge of the crime scene tape and got out of the car. "I just want... I need to know if it's possible. If there's a chance that I can one day just pass the mantle to Aissa and move into a retirement home with Gillian."

"I don't know. I'm not certain. I can ask."

"Thanks. Gillian will appreciate it. So will I."

A uniformed officer met them near the body lying in the street. "Detectives. One victim, name of Vaughn Fairbanks according to his friend. Shot twice in the chest."

"Witnesses?"

The cop sighed. "The friend was across the street trying to score, so he had his back turned when the shots rang out. By the time he realized they weren't shooting at him, the shooter was long-gone. We do have one other possible witness, but ah... probably not helpful."

"Blind?"

"In a way." He pointed and Riley followed his finger and resisted the urge to groan in dismay.

One of the Good Girls was standing near the doorway of a nearby building, her hood pulled down over her eyes and her hands folded in prayer. She was facing toward the crime scene, but the hood may have obscured her line of sight.

The cop bumped his hat higher on his forehead with one knuckle. "My partner tried talking to her, but she won't budge. The only thing she'll say is that she has religious freedom not to get involved. I mean, what kind of crap religion is that? Letting someone get away with murder?"

Riley said nothing, but she agreed with the sentiment. Over the past week, they had encountered the Good Girls on several occasions. Each time was more frustrating than the last. Riley had come close to arresting one Mother for obstruction of justice when it was clear she had witnessed a crime, but Priest told her it would do more harm than good. Unfortunately the commissioner wasn't willing to risk offending a religious order. Three more bodies had been found, and all evidence pointed toward Good Girl involvement. Commissioner Benedict's stance was firm; the Good Girls were to be left alone.

On the bright side, word seemed to be spreading among the population of No Man's Land; the women were not as vulnerable as they might seem. The cops might have been ordered to leave them alone, but it was becoming increasingly apparent that the leader of the Five Families had set down the same edict.

Riley waved off the cop's irritation. "Ignore them like Benedict says. They're statues, for all the good they'll do us." She looked back as the medical examiner van arrived, and allowed herself a moment of relief at the familiar setting. She was back where she belonged. She was working homicide with Priest, and Gillian was on her way to poke and prod the body to make it give up all its secrets. It was almost like the old days.

But when she turned back around, she couldn't help but see the Good Girl standing silently twenty feet away from a dead man. The city was definitely changing.

Whether the changes were for good or bad remained to be seen. But whatever was in store, she was positive that she could handle it.

RUIN UPON RUIN

Due to the fact they didn't necessarily require sleep, Priest and Sariel often remained awake through the night. Priest managed to get back the apartment she'd given up during her brief foray of being a mortal. The church still offered services every few hours, which permeated the walls of her home like ambient heat passing through a porous surface. When Sariel felt it for herself, she began spending less time in her apartment and effectively moved in with Priest. They often timed their lovemaking to coincide with the choir's singing. Priest called it feeding their spiritual and physical selves with the same meal.

They didn't always make love in bed. In fact, that was probably the rarest location of their coupling. Sariel preferred the floor, as it provided more room for a variety of positions. Priest liked the couch. The back was tall, and the arms made her feel enclosed. She wanted to try a casket, with its plush lining and walls on all sides, but she knew how mortals would view that sort of thing. The trappings of death made them anxious and twitchy. But it was a fantasy she entertained from time to time.

Some nights Priest insisted they at least feign sleep. Sometime around two or three in the morning, they would finish whatever they were doing and put it away for the night. They would change into pajamas and adjourn to the bedroom where they got into bed together. Priest was better at sleep than Sariel, having experienced it as a necessity for close to a year. Sariel frequently lay awake and stared at the ceiling until her fidgeting woke Priest or their alarm clock said the ruse could end.

Priest woke on her stomach with Sariel on top of her. She slipped free, careful to disturb her partner as little as possible, and walked quietly to the bathroom. She took off her pajamas and stepped into the shower, gasping at the temperature of the water until it began to warm. She cupped her hands under the flow and let the water pool. When she tilted her hands, the water flowed over her forearms and gathered in the crooks of her elbows.

She had loved showers even before she became a true mortal, but now she truly appreciated her body's response to the activity. Her nipples, small and pink, responded by hardening. She ran her fingers around the pink areole and stared at the small goosebumps that appeared. Being mortal had affected her weight, adding ten pounds that she didn't need. She could have erased them with just a thought, but she had garnered enough compliments that she decided to leave it.

After fulfilling the purpose of the shower, she wet her middle two fingers on her tongue and rested her other hand against the wall. Pleasure with Sariel was one thing, but pleasuring herself was another, different joy. She stroked her pubic hair and circled her clitoris with her middle finger, stretching out the ring finger along her labia. Her touch was gentle, almost utilitarian, but her shoulders trembled as she continued moving her hand in slow circles.

She sagged forward and let the shower hit the top of her head, the spray flattening her hair against her skull and shoulders before it cascaded down her back and over her ass. Her fingers curled on the wet tile, and she climaxed with a quiet cry of release. She loved the way her body felt after an orgasm and treasured the memory of how pure it had felt when she was a mortal.

After her toes uncurled, and after she realized the water had run cold, she turned the faucets and left the tub. She dried herself with a towel, enjoying the ritual of warm cloth against cool skin, and wiped the condensation from the mirror. She ran her hand over her stomach and turned sideways to admire it. As she did, she noticed how long her hair had gotten. She could have stopped it, but she had gotten two haircuts during her time as a mortal and she had to admit she enjoyed the ritual of it. Maybe she would treat herself to another soon. She finished drying herself and left the towel in the hamper as she stepped naked into the bedroom.

Sariel was awake and already dressed in dark gray slacks. She was topless, examining the closet for an appropriate blouse. Priest embraced her from behind, slipping her hands under Sariel's arms to cup her breasts. Sariel leaned back against her in acknowledgement of the touch, but did nothing to prolong it.

"I don't want to be late for my first day of work."

"You sound ambivalent."

Sariel made a noise that wasn't quite rude. "I'm not certain about needing to lead a mortal life. I want for nothing."

"Society requires~"

Sariel turned in Priest's arms and stepped away from her. "We're not part of society. Not their society. Why do we have to pretend?"

Priest's mood darkened. "We went over this, Sara." Sariel scoffed at the human name, but Priest ignored her. "In order to better protect Riley, we have to blend in to her world. I watch over her when she's at work, and you can effect change by taking over Gail Finney's job at the newspaper."

Sariel rolled her eyes. The job interview had been a lark, suggested off-hand by Riley. Sariel typed up a few sample articles and the job was offered to her on the spot. Sariel understood the benefit of having an agent for good in the media, but she didn't anticipate filling the role herself. Priest reached into the closet and took down a plain white blouse.

"Wear this with a blue tie. It brings out your eyes." She used both hands to tuck the hair behind Sariel's ears, then leaned in and kissed her. "If you need anything, I'll be a phone call away all day."

"I'm not hesitating because I'm nervous. I'm hesitating because I feel we would be more effective abandoning the pretense. We are seraphim. Confining ourselves to these mortal bodies limits our strength."

"We're no less powerful than before. In fact, we have greater power. Living above this church imbues us with such strength that we can face any threat that may come after Riley. I was mauled by hellhounds and I recovered."

Sariel sighed and stepped around Priest so she could get dressed. "And what about when she dies? You can't simply ignore the fact that she will, one day, die and won't require your services. You'll move on to the next soul. Will you be Caitlin Priest for them as well? Or will you allow her to die with Riley and return to your true self?"

"When the time comes, I will not hesitate."

"Zerachiel." Priest turned to look at her, and Sariel was smiling ruefully. "You hesitate to respond to that name. It's brief, it's hard to notice even for me, but it's true."

Priest shook her head. "When we're in the mortal realm, Caitlin Priest is who I am. When I am called Home, I will be Zerachiel and... as much as it pains me, Priest will become a memory."

"I hope that is so." Sariel had her shirt halfway buttoned.

Priest turned and walked out of the room. A malicious part of her, a part that was angry at Sariel for questioning her, said, "You forgot to put on a brassiere again."

Sariel's frustrated sigh followed Priest out of the room. She gathered her things from the living room and draped her coat over her arm as she left the apartment. She had watched over countless people, spanning continents and centuries. She had stroked the hair of a Queen as a poisonous asp slipped out of her hand. She had cradled a pioneer aviatrix as she took her last breath on a desolate isle. She loved them all as she loved Riley, and when the time came and it was time for Riley to pass~

Priest's steps faltered and she gripped the railing, twisting to press her stomach against it as she fought the clenching in her chest. She was surprised by the intensity of her reaction to the thought, and she rubbed her chest through her shirt as she cautiously continued down the stairs. She tossed her jacket into the backseat of her car and fumbled with the keys.

Riley's temporary transfer to traffic had afforded her with the opportunity to give Priest official driving lessons. She took to it well enough that she wanted a car of her own. She had enough saved to buy herself something nice, but she became enamored with a used Datsun 260z. It needed a lot of work, but Riley insisted Priest cheat and "sprinkle some angel dust on the engine." The result was the smoothest running used car in the city.

Priest passed Riley and Gillian's building on her way to work, more out of design than necessity, and she noticed Riley's car was still parked at the curb. She smiled and slowed down to park. Riley was eager for a chance to drive Priest's new car, and just as eager that she assign it an arbitrary name, so she would offer to let Riley drive it to work.

She loved being out in the morning. Seeing people on their

way to work, fresh-faced for the day and mostly well-rested. It was a time of possibilities. She greeted the people she passed in the foyer of Riley's building, strangers who had become familiar to her over the past few years. She looked at her watch before she knocked on Riley and Gillian's door. It was close enough to work time that they would probably be rushed, but she could smell breakfast cooking.

Gillian answered the door and they exchanged smiles. Gillian's hair was up, and she was already dressed in scrubs. "Good morning, Caitlin."

"Hello. I just stopped by to see if Riley wanted to drive my car to work today."

"Oh, man. She's going to kick herself, but she went in early. Come on in, I'll give you some eggs or toast."

Priest's smile faded as she followed Gillian to the kitchen. "She left early? How early?"

"About fifteen minutes ago. She got a call, and she said she had to go in."

Priest had an uneasy feeling in the pit of her stomach. Fifteen minutes ago, she had felt a painful twist in her chest. "Did she get a ride from someone?"

Gillian sensed her tone and turned around. "I don't think so. Why? Is something wrong?"

"I don't know. Her car is still parked in front of the building."

"Well. That's not terribly unusual. Maybe she walked to the train or something." She rubbed her arm and looked toward the window, as if she could see through the buildings and into the elevated train to make sure Riley was on board. "Maybe whoever she had to meet lives in a bad part of town, and she didn't want to leave her car there."

Priest nodded. She was disturbed that she couldn't feel Riley's presence. "I'm going to find her. Just give me a moment." She closed her eyes and focused on Riley, on how she smelled and the feel of her soul.

In her mind's eye, she pictured a small closet converted into a nursery. A second-hand crib took up most of the space. Zerachiel didn't enter the room but she simply appeared beside the bassinet. The child was restless, a state she would rarely leave even when she was grown, with both fists balled up near her face. She stuttered and fussed, but the voices in the other room didn't even pause.

"Riley Jacqueline," Zerachiel said. The child opened her eyes as the angel touched her cheek. "You will do great things."

The baby spluttered and began to cry. Zerachiel moved to the foot of the crib as the child's mother, already weary and worn, stepped into the doorway. She watched her child and then turned away, leaving her to cry. Zerachiel knew the night would be cold, so she spread herself over the crib to keep the worse of the chill away from the baby. She glowed, and the baby ceased her cries to watch the colors play against the ceiling of her room until she fell asleep.

Caitlin?

The voice came to her from a distance. She was swaying on her feet and she felt an ache in her cheeks from smiling. She kept her eyes closed but felt herself returning to the Now, in Riley and Gillian's kitchen. "I can feel her. I'll go to her."

"And chew her out for worrying us."

"Yes, ma'am. I'll see you soon, Gillian."

Priest let Zerachiel's divinity envelop her. It grew brighter as she faded, pulled by her connection to Riley. When the glow dimmed, she opened her eyes and exhaled as she examined her new surroundings. She was beneath an overpass, and the tires of passing cars echoed with hollow thuds above her. The hollow sound echoed among the concrete pylons as she examined the piles of trash for signs of Riley. She turned and saw a man staring at her.

He smiled, and she knew he was a demon.

"Do not disturb." He moved faster than Priest could react, his hands closing around her throat. She dug her fingernails into the backs of his hands as they grappled. His lips curled into a sneer. "Bye-bye, angel."

There was shattering sound, and Priest felt herself cast into a vacuum. When gravity returned, it was pulling her wrong. She seemed to be pulled sideways as she was propelled backward. Something shattered against her back and she slammed into the wall (or the ground) before she fell. Her ears were ringing, so she lashed out at the person who knelt next to her. Gillian's cry of pain was loud enough to break through the din, and Priest muttered an apology.

"It's okay. What the hell just happened?"

Priest opened her eyes and winced at the stinging. She knew the whites were filled with blood. "A demon. Following my connection to Riley took me to... a demon lying in wait."

Gillian's face revealed she already knew the answer to her question, but she asked anyway. "What does that mean?"

Priest shuddered as the pain came back in a fresh wave. "It

means that Marchosias has her."

"That can't be possible."

Priest shook her head. "The only other explanation is that Riley went to him willingly." She stood and touched her throat. Her windpipe had been crushed by the demon's grip, but Zerachiel's divinity had already started fixing that. "Only one is true."

"Great. So we get to decide which impossible thing we believe before breakfast this morning."

"No," Priest said. "We don't have to know why or how. We know enough. Marchosias has Riley. We have to bring her back, whatever the cost."

After several unsuccessful attempts to call Riley's cell phone, Gillian decided the time had come to panic. She used the landline to call work and became wrapped in the cord as she explained she couldn't come in. She retraced her steps to free herself as she thumbed through a directory for the number of someone to fill in. When work was dealt with, she returned to the living room and sat next to Priest on the couch.

"What do we need to do?"

"Are you certain you wish to help?"

Gillian took a calming breath and nodded. "I'm fine. I promised I wouldn't freak out every time Riley got in trouble, so I'm holding off until we have more information."

Priest took Gillian's hand. "Okay. You said Riley received a telephone call that made her leave early. Did she say anything about where she was going?"

"Nothing specific, but that's not unusual." She closed her eyes. "We were in the kitchen and I was making breakfast. She had just gotten out of the shower. Her phone rang and she spoke to someone~"

"Do you remember what she said?"

Gillian sighed. "Uh, I wasn't really paying attention. She identified herself, and she listened to someone for a long time. She said, 'are you sure?' and then said she would be right there. She didn't seem anxious. I figured it was just an ordinary call about a murder somewhere." She leaned back and tilted her head to the side. "When I got out of the shower last night, she was on the phone. She hung up quickly, and she told me Aissa called to say goodnight."

"Is there any reason you might think she wasn't telling the

truth?"

"No. Aissa has called a few times since she started working at the shelter. It's only suspicious looking back on it." Gillian looked at Priest. "Do you think she might have gone to Marchosias willingly?"

Priest tilted her head to the side as she considered that possibility. "Why would she do that? And why would she block my attempts to find her?"

"Maybe it didn't go the way she thought it would."

Priest was horrified by the thought, but she couldn't immediately discount it. "Do you have a Caller ID on the bedroom phone?"

Gillian was already up. "Yeah. I'll go check."

Priest closed her eyes and tried to focus on Riley again. A guardian angel could always feel those who were under their protection. Normally she didn't hear it unless she tried. Now she was focusing with everything she had, and there was nothing. It was like the deep silence following an air-conditioner shutting off. She folded her hands in front of her face and said a quick prayer as she heard Gillian return.

"This is the only call we received last night. It's local, but I don't recognize it. I tried calling it from the bedroom, but it's been disconnected."

Priest stood and took the paper Gillian had written the phone number on. "I'll see what I can find out."

"No. Not you, we. I'm not going to freak out when Riley's in trouble, but I'm also not going to sit at home and pace. Wherever you're going, I'm going, too."

Priest considered arguing, but Gillian's expression told her that it would be fruitless. "Fine. Come on."

Priest led her downstairs to her car. "I think Kenzie and Chelsea have some gear to back-trace phone numbers. I don't know if it will work if the number is unlisted, but it's worth a shot."

Gillian nodded. "Should you call in and let Lieutenant Briggs know what's happening?"

"Right. Yes." Priest let the car idle as she dialed Briggs' number. "She won't be pleased. Riley has been doing well since she transferred back from traffic, but Lieutenant Briggs has been acting unusual of late."

"Riley's told me about it. She's concerned, but as long as you're certain it's not demon-related, she's willing to let it play out."

"Definitely not demonic. It's~" The phone stopped buzzing in her ear and went to voicemail. "That's odd. Lieutenant Briggs, this is Caitlin Priest. Riley and I are in the midst of an investigation, so we won't be in the office today. I didn't want you to be concerned. We'll be in touch." She hung up and stared at the phone. "She didn't answer."

"Maybe she's not in her office."

"I called her cell. It should have either reached her wherever she was, or been forwarded to her office as it usually is during work hours. Do you think she and Riley could be together?"

Gillian furrowed her brow. "Do you think Riley finally decided to deal with whatever's been bugging Lieutenant Briggs? Why wouldn't she tell us?"

"Maybe she was told not to. If Briggs is dealing with something sensitive that could affect her employment..."

"Ah... you mean the Hyde family." Priest raised an eyebrow. "She didn't tell you?"

"No."

Gillian cleared her throat. "Oh. Ah, apparently Lieutenant Briggs married into the Hyde family. They're divorced now."

"I understand why Riley would keep that from me." She considered the new information and made a decision. "We'll check with her before we visit Kenzie. Riley may just be working on a special project."

"A special project that neither of us are allowed to know about in advance? One that involves a demon halo-blocking you from finding Riley?"

Priest sighed. "I don't know. Right now I'm grasping at straws."

"You and me both, Cait. Let's get going."

Neither of them spoke during the drive. Gillian was obviously fretting over her wife, and Priest was thinking about her argument with Sariel that morning. Eventually there would be a situation where Riley was in danger, or went missing, or stormed into a fight, and she wouldn't succeed. There was more than a good chance of it; it was an absolute certainty. One day Riley would die, whether of natural causes or at the hand of an enemy, and Zerachiel would move on to her next assignment.

"Caitlin? You're speeding."

She eased her foot off the accelerator. "Sorry. My mind wandered."

"We just need to take our minds off it. Has Riley asked you about retirement?"

"Yes. I've requested more information from Michael, but he's being stubborn about returning my calls. He's also pretty busy elsewhere in the world. But I promise you, I will do everything in my power to get an answer."

Gillian looked at her. "Do you think the answer will be yes? Honestly. I don't want some platitude to make me feel better."

Priest considered the question. "There are champions all over the world. It stands to reason at least a few have found a way to pass the torch without dying, but I've never heard of one. If anyone will know, it's Michael. We just have to wait until he deigns to respond. Riley has defeated her evil counterpart. If that doesn't earn her a bit of peace, then I don't know what will."

"Thank you."

"You're welcome. Riley has chosen her successor, and she has started training to take over someday. Riley has caused a shift in the balance of power over this city, and she's kept the Ladder from falling into the wrong hands. She caused the destruction of Gremory, and she felled an angel. She's done more in three years than most champions do in a lifetime. I'll fight for her chance at freedom if it comes to that."

Gillian smiled as they pulled up in front of Lieutenant Briggs' building. A blonde member of the Good Girls sect was positioned at the intersection, her head bowed in prayer as a crowd of people gathered around her to take pictures with their cell phones. Gillian eyed the woman as they drove by and Priest caught the worry in her eyes.

Priest seemed to read her mind. "The Good Girls are merely positioned in areas that are most susceptible to an incursion by Marchosias' forces. Lieutenant Briggs, as Riley's immediate superior, is at risk for being used as a potential weapon. There is at least one Good Girl outside of your building as well. Their presence doesn't indicate a crime will occur."

"Here's hoping."

They parked and went inside, putting the Good Girl out of their minds. Briggs' apartment was on the second floor, accessed by an enclosed stairwell filled with detritus, both physical and emotional, of the people living in the building. Priest couldn't ignore it, so she just lowered her chin and carried on. Their footsteps echoed off the walls and she was grateful when they stepped out onto the landing. Priest heard music playing inside Briggs' apartment and knocked, turning to make sure Gillian was still okay.

"Maybe the Lieutenant is sick and Riley brought her soup."

Priest smiled. "Maybe. Riley is very considerate." She knocked again and stepped closer to the door. "Lieutenant Briggs?"

"Priest? Shit-damn, hold on."

After a moment of fumbling, the door opened to reveal Briggs dressed in a wrong-buttoned dress shirt. Her legs were bare, and her hair was hanging in her face like a veil. She swept it back and looked between her two visitors.

"What?"

"Why aren't you at work?" Priest asked.

Briggs started to look over her shoulder, but caught herself. "That's none of your business, Detective Priest. Did your partner send you up here?" She looked at Gillian again.

"No. We were concerned for you."

Briggs' expression softened. "I'm fine, Priest. I'm just a little... ill right now." She crossed her arms over her chest. "Thank you for your concern."

Priest offered her hand. "If you need anything, official or not, call."

"Thank you. I will." Briggs took Priest's hand and squeezed. She didn't seem to notice anything until she broke contact, but she quickly shrugged it off and focused on Gillian again. "Why are you here? I... don't mean that the way it sounds, but you're~"

"Caitlin is giving me a ride."

Briggs nodded. "Okay then. Anything else?"

Priest shook her head. "Sorry to have disturbed you. Feel better soon."

"Yeah. Hopefully."

She shut the door, and Priest gestured for Gillian to lead the way downstairs. "She doesn't know anything about Riley."

"That handshake thing. You... scanned her or, or whatever you call it?"

"I didn't want to let her know what I was doing, so I could only get a quick glimpse. Whatever she's doing, she's ashamed. But it's a personal shame. It has little to do with us, at least for the moment."

Gillian grimaced. "If she's cutting out of work because of it, I'd say it has a lot to do with us. We're going to have to deal with it eventually."

"Yes. Eventually, but not now."

"Now to Kenzie's?"

Priest stopped on the sidewalk and looked toward the Good Girl. The crowd had dispersed, and she stood alone like some sort of urban art project.

"Caitlin?"

Priest walked to the hooded woman, the glow around her body expanding as she grew nearer. She felt the waves of the woman's prayer, and the woman felt the angel's approach. She looked up when Priest was only a few steps away and she ceased her litany to drop to one knee.

"You know who I am."

"Yes. It's an honor."

"Rise and tell me your name."

The woman stood. "I am Mother Paladin Badel. You may refer to me as Mother or Paladin."

"Paladin? Is that a rank?"

Badel nodded once. "We are the soldier class, chosen for this mission specifically for our specialty in the physical arts. We are the bravest and strongest members of the Good Girls." Her eyes cut toward Gillian and she dipped her chin in greeting. "The champion's consort. It is an honor to meet you and the angel."

Gillian bristled at the derogatory term but let it slide.

"I wish to know if any of your people have seen Riley this morning."

"Our code is one of strict non-interference. We will act, if acted upon, but~"

Priest grabbed the front of Badel's robe and shuffled her back toward the wall. Badel was too stunned to react until her back was to the bricks. She brought both hands up and swept Priest's arms away, then punched her in the face. Priest barely acknowledged the jab and took a handful of the woman's thick, blonde hair and shoved her down to her knees. Badel struck out at Priest's midsection with her elbow, but Priest stepped aside and avoided the blow. She wrapped her arms around Badel's neck and pulled, burying her knee in the other woman's back. Badel clawed at Priest's arms, but she quickly surrendered.

The fight was over in a matter of seconds, but Gillian seemed to be the only one who even noticed it was happening. By the time she decided helping was unnecessary, the Good Girl was subdued and on her knees. Priest didn't release her hold, but Badel accepted her fate by dropping her arms.

"Detective Parra is missing. My attempt to track her down was prevented by a demon. If any of you saw something, I demand you tell me immediately."

Badel growled.

Gillian stepped forward and crouched to look into Badel's eyes. "My wife is missing. Possibly being held hostage by demons. Everything you have done for her in the past, the prayers and coming all this way just to hold back the darkness, the least you could do... the very *least* you could do is point."

Badel's expression softened. "I saw nothing. But there was a disturbance near your home this morning. Wrenne knows more than I do. I will... I will contact her and tell her to cooperate."

Priest relaxed her grip. "How do we find Wrenne?"

"Go home, and she will find you."

Gillian nodded. "Thank you for your help, Paladin Badel."

Priest let Badel go and joined Gillian for the walk back to the car. They were nearly there when Badel called out Gillian's name.

"Champions rarely find lasting love. Few of them even look for it. We were... not surprised when you left town but we were astonished when you returned. We are amazed by your strength."

"I was coming back for Riley," Gillian said. "No strength required."

Badel nodded and flipped her hood back over her face. Gillian watched her for a moment and then gestured Priest onward. "Come on. Let's go wait for Wrenne to find us."

The Good Girl was waiting outside the building when Priest returned to Gillian and Riley's apartment. Her hood was flipped back to reveal short red hair, and she assumed a more relaxed pose when she saw Priest approaching. "The angel and the champion's consort."

Gillian sighed. "Can we come up with a new title besides 'consort'? We're married."

Wrenne ignored her and focused on Priest. "My Mother Paladin told me to wait here to tell you what I witnessed this morning."

"Nice system of communications you have," Gillian said. "Is there a cell phone clipped under the robe of yours?"

"We have ways of communicating with each other when necessary." She focused on Priest. "I will tell you what I saw and nothing further. I was stationed outside of the bakery on that corner." She pointed to a spot northeast of the entrance to their building. "I was in the midst of prayer when I saw the champion exit. I admit to being overwhelmed by the sight of her. Being assigned this location is quite an honor. She met someone on the sidewalk. He put his hands on her shoulders and they were gone in a blink of the eye."

"Angel?" Gillian was obviously still hoping for the best-case scenario.

Priest shook her head. "Doubtful."

"Impossible. The man was dark, his soul twisted. He was a demon without a doubt."

"And Riley just let him take her? Did she fight?"

Wrenne shook her head. "Their conversation seemed amicable."

"Thank you for your assistance, Wrenne. You may return to your position. We're sorry for disturbing your prayers."

"The honor was mine, angel. Cons~" She caught herself. "Mrs. Parra."

Gillian watched the girl go and shrugged. "Still not exactly accurate, but I like it." To Priest, she said, "What do we do now?"

"Under normal circumstances I could find a trace of the demon's passage and follow it. I'm not looking forward to another detour." She looked down at her hands and then looked into Gillian's eyes. "Do you have a detailed map of the city in your apartment?"

"I think I might have something. What do you need?"

Priest led Gillian upstairs without answering, returning to the apartment. It was still mid-morning, and the light cast odd shadows on the far walls. Gillian went to the kitchen and returned with a large roadmap. "I'm hardly ever home this late in the morning. It feels off." She considered the possibility that the off feeling was due to not knowing where Riley was and focused on trying to find her. She unfolded the map on the kitchen table and held the ends down with both hands. "What are you looking for?"

Priest moved the empty sugar bowl and the honey jar that had been left out after breakfast to hold down the edges. She held out her hand, and Gillian placed hers in it without question.

"I need you to pray for Riley, Gillian."

Gillian smiled. "You never have to tell me to do that."

"No. I don't mean... kneeling by your bed and whispering. The prayer I require is deeper. I need you to push away everything. Your thoughts, your memories, your fears, and focus everything you have on Riley and her well-being. It needs to overwhelm the fact you may be hungry, or cold, or tired. You need to focus your entire being on this prayer. It will leave you weak, but~"

"Will it help Riley?"

"It will help me find her."

Gillian squeezed Priest's fingers. "Then what are we waiting for?"

"I'm going to speak, but you need to ignore me. Just focus on Riley as hard as you possibly can." Gillian nodded and Priest slid her hand back until their fingers were overlapping. Gillian closed her eyes and took a deep breath. Priest watched as Gillian's shoulders relaxed and her chin lifted slightly. Her eyes moved behind their lids, and Priest held her free hand flat over the map. The palm began to glow with her divinity and Priest closed her eyes as well.

She pictured the apartment as a skeletal framework of yellow energy. Gillian's energy was a comforting forest green. It swelled as Gillian's prayer gained power, and it rose from her in waves of light. The map of the city appeared in Priest's mind as Gillian's prayer rose above and spread in an unseen wind. Priest furrowed her brow and followed.

"North." Through streets and spreading down alleys until the two trails met again at a nearby intersection. "East, north. West. West. North. South." She murmured the directions to herself, the energy of the prayer constantly breaking and meeting up again. Occasionally it would slow, and Priest saw the dark red-black energy of a demonic body. The prayer hovered over these traps briefly before traveling on. Gillian's hand trembled against Priest's, but she couldn't spare her concentration to calm her. Instead she wrapped her divinity around Gillian's entire hand and let it spread down her arm to give her strength.

"It's a web," Priest whispered. The pattern was becoming clear. Any attempt to find Riley would have gotten her caught in the web. But if they took the time to construct something so complex, then they hadn't been focusing their power on keeping Riley prisoner. "They built a web around the city."

"Caitlin. My head hurts."

"Just a bit more, Gillian." She wet her lips and furrowed her brow. The disparate threads of the prayer had rejoined in No Man's Land, growing in strength and color until it reached a large building that was familiar in Priest's mind. She identified it and, tracking finished, let the energy dissipate.

Her mental map of the city faded. Priest's hand dropped to the map and she sagged forward, exhausted from what she'd just done. "You may cease your prayer now, Gillian."

There was no response, so she opened her eyes and was horrified by what she saw. Gillian's head was tilted back, her eyes closed, and she was mouthing Riley's name in an unending chant. Blood streamed from her nose and stained her lips, but she didn't notice.

Priest grabbed Gillian by the shoulders and lowered her to the ground. Gillian's eyes opened with a gasp of surprise, and her lips stopped moving as she looked around her apartment. Priest knelt on the floor with Gillian draped across her lap like a child. She touched her lip and frowned at the bright, wet blood.

"What happened?"

"I forced you to pray like an angel. You have my sincere apologies, Gillian. I should have had Sariel here to balance the strain."

"Did you find Riley?"

Priest nodded slowly. "I know where she is."

"Then I don't care." She reached onto the kitchen counter and groped until she found the paper towels. She broke off two and pressed them to her face. "It's not like I had an aneurysm." A worrying thought gripped her. "It's not like that, right?"

"No. The physical effects are fleeting. If I hadn't stopped when I did, however, it might have been much worse."

"We don't have time for might-have-been. You found Riley. That's all that matters right now. Let's go."

"No. The place I have to go is extremely dangerous. I will not rescue Riley just to have her kill me for bringing you there."

Gillian chuckled behind the wad of paper. She moved off of Priest's lap and pressed her back against the counter. She examined Priest.

"You're scared."

"Yes. To get Riley back, I'll have to go somewhere very... bad."

"Take Sariel with you as backup."

Priest shook her head. "As Riley's guardian angel, this is my battle. I won't ask Sariel to intervene." She wet her lips and looked down at her hands. "I'll require my sword."

Gillian raised her eyebrows. "Sword? You have a sword?"

"All angels wield a sword. Ridwan's sword was the key to Riley finally discovering the truth about this city."

"I've never seen you with it."

Priest smiled. "I haven't needed it. As Caitlin Priest, I am armed with the weapons of a mortal." She touched the gun holstered on her hip. "The sword will grant me passage. And if I cannot talk Riley's captors into handing her over to me, then it will give me the strength to kill them." She put her hand on Gillian's shoulder. "Will you be okay here?"

"Just bring back my wife in one piece."

Priest nodded and kissed Gillian's forehead before she stood. She needed time to prepare for what she was going to do. She just hoped Riley could spare the time.

It was noon by the time Priest got back to her apartment. She stripped to her underwear, draping her clothes over the back of the sofa as she knelt in her living room. She would have preferred the bedroom, but she chose to use a spot directly over the sanctuary of the downstairs church. She held her hands to her sides, palms facing out, and touched her chin to her chest. She closed her eyes and felt the ambient energy from the prayers and worship below her washing through her. Hope and fear and stress. Prayer for surcease from sorrow buffeted her from all sides and she felt it seeping into her body. It was like applying heat to an ice sculpture, and she felt stronger almost immediately.

Her wings spread from the center of her back and feathered, stretching out before curling inward around her body to shield her as she spoke. "At your command, Father, I have sheathed and kept still my sword. Now I require my righteous blade, to protect and extend Justice to those who would defy Your Word. Entrust me with the sharpened weapon of Your Armor, and I shall sheath it once again upon the completion my mission."

The fingers of her right hand curled around the grip, and she felt the weight of an impossibly sharp blade resting on the fingers of her left hand.

"Thank you, Father."

She stood and examined the weapon. She'd last held it in 1566, but the weight and heft were still familiar. She rested the sword on the couch as she dressed. She left her suit behind, choosing instead a white turtleneck and tan slacks. Riley would have chastised her for not wearing black, but she preferred to dress in the color of purity if she was going into a den of evil. A scabbard had appeared on the dining room table, and she slung it over her shoulder so the sword would hang along her left side. The prayer had replaced the energy she'd spent by tracking down Riley, but she still feared it wouldn't be enough for where she was going. She took a moment at the doorway before she stepped out of the apartment.

On the sidewalk, people stepped around her extended wings without a second thought. They chose to disregard the sight, focusing on the mundane and explainable as they went about their days. She lifted her gaze to the skies and pushed off the ground with both feet. Her wings caught the wind and she flexed them to gain altitude. She shifted the sword to lay against her back as she angled herself to the south and crossed the city with quick, sure beats of her wings.

She felt the building before she saw it. Every angel in the city tried to avoid it, but Priest more than most. Last time she visited, she stood on the roof between Riley, a demon, and an angel that was moments from falling. She'd wept when Riley made the correct choice and sent Samael to his destiny. Her tears were relief for Riley's safety and anguish for Samael. It was a dark place, where Riley's first victory as champion had, in actuality, been a victory for Marchosias and his demons.

Priest landed softly on the roof of the building and fought the urge to gag. She drew her sword as the stairwell door swung open and a pair of demons emerged. Priest aimed the point of her sword at one's throat and leveled her eyes at the other. She walked forward with only the slightest hesitation in her gait.

"I am here to rescue Riley Parra. You will not stand in my way."

The demons exchanged glances, but they stepped aside to let her enter the building. The stairwell was dark, and Priest was beset by savage emotions. The sword dipped slightly, but she brought it back up and focused on her mission. She tried to focus on Riley, but there were far too many conflicting and dark emotions swirling between the walls of the godforsaken fortress.

"Riley," she whispered. "Where are you?"

The person who answered her wasn't Riley, and Priest's skin crawled at the sound of his voice. "Zerachiel. All that time spent in the closet last year seems to have made you more comfortable in dark places."

Priest continued down a few more steps before she turned to face him. Marchosias wore a blood red shirt and tie with a tailored charcoal jacket hanging open over it. He looked like a host who had stumbled over an uninvited but not unwelcome guest in his parlor.

"Where is she? You had no right to take her."

He remained on the landing, leaning forward to rest both arms on the banister. "I actually had every right. That's why you kept Gillian Hunt and your little lover angel, Sariel, as far away from here as possible. You're the one stepping out of bounds in this little game. You have no right to be here, to interfere with what I'm doing."

Priest lifted her sword and aimed it at Marchosias. "I turned my back on Riley for her trial. I held my tongue during the Angel Maker crisis. I will not fail her again. If I have to slaughter you and all your demons to get her out of this place, I will not hesitate."

"Then your side will lose."

"But she will be safe."

Marchosias smiled and pushed away from the railing. "Impressive. I wish I could help you, but there's nothing I can do. You know that. I have no control over when this ends."

A door at the far end of the corridor swung open, drawing their attention toward it. Riley stepped out, still dressed for work but looking as if she'd been awake for a week instead of just a few hours. Her hair was loose and tangled, and her shirt was unbuttoned to reveal a dirty undershirt.

"You have to admit, the whole thing would have ended a lot sooner if you'd just told me I was in charge, Marko."

Marchosias smiled. "Then we would have missed out on all the fun. So you've made your decision, I take it?"

"Yeah. No dice."

Marchosias shrugged. "The window was open. I had to take the chance. You can't blame me for it."

"The hell I can't. My things?"

He reached into the inside pocket of his coat and withdrew Riley's badge and wallet. He handed them over and took her cell phone from his pants pocket. "I made a few long distance phone calls on that. I'll reimburse you if you send me the bill."

"Call it my treat, March Hare." She brushed past him and continued down the stairs. Priest kept her sword leveled at Marchosias until Riley passed her, and then she followed Riley down. Marchosias trailed behind them at a respectable distance, his hands held up to show he wasn't going to try anything. The few demons that lingered in dark doorways hissed and recoiled at their passage.

"Why aren't they attacking?" Riley said.

"It's part of the agreement. You decided to leave, so they can't keep you here."

Riley nodded. "Good to know."

She didn't let down her guard as they descended. She could hear the demons in the rooms they passed, and she could feel their impotent anger. A vase was standing on the newel of the banister and, as they passed it, Riley bent her elbow and bumped it.

Marchosias gasped and then clucked his tongue as the vase shattered. "Tsk. Now that was simply malicious."

"I'll reimburse you if you send me the bill," Riley said snidely. "Better yet, let's just call it even."

They walked outside and Priest finally relaxed. Riley took a deep breath of fresh air and visibly relaxed. "How long was I in there?"

"Approximately six hours."

"Hm. Felt longer." She looked at the sword as if she had just noticed it. "Nice knife. Is that standard issue?"

"For my profession, yes." She returned the weapon to the scabbard as Riley scanned the cars parked along the street.

"Where did you park?"

"I flew."

Riley grunted and rubbed her neck. "Great. If I remember right, there's a train station not far from here. It'll take me near Gillian's place."

"You have a good memory."

"That day kind of sticks in my memory." Riley suddenly lurched to one side, and Priest caught her. "Ow. Thanks."

"Are you certain you're okay?"

Riley nodded and took a moment before righting herself. "Yeah. Just a little weak." She patted Priest's shoulder and stood up on her own. "Is Gillian okay?"

"She will be, once you're home and safe."

"Good." They walked on in silence for a few minutes before Riley couldn't stand it any longer. "Did you know about this whole thing?"

Priest looked down. "Yes and no."

Riley considered the answer. "Zerachiel knew, but she didn't tell Priest. So Priest had to figure it out on her own."

"Yes, actually. Zerachiel didn't want to interfere, and she knew that I... that Priest would knock down the doors to get you out. So she let Priest run the investigation."

"Does it ever get confusing to you? Dealing with Priest and Zerachiel as two different people?"

"They're not different people. Caitlin Priest is human, fraught with emotion and frail. Zerachiel is an angel who has existed since the dawn of time. But they're both... me. My actions depend on which one is currently the strongest."

"So which one are you right now?"

"I'm your friend." She put her arm around Riley, who had started to slow down again. "Let me carry you home, Riley." She scooped Riley into her arms and flexed her wings. Riley was unconscious before Priest's shoes left the ground.

Riley woke in her own bed, wrapped in the thick blankets from the top shelf of the closet. Her clothing had been removed and exchanged for a pair of soft cotton pajama pants and a clean tank top. The clothes made it obvious she had been pampered even before she noticed the basin of water on the nightstand. She knew that her face and hands had been dirty, but now they were clean. Her heart swelled with love and she twisted to confirm Gillian was lying beside her. It was dusk, but it was still bright enough to see the details of the room as Riley rolled over to put her arms around Gillian's waist and draw her close. Gillian stirred and looked over her shoulder. "Hey. You slept all afternoon."

"I was tired." She kissed Gillian's neck. "I'm sorry."

"You came home safe." She stroked Riley's arms. "That's all that matters."

Riley kissed her way to Gillian's ear and shifted her weight. Gillian responded by rolling stomach and crossing her hands under the pillow as Riley settled in the small of her wife's back. She sat up and gripped Gillian's shoulders, beginning a gentle massage. Riley kneaded until the tension faded, moving her hands up into Gillian's hair to massage her scalp.

"Where should I start?"

"Mm, right there is good."

Riley smiled. "I meant where should I start explaining what happened today?"

"Oh. The phone call last night."

Riley nodded. "Okay. The call was from a demon that runs a cremation service. I didn't like dealing with him, and I didn't want to worry you, so I just kept quiet about it. I wanted to know about Gail Finney's remains."

"Mm. I signed those over to... to, um..."

"Baron Saturday Crematorium."

"Right. Yeah, them."

"Run by a demon named Baron Samedi. I came to him peacefully, for information. I wanted to know about Gail's tattoo so I would recognize it if I saw it on someone else. I was just trying to find..." She focused on a knot in Gillian's shoulder, pausing in her explanation as Gillian sighed. "Better?"

"Mm."

"I was just trying to find out if Gail had a replacement yet. Priest told me I would know, but it was bugging me. This morning I got a call from Samedi, and he said that he had photos of the tattoo for me. I went downstairs and met him, and he told me that he regretted lying but I had to go with him to Marchosias immediately."

"Why?"

"He refused to tell me. We ended up at the building where I first went after Marchosias, and he locked me in a room. He explained that he could try to convince anyone in the city to be his new champion with only one exception. He couldn't resist trying to snipe good's champion. He wanted to Darth Vader me."

Gillian frowned. "But you~"

"I named a successor. If Marchosias had succeeded in turning me, Aissa would have taken over for me. There wouldn't have been a void, so I was fair game. He followed the letter of the law, so there technically wasn't anything Zerachiel could do. Luckily Priest was free to investigate. How's that feel?"

"That feels great," Gillian whispered. "So if he'd turned you~"

"I'd be a bad girl right now." She bent down and kissed the back of Gillian's neck. Gillian squirmed and chuckled. "I managed to stand my ground. I knew you or Priest would find me eventually and I'd get out. I just had to be strong."

"How strong did you have to be?"

Riley thought to the moments during her apparent-captivity. Marchosias' tactic had been to convince her that she was truly working for evil anyway. He pointed out the times angels had lied to her and kept back information. He itemized every moment that the angels had put one of Riley's loved ones in danger. He'd made her relive the moment of Sweet Kara's death, and the sickening aftermath in Lieutenant Hathaway's office when Riley had debased herself. She blushed with shame and ceased her massage.

"Honey?" Gillian pushed herself up and twisted to look at

Riley. "Whatever happened, and whatever he said to you doesn't change who you are. We all have bad moments, and we all do bad things. You're not a saint. That doesn't mean you're not good. You're good, Riley. You are so, so good." She stroked Riley's cheek, and Riley leaned in for a kiss.

The kiss lingered long enough that Gillian threatened to undo all the work Riley had done with the massage, so Riley lifted just enough for Gillian to twist underneath her. Settled on her back, Riley deftly lifted Gillian's shirt and cupped her breasts. She teased the nipples as they responded to her touch, and Gillian also explored under Riley's top with soft, sure strokes with just her fingertips.

Gillian broke the kiss. "Next time, tell me. I don't care who you're dealing with, or what they're doing. Today I proved that I won't freak out just because you're in danger. I trust you. You have to trust me."

Riley nodded. "I swear."

"Take this off."

Riley wasn't sure which shirt she meant, but she settled for taking off Gillian's. Once it was gone, Gillian took off Riley's tank top and stroked the sides of her breasts. They proceeded to undress each other between kisses, taking the time to explore before moving on to the next part. Gillian rolled Riley onto her back and moved down her body, running her tongue along Riley's hip as she curled two fingers over Riley's center and then pushed them inside of her.

"I'm glad you're still a good girl, Riley," she said, and kissed the spot below Riley's navel.

"God, me too..."

Gillian smiled and withdrew her fingers to replace them with her tongue. Riley remembered her first night in Gillian's apartment. She was weak, bloody and battered, and everything she thought she knew about the world had been flipped sideways. Gillian was her safe harbor, her eye of the storm. She didn't consider herself lucky for escaping Marchosias' clutches that day; she considered herself lucky that Gillian reciprocated her feelings.

And with reciprocation in mind, Riley tapped Gillian on the shoulder with two fingers. Gillian looked up, and Riley made a twisting motion with her right hand. Gillian smiled and shuffled up onto her knees. She turned around, brushing her cheeks against Riley's thighs before she lowered her head again. Riley wrapped her arms around Gillian's legs and spread her fingers on Gillian's ass.

She closed her eyes and inhaled, then wet her lips and kissed Gillian's sex.

Their orgasms weren't simultaneous, but Riley hesitated only briefly during her climax. Gillian brushed her cheek against Riley's thigh until she came, her thighs tightening around Riley's head as her hips gently bucked against her partner's now-gentle tongue. She turned her head and kissed Gillian's inner thigh and inhaled again, letting Gillian's scent fill her mind.

"How much longer do you think you can resist, Riley? It's the truth. There are no lies here. You should know; you lived through everything I'm telling you. I'm just doing the math for you. You are a bad person. You need to be on the right side."

The door closed and Riley drummed her head against the wall of the room. She wasn't listening to Marchosias anymore. She had done bad things, there was no contest in that. His argument that she was on the wrong side, though... that was flawed. She ran her thumb over the ring on her left hand.

She belonged on whatever side Gillian was on. And there was no doubt in her mind that Gillian was on the side of the angels.

"Love you, baby."

Gillian chuckled. She had shifted her body so that she was mostly lying on the mattress with her body draped across Riley's. "Welcome home, Riley."

Riley stroked Gillian's hip and rested her head against the pillow in the hopes she could drift back to sleep.

Zerachiel had been very young, inexperienced and childish in her beliefs. She thought of her first charge, Delbora, as a sister. It was her first taste of human emotions, and Delbora taught her happiness and anger and sorrow in equal measure. Delbora was only eight when she fell from her father's arms during an exodus. Zerachiel tried to protect her, but the girl fell under the hooves of the following horses and was trampled.

The next day Zerachiel met Keziah and was told to watch over her.

In the lifetimes since, Zerachiel loved and watched over so many souls. She remembered each one, carrying their memory in her heart. Priest could remember them all, but there was a special kind of pain associated with thinking Riley would one day join their ranks. Riley's death was inevitable, and Zerachiel would move on to the next soul in need of shepherding.

Priest washed her hair in the bathroom sink and combed out

the kinks. She let it trail down her back and wrapped a towel around her shoulders, pinning the hair against her shoulders.

Sariel was standing in the doorway watching her. She was dressed for bed, exhausted and cranky from her first day at work. She had become even crankier when Priest explained how she had spent her day. Their argument had lasted through dinner, and Priest had finally taken a shower just to get some peace.

"Are you going to argue again? I'm tired."

Sariel crossed her arms over her chest. "You could have caused a lot of problems for both sides today."

"I understand that," Priest said.

"I still cannot believe you took your sword into Marchosias' territory and demanded Riley back. What if he had refused?"

"Then I would have run him through with my sword and carried her out."

Sariel shook her head. "He was well within his rights, per the rules that were laid out long ago. You have so little faith in Detective Parra's ability to withstand his torture that you would risk everything to stop it?"

Priest sighed. "It wasn't a lack of faith in Riley. I knew that she would come through in one piece."

"Then why did you do it?"

Priest closed her eyes. "Because I have grown too fond of her to watch her be tortured in that way. I knew she would never agree, so what good was it to torture her? I couldn't bear the thought of it."

Sariel stepped into the room and massaged Priest's shoulders. She kissed her wet hair and their eyes met in the mirror. "You should have stepped down after you were resurrected. You've grown far too personally involved with this one. You should have let me take your place. It's what I was assigned to do. Now that you're back, I have no purpose here."

"You're a guardian angel. Your duty is to protect mortals. There is a mortal in this city that has gone without since the day she was born."

"Who?"

"Caitlin Priest," she said softly. "She picked up some bad habits last year, and sometimes she makes very human decisions. She can be quite stubborn."

Sariel squeezed Priest's shoulders and kissed her ear. "I'll be sticking around for a while," Sariel said. "I suppose it wouldn't be out of my way to look in on her from time to time."

"Thank you, darling."

Sariel kissed Priest's cheek. "Come to bed. You're abuzz with energy, and I would like to share it."

Priest smiled. "I'll be there in a moment."

When she was alone again, she allowed her smile to fade and stared at herself in the mirror. She wasn't mortal anymore, but she was still Caitlin Priest. Being separated from Zerachiel for so long had given her human side a dominance that most angels couldn't understand. She was as much Caitlin as she was Zerachiel. She didn't know how she would give up her identity when the time eventually came.

Even if Priest knew of a way to allow Riley to live forever, she doubted Riley would take immortality as a gift. All she could do was try to find a way to grant Riley some peace in her twilight years.

If she had to call in every favor she had, if it required burning every bridge she had in Heaven, she would find a way for Riley to one day retire as champion. She would make it her duty to discover everything she could about past champions for precedent and, if she found none, she would find a way for Riley to set it. It wasn't something Zerachiel would have done, but Zerachiel wasn't calling the shots anymore. Her body was now a democracy of two. Even if Zerachiel had long ago hardened her heart against losses like Delbora and Keziah, Caitlin Priest still had some hope left. She wasn't going to become fatalistic about Riley.

She opened the drawer and removed a pair of sterling silver shears. She twisted her arm back and spread the blades just above the towel. She held the pose for the length of a slow breath and then cut. She pulled the towel away and let her hair shower to the floor around her feet. She ran her fingers through the remaining strands, letting it fall against the sides of her neck. It wasn't quite long enough to reach her shoulders, and her neck felt naked.

If she decided she hated the new look, she would let it grow out slowly rather than let Zerachiel "fix it." It was a new day, and that deserved a new Priest. She smiled and went to get the broom to sweep up the hair.

HIS FORMER NAME

Joey remembered waking up at this time of day to catch the school bus. This was back when he still went to school, before his father got killed and he'd dropped out to support the family. It was up to him to knock on Nate's door, get him out of bed and dressed, and make sure he was fed before he walked him to the bus stop. Nate was only ten, and Joey was barely fifteen, but he'd lied about his age to get the job at the garage.

Nate dragged his feet, but Joey didn't let him fall too far behind. "C'mon. Bus leaves without you, I gotta walk you all the way to school. That'll make me late for work, and Mr. Starr might take a harder look at my application. You want him to do that? Want me to get fired?"

"No." Petulant and pouting, just like Joey would have been at that age. It was barely six, which meant all Nate had to look forward to was sitting on a cold bus for an hour, and then waiting in a drab common room until the first bell rang. Joey sighed.

"I'm movin' fast as I can, jerk!"

"I'm not sighing at you, Nate." He punched his brother's arm in a playful way and then slid his arm around his shoulders. "Things are going to get better, kid."

He heard footsteps behind him and tensed. He casually tucked his hand into the pocket of his coat and gripped the small gun he'd hidden there. His friend Roscoe had called it a lady's gun, but it was small enough to hide and it was just as deadly at close range. He twisted to look behind him to see if whoever was coming was a threat. His eyes widened and his eyebrows knit together in confusion as he pushed Nate off the sidewalk.

"Hey! We're goin' miss the bus."

"Sh. Shut up." He covered Nate's mouth with his hand and held him close, trying to disappear into the brick wall of the alley.

The woman passed by the mouth of the alley without a glance in their direction. She wore a white hood pulled forward over her face and her hands were clasped in front of her chest. Her robe obscured her feet and made it look as if she was gliding a few centimeters above the pavement as she walked.

Joey had heard about these women at the garage, but until now he'd never actually seen one. According to one of the other mechanics, they were badass nuns or something. Anyone who tried to hurt one of them ended up in the hospital. And that was only if they were lucky and didn't get a one-way trip to the morgue. So far he'd only heard of two people who ended up on a slab. The rest of the heavies in No Man's Land weren't willing to take the chance.

Joey didn't trust them. Religious people were the ones you had to watch the closest. Hypocrites, the whole lot of them. He waited until the jujutsu nun was out of sight before he pulled Nate out of the alley. "C'mon, squirt."

They had barely reached the corner when an old-model sedan pulled up to a stop sign. It idled at the stop sign as they approached, which was unnecessary considering there was no opposing traffic. Joey tensed again.

The passenger door of the car opened and a man climbed out. He was dressed much nicer than most people who came to this part of town, and he looked pissed. The part that made Joey most nervous, however, was the fact the man was white. Well-dressed white guys never came to this part of town unless they were planning something.

Joey tightened his hand on Nate's collar and turned him around. "You ain't going to school today."

"What?"

"Use Mr. Green's computer to look at Wikipedia. It'll make you plenty smart." He was practically running now, and Nate was tripping over his feet to keep up.

The gunshots echoed, and Nate screamed. Joey wrapped his

lanky body around his brother and forced him down, ducking his head and covering it with his hand. As if fingers could protect his head better than his skull could. They cowered against the brick wall of the nearest building, both of them waiting to feel the tear of bullets through their bodies. Joey risked looking back and saw the well-dressed man was now bleeding from two holes in his shirt. His left arm was held across his wounded stomach and his other hand brought up a gun. Joey covered Nate's head as the guy shot at the car he'd just gotten out of.

Tires screeched as the old car pulled away from the stop sign. The shot man tried to run off the street, but the car clipped his hip and made him twist through the air. Joey was cursing under his breath as he pressed Nate's head to his shoulder so he wouldn't see the body land. The car slammed on its brakes, reversed, and Joey knew that he would never forget the sound of impact for as long as he lived.

The car's engine revved again and it sped away. There was a thumping sound and Joey realized with a lurch that the body was being dragged behind it.

Joey held Nate for a long time after the sound of the car's engine faded. He realized he was crying, and his brother's body was quaking.

"You okay?"

"Yeah. You kinda hurt my shoulder."

Joey sniffled. "Don't be a baby."

He looked over his shoulder. There was a gory trail in the middle of the road, but that wasn't what caught his attention. The white-robed nun was back, standing near the stop sign. She had apparently been drawn by the sound of gunfire. She looked at Joey, meeting his gaze for a long moment before she closed her eyes and bowed her head in prayer. Without her there, Joey knew he could have just moved on and tried to forget what he had just seen. But now he would wonder what the nun would think of him if he didn't do something.

"No school today," Joey said again. "C'mon. Back home."

He hustled Nate to his feet and hurried him back the way they had come. He would use the common phone in the lobby to make the call.

The body was found five blocks away from the initial impact sight. Patrol officers were trying their best to keep the scene preserved, but it was next to impossible thanks to the morning commute. Several streets were confined to a single lane, while others were catalogued and photographed as well as possible before the evidence was obliterated. Riley and Priest went to the initial crime scene first and met with the first officer on the scene, a pale young man named Patton.

"Witness was Joseph Tidwell. Car pulled up to the stop sign, sat for a while, and then Don Draper gets out. They argue, Mr. Suit starts to walk away, bang bang bang~"

Riley held up a hand to pause the story. "Three shots? The witness counted?"

Patton shrugged. "No idea. He said he was pretty sure Mr. Suit was hit twice, but he said he thought he heard at least three shots. Whether there really were three, or he just heard an echo of one, who knows?" Riley motioned for him to continue. "The guy returns fire, and the car takes off. Hits him, backs up to hit him again, then takes off south." It wasn't necessary for him to point; the rising sun had made the disgusting trail in the center of the road unavoidably visible.

"Make and model of the car?"

Patton checked his notes. "And I quote: 'Some old sedan. Maybe dark red.'"

"Sounds open and shut to me." Riley grimaced and scanned the opposite side of the street. If the shooter was sitting in the car, he would have been shooting toward the waterfront. The hypothetical missed shot would have gone into the water and disappeared with the tide.

"Okay. Let me know if you get lucky on the scene. Body is..."

"Five blocks that way." Patton pointed again and smiled. "Enjoy your walk, ladies."

Riley smiled tightly and walked away. Priest followed behind with her attention on the bloody asphalt.

"It could be worse," Priest said as she fell into step beside Riley. "It could be raining."

Riley smiled and checked the sky. Police cars with their lights flashing were parked every half-dozen yards, and police were looking for the weapon the witness had seen the victim using.

Riley looked back toward the initial crime scene and then looked ahead. "Five blocks is a long way to walk. Even longer to be dragged on your face. Where was this guy's guardian angel?"

There wasn't anger in the question, but Priest still looked down at her feet. "We can't always stop every bad thing that may happen. I've told you that before."

"Yeah, but... you'd think it would be okay to just pluck the guy from the bumper once he was dead. Save him a little dignity."

Priest looked at the trail. "Maybe that's what happened. It could have taken him five blocks to die."

Riley shuddered at the thought. "Bad, bad way to go."

They walked in silence until the blue-and-white van from the Office of the Chief Medical Examiner came into view. This portion of the crime scene was completely closed off to traffic, but the patrolman either spotted the badge on Riley's belt or recognized her in time to move the barricade to let her through. Gillian was crouching next to the body when Riley approached her from behind.

"I can save you the trouble," Riley said. "Clearly this man died of diabetes."

Gillian tilted her head to the side. "I thought I told you to stay off my crime scenes, Sherlock."

Riley gave the body a wide berth so she could see the face. She immediately wished she'd left it to her imagination. Not a lot could turn her stomach, but this man had definitely not survived five blocks. She shuddered and focused on the body. His clothes were shredded and the skin underneath was scraped various shades of red from his impromptu journey.

"Three fingers on his left hand are broken; I assume that happened when he lost his gun. I found two bullet wounds in the abdomen, which would likely have caused his death given a few minutes. The actual cause of death, though, is... apparent."

"So the killer fatally shot him, then hit him with the car, then dragged him five blocks. Maybe we can get him on three counts of murder."

Gillian held her hands out palm-up.

"Any ID?"

"Nothing in any of his pockets. I took images of his fingerprints with that new scanner thingamajig they gave us. We'll see if it does any good."

Riley sighed. "You get new gadgets, and yet we're still brewing coffee in the first Mr. Coffee off the production line."

"Whine, whine, whine," Gillian said under her breath as she bent down to continue examining the body.

Riley knelt down and twisted her neck to look at the dead

man's wrist. "Jill, what's the tattoo?"

Gillian looked and gingerly lifted the arm. "Looks like a stylized letter H. Two daggers with the hilts forming the crossbar."

Something tickled the back of Riley's mind, but she couldn't place it. "Okay. I'm going to go talk to the witness and see if he can tell me anything new. Priest, maybe you can help the officers look for the missing weapon?" She raised an eyebrow.

Priest read the hidden meaning. "I think I could speed things up a little."

Gillian watched Priest go and checked to make sure her assistant wasn't close enough to eavesdrop. "Scavenger hunt?"

"Priest has seen the body, felt the chakras or whatever she does. She'll have a better chance of finding the gun now."

Gillian shrugged and stood up. "I'll give you a call when the fingerprints come back."

"Okay." Riley said, "Do you have my phone number?"

"Yeah. It's written on the stall of the bathroom at the precinct. 'For a good time, call...'"

Riley shook her head. "Don't blame me. You're the one who wrote it." She blew Gillian a kiss and started toward the witness' address. She was on the front steps when her cell phone rang. "Could have just shouted," Riley muttered, but the display showed a different number. She stopped at the doorway and turned around to take the call before she went in. "This is Riley Parra."

"Riley. It's Briggs. Where are you?"

"Work."

"What? What time is... shit. Sorry. You got a call?"

Riley moved back down to the sidewalk. "Yeah. Where are *you*?"

"I'm... home."

"Everything okay?" She looked back to where Gillian and her assistant were loading the victim into a body bag. Briggs had been a mess for the past few months, since Riley hit the 'reset' button and changed everything. She felt responsible. "I could leave Priest in charge if you need~"

"No. No, work the case. I won't be in today."

Riley sighed. "Boss, you have to tell me what's going on. We can help you."

"I'll let you know. Wait. There's something you can do. When you get to the office, there might be someone there waiting for me. I need you to get rid of him as... politely as you can."

"Sure, boss. What's he look like?"

"Six foot something, long nose and a thin face. Blue eyes, dark hair. Probably dressed in a nice suit." Riley glanced toward the OCME van with growing dread. "Just tell him I won't be in. Whatever you have to do to get him out of there."

The OCME van neared Riley, and she stepped toward the street with her hand raised to stop it. The van pulled to the curb.

"Boss, we may have a situation here. Stay on the line."

Gillian rolled down the passenger side window. "Everything okay?"

"I need you to open up the back."

Gillian got out of the car and followed Riley to the back of the van. She opened the door, and Riley climbed inside and knelt next to the body bag.

She gestured for Gillian to unzip the bag. "This guy you suspect might be at the office. Does he have a tattoo on the inside of his left wrist?" The buzzing silence on the other end of the line went on long enough that Riley thought they'd been disconnected. "Boss? You~"

"He's dead?" Briggs' voice was raw, emotional.

"Yeah."

"Where are you?"

Riley looked at Gillian. "We're taking him to the morgue right now. Who is this guy?"

"Sean Hyde."

Riley closed her eyes and sagged against the side of the van. She covered her eyes with her hand, wishing she had just stayed in bed after all. Sean Hyde, a member of the Hyde family, twenty percent of the Five Families that ruled No Man's Land under the banner of Marchosias. He was also Lieutenant Briggs' ex-husband.

"Maybe you ought to come into work today after all, boss."

Riley stayed in the van for the ride back to work, calling Priest on the way to let her know about the new developments in the case. When they arrived at the garage, Riley climbed out of the back to let Gillian and the assistant take their new client out on a gurney. "I'll bring the lieutenant in for the identification. Everything you heard in the van is strictly need-to-know."

Gillian nodded. "I understand. I'll sign him in as a John Doe. But as soon as his fingerprints come back, it'll be out of my hands."

"Do what you can. Hopefully by then I'll know Briggs' side of the story." She pecked Gillian on the cheek. "Be safe."

Gillian held on to Riley's wrist. "Tell me it's need-to-know again."

"You'll be punished to the fullest extent of the law. I am very serious about this, Dr. Hunt."

"Ooh." Gillian shuddered visibly and rolled her eyes back in her head before she let Riley go. "So sexy when you're in charge."

Riley winked and went to the stairs. She reached the lobby at the same moment Briggs stepped in from the street. She wore little or no makeup, and her hair was limp and unwashed. She had forgone her usual business-casual for a gray sweater over a T-shirt and black leggings. She looked unbelievably broken and vulnerable.

Riley whistled and motioned her over, and Briggs crossed the lobby in what could only be called a death march. She spoke in a whisper as soon as she was close enough for Riley to hear. "It's him."

"We don't know that. I remembered where I saw the tattoo before; every male member of the Hyde family gets it for their eighteenth birthday. Until we know for sure~"

Briggs stopped Riley by brandishing her cell phone. "It's *him*. Alan Hyde called me himself to let me know."

Even though she was fairly sure she knew the answer, she asked anyway. "And how does Alan Hyde already know?"

Briggs glanced over her shoulder as a pair of uniformed cops strolled by. She rubbed her neck until they were gone, then gestured at the elevator. "We should do this someplace a bit more private."

"Of course we should," Riley whispered. She gestured for Briggs to lead the way and followed her to the elevator.

They rode up in silence, even though they were alone in the car. Riley drummed her fingers against her arm, trying to brace herself for the revelations to come. When they reached the right floor, Riley stepped out of the elevator to see Priest had just arrived. She eyed Riley and Briggs and started to rise, but Riley motioned for her to stay where she was.

Briggs went into her office and Riley followed, shutting the door and ensuring the blinds were closed before she spoke. "So you and your ex got back together?"

"Yeah."

"How long?"

Briggs sat behind her desk and withdrew a bottle and glass from the bottom drawer of her desk and poured herself a drink.

"Just a few months. He showed up not long after Gail Finney

shot up our lobby. He called to check up on me. At first I didn't want anything to do with him, sent him away. But then he did something I didn't expect." She took a drink, her hand shaking enough that it rattled against her teeth. "He left. He didn't try to make me see his point of view, he didn't insist on being there for me. He just wanted to make sure I knew he was there if I needed him. I think you know how comforting that is."

Riley thought of the nights she'd glanced over to see Gillian sitting on the couch, legs tucked under her, quietly reading. "Yeah. I know exactly what it feels like."

"Once I was convinced he was authentically worried about me and not just trying to get into my pants, I called him. We had dinner and drinks, and he was a perfect gentleman. In the end, I was the one asking him to bed.

"We were good for a while. Like the old days. But then I came home one night to find Sean in the kitchen with his brother Timothy. Apparently one of their sisters had been arrested, and they wanted to know what I could do about it. I kicked Timothy out, and Sean and I had a pretty big fight. He said it was nothing major, that she would probably get off even if it went to court. I was just saving them some time. I kicked him out."

Riley made a 'get on with it' gesture with two fingers. "I think you can skip to the end."

"When it became apparent I was repeating history, I got scared. That's one of the reasons I sent you to traffic. That, and you deserved it."

Riley shrugged. "What happened last night?"

Briggs took another drink and held the liquor on her tongue for a long moment before swallowing. "I gave Sean an ultimatum. Either we go our separate ways, or he cut ties with his family. I refused to be his tool."

"Wow."

"He said yes."

Riley's eyes widened. "I think I wasted my 'wow.'"

Briggs shrugged, her eyes locked on a spot on the wall beyond Riley. "I was surprised, too. He said he'd been pining for me since our breakup. Now that he had me back, he wasn't going to risk losing me again. He proposed." Her voice broke. "I said no, and he insisted that he was going to do it right. He said he would take my name so he wouldn't be a Hyde anymore. I kicked him out." She touched her knuckle under her eye and looked down at her feet.

"So you thought maybe he'd show up here and make trouble."

Briggs nodded. "Apparently he decided actions speak louder than words. Alan Hyde stopped just short of admitting it when he called me, but he implied that Sean stopped by and they had a disagreement about his 'mistake.' He apologized."

"Did you think he was threatening you?"

"With him? It's hard to say."

Riley considered the possibility. "Okay. For now, we'll keep you out of it. Gillian ran the prints, so it shouldn't be long before we have an official ID on him. Priest and I will check it out and keep the connection to you as quiet as possible. Where was Mr. Hyde when he called?"

"His restaurant. It's where he always is this time of day." Riley stood up to leave, but Briggs stopped her. "I appreciate this, Riley." She looked at the glass and put it on the desk at the outer edge of her reach. "I've been really horrid to you during this whole... mess. I owe you an apology."

"It's fine. I'll let you know when we have anything solid to report."

"Thanks, Riley."

Riley left the office to find Priest leaning against the wall next to the door. She motioned for Priest to follow her and started toward the stairs. "How much did you hear?"

"Enough. It explains her unease and state of undress when Gillian and I visited her at home last week."

Riley twisted to look at her. "You and my wife were in Lieutenant Brigg's apartment, and she was undressed?"

"Only partially." Priest realized what Riley was saying. "It was innocent. We were looking for you."

Riley let her off the hook. "I'm pulling your leg, Cait. Gillian told me about it. Apparently Briggs has really great legs." They took a detour into the morgue and found Gillian preparing the body for the examination. "We came by for the official ID."

"Fingerprints confirmed it. Sean McIntosh Hyde."

Riley flinched as if someone had thrown a punch. "McIntosh?"

Gillian shrugged. "Don't blame me. I didn't name him."

"So now we have a name. Any surprises on your initial examination?"

"Nope. Shot, run over, dragged. It's still up in the air about which one actually killed him, but that's just for the paperwork."

"Okay. Let me know if you find anything."

Gillian looked wary. "And you'll be...?"

"Dealing with the Hyde family."

"That's what I was afraid you'd say. Be safe, Riley."

Riley touched two fingers to her heart and held them out toward Gillian. Gillian snatched it out of the air as Riley left.

"Did you find out anything at the scene?"

"I spoke to the witness and calmed him to the point where he was able to remember more details about the car."

"Calmed him. You mean you hypnotized him?"

Priest shook her head. "That's a parlor trick. I merely erased his anxiety and unclouded his mind so that the information was available to his recollection. I compared his description online while you were speaking with Briggs and came up with a match. The car was a Chrysler LeBaron, probably from 1979 or so."

"Wow, that is late-model. Did you do a registration search?"

Priest smiled as they crossed the lobby. "On a whim, I decided to see if Alan Hyde happened to have a car like that registered in his name. He didn't."

"Let me guess. He has two?"

"Four, actually."

Riley smiled and patted Priest on the shoulder as they left the building.

Hamlet Lane was a short alley that mainly served to connect two other streets. The only business with an address on that street was an exclusive restaurant that was also called Hamlet Lane. The door was shaded by a blue awning that prevented Riley from seeing the bouncer stationed in the atrium. He came outside as Riley parked at the curb and assumed the position of gatekeeper with his hands clasped loosely behind his back. He had ten inches on Riley, both vertically and horizontally, and wore a white dress shirt tight enough he had to have been sewn into it. He gazed at the badge she presented without interest.

"We open at six. Cops don't eat free."

"Good to know. Detectives Parra and Priest. We're here to see Alan Hyde."

He rolled his shoulders in a disinterested shrug and scanned the street to the north of them. "Anything could happen, I guess, if you stay here long enough. Might catch a glimpse when his car leaves."

Riley unclipped the badge from her belt, making sure her

jacket opened enough that he saw her gun as well. "Maybe you have problem reading from a distance. Maybe it's the big words that trip you up. This is an all-access pass."

"Not here."

Riley moved to step around the bouncer and he moved to block her. It put him in the awkward position of resting his weight on his left foot. When he grabbed her arm, Riley brought up her foot and stomped on the back of his left knee. He made a strangled noise as he went down, and Riley grabbed two of his fingers and twisted them back. His strength seemed to evaporate as Riley slung her free arm around his neck.

"I know you didn't mean to put your hands on a police officer, because the difference in our sizes means I'd have to take that as an act of aggression. You wouldn't want me to think that, would you?"

"No... Detective."

"In retrospect, gentleman that you are, I think you were just going to open the door for me. Is that right?"

He grunted a response and Riley relaxed her grip on him. He stood and Riley took a step back in case it was just a ruse. He glared at Riley, avoiding Priest's gaze as she was a witness to his humiliation, and stepped past her to open the door. Riley smiled sweetly as she entered with Priest, pushing through the inner door without the bouncer's help to enter the main dining room.

Alan Hyde seemed to believe he lived in a mobster movie. He reigned from a large table at the back of the room, with doors to the kitchen on either side of his seat. The rest of the tables were set up so that other diners in the restaurant were unwitting extras in his power play. He was a king and the meal was his feast. The bouncer brushed roughly between Riley and Priest in a lame attempt to reassert his dominance even as he massaged his sore fingers.

Currently, Hyde's table was the only one occupied. Riley recognized two of the men as members of the family, but the other two were unknowns. Alan Hyde himself was seated in the center of the table, a tortoise in a tailored suit. He wore thick-framed glasses and lifted his gaze as the bouncer approached, leaning to one side to see around him to their uninvited guests.

"Bailey, we didn't invite these women. Please escort them out."

Riley kept her voice low enough that only Bouncer Bailey could hear her. "Yeah, Bailey, you wanna give that a shot?"

He ignored her. "Detectives Parra and Priest, Mr. Hyde. They said they just want to talk with you."

Hyde sat up straighter. "Parra? Yes. I think I've heard the name. You're dismissed, Bailey." The bouncer turned to leave, but Hyde wasn't finished. "By which I mean you are no longer employed at this establishment. Police or no police, I should have been informed they were here before you allowed them inside. Your final paycheck will be mailed to you."

Bailey was frozen in mid-turn for a moment, but he finally nodded. "Yes, sir, Mr. Hyde. My apologies."

Riley watched him go and then looked at Hyde again. "That was a little harsh, don't you think?"

"Let him be an example to the next one. Now what can I refuse to do before I throw you out of here?"

"We're here about the death of your son, Sean Hyde. We were hoping you might be able to shed some light on the circumstances surrounding what happened."

Alan picked up a napkin and thoroughly wiped his fingers with it. "A tragedy."

"Sure it was." Riley eyed the other people at the table. It was impossible to tell if they were armed, but she wasn't taking any chances. She rested her hand on the butt of her gun as a show of readiness. "And it's come with quite a mystery. Care to explain how you knew the victim's identity before we did?"

"Your medical examiner used a Portable Print Scanner at the scene. The results of that test were flagged when a member of my family was identified. It helps to have friends in the right places, my dear."

Riley said, "A late-model Chrysler LeBaron was spotted at the scene. Would you mind letting us have a look at any cars you might own that match the description?"

Alan smiled. "Do you happen to have a warrant, Detective Priest?"

"I'm Parra. She's Priest. And no, we don't have a warrant."

"Then we're done speaking. I would like to be informed when my son's body is available for funeral services." He looked at Priest. "Send her. Despite your celebrity, I dislike speaking to minorities and avoid it whenever possible."

Riley bristled as she took a card from her jacket pocket and leaned forward to flick it onto the table. "Choo dealin' wit' me, *papi*. Deal wit' it." She turned and motioned for Priest to follow her out of the restaurant.

Priest waited until they were outside to speak. "That didn't accomplish much."

"We know that he has access to the PPS. That needs to be investigated. And we kicked the hornet's nest. Now we can sit back and watch what happens." Riley saw a shadow on the sidewalk coming up fast from behind her. "Priest, take a big step to your left, please."

Priest did as instructed and Riley spun on her heel. She curled her fingers against her palm and thrust her hand up, the meaty heel of it impacting Bailey's chin just before he was close enough to grab her. She shot her other fist into his gut like a piston, realizing only as he was falling that he had both hands in his pockets. She didn't feel guilty as he hit the ground; he'd already attacked her once and he was approaching her at a fast clip. He cried out as he hit the ground, his hands coming up in a defensive pose. The seams of his too-tight shirt had popped when he fell, and the resulting look was purely pathetic.

"If you want to make me pay for what happened in there, I'd suggest you just let it go. This won't end well for you."

Bailey stayed on his back but looked toward the restaurant to make sure no one was looking. "No. I, uh, it... no. Hyde's always been a bastard. He was just looking for an excuse to kick me loose." He sat up, cupping his jaw in one hand. He looked like an overgrown toddler who had just fallen off his bicycle. "I waited because if that prick ain't loyal to me, no reason I should be loyal to him. You're here about Sean, right?"

"Yeah. You happen to know anything about that?"

He sighed. "I know enough. But I'm not going to talk about it here."

Riley held out her hand. "Sorry. You understand my confusion."

"Sure. Whatever." He took her hand.

"Come on. My partner and I will give you a ride to the unemployment office." It took nearly all her strength to keep from toppling over when Bailey pulled; he was a hefty boy. She brushed off the back of his shirt, the closest she would come to an apology, and glanced over her shoulder as Priest walked him to the car.

A man she hadn't seen at Hyde's table was standing at the front door of the restaurant. The door was propped open against his right foot, and he held a lit cigarette outside so that the wind would catch the smoke. He had dark eyes and shaggy yellow-blonde hair, his lips pursing in the center in a way that reminded her of a lion.

Riley saluted him with two fingers, and he responded with an upward toss of his chin. She walked around the back of the car and got behind the wheel.

"Got bad news for you, Bailey. No matter what you tell us, your boss is going to know you talked."

"Screw him. He brought it on himself."

Riley glanced at Priest, shrugged, and pulled away from the curb. When she glanced back, the smoking man was no longer standing in the doorway.

They drove to a diner outside the amorphous boundary of No Man's Land, and well outside the Hyde Family territory, and Riley escorted Evan Bailey to a booth near the back. She sat facing the door, and Bailey seemed desperate to fit his bulk as close to the wall as possible. "You can relax, Mr. Bailey."

"Are you kidding? You think we're safe just because we drove a mile or two? Mr. Hyde has eyes everywhere."

"I didn't mean to imply he wouldn't find out. I'm telling you to relax because he already knows you're talking to me. One of the Hyde brothers saw you leave with us. Blonde guy, kind of looks like a lion."

Bailey looked confused for a second and then rolled his eyes. "Ah, cripes. Danny Falco. He's not a brother. He works for the big cheese."

Riley met Priest's gaze. "Big cheese. Guy named Marchosias?"

"Nah, the Marquis." He rubbed his face. "Well, if *he* saw, then it's really all over for me. I might as well go and jump off the waterfront myself."

The waitress brought over three water glasses, but Riley waved her away when she offered menus. She folded her hands on the table and leaned forward. "Well, if you could tell us what you know before your swim, I'd be greatly obliged."

Bailey pulled his lips back against his teeth and drained his water like a horse drinking from a trough. When he was done, he wiped his mouth on the cuff of his sleeve and leaned back.

"Sean Hyde called his dad last night and they had an unscheduled meeting. That's about as odd as if the President walked in here right now and ordered chocolate chip pancakes. I drove Mr. Hyde to the meeting~"

"Which Mr. Hyde?" Priest said.

"The father, Alan. I drive... *drove* him wherever he needed to go."

"When and where did they meet?" Riley asked, hoping he would say it was the waterfront around the time Joey Tidwell saw the shooting.

Bailey took Priest's water without asking and downed it as well. "Close to midnight at that shut-down mall on Franklin. Just in the parking lot. They had words, it was acrimonious."

Riley couldn't help laughing.

"What?"

"Sorry. Acrimonious?"

Bailey showed his hands. "That's what Mr. Hyde said it was. If it's the wrong word, laugh at him, okay?"

Riley shook his head. "Okay, so after their acrimonious meeting, what happened?"

"Mr. Hyde, uh, Alan... he told Sean that if he wanted out of the family, it could definitely be arranged. Sean said he didn't care and he was done. He walked away. Alan was totally thrown by that. I mean, no one walks away from him. So he called after him and said that he was no longer his son. Sean didn't even react; he just got into his car and drove off."

"And what did Alan Hyde do?"

Bailey shrugged. "Got back into the car and sat there for a long time. He didn't tell me where to go, so I just sat there with him. Finally he told me to take him home. I did."

"He didn't make any calls? No Chrysler LeBarons came into the picture?"

"No. I mean, he might have called from home once he went upstairs, but I stay on the ground floor after hours. And boss has a couple of LeBarons, but last night we went to meet Sean in a town car."

Riley took a drink of her water before Bailey could take it as well. His information wasn't the smoking gun she hoped it would be, but it still filled in a lot of blanks in the timeline of Sean Hyde's death. "All right. Let's go."

"Huh?" Bailey looked at them both. "Where are we going?"

"We're not going to just turn you loose with someone like Alan Hyde gunning for you. We'll get you some protective custody."

Priest slid out of the booth to let Bailey up. He cleared his throat and nodded past Riley. "You mind if I, uh, visit the little boy's room?"

Riley rolled her eyes and hooked her thumb over her shoulder.

"Hurry up." When he was gone, Riley lowered her voice and stepped closer to Priest. "What do you think? Is he telling the truth?"

"I'm pretty sure he's telling the truth as he knows it." She was watching the bathroom door the former driver-slash-bouncer had gone through. "I can feel some kind of barrier in his mind, but it's small. It may be something as simple as his will to forget something rather than outside influences. Do you really think he knows anything useful in Sean Hyde's death?"

Riley shrugged. "It's possible he doesn't even know what he knows. But even if he can't help us find Sean Hyde's killer, as Alan Hyde's driver, he'll know enough to justify protective custody. Hell, he might even get Witness Protection."

Bailey came out of the bathroom daintily wiping his hands with a paper towel. Riley led him out with Priest bringing up the rear of their group. Riley called Briggs before she started the car. "It's me. Are you still at the office?"

"Yeah. I decided I might as well make myself useful."

"We're bringing in Alan Hyde's driver. He may be able to shed some light on the victim's last few hours."

Briggs exhaled sharply. "Well, that's a relief. Thank you for calling."

"No problem. We'll take him to Interrogation Room One when we show up."

Priest had gotten into the backseat with Bailey, and she put a hand on his shoulder when he tried to lean forward. "I'm not... I'm just making sure... you're not arresting me, are you?"

"Not yet. But the day is young. Buckle your seatbelt."

The drive to the station was spent in silence, with Bailey brooding in the backseat. The intimidating bouncer had all but evaporated and, in his place was an overgrown elementary school child. Riley was less afraid of him overpowering her than she was dealing with him if he decided to start crying. She stopped herself before she started feeling bad about hurting his hand; he'd definitely been asking for that at the time.

They took the elevator and Riley used the ride to explain what was expected of him. "The more you can give us about the Hyde family and their activities, the more we'll be inclined to help you out. You've already spilled the beans about one thing, so they're already mad at you."

The doors opened and Riley preceded Bailey into the main room. Briggs was coming out of Interrogation Room One and spotted her, changing direction to meet with her instead of returning to her office. "Boss, this is~"

Bailey punched her in the neck, throwing his full weight behind the rabbit punch to the spot where her skull met her spine. As she dropped, he reached into her jacket and removed her weapon. Priest slammed into him from behind but he elbowed her in the gut and twisted. He pressed his hand flat against her face, muttered a phrase in a foreign language, and Priest twisted away from him with a shout of pain.

Briggs was halfway across the room with her own gun drawn by the time Bailey returned his attention to her. "Meddlesome bitch." He aimed at her head.

Riley managed to clear her head and threw herself at Bailey's right leg. When in doubt, take out the knees. She twisted his leg the wrong way and Bailey dropped to one knee. His shot went wild and Briggs took her shot. The bullet hit Bailey in the chest but didn't slow him down. He cocked the hammer again and bared his teeth.

A black woman dressed in rags was the closest person to Bailey other than Riley and Briggs. She brought her gun up in a mirror image of Bailey's move, but she was faster on the trigger. Her shot took off the top of his head, and the big man finally went limp. He fell backwards, his shirt soaked with blood from Briggs' shot. Riley pulled herself away from the man as he went down. She clutched the back of her head where it felt as if he'd rammed a spike through the skin.

"Riley, you okay?" She nodded and Briggs looked toward the elevators. "Priest?"

Priest had one hand over her eyes, but she waved off their concern.

The apparently homeless woman broke her firing stance and joined Briggs and Riley over the body. Briggs nodded to her. "Nicely done, Detective Kane."

Wanda Kane exhaled and rubbed her wrist back and forth over her forehead. "The one day I come in to do paperwork, there's some actual excitement."

Uniformed officers appeared at the top of the stairs and Briggs held up her hands to let them know the excitement was over. Riley had recovered enough from the surprise blow to kneel next to Priest.

"Are you okay? What did he do?"

Priest's eyes were red and overflowing with tears. "Sulfur. I'll be fine, but it hurts very badly. Are you all right?"

"Comparatively."

"No," Briggs said. "Have someone check you out, even if it's only Dr. Hunt. The way he hit you, and the way you went down, I want to make sure there's no damage."

Riley nodded. "All right. I'll take Priest down to get checked out." She paused. "Boss, I don't know what to say. If he'd shown any sign~"

Briggs stopped her. "I'm sure it's a long story and you'd rather not go into detail here. We'll debrief later in my office."

Riley nodded, thankful for the reprieve. She ushered Priest into the elevator as Riley, Briggs and Wanda Kane handed over their weapons to another detective according to standard procedure after a shooting. Riley looked at Priest again, checking her eyes. "Sure you'll be okay? They look pretty red."

"It's the equivalent of blowing cinnamon into someone's eyes. Enough to briefly incapacitate. My eyesight is already coming back."

The doors pinged as they opened, and Riley helped Priest out into the corridor. There were three bodies laid out in the morgue, and Gillian was in the midst of examining one when Riley entered. She pulled down her mask, almost successful in hiding her anxiety.

"Detective DiMarco said there were shots fired. Shots. Fired."

Riley crossed the room in fewer steps than she would have thought possible. "We're okay. The bad guy is the only one who got hit."

Gillian held her hands out to the side, unable to hug Riley with her scrubs, apron and gloves on. Riley put a hand on either side of Gillian's face and touched their foreheads together. They held the position until Gillian whispered, "Okay," and turned her head to kiss Riley's palm. "What's wrong? You look fish-eyed."

"I got hit in the back of the head. But you should check out Priest first~"

"I'll be fine. Riley's head~"

"Quiet," Gillian snapped, her fear dissolving into anger. "Either one of you, on the table. Now."

Riley knew better than to argue with that voice. She walked to the empty exam table while Gillian removed her gloves and put on a fresh pair.

"So what happened?"

Riley explained about their visit to Hamlet Lane. When she got to the part about Bailey going crazy, Priest took over. "I felt a black spot in his mind and thought it was just his attempt to block painful or traumatic memories. The moment he saw and recognized Lieutenant Briggs, however, it shattered. It was a trap set by the demon he mentioned, Danny Falco."

Gillian said, "Shouldn't you have felt that? I don't mean to cast blame, Caitlin, I'm just~"

"No, you're absolutely correct. If he had added something substantial, I would have found it in a heartbeat. But he formed his mousetrap out of Bailey's existing aggression. He wrapped it up like a spring and filled it with just a touch of demonic energy. It's what gave him the ability to disable me so effectively. That's why Bailey was acting so conspicuously..."

"Infantile," Riley suggested.

"Yes. His mind was only partially present during our talk at the diner. The rest of him was coiled around the trap waiting to be sprung. All the violence of his soul was unleashed in that moment, combined with the demon's aggression and his humiliation over what happened at the restaurant."

Gillian said, "You provoked him?"

"No more than anyone else trying to kick my ass." She squeezed Gillian's forearm. "There was going to be violence either way. I just made sure I got in the first blow."

"Well, then. Good girl." She pecked Riley's lips and stepped back. "I diagnose you with minor whiplash. I can give you some painkillers and keep an eye on it."

"Do you make house calls?"

"At your house, I do." She stepped back and gestured for Priest to take her place. "Next patient."

Priest shook her head. "I'm fine~"

Riley cut her off. "Don't even try. Get on the table, Caitlin."

Priest gave in. "What's our next step?"

"We go back to Hamlet Lane and I'll take Alan Hyde into custody. Whatever the cause, his bodyguard just opened fire on a police officer. While I'm doing that, you can have a conversation with Danny Falco. Between the two of them, we should be able to get some semblance of the truth about what happened to Sean. Do you think he knows about Falco's... real connections?"

"Anything's possible. We should tread lightly when we return."

Gillian looked at Riley. "Very lightly. Feather lightly."

"Yes, dear." Riley kissed Gillian's cheek. "Is she cleared for duty?"

"Considering her eyes were healing as I looked at them, I'll say yes." She aimed her finger at Priest's face. "Keep an eye on her, Caitlin. Tell me if her whiplash gets exacerbated."

"Great. My guardian angel is tattling on me to my partner. C'mon, Cait."

Gillian swatted Riley on the rear end before she got out of reach, and Riley ushered Priest out of the morgue. Priest said, "She took that well."

"She hides it well." Riley's smile faded. "It'll come out tonight."

"Oh."

"It's okay. I'll be there to hold her." She snapped her fingers and pointed at the elevator. "Let's go confront a mobster and a demon."

Riley parked two blocks away from Hamlet Lane so her car wouldn't be spotted. She and Priest both wore bulletproof vests, although Priest's was mainly to keep up appearances, and covered them with their jackets to reduce the amount of odd looks they got as they walked to their destination.

Instead of going to the front door, she and Priest cut through the alley that ran behind the restaurant and found the kitchen entrance. She had her badge ready when she knocked, and she made sure the cook who answered saw it before her weapon. His hands went up, and Riley gently pulled him out into the alley.

"We're not here for you. We just want Mr. Hyde and his people. All you have to do is step aside and let us into the building. Can you do that?"

The cook nodded and stepped aside. Riley nodded her thanks to him and led Priest inside. The other cooks and the wait staff that was loitering all tensed at the sight of Riley and her weapon, but they left silently when Riley motioned at the door with her head. She stopped the last one and said, "Anyone else out there besides Hyde and his cronies?"

"No. It's the slow period."

Riley nodded. "Thanks. Go on, get out of here." To Priest, she said, "Is Falco going to be a problem?"

"Not for me."

Riley smiled. She peeked around the corner and saw Alan Hyde sitting at his table with a laptop in front of him instead of a plate. Only two men at the table were eating. Falco was lounging in a booth by the front door with his eyes cast down. Riley held up her free hand to show Priest there were five people present just as Falco's head snapped up and he spotted her.

"Hands where I can see them." Riley stepped into the room and took position behind Hyde's table. "Gentleman... hands on the table, palm down. Reach for the opposite edge of the table and don't move a muscle." The men reluctantly did as they were told, their chins on the table as their arms stretched forward. The only one who didn't comply was Alan Hyde, while Falco was still in position by the front door.

"Mr. Falco, hands on the back of your head, please."

Priest stepped around the table and approached him with her gun drawn. Their eyes met, and Falco's lips curled into a smile. He showed her his palms and casually put them on top of his head. Riley turned her attention to the back of Alan Hyde's head.

"Are you armed, Mr. Hyde?"

"Why would I be armed? I have so many people willing to dirty their hands for me, Detective Parra. Is this still about my son's death?"

"Indirectly. Your former doorman, Evan Bailey, attempted to murder a police officer after he left here. Your comment about people dirtying their hands for you makes me wonder if he was just following orders. So we're going to have a conversation about that."

Hyde looked at the man next to him. "Oh-oh. They're going to take me downtown."

The men chuckled, which was made difficult by their positions.

"Stand up slowly and put your hands behind your back, Mr. Hyde."

Falco cleared his throat. "Not to interrupt, but I may have some information that could end this entire matter without further humiliating Mr. Hyde."

Riley looked at him. "Yeah? Maybe we should take you downtown, too. We have a special Cell to put you in."

Falco's smile widened. "I've heard about that Cell of yours, Detective Parra. Managed to get many of my kind into it?"

"Not really. It's easier to just kill them outright."

Falco turned his eyes to Priest like a predator sizing up potential prey. His hands were still on his head, but he seemed more relaxed than submissive.

"Sean Hyde was the heir to this family. He was going to take over when Alan here finally kicked the bucket or retired. The news he was going to turn his back on his birthright was not well-received."

Alan finally showed emotion. "Danny, what the hell are you doing?"

Falco said, "The police are here, Alan! They have us dead to rights!" His uncharacteristic display of emotion faded as quickly as it appeared, revealing it as an act. "Alan wanted to convince Sean that he was making a mistake, so he took him for a drive around his fiefdom. When Sean refused to hear reason and tried to walk away, Mr. Bailey was ordered to kill him."

"Shut your—" Alan Hyde suddenly choked on his words, gasping and sputtering as he tried to force them out anyway. Riley hadn't seen Falco do anything, but she knew it was his doing. He watched Alan for a moment and then continued his confession.

"Mr. Bailey was also ordered to eliminate Sean's former wife. She knew far too much about our operation to be allowed to roam free."

One of the men sitting beside Alan Hyde rose to his feet with an enraged roar. He pulled a gun from under his jacket, but Falco nodded at him. The man shouted, "You son of a bitch!" Then pressed the barrel under his own chin and pulled the trigger. The rest of the men at the table hit the ground, and Riley grabbed the back of Alan Hyde's chair and pulled it backwards. Her actions saved him from catching a bullet in the temple.

She managed to roll his bulk and shoved him toward the kitchen door. By the time they were safely inside, the gunfire had stopped. Riley kept her hand on his shoulder to keep him from running as she peeked into the dining room.

"Priest?"

"I'm fine." She was at the table, kneeling to examine the men who had just opened fire on each other instead of Falco. "They're dead."

Alan Hyde gasped in horror. "No. They can't be."

"Falco?"

Priest glared at him. "Never took his hands off his head."

Riley rose and saw Falco shrug. He was the picture of cooperation. "Feel free to take me to your Cell, Detective Parra, but you may want my testimony on file. Without it, you may find Alan Hyde's prosecution rather difficult. The choice is yours."

Riley looked down at Alan Hyde. His sons were dead. Putting him in prison would create a power vacuum. Riley met Falco's gaze and read the calculating grin on his lips.

"How hard did you push? How much power did you exert to make this happen?"

Falco smiled. "You mean how much did it take to convince Alan Hyde to order the death of his eldest child? None at all."

Priest moved closer to the demon. "That wasn't your doing at all. You couldn't convince these men to kill themselves until they drew their weapons on you. You didn't affect Alan Hyde at all. You affected his son."

Falco winked at her.

"Which son?" Riley said.

"Sean Hyde. Falco found the love he had for Lieutenant Briggs and reignited it. That's why he seemed so different with Lieutenant Briggs. His love was brought out the same way Bailey's aggression was suppressed. Everything else, Alan Hyde did of his own free will."

Falco sighed and shook his head in wonder. "Free will. Such an amazing trait. You see, Zerachiel, anyone can make a person pull a trigger. The real joy comes from making them *want* to pull the trigger." He rose and looked at Riley. "Have you made your decision yet, Detective Parra? Alan Hyde's prosecution and the crumbling of the Hyde Family in exchange for my freedom."

"The money and power of the Hyde family has to go somewhere," Riley said. "I assume you'll be taking control of it?"

Falco raised an eyebrow. "Well, I've been a very close friend to the family for years now. Alan trusted me. And when Sean began to turn his back on the only family he'd ever known... I became like a son to him."

"You're taking control of everything Hyde controlled?" Priest said. "But if Marchosias wanted someone else in charge~"

Riley interrupted her. "He's not working for Marchosias. We saw a demon working for one of the Five Families, so we assumed he'd been put there by the big boss. But that's not it is it?"

Falco winked at her and chuckled. "A demon once owned a bar in Tallahassee, Florida. It was one of his minor projects; he probably forgot about it decades ago. But I walked in, proved that I was a demon, and let the owner assume I had been sent by his employer. I took the profits of that bar for ten years before anyone caught on and then, well... alcohol is so flammable and accidents do happen."

"And now you're setting your sights on Marchosias."

He shrugged. "He's in the game, and yet he refuses to play. A champion to oppose you should have been chosen weeks ago, and the longer he waits the stronger you get. Either I will succeed and evil will have a truly motivated hand on the tiller, or Marchosias will have a fire lit underneath him and start working toward waging a proper war. First I'll take the Five Families from him, and then I'll use them to wrest the throne from his feeble grip." His face hardened and his eyes become smoldering bits of charcoal. "And then I will come for you, Riley Parra, and you will know an enemy the likes of which you have never seen."

Riley returned his stare unflinchingly. "Come on, Priest."

"Riley..."

"We have a prisoner to process." She looked down at Alan Hyde, who looked like he'd aged ten years during the conversation. "Let's go."

Priest backed away from Falco, who finally took his hands from his head.

"We'll see each other again, Mr. Falco. Soon."

He winked again. "Count on it, Detective."

Riley holstered her weapon and pulled Hyde to his feet. She handcuffed him and read him his rights as she ushered him out of the building.

Priest kept her voice steady. "We can't just let him go."

"We're not. We're giving him time and space. If Marchosias and Falco want to waste resources fighting each other, it's no skin off my noise. Let them erode their own forces for a while."

"And the collateral damage?"

"That's what we're here for, Priest."

Priest considered that and finally nodded. She looked over her shoulder at the restaurant. "We exchanged the human head of a criminal organization for a demon. I only pray we're not setting Marchosias up for a fall only to have something worse take his place."

Riley didn't say anything, but the thought had definitely crossed her mind.

Riley knocked on Briggs' office door, entering only when she finally answered. "Hey. I thought you would want to know. Alan Hyde is being processed as we speak."

"Thank you, Riley." Briggs was still dressed in her day-off clothes, her hair in a ponytail. She still had the bottle of liquor on the desk, and the level was much lower than it had been that morning. "Have a seat. You're almost off-duty. Have a drink with me."

Riley thought about refusing, but she decided a drink might hit the spot. She shut the door and Briggs poured her a glass. Riley tapped their glasses together before she took a seat.

"Are you okay?"

Briggs closed her eyes. "A demon convinced my ex-husband to recommit to me as part of a plan to have said ex-husband killed by his father. I'm not even sure how to begin processing that."

"You look at the bright side." Briggs looked at her, incredulous, and Riley shrugged. "You got to reconnect with Sean, just the good stuff. The stuff that made you say yes the first time. Right?"

"I suppose."

"And you got to have great sex for a few weeks."

Briggs laughed. "Well, I don't know about great. But what it lacked in quality, it made up for with quantity."

Riley smiled and they drank in silence for a while.

Finally Briggs put down her glass. "I'm resigning first thing in the morning."

"What?"

"I've been compromised twice. Fool me once, fool me twice... I feel I shouldn't gamble on a third time."

Riley shook her head. "The Hyde family is essentially gone now, boss. They won't come after you again."

"Can you guarantee that?"

"As much as I can guarantee anything when demons are involved. Maybe you let your heart call the shots one time too many, but you're a good cop."

Briggs shook her head. "I let bad guys get away. I looked the other way. There have to be consequences."

Riley leaned back in her chair. "You leave, I guarantee you someone ten times worse will take over your job. Priest and I will have our hands tied up again in secrets, and we won't be as effective in No Man's Land."

"So I can't retire because it would be inconvenient to you."

Riley smiled. "You can't retire because you're the best person for this job. You're the only person for this job. You got a little smudge on your conscience, but that'll only make you work harder to do right."

Briggs shook her head. "I don't know."

Riley put her glass on the desk with great deliberation and folded her hands together. "About three years ago, right before I realized what was really happening in No Man's Land, my partner

Kara Sweet got paid off by a demon to stop an investigation. At that point I didn't even know angels and demons were real, but I knew my partner was holding a gun to my head. We fought, the gun went off, and she died. Your predecessor, Nina Hathaway, knew the entire story. She agreed to help me cover up what happened, kept me from being suspended or worse, in exchange for oral sex."

Briggs was holding her glass against her bottom lip.

"I did it, and she held up her part of the bargain. I never..." She lowered her head. "I was never held accountable by the law, or by Kara's family. I keep in touch with them. Kara was sending them money, so I keep that up, too."

"Why?" Briggs' voice was raw. "Why tell me that?"

"Mutually assured destruction. I know something bad you did, and now you know..."

Briggs scoffed. "So it's a wash? We can both call ourselves good cops now?"

"Sure. Comparatively."

"That's a slippery slope, Detective."

"We can't always be punished for the bad we do. We're not saints, and trying to be one guarantees we'll crash and burn. Just be the best cop, and the best person you can be. Learn from your mistakes. If that's not enough, then you can decide to resign. But give it time."

Briggs said, "For you?"

"No. Because if something bad happens and I get taken out of the game, I want to know someone like you is still around keeping things under control."

Briggs laughed. "Honestly, Riley. If you're dead, I'll have already been dead for a very long time. But I get your meaning."

Riley picked up her glass again. "To good cops. Flaws and all."

Briggs stared at the glass before she clinked her glass against Riley's.

Riley did paperwork until Gillian was finished downstairs, and then they drove home together. They stopped to get takeout for dinner, and Riley served it onto plates when they got home. They ate in the kitchen, with only the light over the stove turned on, and then adjourned to the living room to watch the news. Riley leaned back against the arm of the couch with Gillian lying on top of her. During the commercials, Riley flipped through the channels with one hand while playing with Gillian's hair with the other.

Gillian moved her hand up and lightly touched the back of Riley's head. "Are you sure you're okay?"

Riley nodded and kissed Gillian's forehead. "Yeah. But I'll let you give me a full check-up later on so you can convince yourself."

Gillian smiled and slid down to rest her head on Riley's chest. Riley tangled Gillian's hair around her fingers and went back to the news. The day had been endless and the night was going by far too quickly. She held Gillian tighter, determined not to let the minutes slip away from her.

STATIONS OF THE CROSS

The faded ochre walls of the precinct's lobby reflected off the pale yellow tiles and, combining with the early morning sun coming through the arched windows, made the entire ground floor look like it was outlined in tarnished gold. The sergeant's desk was on a raised platform next to the front door, facing the bank of elevators and the wide staircase. Visitors to the 410th Precinct, willing and not, sat on wooden benches in the center of the space.

Riley held the door for Priest and guided her in. "...it's like musical chairs, but with lesbians."

Priest started to respond, but the desk sergeant interrupted her by calling out Riley's name. "Detective Parra. You have a visitor."

Aissa was sitting on the end of a bench and stood up with a smile. "Detective!"

"Aissa. I told you to call me Riley." She hugged the girl, who then hugged Priest. "Is everything okay? The shelter..."

"It's amazing. I love it there. I feel as if I'm continuing my mission. Thank you so much for finding a place for me."

Riley smiled. "It was my pleasure. You can do a lot of good even without your sisters. So what brings you down here? You could have come by the apartment."

Aissa hesitated. "Actually, I'm not the guest he was talking about. I'm not here to talk to you." Riley raised an eyebrow. "I-It's a perk, for sure, but... oh, goodness."

Riley laughed. "It's all right. You can have business that doesn't involve me."

"It actually involves the shelter. Eddie asked if I would come down here and speak with someone in~" She looked at a sheet of paper clutched protectively in her left hand. "Narcotics."

"Drugs?"

Aissa nodded. "It's a big problem with the people we're helping. Eddie wants to know about a new drug that's been making the rounds."

"Keep me in the loop, okay? Might be some overlap."

"I will. Good to see you again, Det~ Riley." She stopped short of bowing to Priest. "Zerachiel."

Priest smiled. "Be well, Aissa."

Riley turned to the desk sergeant. "If she's not my guest, who are you talking about?" He pointed with his pen, and a slender black man rose from a back bench. He looked ordinary from a distance; it was only when he stood next to someone that it became clear he was well over six feet tall. He wore an old army jacket with the patches torn off, layered over a pair of dress shirts with missing buttons.

"Radio! Long time no see."

"Hello, hello, I'm back again."

Riley wrinkled her nose. "Gary Glitter?"

Radio shrugged. "Desperate times."

Riley first met Russell Miller three years earlier when Kenzie first returned to town. He was a member of her unit. A traumatic experience left Kenzie and Radio both scarred. Kenzie's scars were physical and Russell's were emotional. His quirk of being able to use song titles as everyday conversation became the only way he could communicate with others. Riley had never quite gotten the hang of translating it, but Kenzie was a pro.

"You remember Priest."

"Angel of the morning." Radio nodded to her and shook her hand. "Can we talk?"

Riley gestured at the elevators. "Sure. We can talk upstairs."

"Show me the way."

Riley chuckled and waved to Aissa as she led Radio and Priest to the elevators. Aissa wore a knit hoodie that was a few sizes too big for her, and she had the sleeves twisted around her hands as she waited for a narcotics officer to become available. She looked like a normal girl and, even though Riley knew she was still new to this world and No Man's Land, she seemed to be making rapid progress.

Riley stopped on the second floor and spoke briefly with the head of narcotics. She made sure he knew that a friend of hers was downstairs and needed to speak with someone. A detective was assigned before Riley caught up with Priest and Radio. "We can talk in the on-call room. Should I call Kenzie?"

Radio raised his eyebrows. "Have you seen her?"

"Yeah. We see her all the time. She's here in town, working as a private investigator. Our paths cross now and again."

Radio nodded and sat on the sagging couch where Riley had taken countless naps. He thought for a second and then, apparently unable to think of an appropriate song title, nodded.

"I'll go call her." Riley nodded her thanks as Priest went to her desk to make the call.

She sat on the table in front of Radio. "I take it this isn't just a social call?"

Radio shook his head. "Bad moon rising."

"Okay. I'm listening... for what it's worth."

Radio managed a smile, closed his eyes, and then spoke. "Where the streets have no name. War. When Johnny comes marching home again. Bad. Soldier boy." He looked at her, hopefully.

"Ah. Right." She tried to make the connection and failed. She winced and said, "You gotta help me out a little more, Radio."

"Ahh." He groaned and covered his face with his hands. Finally he straightened and framed each song title as if in its own individual box. "Walk like a man... Show me the way... Teach your children."

Riley twisted and looked out into the bullpen. Priest was still on the phone. "Kind of wish Kenzie was already here. One more time?"

He nodded and patiently recited it again, this time mixing up the first batch with the second. "War. Walk like a man, show me the way. When Johnny comes marching home again. Bad, soldier boy, teach your children."

Riley said, "There's a bad soldier?" Radio smiled. "He... went bad."

Radio groaned and made a spinning motion with his hands. "Never any good."

"Never... he didn't go bad, he was always bad." Radio's smile widened. "He went to war. He enlisted, or got drafted. He went to war..."

"Walk like a man. When Johnny comes marching home again. Teach your children."

Priest came back and started to say something, but Riley held up a finger. "He was always bad. Lived on the streets. He went to war where he..." She muttered under her breath. "Walk like a... He was trained. He was trained by the army. Then when he came 'marching back home' he... taught his children."

Radio was nodding enthusiastically now.

"How to fight?"

Radio exhaled sharply. "Hallelujah."

Riley sat up. "Hold on. Someone... involved in gangs?" Radio nodded. "He joined the army and was trained in military tactics. Then he came home and he's teaching those tactics to his gangs for use in street fighting. Do you know his name?"

Radio nodded. "A horse with no name."

"So you don't know it."

"Don't know much."

Riley thought for a second and then looked at Priest. "Is Kenzie on her way?"

"She was getting in the car when I hung up."

"We'll get Detective Wyatt from the gang unit to help us out on this one. Radio, you can stay in here for now. Can we get you anything while we're waiting on Kenzie?"

"I'm all right."

"Okay. Hang tight." She motioned for Priest to follow her out of the room and asked another detective for Chris Wyatt's extension.

Priest waited until they were at Riley's desk before she spoke. "I hoped he would have gotten better since last we saw him."

"I'm sure Kenzie was hoping the same thing. Looks like he's still living on the street." She picked up the phone and called Wyatt's desk, two floors up. "Wyatt, this is Detective Parra, Homicide. I have some information you might want to hear..."

Chris Wyatt was a former football star gone to seed, his muscle traded for flab. His hair, now more salt than pepper, was still cut into the George Reeves Superman style. He was still handsome, and had the lantern jaw to prove he could once have knocked through a wall of guys in helmets and shoulder pads without breaking a sweat. Now his uniform was a rumpled suit without a tie, and he groaned as he cleared off the empty desk next to his for Riley and Priest.

Despite the fact he looked like he'd let himself go a little, he had apparently spent the time between Riley's call and their arrival on the fifth floor to do a fair amount of work.

"I asked around the office, got some updates on guys who are currently, uh, taking their talents to the gasoline countries. We've got a couple former troublemakers who went through Do-Over, Bootstraps, those redemption places that give kids a second chance and helps get them on the straight and narrow. A couple of 'em signed up as an alternative to prison time. I know some judges who love giving them that choice."

Riley said, "Any of them seem like the kind who would parlay it into a business opportunity like the one my friend suggested?"

Wyatt passed her three files. "Take your pick of them. They did their time overseas, rotated out recently and are back on friendly soil as of last month. So the timing is right. Can your guy be more specific about when this all started or where he got the information?"

Riley grimaced. "Specific is kind of a problem with this guy. But we'll do our best." Riley glanced at the photos just to make sure she didn't recognize any of them. "So these are your three top choices?"

"Yep. On top of the timeline, I can see any one of them pretending to go straight just to get the training."

"How about the theory itself? Have you guys had any trouble with gang members becoming more cunning or harder to catch?"

"Harder to catch." He rubbed his cheek with one thick finger. "Ah. We're stopping floodwaters with cardboard down here. I'll ask around, but I don't think you're going to like the answers I get."

"Right. Do you mind letting us take the lead on this one?"

Wyatt shook his head and held up both hands. "Your guy has the inside track. I'm just your guide. I know the lay of the land, so I'll take a backseat."

"Thanks." Riley stood up. "We've also asked a private investigator to help out. Mackenzie Crowe. She's former military, so we figure she'll be helpful."

"The more the merrier." He leaned forward in his seat as Riley stood. "You know, we've heard about you up here. The Angel Maker case? That was some badass police work."

Priest looked down at her shoes and rubbed the back of her neck. Riley didn't look at her. "Yeah, it was... a group effort. We'll check these three guys, see what we can find out, call you down when we need a guide. Sound good?"

"Works for me."

Riley nodded and motioned for Priest to follow her. On the stairs, Priest said, "I thought we were going to give Kenzie and Radio some time to get reacquainted."

"We are. We're not going straight to her. We need someone with inside information on the gangs. I think I know where we can get it."

The name SARA ELMORE was written on the plate at the front of the desk, and Riley picked it up to polish the vowels with her thumb. Sariel snatched it away from her and replaced it. "I like an immaculate workspace," she said as she took her seat. "If I must work here, I would prefer to keep it from becoming slovenly."

Riley sat down while Priest remained standing. Sariel hadn't taken Gail Finney's old desk; she claimed there was a lingering presence over that entire section. Instead she had applied for and won a position next to a window and in the far corner of the newsroom. The room was mostly empty except for them, with the sole exception being a mumbling man who kept crossing from his work station to the printer without once looking in their direction.

"You could just look up their records on your own computers."

Riley shrugged. "Sure. But I think we'll get a much better view of their activities if we look through yours. Police reports will just tell us the bare facts." She smiled. "Besides, what better opportunity to see you at your new job."

Sariel glared at her. "This is not my job. This is a... distraction." She pulled the files forward and typed the first name into the search engine. The name was Dawson Embry, and it took her twenty seconds to type the eleven letters and hit Enter. She read the screen. "He has a record. Unsurprising. Mostly involvement in gang activities. He was arrested several times up until six years ago, when his name appeared in a Hometown Heroes section, announcing he had signed up for the army."

"And when he came back?"

Sariel shrugged. "A report announcing his return. He hasn't gotten into any trouble since then that we've heard about."

Priest said, "He might have actually gotten clean, stayed on the straight and narrow."

Riley shrugged. "Always a possibility. Leopards can change their stripes, right?"

"Leopards have spots," Priest said.

"See what I mean?"

Priest frowned and Riley waved her off. "It's not important. What about the other two names?" Sariel began to type and Riley rolled her eyes. "Good lord, how do you survive as a reporter?"

"As I'll remind you, I did not choose this job. I manage to fulfill the requirements of it without... much strain."

Riley picked up the keyboard and turned it around, quickly typing the other name. Kevin Waller and Daniel Reynolds were pretty similar to Embry when it came to a history; for the most part, only the dates were different. Riley noted that in most of the stories, Waller and Reynolds came off as foot soldiers. Whenever they were involved, there was usually someone else higher up that took the fall or caught the blame. Embry seemed to be his own man.

Priest said, "It could be that Embry is using his new training to build an army for himself."

"Alternatively, Waller and Reynolds may be using their new tactical know-how to rise up in the ranks. Whichever it is, we still can't rule anyone out." She turned the keyboard around and returned it to Sariel's side of the desk.

Sariel rearranged it so that it was lined up perfectly with the edge of the desk. "I'm sorry I wasn't of more help."

"It's all right. The main goal was to see where you worked." She stood up. "Ask around with some of the other reporters. Could be there were things about these three kids that didn't make it into the papers or the police reports. And you journalists are always sticking your noses where they don't belong." She winked and smiled. "See you around, Sariel."

Priest followed Riley out of the building, waiting until they were back at the car before she spoke.

"Are you okay, Riley?"

"Fine and dandy."

Priest turned and looked at her. "You're... chipper. Happy. You're smiling so much. And it can't be explained by something even as impressive as seeing Radio again. He made an impression on you the first time he was here, but this is different. You weren't even this giddy when Kenzie came back. I haven't seen you smile this much since the morning you married Gillian."

Riley's smile widened. "That was a pretty good day, wasn't it?" She looked out the window, momentarily lost in thought, and then shook her head to clear out the cobwebs. "I don't know, Priest.

Radio is back, and I really enjoyed meeting him. It's nice to see him again. It's nice to work with Kenzie. I saw Aissa at the police station, and she seems really content, if not flat-out happy. And I started the day with my wife waking me up with her tongue." She raised her eyebrow. "If that's not an excuse for being a little extra chipper, then I don't know what is."

Priest smiled and blushed a little. "I see. Well, then carry on."

Riley nodded. "I'll let you know if there's any cause for alarm." She checked her phone. "I told Kenzie we would meet up with her and Radio for lunch. Hopefully they had more luck knocking on doors than we did with the files."

Kenzie picked Radio up at the station and drove him to a steakhouse. It was mostly abandoned in the middle of the day, with only a handful of people holding business meetings over lunch on the far side of the dining room. The hostess escorted them to a booth as far from the businessmen as possible and neither she or the waitress raised an eyebrow at Radio's disheveled appearance. Kenzie reminded herself to leave a big tip for that alone.

"I got you something," she said. "Well, technically it's mine. But I've been meaning to upgrade and I want you to have it."

She passed the iPod across the table. "It has about ten million songs on there. Pretty much everything anyone has ever recorded, basically. So, you know, if you ever get stuck in a conversation."

Radio grinned and scrolled through the menu. "I thank you," he said.

"Hey, I owe you. The charger is out in the car..." She hesitated. "Ah. That is, uh, if you have somewhere to charge it..."

"I get by with a little help from my friends."

Kenzie pointed an accusing finger at him. "That's a lyric, not a song title."

Radio shrugged. "I'm getting better all the time."

The humor faded from Kenzie's face. "That's... not even a lyric. Radio, have you been really been getting better?"

He sipped his water and looked down at the iPod. After a moment, he took a deep breath and said, "Yes, Kenzie."

Kenzie pressed back against the vinyl of the booth. It would have been less shocking if he'd started speaking Arabic.

"How? When?"

Radio shrugged, thumbed through the menu of songs, and furrowed his brow as he scanned the titles. Finally he shook his head and gave up. "Long, long time."

"Well. Maybe I'm amazed."

Radio grinned.

The waitress came by for their orders. Kenzie assured Radio that she was treating for whatever he wanted in honor of his return. He pointed to his order on the menu.

"How would you like that cooked?"

"Medium rare."

Kenzie gave her order and smiled at Radio. "You can't say 'porterhouse,' but you can say medium rare?"

"Foo Fighters."

"Ah. Well, you can say the band name. That's a start." She crossed her arms on the table in front of her, resting on her elbows. "Look, Radio, coming back to town has been great for me, but there was a part of it I regret. I let you go. The past three years, every homeless person I pass makes me think of you. Where you are, if you're okay. Stay here. You can stay with me and Chelsea until you get on your feet."

Radio blinked at her. "Who's that lady?"

"My partner. Chelsea Stanton." She smiled. "That's something else I owe you for. If you hadn't saved my life, I would have died hating the woman I'm now going to spend the rest of my life with. I knew her from my time on the force, but she did a... very bad thing. She soured me on the job I'd loved my entire life. So I signed up and became a different kind of cop. When I came home, after our little underground journey to find you, I ran into her again. She made amends and I... fell in love." She smiled. "She caught up eventually. So I don't just owe you for saving my life. I owe you for giving me enough time to find her. Let me pay you back with more than just an iPod."

"I need time."

Kenzie nodded. "Okay. Take as much as you need, but remember that I'm here for you. Riley is, too. She has friends in high places." She chuckled. "You wouldn't believe how high."

Radio raised an eyebrow, but Kenzie shook her head.

"It's not my place to say. For now let's just focus on what you've been doing."

"Talking in the dark. Don't let me be misunderstood."

Kenzie smiled. "Hit me with your best shot."

Radio laughed.

Priest convinced Riley that they should wear bulletproof vests to check on the names from Wyatt's list. Heading into gang territory was dangerous enough without the added threat of military training. Riley parked in front of the address from Embry's file and took a moment to look up and down the street. Priest waited until she had completed her survey before she spoke.

"Is something wrong?"

"The yellow house, three doors down. Let's say your friend lived there and you came by for a visit. What would you do?" Priest stared at her and Riley shrugged. "Humor me."

Priest looked at the house. "I would go up the front walk, onto the porch and..." She leaned forward to get a better look at the porch and frowned. "That's peculiar. The front door seems to have been boarded up."

"And look at the fences between the houses. No gates, except on every... fifth house or so." She twisted in her seat to look back the way they had come. Trash cans stood by the driveway of each house, an occasional tricycle or playhouse was abandoned in a lawn but no kids were visible anywhere around. "It's set dressing."

"The neighborhood is fake?"

"I think Dawson Embry made himself a base of operations. Fortified. This house is the only point of access. I think we picked the right place to visit first." She unfastened her seatbelt and checked to make sure her gun was ready to fire before she slipped it into her shoulder holster. "You ready?"

Priest nodded. She didn't like using her gun, but she accepted that certain situations made them necessary. She and Riley emerged from the car together, and Riley led the way up the front walk to Dawson Embry's front door. Riley kept her posture casual and unthreatening as she examined the center of his personal forward operating base.

The lawn was nearly mowed, unlike the other houses that sported weeds and inch-high growth. Instead of a false front, the porch was an inviting platform. Four wide wooden steps led up to the front door, which was brand-new and painted red with gold fittings. A window on the second floor was open and a curtain flapped lazily in the breeze. Riley kept her eye on the door but saw movement in her periphery.

"Riley."

"Spotter upstairs. I saw him. Armed?"

Priest took a moment to make sure before she answered. "I

don't see a weapon."

Riley didn't move to make sure he would see her weapon. The word POLICE stenciled across the front of her vest was all the warning she was willing to give him. When they reached the bottom step of the porch, the door opened and two men stepped out. Both were dressed in form-fitting safari shirts, khaki pants and matching boots. Neither was openly carrying a weapon, relying on their superior height and weight to get them through any confrontation with two female police officers.

"Afternoon, gentlemen." Riley gestured at their outfits. "Did you guys call each other this morning to set up your outfits? It's cute."

"How can we help you, miss?"

"Detective Riley Parra. This is my partner, Detective Priest. We'd just like to have a few words with Dawson Embry."

The man on Riley's left had been the first to speak, but the one on her right spoke next. "Do you have a warrant?"

Riley shrugged. "We have no reason to get one. Yet. We're not here because we think Mr. Embry has done anything wrong, we just want to talk to him."

"Then he's well within his rights to refuse to speak with you." This came from Left again. "He's a private citizen and you have no cause. He cleaned up his life. Got on the straight and narrow. Served in the military."

"That's why we want to speak with him," Priest said. "We're afraid someone has been making a mockery of the oaths your friend took. We think they're using the training they received from their country and using it to terrorize."

Riley nodded. "That's right. We figured Mr. Embry would want to help us stop these reprobates before they do any serious harm. You can understand that, right? The military saved Mr. Embry's life. Made him a better man. And now someone is using that like a weapon against good, hard-working American citizens?" She held her hands out. "Something like that probably makes a good soldier like Dawson Embry sick to his stomach."

Right stepped forward. "I think we've given you our answer, Miss Detective. Mr. Embry is a private citizen. He's done his duty. Why don't you go and do yours?"

"Do you do all of his speaking for him?"

Left straightened his shoulders. "We make sure Mr. Embry isn't bothered by insignificant people or problems."

Riley rubbed her cheek and looked down the street. The garage door of the house next door had rumbled up, and a man stepped outside with a garden hose. He wore a pastel yellow polo shirt and plaid shorts. He idly began to water a random spot of grass with one hand in his pocket. He was watching the street and, Riley knew, the current confrontation out of the corner of his eye.

"We could always make this official, sir. Get paperwork involved, force Mr. Embry to come out and say hello to us. But why go to that trouble?"

Right shrugged. "My job is to make Mr. Embry's life calm, not make *your* job easier. Bring us something that says he has to talk to you, and he'll oblige." He smiled. "Dawson Embry is a law-abiding citizen now."

Riley nodded. "I'm sure he is." She looked between the two men and focused on Left. "If I ask your name, will he be the one to answer me? And will it be his name or your name?"

The men looked at each other. Left coughed into his hand and went down onto the third step. It wasn't a threatening advance, but Riley read volumes into it.

"We'd like you to leave now, Detective. You're making our neighbors nervous."

Riley grinned. "Yeah. Your, uh, neighbors." She waved to the man who was still watering the same patch of ground. He didn't acknowledge it. "You know how complicated things get when we force people to talk to us. Once their name is officially connected to a case, things get misfiled, it could look bad down the road."

"You won't get any warrants because you have no reason to bother Mr. Embry," Right said. "So it's been nice meeting you, but I think we won't be seeing you again."

Riley whistled. "Be careful, sir. A more paranoid detective might take that as a threat." She looked up toward the window. The man partially hidden by the curtain was leaning against the wall pretending to smoke a cigarette. He didn't bother hiding the fact it was unlit. She sighed, shrugged helplessly, and turned to walk back to the car. Priest fell into step behind her, casually blocking Riley from any attacks.

When they were back in the car, Riley looked to see the inept gardener had disappeared back into the house. Left and Right were still standing on the porch, but at least were making an attempt to appear casual.

"Did we learn anything useful from that?"

"The outfits were uniforms," Riley said. "The guy in the window and the 'neighbor' were back-up in case I didn't go willingly." She scanned the street and wondered how many other people she hadn't spotted. How many gun sights had been on her during that conversation? Right was watching her from the porch and she waved and offered him a friendly smile as she started the engine. "Dawson Embry is definitely the guy we're looking for. But unless we have probable cause, Briggs is going to shut us down."

"So what do we do now?"

Riley pulled away from the curb. "We hand it over to someone who can actually do something."

Walter was standing by the door when the beat-up Chevrolet pulled up in front of the house. "Ronald. C'mere." They stood at the small curtained window beside the entrance and watched as the driver put her hands on top of the steering wheel and rested her head against them. Finally, after what felt like five minutes had passed, the door opened and she got out onto the sidewalk. She tugged nervously on her coat and made her way to the porch. Walter and Ronald stepped out and she stopped in her tracks.

She straightened into a military posture that both former-Navy men recognized. "Major Mackenzie Crowe."

"State your business."

"I'd like to speak with Dawson Embry."

Walter shook his head. "He's not accepting uninvited guests. Sorry."

"I'm not a guest. I'm..." She shoved her hands into her pockets and looked around. "I'm here for my friend. He hasn't been able to get back on his feet since coming back home, and he thought maybe there was a place for him here."

"Can your friend not speak for himself?"

Kenzie winced. "It's complicated. Please, this is his last hope. He's living on the streets. He could be useful if someone just gives him a chance."

Walter glanced at Ronald, who shrugged almost imperceptibly. "Okay. Come on inside and we'll see if the boss wants to hear about your friend."

Kenzie went up the steps. When she was close enough, Walter grabbed her arm. Kenzie tried to pull away but his grip was like a vice.

"Easy. Just want a closer look." He brushed the hair away from her face and Kenzie tensed. She kept her eyes forward, refusing to look away or be ashamed of her scars. They hugged the right side of her face. It just barely missed her eye, but her ear was misshapen with scar tissue. Walter let the hair fall back over it and let go of her arm.

"How'd it happen?"

"Roadside bomb. I accidentally triggered it, and the guy I'm trying to help saved my life by knocking me out of the way."

Ronald nodded. "Takes courage. Let's go see the boss."

Kenzie followed Ronald into the house, with Walter coming in behind them and shutting the door. Kenzie tried to make sense of the house's original layout, but it was difficult. The walls had been knocked down to turn the living room and kitchen into a single large common area. The bedrooms had also been taken out and replaced with cubicles. The construction was obviously still underway, some parts of the house still showing signs of recent habitation. The walls were bare drywall and, in some places, just naked support beams.

"What is this?" Kenzie said.

"Base of operations. Come on. Colonel Embry is next door."

Kenzie raised an eyebrow. "I heard he was a major. Did he give himself a promotion?"

"Well-deserved, believe me. I respect him more than any commanding officer I had over there. If he doesn't deserve the title, I don't know who does."

Kenzie nodded and followed Ronald through what had once been a closet and into a makeshift tunnel that connected the main house to its neighbor. Walter kept an eye on the back of her head as he brought up the rear. If Colonel Embry decided she and her friend were good additions to their army, she would be welcomed. If not, then he and Ronald would have to make sure she didn't tell anyone what she knew.

He started thinking of places in the backyard cemetery where their bodies would fit.

"Your girl is good under pressure," Riley said.

From the backseat, Chelsea Stanton chuckled. "Well, once I erased all the bad habits her former partner taught her, it was easy to make a good detective out of her."

Riley smirked and adjusted the volume as Kenzie was led into a room with better acoustics.

The bug was in Kenzie's sneaker, hidden behind the blue mesh on the side. The receiver was affixed to Riley's dashboard. Riley and Priest were in the front seat with Chelsea and Radio in the back. Chelsea insisted on coming along in case Kenzie got into trouble. At first she only asked how dangerous Embry was, and Riley's description of his suburban fortress was enough to convince her they needed all the bodies they could spare.

Riley was reluctant, but she couldn't exactly call for official backup until Embry actually did something illegal. If they waited until then, they would be going up against a well-trained army. They had to stop him while he was still gathering his forces.

The shuffling noise of Kenzie's footsteps stopped, and there was a knock on the door. Kenzie's escort went into the room without waiting to be acknowledged.

"Colonel Embry."

"Yes, Walter... who is this?"

Kenzie answered. "Major Mackenzie Crowe, sir. I'm here on behalf of another soldier. A man from my unit, who was very badly injured saving my life." Riley heard a whisper and just barely made out someone saying 'show him your scar'. "You can see the damage from that day."

"Hm. Must be hard looking at that in the mirror every morning."

"I'm grateful for it, to be honest, sir."

"Grateful?"

"Yes, sir. The explosion that left this could killed me instantly. Thanks to my friend, I lived. I was honorably discharged and came back to the city where I grew up, and I fell in love. The scar is a reminder that my life almost ended before it really began. It reminds me to be grateful of what I have. And it reminds me of the debt I owe to my friend."

Riley looked in the mirror and saw that Chelsea was looking out the window, the street beyond reflected in the glasses that hid her mostly-sightless eyes.

Embry was silent for a long moment before he spoke again. "Does your friend have a name?"

"Sergeant Russell Miller. But we call him Radio. He was traumatized. He only speaks in, ah, song titles."

Riley heard someone chuckle at that. Radio shifted his considerable weight in the backseat. "Don't listen to 'em, big guy. Not everyone appreciates you like we do."

"Well, that's certainly unique. What do you think your man can do for our little... organization?"

"I'm not entirely sure what your organization is, Mr. Embry. All Radio knew is that you were a recently returned soldier who had put together a place for people like him. People who have nowhere else to go. If that's wrong, I can turn around and walk away right now, no hard feelings."

"Walt, Ronald, would you excuse us, please?"

Chelsea said, "What's the plan if they don't let her go?"

"Go in guns blazing."

"No reason," Radio said.

Priest said, "He's right. We have no cause. That's the whole reason we sent Kenzie in."

"Not at the moment. But if he tries anything, that will be an attack on a private citizen and we'll be responding to Kenzie's distress."

Chelsea smiled. "That's a thin line, Detective Parra."

"We're fine as long as we stay on this side of it." She winced. "Sorry, Chelsea. I didn't mean~"

"I know." Chelsea's voice was soft. "I'm not offended."

In Embry's office, the door closed. "Have a seat, Major Crowe."

"I'm fine standing, sir."

"Suit yourself. Something tells me you're not just here for your friend. I think maybe you're here for yourself. I can tell you're scoping things out. It's okay. Feel free to look around. But turnabout is fair play, and I'll be checking in on you as well. We can't have people we don't know running around."

Kenzie chuckled. "Let me save you the time, Colonel Embry. Before I was a soldier, I was a police officer. Currently, I'm a private investigator."

Riley whistled. "Ballsy."

"Foolhardy," Priest said.

Riley shrugged. "Same thing. There's a chance he already knew who she was. Telling the truth will make him trust the rest of her story."

"Being a private investigator means I answer only to my client. Right now my client is Radio. If I think this place is good for him, I'll tell him so. If I think it's not, I'll tell him that, too. But that's where my involvement will end. Whatever you're doing here, I don't really care. I just want to do right by Radio."

Embry was quiet for a long time. "I appreciate your honesty, Major Crowe. Of course, any friends you still have on the police force may not fully appreciate what we're doing here."

"I have no friends on the police force. The only connection I still have to them is a woman who was kicked out and sent to jail for being a junkie."

Riley, Priest and Chelsea were all silent. Riley coughed into her fist. "She's, uh. She's a really convincing liar."

"Mm-hmm," Chelsea said.

Riley twisted in her seat and looked at Chelsea directly. "Hey..."

Chelsea smiled. "Riley, if you think Kenzie and I haven't discussed her anger toward me, then you don't know us very well. We had this fight... we're past it. That doesn't make it any easier to hear her say those words."

The conversation inside the complex was continuing. *"The war isn't just over there, you know,"* Embry said. *"It's all around us, every single day. You've been out there. You've seen what the animals of this city are capable of. And the cops can't do anything to stop it. The criminals are just getting stronger. Craftier."*

"So you're... what, vigilantes?"

Embry laughed. *"No. I'm just one soldier. I can't stop this war. But I can grab for the biggest piece of the pie I can get. You've heard of the Five Families?"*

Riley glanced at Priest. Her eyes were closed and she was slowly shaking her head.

"I'm familiar with them. I heard there was a bit of a shakeup in the Hyde family recently. New management."

"Oh, yeah. And that's just the beginning. New boss of the Hyde family is a guy named Falco. Hyde's don't exist anymore; it's just Falco now. Down to Four Families. Falco's next step is to absorb the others. One by one, the rest of the families are going to fall, crashing to the ground. Burke, Pierce, McGowan, Rowland... their days are numbered. Falco's gonna be the last man standing. Falco is our commander-in-chief, and we're his military."

"And you think being a foot soldier in this guy's army is going to be good for my friend?"

"I think it'll be the safest place to stand in a few months. See, once the other families find out what Falco's up to, they're going on the offensive. There's going to be a civil war in No Man's Land. Last man standing takes the prize."

Riley murmured a curse under her breath and shook her head.

"Sorry," Kenzie said. *"I don't think this is the place I thought it was. My friend needs a safe environment."*

"Then send him to Disney World. This city has never been safe, but it's about to get a whole lot worse."

"I'm sorry to have wasted your time." They heard the muffled sound of a door being opened and Kenzie said, *"I don't need an escort. I can find my own way out."*

"They're not an escort, Major Crowe. I'm sorry, but you knew the

moment you walked through the door you weren't going to be able to just walk away."

Riley was already out of the car, with Priest and Radio right behind her. Chelsea brought up the rear, her diminished eyesight making her a liability in the upcoming fight but unable to stay away. Riley checked her weapon and looked over her shoulder at Priest.

Radio said, "For those about to rock, we salute you."

"Is that your way of saying locked and loaded?" Riley asked.

"You got it."

Riley managed a smile as they approached the front door of Colonel Embry's property. The front door opened and one of the musclemen from earlier stepped out onto the porch. He looked at the crowd coming up the front walk.

"Is one of them holding a warrant? 'Cause unless they have one~"

"We got a call about a woman in distress." Riley didn't slow down as she ascended the steps. "Probable cause gives us a reason to enter the premises."

"The hell it does~"

Radio brushed by Riley. The guard went for his gun, but Radio grabbed the man's elbow and squeezed. He went down to one knee and Radio stepped behind him. He pulled the guard's arm back and twisted.

"Why can't we be friends?"

Riley ignored the guard's cries of pain and drew her weapon as she entered the house.

"Colonel" Embry's office was a former master bedroom with a set of French doors that led out onto a shaded patio. Kenzie eyed the glass doors as a possible escape route, even though Embry's desk and the guard called Ronald were in the way. She mentally ran through ways to disable the meathead and vault the desk before Embry could draw the gun tucked into his belt. The walls were covered with street maps of the city, focusing on No Man's Land. Each of the Five Families had territory marked off. The name HYDE was crossed out in red with FALCO written in its place.

"You'll be a guest of this compound until you've come to your senses."

"A prisoner," Kenzie corrected.

Embry held his hands out palm-up. "Call it what you like. This is a very delicate time. The more people who know about this, the more chances it'll go wrong and there will have to be bloodshed."

"I think we're already past that point, Mr. Embry."

"Colonel," he corrected.

Kenzie couldn't keep character any more. "No, Major. You haven't earned that right."

Ronald stepped forward. "You'll show him respect."

"He hasn't earned my respect." She kept her gaze locked on Embry even as Ronald stepped into her personal space. Like Embry, he had a gun stuck down the front of his pants. Without looking, Kenzie grabbed the butt of the weapon and curled her finger around the trigger. "Saw this in a TV show once," she said without emotion. "You move, Mr. Ronald, and I pull the trigger. It's probably not an immediately fatal shot, but I think you'll wish it was."

Ronald had frozen with his hands forming parenthesis on either side of his torso.

Walter's voice echoed through the makeshift hallways from what had once been another house. "Boss! That cop is back."

"Remember what I said about my friends on the force?" Kenzie said. "They're actually pretty dependable."

Embry surged forward at the same time Kenzie yanked the gun free of Ronald's trousers. She buried her knee in his groin and he went down, anguished but probably grateful for the lesser of two evils. Embry slammed into Kenzie before she could get a shot off. She hit the wall and felt the drywall cave under her weight before she went down.

"Been a while since your last fight, soldier?" he growled. He spit when he talked, and Kenzie cringed away from it. "There aren't rules. It's just whatever keeps you alive and gets the other guy dead."

From outside, she heard Riley's voice. She twisted her neck. "Riley! Back here! Next door, to the so~"

Embry jabbed her throat with two fingers and her voice cut off into a choking gasp.

The sounds of his soldiers scrambling was too loud to ignore now. Kenzie heard Riley and Priest announcing themselves as police officers and ordering people onto the ground. Embry looked toward the door with a sneer, then grabbed Kenzie by the collar of her blouse. "All right. All right..." He stood up and hauled her up, spinning her around to use as a human shield.

The soldiers of Embry's little homemade army immediately surrendered, ignoring the powder keg of weapons strewn about the living room and hitting the floor without as much as a vocal argument. They laced their fingers on top of their heads as Riley moved through the living room toward the sound of Kenzie's voice. She hadn't liked how it had cut off.

Chelsea followed her. "Chels, I appreciate the support, but~"

"Tell me to leave, and I'll knock you down and take your gun away."

Riley pressed her lips together. "Noted."

Embry stepped into the hallway ahead of them. He had his arm around Kenzie's throat, his gun pressed to her scarred temple. He was a few inches shorter than Kenzie, his chin obscured by the barrel of his gun. Her hair was also fanned across his features like he'd walked through thick brown cobwebs.

"Detective Parra, I presume. My boys told me about your visit earlier. I should have put two and two together. Nice to put a face to the pain in my ass. Now just put your gun down, and your friend will~"

Riley fired toward the ceiling above Embry's head. Embry's knee-jerk reaction caused him to swing his gun fractionally toward the woman firing at him.

At the moment the pressure of the gun was off her temple, Kenzie grabbed the arm crossing her throat and flung herself forward. Embry was lifted up onto her back, his feet leaving the floor. Kenzie twisted at the waist and dumped him on the ground. Riley and Kenzie pounced on him at the same time, holding his arms down as Riley freed her cuffs from her belt.

"Looks like we still make a pretty good team," Riley said.

Kenzie smiled and coughed. "Yep. Just like the old days." She looked up and saw Chelsea. "Hi, honey. Did you get tired of waiting in the car?"

Chelsea nodded. "You always take so damn long."

"I told you to bring something to read."

Riley hauled Embry to his feet once his hands were safely cuffed behind his back. She walked him through the ramshackle corridor that connected his house to the neighbor's. Priest was keeping an eye on the erstwhile soldiers. She could hear sirens closing in outside, the backup that Priest had no doubt called while Riley and Chelsea were dealing with Embry.

Riley stopped Embry in the entryway of the house and turned him to look at his troops. "See that, Mr. Embry? When Mr. Falco visits you to see what went wrong... and trust me, he's going to hold you responsible for what went wrong... I want you to tell him about this. I want you to tell him how quickly his army gave up."

"It won't stop him. This is too big. He's probably got other cells all over town."

Riley chuckled and him out of the house. "Is that supposed to scare me, Embry? This isn't even a case. I was never called in on this. Taking you down was just how I chose to spend my day off." A squad car pulled up in front of the house with its lights flashing and Riley nodded to the officers as they came up the walk. "Look at that. Your ride's here."

She handed him over and went back into the house. Kenzie and Chelsea were standing against the wall, staying out of the way to let the police do their jobs. Radio was in the main room, intimidating the soldiers who were still waiting to be handcuffed, while Priest returned from deeper in the complex with a few other teenage gangbangers in tow. Riley moved toward her as the kids assumed the position on the floor.

"How many?"

"I found half a dozen in various rooms throughout the complex."

"Did any of them fight?"

Priest shrugged. "A few. But they capitulated soon enough."

Riley chuckled. "I'll bet they did."

"You were right, by the way; all these houses are connected to a varying degree. In some cases it's just a knocked-down fence or a covered walkway. But he was turning it into something big. If Falco had managed to keep this quiet for another few weeks, Riley, it would have taken an army of our own to take it down."

Riley looked at Kenzie, Chelsea and Radio. "Well, throw in you, Sariel and Briggs and I think we've got a pretty good army." She looked at the kids on the ground. "Do you think Embry was telling the truth? Does Falco have other cells hiding elsewhere in the city?"

Priest shrugged. "If he wants to take down the remaining heads of the Five Families, he's going to need as much firepower as he can muster. I would be very surprised if this was the only stronghold he had."

Radio cleared his throat. "You're going to need help."

Everyone looked at him. His eyes were closed and each word he said seemed to be an effort.

"I helped... today. I can help again. Find more." His jaw trembled. "I can help. Detective Parra."

Riley walked over to him and held out her hand. "We'll take all the help we can get, Sergeant Miller."

Kenzie said, "Yeah. You can coordinate with me and Chelsea. We'd be happy to have an extra hand around the agency."

He nodded. "I can help."

Riley could now recognize the difference between Radio speaking for himself and reciting song titles. She patted him on the shoulder. "It's a start, Russell."

He took a deep breath and nodded as more uniformed officers arrived. Riley assumed the leadership roll and stepped forward to address her troops. "Okay, folks. Hope you brought a lot of zip-ties. It's going to be crowded in the holding cells tonight."

Radio declined Kenzie's invitation to stay at their apartment, opting instead to stay the night at a nearby shelter. Priest offered to walk him while Riley drove Kenzie and Chelsea home. She called to update Briggs and Detective Wyatt on the day's events with a promise to give them both a full debriefing in the morning. In the meantime, almost three dozen young men and women with outstanding warrants were dragged out of Embry's compound and taken in for processing. It was going to be a long night, but for once Riley was saved most of the paperwork.

Chelsea and Kenzie lived in a surprisingly spacious apartment above their offices. When Riley parked at the curb, passing headlights illuminated the new scrolling letters across the office's front windows that identified it as Stanton & Crowe Investigations. Riley smiled and said, "Looks like you guys made it an official partnership."

Chelsea said, "Yeah. I decided to keep her around."

"Wise decision."

Kenzie, sitting in the passenger seat, turned to look at Chelsea. "Hon, I'll be up in a second. I just want to talk to Riley."

"Okay." She leaned forward and pecked Kenzie's lips. "I'll start dinner. Don't sit down here talking all night."

Riley said, "We won't. Gillian gave me a curfew."

Chelsea chuckled and climbed out of the car. "Good night, Detective Parra. Thank you for another exciting afternoon."

"I aim to entertain," Riley said.

They watched her go inside, and then Kenzie slumped back against her seat. "Sorry. It's not that I don't want her to hear this, I just would have felt awkward saying it in front of her. I cannot get used to... that." She pointed at Riley's hands that were resting on the steering wheel.

Riley extended her fingers and looked at them. Her eye was drawn to the simple gold band around the third finger of her left hand.

"Yeah. It took me a while to get used to it, too." She clutched the wheel again. "Sorry about, uh, not inviting you to the wedding~"

"No, that's fine. It would have been a little strange to invite your ex. I understand." She looked out the window and rubbed her chin, her finger straying higher and closer to where her scar tissue began. "For a long time, you were a godsend to me, Riley. I never thought I'd find someone willing to deal with my bullshit... someone who came with their own unique bullshit for me to deal with. You made me happy. You were my safety. I always thought we'd end up together."

"I kind of thought the same thing, Kenzie."

"So how did you end up married and I'm..." She sighed and rubbed the back of her neck.

"Kenzie, what's wrong? Is everything okay with you and Chelsea?"

Kenzie laughed. "Perfect. Wonderful. That's sort of the problem. I want to marry her, Riley. But not just because I love her. I want to marry her so I can stop worrying she'll leave me. I look at myself in the mirror and I wonder if Chelsea would stick with me if she could see... this." She flicked her hair and momentarily exposed her scars in the darkness. "When I think about asking her to marry me, my main motive is to keep her with me. Selfish, huh?"

"I think that's just... a really intense form of love. Talk to her about it, Kenzie. Get it out of the way and see if she feels the same way about you. I'm pretty sure I know what the answer will be. You don't have to marry her to make sure she won't run away. She loves you, Kenzie. Just talk to her. Don't... don't try to trap her. It would be wrong and, more importantly, you don't have to."

Kenzie exhaled sharply and nodded. "Thanks, Riley."

"Yeah. You guys are really great together. She might be worrying the same thing about you. Go set her mind at ease."

Kenzie smiled. "Night, Riley. Kiss Gillian for me."

Riley saluted and waited until Kenzie was inside before she pulled away from the curb. She drove toward home, stopping at a red light and fishing the small pill bottle from her pocket. She held it up to the light from the lamppost streaming through her window.

The capsules were two different shades of green, light-green and forest, and clunked quietly against the sides of the container as she twisted it. She could just make out the tiny white letters on the side of each capsule: U4ic.

She thought she had been careful with her experimentation, but Priest had picked up on her elevated mood immediately. She got the pills from Muse, who assured her they were one hundred percent legal. She found some information about them online and didn't find anything about potential side effects. As far as she could find, there weren't any. She'd never heard of a pill with absolutely no side effects whatsoever, but the first dosage left her mind clear when she needed to think, and she'd been alert and ready during her confrontations with Embry and his people. The only difference was her happiness level.

She popped the top of the bottle and shook one of the pills into her hand. She dry-swallowed it just as the car behind her honked. She waved an apology, silencing the voice in the back of her head that told her she should have flipped the guy off. Had she done that, it would have made her angry. Therefore she would have arrived home in a foul mood.

Instead, she parked and went upstairs with a smile. She took the time to hang her jacket on the back of the door before she went into the kitchen.

Her wife, her partner, the love of her life, was still dressed for work in a pair of baby blue scrubs. Her hair was down as she prepared a sandwich for herself. She looked up, and a few rust-brown strands of hair caught in the frames of her eyeglasses. She smiled and Riley's heart swelled. Who needed pills for an elevated mood?

"Welcome home."

"Thanks. Good to be here." Riley left the kitchen doorway and approached Gillian slowly. "Been here long?"

"Just got in." She wiped mayonnaise off the crust of her sandwich with her thumb and presented it to Riley. Riley took it into her mouth and sucked it clean. "Want a sandwich?"

"No." Riley pressed against Gillian from behind and began to move her hips. Gillian was forced to dance with her and chuckled. "How was your day?"

"Slow. I missed seeing you. No dead bodies?"

"No dead bodies."

Gillian sighed. "That shouldn't make me sad. But a busy day?"

"Not too bad." Riley kissed Gillian's neck, and Gillian arched her back and closed her eyes. "Stopped a bad guy. Hung out with Kenzie."

"Oh... so that's why you're so hot and bothered..."

"Nope. All you, babe." Riley moved her lips up to Gillian's earlobe and nipped it. "How hungry are you?"

Gillian twisted so she could see Riley. "Depends on what you have in mind."

"You woke me up in a very nice way this morning, and we didn't have time for me to reciprocate. I'm calling in my rain check." She hooked her thumbs in the waistband of Gillian's scrub pants and kissed down to the collar of her shirt. "So... what do you say?"

Gillian added lettuce to her sandwich and pressed her hips back against Riley. She carefully closed the sandwich, picked it up, and stretched to open the fridge door. She placed the sandwich inside, closed the door, and twisted to face Riley. They kissed, and Riley pushed Gillian's scrub pants down. She splayed her fingers over Gillian's rear end and sucked her tongue.

"What about you? Don't you want something for dinner first?"

Riley shrugged and bent her knees, sinking down Gillian's body.

"Oh... I could eat."

Gillian grinned and braced herself against the counter.

Kenzie stepped out of the shower and wrapped the towel around her waist. She dried herself off in front of the mirror and then wiped away the steam to see her reflection. Staring at her face, she reached up and carefully lifted her hair away from the twisted burns. Her hair started about an inch above her ruined nub of an ear, a fact she hid by growing it long and combing it over. The damage curled around her ear, stretched out toward her eye, and meandered down onto her cheek. It stayed far enough from her lips that her speech and facial expressions weren't affected, thank God, but the damage was vast. If her head was a globe, the scar tissue would cover both North and South America. Maybe even some of Europe.

Having two strangers gawk at the wounds in the space of one day made her self-conscious. She didn't like anyone touching it, looking at it... hell, she didn't like people *knowing* about them. And yet, when Priest offered to heal them, she refused. Why? She turned her head so that the undamaged side was hidden. She then turned the other way so she looked undamaged.

She stared at herself full-on. The scars were a part of her now. She traced one curled piece of skin with her index finger, bracing because she still expected it to hurt.

Finally, she finished drying off and pulled her hair back into a ponytail. She put on a pair of baggy cotton shorts and left the bathroom.

Chelsea was in bed wearing a T-shirt two sizes too large for her. She was swimming in it, with one shoulder and both legs exposed. She was reading, the book of Braille open in front of her and her left hand skimming over the page. She paused in her reading and looked toward the bathroom door. Kenzie knew that Chelsea saw in shades and variants of light. Her view of the world was a movie seen out of focus, a television show watched through fogged glass.

"You were in there for a while."

"Just... looking at something."

Kenzie crossed the room and turned off the overhead lights. She crossed the room in darkness, crawled into bed, and straddled Chelsea's thighs. Chelsea put her book aside.

"Are we making love?" Chelsea whispered.

"Maybe." Kenzie took Chelsea's left hand and lifted it to her face. She let the palm rest on the scars, holding her breath as Chelsea realized what she was touching and stroked it lovingly. She swallowed her emotions - damn things, she didn't know where they had come from; she'd done just fine without them before - and said, "This is my face. Do you wish it was different?"

"Absolutely not, Mackenzie."

Kenzie turned her head and kissed Chelsea's palm. "I love you. So much. It scares me sometimes. I remember you. All those years ago, I remember how you made me feel. Awe. Lust." Chelsea chuckled. "And then anger and... hurt. You make me feel more than anyone ever has. I don't like being an emotional wreck. But for you... I'll suffer through it."

Chelsea laughed. "Good to know."

"I've been thinking I want to marry you, but I don't think I do. But that's just because I don't want to be married to anyone. But I wanted you to know... I'm not leaving you. I can't imagine my life without you in it. And now I'm vulnerable, and I hate that more than I hate *feelings*, so I'm just going to shut up now."

"Kenzie. I'm not going anywhere, either."

"No?"

"Not unless you're going there with me."

Kenzie smiled and bent down to kiss her. Chelsea dropped her hand from Kenzie's cheek to her breast, reading the Braille of Kenzie's goosebumps and then circling her nipple. Kenzie smiled and scooted higher on Chelsea's lap.

"What's it say?"

"It says I'm not getting to sleep any time soon. It's a story about a woman who can't believe how lucky she's gotten... who went through Hell and came out the other side with a life so blessed that sometimes she can't believe it's real. But fortunately, the woman she loves reminds her that it's real. A lot."

Kenzie grinned. "Hm. I like that story."

Chelsea moved her hands to the back of Kenzie's head, tangling her fingers in the wet strands of her hair. "Come here. I'll tell you how it ends."

It was dark by the time Aissa left the police department. She pulled the hood of her sweatshirt up over her hair, stuck her hands into her pockets, and began walking toward the nearest train station. No one in the narcotics department would pay serious attention to her warnings about the drug problem. Eddie had also seemed skeptical, but he supported her decision to go to the police. All the medical reports emphatically stated the pill was harmless. It was just a mood elevator.

Aissa had stayed at the station as long as she did in the hopes Riley would show up. She knew Riley would listen to her about the dangers of U4ic. But apparently she'd been temporarily loaned out to another department, and Aissa hadn't seen her.

She put her hands in her pockets and made the decision to come back another time, as soon as the shelter could afford to spare her for another day.

The pill created a happy feeling, yes, but that was just the start. Soon the pill wasn't necessary for the high, and even the worst-tempered person spent their days wearing a smile. The next step after that was a blissful relaxation in which nothing mattered. Test subjects who used U4ic regularly for six months were found alone in their rooms, smiling at the ceiling, dead from starvation.

She could only comfort herself with the knowledge that U4ic hadn't yet started spreading to the general population. Hopefully they would be able to destroy its limited supply before it got out. There was a chance they could stop a widespread epidemic before it started.

She climbed the stairs to the elevated train platform and took a seat not far from a huge, friendly-looking black man in an old army jacket. He looked over his shoulder when he heard her arrive and smiled. She returned the smile and zipped her jacket up to her throat.

"Cold, cold night," he said.

She shrugged. "Not so bad."

"I like the night life."

Aissa tilted her head and stared at the man. "Excuse me?"

He shrugged and shook his head. "Someone to watch over me?"

"I don't... um." She looked around. The platform was empty, and the man seemed more lonely than threatening. "How about we watch over each other?"

"Strength in numbers."

Aissa stood up and moved to sit next to him. She held out her hand to him. "Aissa Good."

"Russell Miller. F-fo-folks call me... Radio."

"Nice to meet you, Mr. Radio."

She settled back against the bench, hands in her pockets, and waited for the train with her new friend.

Riley kissed her way up Gillian's stomach, pausing between her breasts and breathing deeply. Gillian lifted her head off the kitchen tile and moaned as Riley's lips met hers. They were lying in a nest of discarded clothing. Gillian brushed her foot along the back of Riley's calf, writhing underneath her. Gillian's tongue slipped into Riley's mouth and then retreated. Gillian shuddered and ran her fingers down Riley's back. "Oh... baby..."

"Pretty good appetizer?"

"Hooo... yeah." They kissed again before Gillian patted Riley's shoulders. "Off me. I'll go get dressed and then I'll buy you dinner."

"You'll buy?"

"Give me head like that, and hell yes I'll buy you dinner."

Riley laughed and rolled off of her. She lay on her back and watched, upside down, as Gillian hurried to the bedroom on the balls of her feet. Riley felt completely blissful, her heart drumming against her ribs. She was sweaty and wet, and the idea of going on a real date with her wife made her giddy. Of course, things could always be better. She scooted over to her jeans, which were draped over a chair at the kitchen table, and fished out her bottle of U4ic.

She tapped one into her palm and popped it into her mouth.

She shook the bottle and made a guesstimate on how much was left. A refill would probably be expensive, but she couldn't put a price on feeling this good. She hid the pills again. She didn't want Gillian to see them and think she needed a boost to enjoy a night with her wife. They weren't necessary, they were just... icing on the cake.

Gillian returned from the bedroom and tossed a black skirt and red blouse at Riley. "If I'm taking you out, you're dressing up." She winked and disappeared down the hall.

Riley smiled. "As you wish." She took the clothes and followed Gillian into the bedroom so they could get ready together.

THE FALLEN

11:54am

Riley lunged for the recessed entry, hit the ground with her knee and turned the tumble into a roll. She spun into the doorway and tucked her arms in tight to her sides, her back scraping against the crumbling brick wall. The door was solid and sturdy, and a quick check of the knob revealed it was securely locked. She checked her arm. The makeshift bandage she'd made out of her shirtsleeve was holding up well. Her ankle was sore, protesting an earlier bad landing every time she stopped moving. Luckily the adrenaline was enough to silence it when necessary.

She leaned out of her hiding place and looked to make sure the Enemy wasn't advancing on her. The alley between buildings was barely wide enough for a delivery truck, with puddles of rainwater shimmering in potholes. Overhead, metal catwalks passed from one building to the next, connecting them like webbing of a massive industrial spider. Some windows were broken, but she didn't want to risk being caught on the fire escape with no way down.

The end of the alley led out onto a thoroughfare that would take her out of this hellhole. She could run, find a cab or a train station, head home, and wait for this to blow over. God, that was tempting. But she couldn't do that. She had to see this through to the end. But the urge to run, the urge to just hide, worried her.

She dropped down and stretched her feet out in front of her as far as the cramped alcove allowed. She checked her watch. She had taken her first pills an hour ago, so she had six minutes until she could take another dose. She cursed and fished the bottle out of her pocket. With the way her adrenaline was pumping, she could easily shave five minutes off the recommended dose. And six was almost five. She unscrewed the cap and poured a few pills into her hand.

She popped them into her mouth and grimaced as she swallowed them. She could take another dose in an hour. She stuffed the pills into her pocket and twisted to look down the alley as a small blue sedan pulled up to the alley entrance.

Riley stood carefully, grunting as aches and pains shouted for her attention. She ignored them and limped forward to meet the car. Lieutenant Briggs parked and climbed out from behind the wheel, her eyes widening as she saw the creature lurching toward her. Riley looked down and saw that her white tank top was filthy and smeared with blood and soot, and more blood had dried on the leg of her pants. Her face was probably bruised as well; a person doesn't get hit that hard without getting a bruise.

"Riley? My God. What the hell is going on?"

"Fight," Riley said. "Did you bring the stuff I asked for?"

Briggs nodded. "But now I'm debating whether or not to give it to you. What the hell is going on, detective?"

Riley swallowed and looked over her shoulder. "I don't have a lot of time to explain, boss. Please, the... the stuff. I need it."

Briggs hesitated, but then she opened the backseat and pulled out a duffel bag. Riley stepped forward as Briggs put it on the hood of the car and unzipped it. Riley did a quick scan to make sure she had everything she asked for: extra ammo, a Kevlar vest, a first aid kit, painkillers, and - the most confusing in Briggs' mind - an extra-large jar of flax and two small blades she had gotten from the bottom drawer of Riley's desk.

"Thanks, boss. I'll owe you." She slung the strap over her shoulder and started to turn away. Briggs stopped her by saying her name. "Boss, I don't really have a lot of time."

"You have two options here, Detective Parra. One, you keep your secret and in five minutes you have a SWAT team knocking down the walls of this place. Or two, you tell me what's going on and maybe, just maybe, I agree to let you run it your way. What the hell are you fighting?"

Riley sighed and checked her watch again. 11:59. One more minute and she could take another dose of her pills. She turned and faced Briggs. "That new drug that people have been talking about. U4ic."

"Euphoric? Narcotics sent out a memo, but so far it's an urban legend. There aren't reports of anyone actually selling or buying any of it."

Riley wiped her hand down her face and looked around to make sure the Enemy wasn't sneaking up on her. "Sure. Muse gave me some information about it. Said he knew where it was being mixed up. The kitchen is here somewhere, in this place. Priest and I were looking for it, but the cookers caught us off-guard. They set up a booby-trap with some of their supply and they dosed her. You know what the drug is supposed to do, right? Gives the user a sense of... peace and contentedness." She shuddered and hoped Briggs didn't notice. "But to an angel, it does something different. It pushes them to the edge. As of two hours ago, Zerachiel has fallen."

"What?" Briggs scanned the sky. "Does that mean...?"

"I don't know what it means. It's an artificial high, so I'm hoping it's temporary. But I need this stuff so I can fight her."

"I can block off these streets to make sure she doesn't get out."

Riley shook her head. "No. That's not necessary, I mean. She's not leaving until she finds the stash of U4ic and takes it for herself. If she overdoses, the high will never wear off and she'll be stuck like this forever. The pills effects are supposed to last for six hours. It's been two. Hopefully by four o'clock this whole mess will be behind us."

Briggs looked at the ground, hands on her hips, and mentally debated for a moment. "What can I do to help?"

Riley patted the bag. "You've already done it, boss. For now, just keep a safe distance away. I don't want to give the Enemy a chance to hurt anyone else."

Briggs frowned. "The Enemy?"

"Yeah. It's not Priest, it's not Zerachiel... if I think of it like that, then I'll hesitate. And I can't hesitate. Thanks. And... when you get back, tell Gillian not to worry."

"You mean lie," Briggs said flatly.

Riley nodded. "Yeah. She'll be mad at me, not you. See you late this afternoon, boss."

She turned and walked away before Briggs could argue with her further. She heard the car door slam and the engine rumbled for a

long minute before Briggs drove away. Riley walked to the far end of
the alley and checked for signs of Priest lying in wait for her. She
checked her watch and saw it was four minutes past noon. She took
out the bottle of pills, tapped a few into her cupped palm, and
swallowed them. She could take another dose in an hour.

After a moment to catch her breath and make sure Briggs had
really left, Riley pushed off the wall and went in search of her
former partner.

12:03pm

Priest stood on the roof and watched the street, waiting for her
guest to arrive while at the same time viewing the maze where her
goal and her quarry both hid. Her clothes had been damaged during
her crash landing, caused by Riley clipping her wing with a tossed
bit of masonry, and she'd removed her shirt entirely. Her suit jacket
was still in good condition, and it saved her from fighting topless.
Her trousers were torn, however, revealing her bloody knees and
calves whenever the wind caught the tatters of material and lifted
them.

Once this block had been a successful clutch of car dealers.
Now the expansive empty parking lots were filled with cracked
asphalt and weeds, framed by empty showrooms and long stretches
of offices and garages. The few office buildings that once coexisted
with the dealerships stood like empty watchtowers on the corners of
the block. Priest watched them for signs of movement, either by
Riley or the U4ic makers, when she spotted a vehicle moving
through the tight, narrow alleys of the industrial area. She stepped
off the parapet of the roof and spread her wings to catch a drift to
the next building. When she identified the car, she extended her
wings and flew down to gently land on the hood. The car lurched to
a stop and Priest bent her knees, leaning down to flatten her palm
on the roof to keep from being thrown.

The door opened and Kenzie stepped out. Priest rose and
looked down at her, hair loose and blown by the breeze.

"Whoa. Caitlin, you look..."

"Different. I am. I'm hunting." She jumped and glided from the
roof of the car to land on the ground next to Kenzie. "What do you
and Chelsea know of a new street drug called U4ic?"

Kenzie shrugged. "About as much as anyone else. It's not real."

"Yes, it is. Riley is an addict."

"What?"

"Apparently she acquired a sample from Muse. He wanted her

to have it tested by our labs to make sure it was as safe as the rumors claimed, but Riley decided to use herself as a test subject. I noticed the odd shift in her behavior, but I ignored it. I'll never forgive myself for that."

Kenzie nodded. "Okay, fine, but how does that lead to this? You all bloody, asking me to bring~"

Priest looked into the backseat of the car. "Ah. You found it. Thank you, Kenzie." She opened the back door and took her sword and scabbard off the seat.

"Tell me you're not going after Riley with that thing."

Priest examined the sword as she answered. "I'm only going to use it as a deterrent. I will show her that I have the superior position and she'll have no choice but capitulate." She slung the leather strap of the scabbard across her torso, letting the sword hang between her wings.

"You didn't answer my question. U4ic is just supposed to make you happy all the time."

"In small doses, yes. Riley was under the influence of U4ic for about two weeks before I discovered the truth. The only side effect is the withdrawal you go through after you stop taking the drug. Imagine being slightly depressed, so you take a pill that makes it all go away. You're happy for the duration of the pill's effect, but then it begins to wear off. You feel sad again, so you boost again. And again and again. If you should run out of the drug, the resulting depression would drive even a strong person to despair and suicide."

"My God. Riley...?"

"She was trying to wean herself off when she revealed the truth to me. Whoever was manufacturing this drug could give away the first doses at a small price, but subsequent refills..."

"They could name their price."

"Precisely. We came to this place in pursuit of a lead that the first marketable batch of U4ic was being prepared here. Riley hoped to stop the onslaught before it reached the streets. But the cooks spotted us. When we infiltrated their building, they hit us both with a massive dose of the unrefined drug."

Kenzie winced. "That can't have been healthy."

"It didn't affect me at all... my divinity protected me. But Riley was already affected by her exposure and the subsequent withdrawal. She became convinced I was her enemy and turned on me. Extreme paranoia is apparently an unforeseen part of the drug leaving your system. We fought, and I was forced to defend myself.

I'm lucky I was able to get away from her in one piece."

Kenzie looked around. "If she's running around, out of her mind, we need to get the police involved. We need to block off these streets."

"No. The risk of exposing other police officers to the drug is too great. It's why I asked you to meet me here, at the outskirts. You should be safe so long as you leave quickly. And Riley won't leave until she's managed to secure a large amount of the drug for herself."

Kenzie frowned. "But you said she was in withdrawal."

"She was. After the dosing, she relapsed. She doesn't have to worry about the withdrawal symptoms or buying more if she has her own stockpile. Go home, Kenzie. Be safe." She cupped Kenzie's face and chastely kissed her lips. "Give my love to Chelsea."

Kenzie nodded. "If you guys aren't safe by tonight~"

"The effects of the drug should wear off in approximately four hours. Hopefully I'll be able to subdue Riley before she can get another dose and this will all end peacefully."

"What if she gets her hands on more of the drug?"

"Then I'll do whatever is necessary to stop her. Leave this place, Kenzie. It's not safe for you." She spread her wings again and flew back into the sky. By the time she landed on a nearby roof and looked back, Kenzie was already back in the car and driving away as instructed. Priest scanned the sky and walked with purpose to the opposite end of the building to continue her search.

12:15pm

Riley found an unlocked door in an office building and let herself in. She shut the door behind her and went deeper into the abandoned shell. Leftover furniture was scattered in a few offices, surrounded by debris left by squatters who'd been run out by the U4ic cookers. They seemed to have taken over the entire block for their own purposes. The drug makers themselves had abandoned ship pretty fast themselves after setting off their little booby trap. Now the various alleys and walkways of the building were creeping her out. It felt like the entire city had been closed off.

She found a room with a table and a metal chair that wouldn't be moldy or too weak to hold her weight. She took the flax out of the bag and poured it in a circle around the table. She knew it would trap an angel inside a ring of it, so she presumed it would also work to keep an angel *out* of a certain area. She dragged the chair across the floor and perched on it as she opened the First Aid kit Briggs brought her. She carefully unwrapped the strip of cloth wrapped around her arm, hissing through her teeth as the dried blood pulled at her wound.

"God... what was that?"

Priest brought up her arm and pressed her nose into the crook of her elbow. "Some sort of smoke bomb."

Riley tasted something on her tongue and vaguely recognized it. After a moment, she identified what it was. "Oh, hell. Priest, it wasn't a smoke bomb." She grabbed Priest's arm and pulled her away from the door. With her other arm, she tugged her collar up over her nose and mouth though she knew it was too little, too late. "They dosed us."

"What?"

Priest started running, so Riley let go of her arm. "This is U4ic. They blew up whatever they were working on."

They were almost to the street when Priest grabbed Riley's arm and twisted. Riley's forward momentum had carried her straight into the wall. She went down and Priest grabbed her from behind, pinning her arms back.

"I'm sorry, Riley, but this is really for your own good."

Riley had lurched upward, catching Priest's chin with the top of her head. Priest was so shocked by the move that she stumbled backward and let go of Riley's arms. Riley spun to face her, touching her bruised cheek to make sure the skin wasn't broken. "What the hell is the matter with you?"

Priest had her gun out of her holster and fired. Riley cursed under her breath and ducked out of the way. She felt the passage of the bullet tearing her sleeve. The sudden movement caused her to miss the next step and she went tumbling. When she hit the landing, she looked up to see Priest coming down after her fast. Riley pulled her own gun, fired, and scrambled back to her feet before Priest could give chase.

She hissed as the antiseptic did its job, then she covered the wound with a square pad. She managed to wrap it with gauze, twisting awkwardly to cut it and secure it with tape. She wished she had asked Briggs to bring a change of clothes, but that would mean involving Gillian. Riley wasn't willing to do that. Gillian didn't even know about Riley's U4ic use and, if Riley had her way, she would never find out. She was ashamed of how close she'd gotten to a true addiction. Now that she knew what the withdrawal could do, she wouldn't touch the stuff. Her skin was crawling though, and she paused cleaning her battle wounds to take the pill bottle out of her pocket.

The dose of unrefined U4ic they'd been hit with had sent her over the moon. She was already starting to feel the need for another hit. The stimulants were helping. As she crashed down, the stimulants pushed her back up a little higher. It was like catching updrafts while falling off a building. Catch enough of them, maybe she wouldn't break every bone in her body when she finally hit the ground.

She still expected to break a couple.

She looked at her watch. It was 12:29, and she had more than a half hour before she could take another dose. She pressed the heel of her hand into the hollow of her eye and muttered under her breath. The drugs were making her foggy. She had to stay focused and stay ahead of Priest at all costs. The pills went back into her pocket, even though she wanted to weep at the wastefulness of not taking one.

Fifteen minutes was much too long to stay in one place. But if she was going to keep taking her pills, she needed to stop losing blood. She was lightheaded enough as it was. She stood up and dropped trou so she could clean the cut on her thigh.

12:37pm

Priest made a circuit of the block, eyeing the streets below for signs of Riley. She knew that Riley wouldn't leave without all the U4ic she could carry. When she first admitted to using the pills, Priest had been devastated and hurt. She'd also been angry at herself for not knowing it in advance. It was a guardian angel's job to know everything about their charge.

But you haven't been a traditional guardian angel in quite some time, have you, Caitlin?

She ignored the voice at the back of her mind and landed on the roof of an office building. She had lied to Kenzie about being unaffected by the drug. She wasn't sure what exactly it had done to her, but she did not feel... right. She rolled her shoulders and scanned the area for Riley. The drug makers had also been able to vanish alarmingly fast, but she knew they probably had what Riley called "rabbit-holes" all over their little corner of the world. She closed her eyes and pressed the tips of her middle fingers to her temples and rubbed in slow circles.

"Oh, hell. Priest, it wasn't a smoke bomb. They dosed us."

"What?"

Priest started to run, and Riley let go of her arm. Riley spoke without turning to look at her. "This is U4ic. They blew up whatever they were working on."

On the last flight of stairs, Priest saw Riley's head drop and her hand went up to the back of her neck. Priest knew that all of Riley's hard work to get off the drug had just gone up in smoke. She needed to be restrained for her own safety. She grabbed Riley to stop her, but Riley's movement caused her to be thrown into the wall face-first. Priest pulled Riley's arms back and threaded her arm around Riley's elbows, pinning her in place.

"I'm sorry, Riley, but this is really for your own good."

Riley slammed the top of her head into Priest's chin. Priest bit down on her tongue and tasted blood as she stumbled backward. Riley spun to face her.

"What the hell is the matter with you?"

Priest saw it then. The anger and darkness Riley had always kept at bay; the U4ic had awoken it. Priest drew her gun and fired a warning shot, just to make Riley take notice. Riley ducked away from the shot, although it clipped her left arm, and lost her footing. Priest watched helplessly as Riley fell down the stairs. Thankfully it was only five or six steps down to the next landing.

Priest went after her, but Riley returned fire and ran. Priest, bleeding and angry, gave chase.

Priest looked down at her right hand, still wrapped with a part of her shirt. Riley's shot had nearly taken off her thumb, but Zerachiel fixed that. The rest of the damage was slowly being knit back together. Riley wouldn't be as lucky. The damage she had incurred as a result of trying to get Riley to listen would linger. Suffering pain and blood loss in addition to her withdrawal depression... she would be an easy target.

And what will you do when you find her, Priest?

Silence, Zerachiel.

The voice in her head laughed, and Priest clapped both hands over her ears in a futile attempt to shut it out. The angel in her, the mortal in her... they had both been dosed by just as much of the drug as Riley. How could she be certain her thoughts were her own?

Simply by what the voices were telling her to do. She would listen only to the inner voice that made the most sense, the one that sounded the most righteous. It had gotten her this far. She silenced the unfamiliar cackle and focused on her hunt for Riley.

And once she was found... then what? Riley had already proven she was adversely affected by what happened. The drug had amplified her paranoia and clouded her mind. Every time Priest had gotten close enough to talk sense into her, Riley had responded violently enough to send Priest running with a new wound. And, unfortunately, Priest had been forced to respond in kind just to keep Riley from killing her.

Unfortunately? You weren't just 'responding' when you tackled her into that pile of broken stones.

Priest felt the sickeningly dark smile spreading across her face but couldn't summon the energy to stop it.

You enjoyed that. Causing Riley so much pain.

"Nn..."

After so long of watching out for her... more than three decades of taking care of her only to have to go into yet another dangerous situation... it was fun to cause some hurt, wasn't it? You're just giving her what she wants.

"Shut up. Shut up."

You liked hurting her. You liked seeing her bleed and knowing you'd done it.

"Yes." Priest didn't recognize her own voice, and it made her skin crawl. She drew her sword from the scabbard and gasped as her still-damaged thumb tried to grip it. She switched it to her left hand and took one last look at the area before she let the wind catch her wings and carry her away. She would find Riley eventually and what happened next would be entirely up to Riley.

A part of her hoped Riley would resist. She ignored that voice even as she unknowingly coddled it and stoked the fires that had brought it to life. She couldn't ignore the fact that the voice was right.

It *had* been fun to make Riley bleed.

She was sickened and excited in equal measure at the idea she might get to do it again.

1:00pm

Riley popped four stimulants and winced as they went down. Bottled water. She should have asked Briggs for bottled water. Too late now. She wasn't going to risk anyone else getting caught up in this. She had taken two of the painkillers while giving herself first aid. She felt woozy, but the adrenaline would take care of that. She hoped the stimulants would also boost her during the inevitable crash. Off the pills, off the adrenaline... She was heading for a fall bigger than Zerachiel's.

She repacked her bag, her pants-leg stiff from dried blood but the bandage keeping it from getting any bloodier, and broke the ring of flax with a sweep of her foot. She was halfway to the door before the window behind her shattered. Riley hit the ground and twisted, bringing the gun up and firing before she had a clear line of sight of the Enemy.

Priest landed, fresh scrapes oozing blood down her features as she flexed her wings and ducked to avoid Riley's shooting. Riley scrambled through the door and into the hallway. Instead of continuing down the stairs, she spun and waited for the Enemy to give chase. Her heart was pounding in her ears, but she heard the slide of Priest's shoes on the floor. Riley held her bag of supplies in her free hand like a slingshot, ready to use it to club the Enemy if necessary, but she never exited.

"Riley?"

"How are you feeling, Caitlin?"

"Not well. How about you? You dropped some of your pills in here..."

Riley resisted the urge to check her bag. "That's okay. I don't really need them. How long is this going to go on? Until you kill me?"

"No." She actually sounded offended by the implication. "Riley, for better or worse, I'm your guardian angel. It's my job to protect you from harm, even if it's self-inflicted. Have you had any luck finding the rest of the U4ic?"

"Why? Need a booster shot?"

"Riley, I told you, angels aren't affected by the drug."

Riley laughed and stepped back into the doorway. The Enemy had been standing against the wall and backed away at Riley's sudden appearance. She held her hands out to her sides.

"I want to help you, Riley. Just put down your gun and~"

"Right. Nice sword. Who brought it to you?"

"Kenzie. She wants to help you as much as I do."

Her grip tightened on her gun. "Yeah. And what part of rehab includes using a sword on me?"

Priest closed her eyes and shook her head. "Please, Riley. Look at yourself! You're threatening me with a gun. You've harmed me grievously."

Riley gestured at her own wounds. "Don't sell yourself short. You've done your fair share of damage to me, too."

"I did what I had to."

"Let's say I believe you. What happens then? You take me to Gillian, she nurses me through withdrawal, and you come back here and find the drugs at your leisure. You said it's your job to take care of me... well, maybe I want to take care of you this time. I've seen an angel fall, Priest, and it wasn't pretty. I won't let you do this. If I have to spend the next three hours kicking your ass until this drug wears off, I'll do it. Even if I'm held together by duct tape by the end."

The Enemy held her hands out and looked down at herself. "Look at me, Riley. Do I look like I've fallen?"

"Did Samael? He lied to me, tried to set up my murder... the whole time smiling to my face. But I know you, Priest. Zerachiel. Something's off."

"Maybe the thing that's off is your perception. You have a massive dose of U4ic in your system, and to top it off you've been popping prescription pills to balance yourself. The only person in this room whose judgment you can be certain is compromised is you. Let me help you, Riley." She stepped forward.

Riley fired twice, both bullets hitting Priest in the chest and knocking her backward. Riley turned and ran before Priest hit the ground, taking the stairs four at a time. When she reached the ground floor, she slung the bag of supplies over her shoulder and shoved through the front door of the building. Her head really was swimming; she had lost track of how many pills she'd taken. She wanted to dump them, just to be safe, but that would be like cutting the ropes of her parachute while she was still plummeting.

She heard Priest shouting her name through the broken window of her erstwhile hideout but didn't turn around. She found a locked door that led into a showroom and kicked it in. The wall of windows was horrible from a tactical standpoint, but Priest would be surveying from the sky when she was back on her feet. Being indoors would give her more cover than running through alleys and between buildings.

There was an abandoned desk nearby and Riley took a moment to push it in front of the door so it wouldn't be hanging open when Priest came after her again. The effort took most of her remaining energy and she dropped the duffel bag on top of the desk to sort through its contents. She dutifully ignored the bottle of stimulants and found an energy bar. She tore the package open with her teeth and ate it quickly enough that she didn't even notice the taste, sagging against the side of the desk as she tried to think of her next step.

She closed her eyes, her hands braced against the edge of the desk.

Muse shook the pill bottle. "It's safe. It's not even on the market yet."

"What is it?" She took the bottle from him and twisted her wrist so

that the pills tumbled against the side.

"Newest thing. You heard of *Five Hour Energy*, right? This is *Six Hour Smiles*. Puts you in a better mood like that." He snapped his fingers.

"You think I need to be in a better mood, Muse?"

He laughed. "Have you met you?"

Riley opened her eyes and realized she'd nearly been dozing. She should have just taken the damned pills in, gotten them tested like Muse said. But his comment had gotten to her, and she decided that if they *did* work, she wanted to give Gillian a surprise. She wanted Gillian to have a happy, relaxed wife for once. Gillian would never have said anything, but Riley felt guilty for everything she'd put her through over the course of their relationship.

So she took a pill and went home. They watched a movie, they made love on the couch, and they went to sleep in each other's arms. It felt so nice, so normal, that Riley decided to keep the pills for just one more day.

That was the real danger of U4ic. The pills weren't addictive, but they made possible certain situations that would have been impossible without them. Riley knew she would never be able to relax that much on her own. If she wanted that experience again, she needed the pills to make it happen.

But no more. She would do whatever was necessary to keep the drugs from hitting the streets, but she was never going to take another one again.

She slapped both cheeks to make sure she was fully awake, pushed away from the desk and started running.

1:28pm

She gave up shouting for Riley to come back; she was long gone. Priest caught her breath and summoned what was left of her energy to dragged herself to the wall. She unhooked her scabbard, propped up under the window as she tried to compartmentalize the pain in her torso. Riley's bullets were still inside of her, and the wounds were large and ugly. Blood dribbled down the front of her jacket as if she had sprung a leak, and she worried about deflating. She smiled and gave a hollow laugh as she withdrew her wings and focused her divinity on healing.

Not a lot left in the tank. Eventually you'll either have to give up the search to find a church, or you'll just fade away.

"Shut up."

She was right, you know. You're lying about the pills affecting you. Do you even know which of us is in charge anymore? Priest? Zerachiel? We're the same, but we're not. Not anymore. Not since your flirtation with mortality. How badly do your wounds hurt?

Priest groaned and squeezed her eyes shut.

There was a time when those bullets wouldn't even have stopped me. You were the Earthly manifestation of an angel. But now you're confused. You think of yourself as mortal even if you don't admit it to yourself. When your divinity was taken away you learned to live as one of them. It ruined you.

"Making... best... of a bad situation."

Give up, Priest. Let Zerachiel take over. You're an angel, and an angel is what is needed to end this.

Priest's eyes opened. "Oh, my Father. Riley was right..."

No. Riley is sick and we must stop her. For her own good.

For the first time, she could hear the desperation in the mental voice. That was why her mind had seemed so fractured. Zerachiel was affected by the drugs. It was Caitlin Priest, the mortal part of her, that was fighting it. If she gave herself over to Zerachiel...

You'll be healed. Give control over to me now, Caitlin, or die where you sit.

The wound over her heart mended, and Priest looked down to see the blood stop flowing.

The body was mine to begin with. I created you as a tool. I should have seen you were damaged when we reconnected. I should have killed you then and started over fresh. If Sariel had done her job properly, it wouldn't have been an issue. But she failed, and you tainted her as well.

"Shut up..."

Stop telling yourself to shut up, Caitlin. Because we are the same. I'm in your head because it's my head, too. As much as it may disgust you after the things I've done, after the Angel Maker fiasco, you and I are one and the same. You are Zerachiel to your core. And as much as it sickens me to admit this, I am Caitlin Priest. I'm a shadow of the angel I once was. I'll never forgive you for doing that to me. You're an-

"~anchor. A millstone around my neck." Zerachiel realized she was speaking aloud and paused to look down at her hands. She smiled and closed her eyes, arching her back as she closed the wounds on her torso. The flesh knit back together and the blood stopped flowing. She visualized the bullets within her body and diminished them until they were nothing more than small flecks of atoms. They wouldn't even set off a metal detector.

She pushed herself up and retrieved her sword. "You made a wise decision, Caitlin. You were nothing more than a mask. I've been protecting Riley since she was an infant. You may think you remember being there, you may claim to carry the memories of the atrocities I've witnessed, but it was never you." She drew the blade from the scabbard and watched as the light gleamed from its edge. "Now sit back and let me do what you were too weak to do. It's time to protect Riley. Or, barring that, ensuring her death is as painless as possible."

2:18pm

Riley skipped taking her stimulant at two o'clock, but she felt the crash coming and finally relented at a quarter past the hour. She needed her wits because now she wasn't just contending with the Enemy; she thought she was closing in on the main laboratory. She kept finding signs of recent activity, like magazines left out and junk food wrappers littering the floor next to milk crates arranged into furniture shapes.

Muse leaned forward between the front seats and pointed at the nearest building. "They're holed up in that place. Not the whole place. They like it 'cause it gives them a lot of room to expand once the U4ic starts rolling out." He wet his lips and looked at Riley. "Look, Detective Parra, if I'd had any idea this shit was... you know..."

"I know, Muse." She unfastened her seatbelt. "So the main lab?"

"I don't have a clue. Guys who brought me here, they took me to that building. Top of the stairs. They had a big theatrical-type thing just to make things look good, but I know that wasn't where they actually made it."

"So how can you be sure the operation is based here?" Priest asked. "Maybe it's just a... façade."

"A storefront," Riley suggested.

Muse shook his head. "No. They showed me the front of their store, but they wouldn't risk taking their product very far away from home. Nah, they're definitely cooking it somewhere in there. I just don't know where."

Riley nodded. "Okay. Thanks for the info, Muse. I'll put it on your tab."

"Hell no. I gave you that bottle, Detective. If something bad had happened to you, I'd've never forgiven myself. So this one is free. Maybe the next one, too."

"That's a good start, Muse. Get out of here. If these guys have more people you don't know about, I don't want you getting caught in the crossfire because you feel guilty."

"So... we're good?"

Riley held out her hand to him. "Yeah, Muse. We're good."

Now it looked like Muse's intel had been correct. She and

Priest had been dosed on their way up to the storefront, their confusion giving the cookers a chance to escape. Riley hoped that once she secured their main lab, she could focus on stopping the Enemy. She didn't know if she was capable of doing "whatever was necessary" to stop Zerachiel from falling, but she couldn't just stand back and let her go to the dark side.

A garage access door at the rear of the showroom had been covered with stickers warning people to keep out of the "environmental hazard" beyond. Riley put down her bag and pressed her back to the wall next to the door. She listened for sounds of movement inside, aware that she wasn't exactly the picture of authority in a tank top that was more black and red than white. She made sure her badge was visible just in case someone was lying low, then tried the knob. The door was unlocked, and she counted to three before she threw it open and went inside, leading with her gun.

The space looked immense without vehicles or machinery to fill it. Thick concrete pillars were evenly spaced throughout the garage separating it into three individual bays. The garage doors that ran down the north and south walls had windows that let in enough light for her to see clearly. In the center bay, several folding tables were set up to support what looked like a high school chemistry class. Cardboard boxes were stacked on the floor at the corner of one table.

Riley walked closer and peered into the highest box. Counterfeit prescription bottles, dozens of them, all ready to hit the streets. Riley itched to take one. Hell, maybe two. If stimulants were like having a parachute, then popping U4ic would be like having a pair of goddamn wings.

She pushed the thought out of her head. The pills would be confiscated. She moved to the table and examined the set-up, trying to figure out how the drug was made. Priest assured her they weren't demonic in nature, but Riley had no idea how they could produce such a high with conventional means. There was some residue on the table but she resisted the urge to touch it. The Hazmat team could deal with all of that from the safety of their spacesuits.

Riley was about to take out her phone to call for reinforcements when a shadow flickered past one of the south windows. She spun toward it as the Enemy blew one of the doors inward. Riley dropped and covered her head as the door shattered and sent a wave of debris past her before the angel strode into the garage. Her wings were spread wide, her sword gleamed in her hand, and she had removed Priest's blazer so that she was unabashedly topless.

"Zerachiel, I presume?"

"In the flesh," Zerachiel said.

Riley backed away and aimed at the angel's head. "How'd you find me here?"

"Oh, Riley. I'm your guardian angel. I always know where you are."

"This isn't you, Z. The drug is making you do this. Why don't you let your head clear~"

"My head is clear enough." She raised her sword and aimed the point at Riley. "You ruined everything. I've been a guardian angel to kings and princesses. I felt the last breath from one of my charges as she perished in what you call the Ice Age. I am ancient, you little piss-ant, and you have tarnished me. Perhaps for eternity."

She swung the sword and destroyed one of the glass beakers. Riley stepped back as Zerachiel advanced. "Because of you, my divinity was torn away from its mortal shell. Because of you, that mortal shell went on living. I am one, I am both. I am neither. Now that we are tied together again, I... feel. I remember being mortal. The frailty of it. I feel as if I've been locked in a box and chained. But if I kill you, I will be reassigned. I will show mercy when I kill Caitlin Priest. Maybe I'll take you both at the same time." She bent her elbow and pressed her blade against her own throat. "What do you think? Put your gun to your head, Riley, and we can do this together."

Riley kept her gun aimed at Zerachiel. "You're not yourself."

Zerachiel sneered and lowered her sword. "So I kill you, and I'm assigned a new charge. I'll do this one right, Riley. I'll stay to the shadows. Hidden. She'll never know me. She'll never drag me down the way you did. You're the engineer of my downfall, Riley. The path I'm on, I'm on it because of you. You made the choice to show Caitlin what it meant to be mortal even before she lost her divinity. You showed her how to survive as a human."

"I showed her how to live," Riley said.

"You taught her sexual desire... you debased the idea of love. And now you have her doing the same thing to Sariel. That will be the third angel whose wings you've clipped. You must be very proud of yourself. You dragged me down to Earth. Now it's just a short tumble down to Hell." She eyed the box of pills and her face brightened. "Ooh. Exactly what I was looking for."

"Z, don't."

Zerachiel's eyes darkened. "You don't get to tell me what to do."

Riley fired and hit Zerachiel in the chest. The wound immediately closed, and Zerachiel swayed as if it had been little more than a friendly punch on the shoulder. She looked down at the spot of blood that surrounded now-unmarked skin and then glared at Riley. "What are you going to do? Empty your gun into me? How many bullets do you have, Riley?"

"I don't have to fight forever. I just have to wait until the drug wears off. Six hour doses. You'll be yourself in..." She risked a look at her watch. It was thirty-eight minutes after two. "Eighty-two minutes."

Zerachiel laughed. "Do you really think you can fight me for an hour and a half?"

"I think I'll do whatever it takes to keep you from falling."

Zerachiel flashed her wings, the feathers glowing momentarily before she rolled her shoulders. "Well, then... catch me if you can." She roared and launched herself forward.

Riley retreated without turning around, forcing Zerachiel to close the distance between them. The angel flew a few feet off the ground, her face even with Riley. She led with her sword, and Riley ducked underneath the vicious blade as it swung at her throat. She bent her knees and, when Zerachiel was above her, shot straight up. She slammed her head into Zerachiel's shoulder and knocked her sideways into the concrete pillar.

Zerachiel slumped to the floor and Riley pounced onto her. She wrapped one arm around Zerachiel's left arm and put her in a hammerlock. She pressed her knee into Priest's back, right below the spot where her wings began. Zerachiel struggled and then looked over her shoulder with hatred in her eyes. "Do you really think *pain* will stop me?"

Riley ignored her and grabbed Zerachiel's other arm. She wrapped both her arms around Zerachiel's elbows and dug her knee into her partner's back. "Not pain. Inconvenience. Sorry, Caitlin." She pulled up with both arms as she pressed down with her knee. Zerachiel cried out in agony as both her shoulders popped out of their sockets, twisting in Riley's grip in a frantic attempt to get free.

Riley let her go and ran for the door in a desperate scramble. She cursed herself for leaving the bag outside. She reached the door as Zerachiel slammed into her from behind. The momentum carried Riley forward and through the door, and they tangled with each other as they hit the ground and rolled.

2:45pm

Zerachiel regained full use of her right arm in a matter of seconds, but her left was still dead weight. She flipped Riley onto her back, grabbed her throat, and leaned down with all her weight. Riley choked and tried to tear the fingers away, but Zerachiel wouldn't let that happen. Her lips were pulled back in a vicious sneer as she focused all her power on her hand. She knew that Riley's windpipe was just a fraction away from being crushed, but she wanted this to be slow. She wanted to look into Riley's eyes when the life faded from them, wanted to see her face slowly turn purple from~

"Shh, darlin'. It's all right. I'm your daddy's friend."

"But..."

"Don't say nothing, all right? Just lay there like that. You're so beautiful, darling."

Zerachiel reared back in horror. The image had been so clear that, for a moment, the woman underneath her had transformed into a thirteen year old girl. The abandoned showroom had been a small, dark bedroom. Zerachiel was still straddling Riley, who was taking the unexpected reprieve to try and reach her duffel bag again. Zerachiel recovered enough to punch Riley hard in the face.

"If you cry, I'm going to have to do something bad. Okay? So just be quiet."

Zerachiel roared. "Stop that!"

No, you bitch. I was there. I watched those men do unspeakable things to Riley. Things like that you're doing now.

Zerachiel put her hands over her ears and closed her eyes. Damnable human bodies and minds. Frail, fragile, weak. She saw the men pushing open Riley's bedroom door and slipping inside. She could hear the voices outside. Zerachiel was aware of a soft sobbing and knew her face was red, but she couldn't put the two together.

"Stop it..."

Riley

"You're nothing but a shell~"

is

"~that should have been destroyed a long time ago."

MINE

Zerachiel twisted and lurched toward the wall. She hit hard

enough to leave a crater in the drywall, and she thrashed as if being held against it by some invisible force. She turned her head, her cheek against the wall, and met Riley's confused gaze. "Now... do it now, Riley. Whatever you have to..." She cried out in pain and dropped to her knees, trembling violently as she wrapped both arms over her head.

There was a snap in her mind, and she lifted red-rimmed eyes to see Riley standing in front of her. The flax had been poured in a wide circle around her, and it burned with a gentle blue light. Riley had made the circle large enough for her to lie down, and she gratefully took advantage of that fact. She curled into a ball with her wings wrapped protectively around her, shuddering through the cold sweats that were suddenly wracking her body.

She could hear Zerachiel inside her mind, bellowing to be released, and it was all she could do to hold her back. She closed her eyes and imagined a wall being formed around the angel's consciousness. It was like pouring a glass of water on a wildfire, but it still helped.

When she spoke again, she spoke as Priest. "Thank... you." She swallowed the lump in her throat and rested her head on the carpet. "You should... call... for help. For b-both of... us..."

Riley nodded. She looked battered and broken, and she turned to walk back to the bag on shaky legs. She managed to take three steps before she tripped herself up and fell flat on her face. Priest stared at her and waited for her to get up. She even reached out for her, but the barrier currently keeping her sane sparked against her fingertips. She hissed and pulled her hand away.

"Riley... get up. Riley, you ha-have to get up." A seizure passed through her body, and Priest's eyes closed tightly as she struggled to keep Zerachiel from taking control again. The seizures passed, and Priest curled into a tighter ball.

The next hour was going to be Hell.

5:21pm

Briggs followed Riley's request to the letter. She waited until one minute to four, and then called in the reinforcements. By the time Riley regained consciousness, SWAT had all the streets around the complex cordoned off. The teams began a systematic search of the grounds and found Riley, Priest and the U4ic lab within a matter of minutes. Priest had regained her faculties enough to conceal her wings before they arrived, but the team members still got an eyeful of Priest's bare breasts.

They were both too weak to move, so they were sitting against the wall when Briggs finally found them. One of the SWAT team members had found Priest a windbreaker, and she managed to get her arms into the sleeves and zip it up. Briggs looked at them both, hands on her hips, and betrayed her concern by skipping the lecture.

"Are you okay?"

"We will be." Riley's voice was still rough from her near-strangulation, but it would heal.

Briggs looked into the lab. "The U4ic?"

Riley nodded. "We think this is the home base. It looked like they were ready to start rolling out supply. Looks like we might have nipped it in the bud and stopped the spread before it could start."

"That's one way to stop a drug war." Briggs looked at them again. "Any idea who was behind it?"

Riley sighed. "No clue. But the way things are going, I'd put my money on Falco."

Briggs rolled her eyes. "Great. Two criminal masterminds in town and my best detectives keep getting caught in the crossfire. Can you walk?"

Riley looked down at her feet as if the question had been directed to them. "In a minute."

Briggs smirked and lifted her radio to her mouth. "Come on in. She's not going anywhere."

The clatter of a gurney drew Riley's attention to the main entrance, and she shuddered when she saw Gillian was the person pushing it. "Uh-oh. I'm in trouble, aren't I?"

"Oh, yeah." Briggs walked past them and went into the lab to coordinate the confiscation of the drug.

Gillian parked the gurney in front of Riley and looked down at her. "Do you need help getting up?"

"No, I think I can stand." She pushed herself up using the wall for support, stepped forward, and gratefully stretched out on the gurney. It wasn't the most comfortable mattress she'd ever slept on, but it also wasn't in the top ten worst. She sighed and let her body relax, sinking into the plushness as Gillian drew the blanket up over her. "Thank you."

"Uh, Caitlin..."

"Don't worry about me, Gillian. Sariel is on her way. She'll take care of me."

Riley stopped Gillian from leading the gurney away and twisted to look at Priest. "Hey. Are we good?"

"Good?"

"Are we okay? Are you carrying any of that residual anger or resentment at~"

Priest stopped her by raising her hand. "That wasn't me, Riley. That was a dark and, under normal circumstances *small* part of Zerachiel. Is a part of me bitter than things have changed so drastically since I met you? Yes. Of course. At my age change is frightening and unwelcome." She smiled. "But I wouldn't trade my time with you for monotony. I wouldn't trade who I am now for... anything, Riley."

She pushed herself to her feet and walked forward carefully. She brushed Riley's hair away from her forehead, bent down and kissed her between the eyebrows.

"Thank you for not letting me fall."

Riley smiled. "Selfish interests, believe me. Make sure Sariel takes you to a good church."

Priest nodded, and then looked at Gillian. "Go easy on her."

"We'll see," Gillian said. She stepped around the gurney and hugged Priest. "I'm glad you're okay. Both of you."

"Thank you, Gillian."

Gillian turned to Riley, sighed, and gripped the end of the gurney. Riley looked up at her, noticing the soft skin under Gillian's chin, not for the first time. Gillian was dressed officially in crisp blue scrubs underneath a blue jacket that identified her as a member of the Office of the Chief Medical Examiner.

When they were outside and away from eavesdroppers, Riley cleared her throat. "I know I'm in deep shit with you, and this is in no way meant to be an attempt to get out of it. I just want you to know how beautiful I think you look right now. After the day I've had, seeing you is just what I need."

Gillian kept her eyes forward. "Thank you."

"Now that that's out of the way, feel free to rip me a new asshole."

Gillian barely managed to hide her smile, but said nothing. She pushed Riley into the back of the ambulance and climbed in after her, crouching next to the gurney after shutting the doors and directing the driver to the nearest hospital. She took Riley's hand, squeezed, and then twisted it to look at her watch. "For the next thirty seconds, I'm just going to be your wife."

Riley nodded.

"Are you really, really okay?"

Riley considered the question. She didn't want to just give a pat, reassuring response. She squeezed Gillian's hand, brushed her knuckles, and said, "My stomach is tied up in knots. I have a splitting headache. I'm nauseated. I think I was two doses away from ODing on those stimulants. I feel like I just got dragged behind a bus. But all things considered... I'll be fine."

Gillian sniffled and wiped her cheek with the back of her free hand. "Okay. Now I'm going to be your doctor and your wife." She squeezed Riley's hand almost hard enough to hurt and leaned forward. "*Drugs?* What the hell were you thinking, Riley? I don't give a shit what they're supposed to do, how safe they supposedly are, or if you *think* you have a handle on it. You had no right to do that to me. You risk your life too much as it is without adding addiction on top of it. What could have possibly possessed you to start taking this shit?"

"They were supposed to make me happy. And I'm happy with you, Jill. I swear it. You're the only thing I can consistently count on to make me happy in this world. So I thought... if the pill could help me do the same for you... then it was worth it. I just wanted to be your bright spot at the end of the day and not just some dark, depressing beast you had to comfort."

Gillian blinked and bent down. She stroked Riley's hair and kissed her lips. "The best part of any day is the time I spend with you. No matter what we're doing, Riley. You know how bad this town is... but I came back because you're here. I could live in Hell if you were there with me. *That* is what you do for me, Riley. Don't you for a second forget it. Understood?"

Riley smiled. "Yes, ma'am."

Gillian kissed her lips. "I love you."

"I love you, too."

Gillian sat up and twisted to look out the windshield. She kept her hand in Riley's, and Riley was looking at their intertwined fingers when her adrenaline finally faded completely. She passed out with Gillian's hand warming her own.

Sariel took Priest to the largest church in town. Votive candles flickered in small red glasses and cast dancing shadows on the walls. Priest groaned as she was lowered into a back pew, and Sariel kept her arm around Priest's shoulders and drew her close. Priest put her head down on Sariel's shoulder and breathed deeply.

A choir was practicing, but a sign in the foyer assured them it was open to the public. As the group worked their way through the litany of songs, Sariel stroked the back of Priest's neck.

"If I had known you planned to kill yourself, I never would have left town."

"Hm." Priest pressed closer to her lover. "It wasn't exactly a plan. Where did you go?"

Sariel was silent long enough that Priest almost thought she was ignoring the question. Finally, she spoke quietly enough that her words were almost covered by the choir's singing.

"I was following a lead on something you requested I investigate. Something for Riley." She stroked Priest's neck and pushed her hands up into Priest's hair. "The situation with past champions, and whether any have... resigned. I've been looking into it for the past few weeks, but I didn't want to tell you anything until I had something solid to report."

Priest sat up. "And you do now?"

Sariel nodded slowly. "I believe I do. There was a man who was the champion in a small southwestern state. After twenty years of dedicated service to the cause, he chose and trained his successor and informed his handler that he would no longer be the champion. As far as I can tell, it worked. His protection was removed, but the other side was focused on his replacement and thus he was left alone. I've heard he's living peacefully in the same town he once fought for."

"And you went to speak with him?"

"No. I went to seek permission to speak with him."

Priest frowned. "Why would you need...? Oh, Father."

"Yes. When he was champion, he represented the side of evil. Now that he's retired, it may not matter. But if he has even a hint of loyalty remaining..."

"Then we cannot possibly bring him here."

Sariel nodded and looked at Priest. Her skin had regained its luster, and she was already looking much better. "I did attain permission to speak with him if you think it would be a wise decision. I thought I would leave it up to you. What do you think we should do?"

"We'll..." She searched for the proper phrasing. "We'll play it by ear. If all else fails, we will bring him in so he and Riley can have a conversation. But only as a last resort."

Sariel turned to face the altar again. She stroked Priest's

shoulder.

"We also must address the... ramifications of this quest. If it's successful and Riley finds a way to resign her post as champion... will you be prepared for that?"

Priest took a deep breath and felt something in her side pinch. She hissed and reached for it, but Sariel found it first and gently probed the injured area with strong strokes of her fingers. Priest closed her eyes and leaned back against the pew. She looked up at the crucifix hanging over the stage.

"Today, Riley kept me from becoming a fallen angel. If there's anything I can do to bring her peace, then God willing, I will do it."

Sariel nodded and drew Priest's head back to her chest. Priest closed her eyes and let the choir's singing lull her into a peaceful doze.

BROKEN HALLELUJAH

The tall blonde woman left her house and hop-walked to her red Ferrari in the driveway. She was late for her job as astronaut, and she was supposed to go into outer space today. Just as she got her legs stretched under the wheel, which was difficult because her knees didn't bend, a dinosaur jumped onto the roof of the house and roared. The tall blonde rich astronaut wasn't scared, because she was also a dinosaur trainer. So she—

The little girl looked up from her toys. Cassie was back, standing in the doorway of her bedroom. She wore a white dress, like always, and her red hair was tied in pigtails. She had freckles, and big blue eyes. She smiled and the little girl looked back at her toys. She walked her Tyrannosaurus across the roof of Barbie's house and waited for Cassie to go away.

"Hi, Gillian."

Gillian Hunt pushed out her bottom lip and focused on making Barbie tame the dinosaur. She had gotten the dollhouse for her fifth birthday, so it was still new. She didn't want to share it yet, but she also didn't want to be rude. She put the T-rex down and wiped her hands on her skirt. "I think I'm done playing right now..."

"Oh. Well, maybe we can play something else."

Gillian guessed that would be all right. "Let me put away my dolls." She picked up Barbie and T-rex and took them to her toy box. As soon as her back was turned, she heard a stomp. She turned around, certain that Cassie was trying to play with her dollhouse without permission. Cassie was in the room, but she was looking at the floor in front of the dollhouse. She had knocked a book off the shelf.

"What are you doing? You're gonna break it." Gillian picked up the book and yelped when she saw the crushed spider underneath it.

"It came out of your dollhouse."

"Grammy said she kept it in the attic but she cleaned it before she gave it to me."

"I'm sure she did. Spiders are tricky and they hide real good."

Gillian bent down and looked at the dead spider. She couldn't tell what kind it had been. Maybe a brown recluse... Mommy said Grammy's house had lots of those kind, but she didn't know what they looked like. She would have to clean it up before it stained the carpet. She looked at Cassie.

"It could have bit me. Thanks for killin' it."

Cassie smiled. "That's my job."

Gillian screwed up her face. "Kids don't have *jobs*. You're funny."

"Yeah." She crossed her arms over her knees and rested her chin on them.

"I'm gonna go clean it up. Then we can go outside and play."

Cassie nodded. "Okay."

Gillian ran into the bathroom and wet some toilet paper. When she got back to her room, Cassie was gone. She didn't think anything of it, even though Cassie would have had to pass the bathroom to go downstairs, and she got onto her knees and started cleaning the dead spider away.

Gillian lifted her head off the pillow and rolled onto her back. The bed next to her was empty. "Riley?" The sound in the bathroom repeated, and Gillian winced sympathetically. She sat up and pulled the blanket around her hip. "Sweetie? You okay?"

"Fine. Just a little nauseated."

Gillian looked at the clock. "You're still getting over your ordeal with the U4ic and the uppers you were taking to balance it out." She tried to keep any recrimination out of her voice. They'd had the fight, and Riley sincerely apologized, but she still couldn't believe Riley had gotten hooked on pills. "Briggs will understand if you need to take some extra time off."

Riley came out of the bathroom and left the light on. "I've already taken off too much time. It's just morning sickness."

"Morning sickness?" Gillian said. "You told me you were on the pill."

"Ha ha." Riley climbed under the blankets and Gillian stretched out next to her. "It'll pass by breakfast." She pulled Gillian close. "Go back to sleep. I didn't mean to wake you up."

"Mm. I'm probably up for the day."

"I've heard that song before. Just give it a minute."

Gillian snuggled closer to Riley. "I'm happy to prove you wrong. We can lie here all morning, if that's what it takes." She closed her eyes. "But I know when I'm up."

"Uh-huh."

When Gillian opened her eyes and saw the sunlight stream in through the window, Riley had the good sense not to rub her nose in it. Gillian went to the bathroom and took a shower to wake up. She had just soaped her washcloth when the curtain pushed back and Riley joined her under the spray. Riley's arms wrapped around her waist and Gillian leaned back into the embrace. Riley slid her hands up, and Gillian reached back to spread soap over Riley's hips.

"Well, I was *going* to take a quick shower."

"The actual showering will still be quick," Riley assured her. "And don't worry... I brushed my teeth, and I'm feeling completely unsick. I think your body wash has curative properties."

"Well, then. By all means."

Gillian's hair was already wet and easily shifted off one shoulder to the other. Riley bent to kiss her neck, drawing quiet sounds of approval from Gillian as the water swirled around their feet. Riley moved one hand down between Gillian's legs, and Gillian matched her movements by cupping Riley's sex. She bit her lip as they began working in concert, Riley moving her lips up and down Gillian's neck. Her palm molded to the shape of Gillian's breast and she split two fingers over one nipple.

Riley turned them so that the water hit Gillian's upper chest, washing down over Riley's arms and Gillian's stomach. Riley bent her wrist so that her palm formed a reservoir to catch the falling water, and she rolled her fingers to guide the water flow toward Gillian's clit. Gillian groaned and leaned back, resting her head on Riley's shoulder as she rocked her hips forward and tried to focus on using her fingers to bring Riley pleasure.

Gillian came first, and she redoubled her efforts to get Riley off. She turned and stepped out of Riley's embrace, dropped to her knees, and kissed Riley's stomach. She added a third finger, forming a pyramid with them as she began to thrust harder, angling her head to take Riley's clit into her mouth. Riley pressed against the wall of the shower, spreading her legs and signaling her orgasm by running her fingers through Gillian's hair. She spread her fingers on the back of Gillian's head and groaned as Gillian pulled back, kissed the hollows of Riley's hips, and stood up to pull Riley to her.

They kissed as the water washed over them, cascading down between their bodies. Gillian finally pulled back and brushed Riley's hair back out of her face. "That was a nice surprise."

"It's been a while."

"A couple of days."

Riley shrugged. "Felt like longer. I know you're still mad about the drugs~"

Gillian shook her head. She ran her finger over Riley's upper arm, tracing one of the mostly-healed scars from her bout with Priest. "I know your intentions were good. You were just thinking of me. But yeah, maybe... maybe I did make it a little difficult to be intimate."

Riley kissed her again. "Well. You're worth the wait."

Gillian grinned. "Want to share the shower? I'll wash your hair."

"Temping. But I'm going to head in early. Show of good faith and all that." She kissed the corners of Gillian's mouth and then her lips. "I love you."

"Love you, too."

Riley pushed the curtain back and left the shower, and Gillian held her hands under the spray and pushed her fingers through her hair. She smiled and closed her eyes as the water washed over her face. She really hadn't realized how long it had been since she and Riley made love, but she was glad the drought ended before it was brought to her attention. If Riley had mentioned it at work, she would have had to do something drastic that could have cost them both their jobs.

She smiled at the fantasy, letting it play out in her mind as she finished showering. Even if she and Riley couldn't *really* have sex on her desk, the topic could come up during their next round of dirty talk.

Riley stared at the box of doughnuts and tall thermos of coffee on her desk and then looked at Priest. She was in her usual three-piece suit, and she'd trimmed her hair again. The short cut had taken some getting used to, but Riley had decided it looked good on her. She was making a show of averting her gaze by staring at her computer screen with an intensity most internet users reserved for watching porn.

"A whole box? How fat do you think I am?"

Priest dipped her chin and finally looked at her. "I felt it wasn't enough of an apology for what... happened. I injured you very badly."

"And I paid you back by breaking both your arms. Let's just call it even." She opened the box and held it out to a passing detective. "Here. Courtesy of Detective Priest."

Briggs came out of her office. "Riley. I was going to let you settle in, but we have a potential weird one. Think you're up to it?"

"I'm always up for weird." She took her jacket off the back of the chair and slipped it back on as Briggs handed her the address. Priest joined her and they walked to the elevator. "You don't have to buy me gifts to make anything up to me, Cait. We've gone through rough times before, and we've come to blows. This time at least we can both blame the drugs."

Priest smiled weakly. "I'm your guardian angel, Riley. To have the memory of holding you down, of drawing your blood... you can't imagine how much that hurts me."

"I hadn't thought of it that way. But it's water under the bridge."

As a show of support, Riley let Priest drive them to the crime scene. Priest was getting better at navigating the city without wings, but she occasionally had issues involving street signals and right-of-way that Riley helped her out with. The building was easy to find; two police cars were parked in front with their lights still spinning.

When they parked, Riley congratulated her on learning how to drive so quickly. "But all that stuff I was telling you about pedestrians and right-turn on red should have been covered when you took your driving test."

"My what?"

"For your..." She squinted at Priest. "You do have a driver's license, don't you?"

Priest blinked. "Yes. I have all pertinent identification necessary~"

"You have one issued by the state, though? By an official agency that tested your abilities before you got behind the wheel of a car?"

Priest cleared her throat and Riley rolled her eyes. "Well, I know where we're heading this weekend." She showed her badge to the officer blocking the door. "Parra, Priest, Homicide."

The officer turned and gestured at the stairs behind him. "Third floor, apartment 3B. It's pretty nasty."

"Aren't they all. Thanks, officer."

They headed up and found the door crossed by yellow crime scene tape. Riley ducked underneath, holding it up for Priest, and put her hand under her nose. The smell was unbelievable. Priest saw what Riley and the other officers in the room were doing and mimicked them even though the smell wasn't exactly pungent to her. The apartment was pristine except for a trail of blood that led from the armchair, through the living room, and disappeared around the corner into the kitchen.

One of the uniformed officers approached. "Detective Parra."

She looked past the white handkerchief covering his face and recognized the eyes. "Sam Cooley. Long time." The last time she remembered working with him had been immediately after Lieutenant Hathaway's assassination on the steps of the precinct. Not a good memory, but he'd always been a solid cop. "What's the story on this stench?"

"Tenant was Hunter Poage. Worked at the supermarket down on the corner there. Boss called when he hadn't shown up for three days, and the landlord came upstairs and found this."

Riley had moved to the kitchen door to follow the blood trail. "He called instead of just firing him?"

"Apparently the kid is a good worker."

The trail went past the fridge and into the pantry. The body was stuffed onto the bottom shelf, several bones obviously broken to make him fit right. Cans and other non-perishable food items were stacked carefully on the floor to make room. Whoever had done it wasn't in any hurry. The body had begun to decompose, which filled the room with an unforgettable reek. An officer wearing a biohazard mask was standing guard beside the door.

"Lose a bet?" Riley asked him.

He closed his eyes and shook his head slowly. "Cooley offered me a steak and lobster dinner if I stood watch."

Riley nearly gagged at the mention of food. "I think you got played, officer." She turned and looked into the living room.

"Where's the medical examiner?"

"Not here yet," Cooley said. "Can't move him until she signs off."

"Of all the times for Jill to get stuck in traffic," Riley murmured. "Is the photographer done with the scene?" Cooley nodded, so Riley walked to the living room window and pushed it open to let the stink dissipate in the fresh air. "Okay, unofficially, what looks to be the cause of death?"

"His throat was cut." Cooley went to the armchair. "It looks like he mostly bled out here, then he was dragged to where he is now before he was all the way empty."

The officer from downstairs appeared at the doorway. "Detectives. Call just came over the radio for available units about three blocks from here..."

Riley nodded and waved him off. "Go on."

The other cop that Riley hadn't spoken with left with the downstairs guard, leaving Cooley and his partner with Riley and Priest. Riley walked to the window and looked down as the two officers got into their car and sped off in the direction of whatever emergency had gotten their attention. She breathed the fresh air and drummed her fingers on the windowsill.

"Okay, let's forget about the body for right now."

"Easy for you to say," Cooley said.

Riley shrugged. "We'll do our best. Priest, look around. See if you can find anything clue-shaped." She pulled on a pair of rubber gloves and began going through the mail. Nothing but bills and bank statements, envelopes with ominous phrases like FINAL NOTICE written on them. She opened one and saw that his electricity was due to be cut off in three days. Priest was at the desk with the laptop open, randomly opening files and closing them again.

"The recycle bin is full of image files."

Riley joined her and looked over her shoulder. "Carly04142011, Carly02282011. Looks like they're all pictures of the same person. Maybe an ex-something or other. We could get lucky and this is just a suicide. Maybe Mr. Poage killed himself, waited for most of his blood to drip onto the chair, and then dragged himself into the kitchen and stretched out on the pantry shelf."

Cooley shrugged. "Stranger things have happened."

Riley looked at him. "Yeah?"

"You ever been in No Man's Land after dark?"

Riley chuckled as her cell phone chirped in her pocket. She fished it out. "More often than I'd like to remember, Officer Cooley." She answered the call. "This is Parra."

"Riley, get to the hospital." Briggs sounded out of breath, frantic.

"Boss? What's going on?"

"There was an accident. She's in surgery right now."

Riley frowned. Priest and Cooley were both staring at her. "Who is in surgery?"

"Gillian."

The stench seemed to vanish, and Riley felt as if all the air in the room had been sucked away to leave her in a vacuum. "What? What happened?"

"There was an accident. I've sent another pair of detectives to take over your case, just~"

"*Where?*" Riley realized she had shouted it when she noticed Priest flinch. She was already out the door, with Priest trailing behind her. Briggs told her the name of the hospital, but Riley had to ask her to repeat it before it registered. "St. Luke's. Right..."

Priest grabbed Riley by the shoulders when they reached the foot of the stairs. "Riley, stop! What happened?"

"Gillian was in an accident. Surgery." She swallowed hard. "I have to get to St. Luke's. Give me your keys."

"No~"

"Cait, I'm not in the mood."

Priest said, "I have a better idea." She grabbed Riley in a tight hug. "Hold on tight."

The floor vanished from under Riley's feet and she stumbled just as it reappeared, the darkness of the stairwell replaced by a sunlit lobby. Riley overcame her dizziness and the world corrected itself as she realized she was in the lobby of St. Luke's Hospital. She grabbed blindly for Priest's hand and squeezed. "You're forgiven, Cait. For anything you've ever done to me. Thank you."

"Go," Priest said.

Riley rushed forward and grabbed the first person in scrubs that got within arm's reach. "Gillian Hunt. She was in some sort of accident..."

"They would have taken her to the emergency room."

Riley nodded and pushed away, following the white arrows on the walls that pointed her in the right direction. It was minutes before she realized that Priest had vanished after delivering Riley to the hospital.

Bezaliel was a handsome son of a bitch. He watched his reflection in the mirror and turned his face one way, then the other. Angels manifested a unique shell when they appeared in the mortal realm, but demons liked taking things right off the rack. A body that had been lived in was so much more fun, with so many options to explore. This host was named Beau, and he had been a naughty boy for the past thirty-six hours. The things he'd done while under the demon's power would destroy his relationship with his wife, and his children would never be the same. All he had to do was slide into Beau's skin, spend a day or two going wild, and his job was done. Being evil was such a damn breeze.

He finished his beer and glanced toward the girls in the corner. High school, if even that, skipping school. Being naughty and seeing how long they could get away with their fake IDs. Bezaliel was still deciding which one of them he would seduce and impregnate and which one he would just disfigure when he was pulled backward off his stool.

He had a glimpse of pale skin and blonde hair as his attacker stood him up, and then an outstanding right hook filled his vision with stars. There were distinct downsides to wearing a mortal's skin as a suit. He was punched relentlessly, unable to bring his arms up for defense as blood streamed over his lips.

Beau's nose was definitely broken, and several of his teeth were loosened by the time the attack finally ended. He faced his attacker with fury that only grew when he saw it was a woman wearing a suit. Her hair was mussed and her tie had been loosened, but otherwise she looked like she had merely jogged down the hall.

Her demeanor flicked a switch in his mind and he recognized his attacker. "Zerachiel. Attacking me without provocation... do you know what a hellstorm you've brought down on yourself?"

The angel punched the wall next to his head and her fist broke through the drywall. Beau heard the sounds of the other patrons fleeing the bar. The door was open and the harsh light of day made the room look flat and ugly.

"Who ordered it?"

"Who ordered *what?*" Bezaliel touched the back of his hand to his nose. It was going to take hours to heal all this damage. Hell, maybe he'd just abandon the body. Leave Beau with a nice parting gift courtesy of Zerachiel.

"The wife of our champion was attacked today. I want to know who ordered it and why. I will drag the information from your lifeless corpse if necessary."

Bezaliel stared at her. "Gillian Hunt has been hurt? Ha. Oh, Marchosias is going to be thrilled." He reached for napkins off a nearby table and pressed them against his nose. Stupid mortal bodies. Once a leak was sprung, it took forever to stop. "Sorry, wings. No call went out. I'd have heard if it had. That's why you came to me, right? Bezaliel, always looking for a quick buck. No one was after your precious champion's precious consort."

Zerachiel backed up a step.

"You know I'm telling the truth. It irritates me that we weren't involved. Hey, what happened to her? Is she still in one piece?" He considered for a moment. Maybe there was still a way to salvage the situation. If she was in a hospital~ The angel's hand closed around his throat and his mind began to focus on ways to get her off of him.

"Tomorrow morning your host will awaken in a mental health facility. He'll be suffering amnesia that covers the past two days. In a month, he will be released into the loving arms of his family so they can begin healing."

Bezaliel rolled his eyes. "You're no fun."

"Leave now or I will pull you out of him."

Bezaliel stuck his tongue out at her. His body twitched suddenly, and his head knocked against the wall twice before he was pulled away from it and dropped onto the floor.

After a moment, Beau Gilchrist touched his face and cried out in pain. He was shaky, terrified, and completely and utterly confused. A woman put her hand on his shoulder and he cringed away from her. When he looked up, he saw that she was quite possibly the most beautiful woman he'd ever seen in his life. The pale blue of her eyes was like the sky on his favorite summer day, and he felt himself relax.

"Who are you?"

"My name is Caitlin Priest. I'm here to help you, Beau."

The corner of the hallway had three blue tiles alternating in a sea of white. The glass walls stretched up two stories, panes separated by thick metal struts. The picture on the wall showed a building with two apparent light sources judging by the way the shadows fell. Four plush chairs were arranged in sets of two, separated by a potted plant with wide leaves. There were five magazines on the table.

Riley dedicated everything in the corner to memory without intending to. She would sit in one of the chairs, push herself up to pace toward the end of the hall, then return because she didn't think the doctors knew to find her anywhere else. She had sat in all four of the chairs, and she knew which of them was the most comfortable. She stood at the window and watched the cars passing on the street outside.

At some point she realized Priest was beside her. She stayed quiet for a long time before she spoke.

"Demons?"

"No."

"Sure?"

"Positive."

Riley pressed her lips together and looked down at her shoes.

"Do they know anything?"

"She's in stable condition. No better, no worse, just more of the same." She was shaking and shoved her hands into her pockets. "Ruptured spleen. It was bleeding into he~" Her breath gave out on her and she had to start pacing again. "It has to be demons, Cait. It has to... it has to be something I can *fight*."

"I'm sorry, Riley. There is no way a demon would deny involvement in this if they were involved. Have they said what happened?"

Riley closed her eyes. "The doctor, uh... he said some idiot was texting. Wasn't looking at the road. Gillian was in the passenger seat of the medical examiner's van, and they got sideswiped. It went onto its side and skidded, rolled, and Gillian..." She swallowed the lump in her throat and wiped her hand down her face. "She was wearing her seatbelt. Her assistant was in the back, broke both his legs. Probably won't walk again. Gillian usually rides in the back."

Priest touched Riley's back and rubbed between her shoulder blades. "Is there anything I can do?"

"Can you heal her?"

"No. Damage this severe is... beyond my abilities. It would cost me my divinity again."

Riley was ashamed of herself for advocating that, but she kept her mouth shut. "Then find Kenzie. Tell her and Chelsea what happened, but... I don't want them down here. I don't need them fawning over me. I just... tell them to pray for her."

"Okay. There's a stop I have to make first, someone I have to find, but I'll tell them. Is there anything I can do for *you*?"

Riley considered refusing, but then she had an idea. "Yeah. Actually..."

After granting Riley's request, Priest went on a search of the hospital. She started outside the operating room, moving between nurses and doctors in bloody scrubs with none of them paying attention to her presence. She moved further into the hospital, ascending the stairs and traveling down long corridors to patient's rooms without a single worker questioning her presence. She was getting frustrated and angry by the time she reached the neonatal wing and found who she was looking for.

"Cassiel."

The angel looked away from the glass. She didn't smile, barely acknowledged who she was looking at before she looked back at the newborns. Priest joined her, restraining the urge to cause violence. It was unseemly for guardian angels to attack one another.

It was Cassiel who broke the silence. "There is nothing I could do for her at this moment. Her soul is in isolation. The doctors are striving to repair her physical form. I can do nothing to help, so I came here."

Priest looked down at the newborns. She could see that they were surrounded by two distinct auras; one was the child's soul, still in flux, and the other was an angel's presence to watch over them. One newborn in the middle row only had one aura. There was no angel, and Priest knew why. Something was going to happen to the child at a very young age, something even its guardian angel couldn't prevent, and it would die.

"In a way, she is lucky." Priest thought Cassiel meant Gillian, but then realized she was looking at the same baby. "The first awful thing that happens in her life will also be the last. She will only know happy things. We should all be so lucky."

Priest couldn't keep the anger out of her voice. "You should have been there."

"I was."

Priest turned, her voice barely under a scream. "Then why didn't you stop it?"

Cassiel turned and met Priest's anger with serenity. "I was there, Zerachiel. I guided Gillian to the front seat instead of the back where she often rides. I guided her hand to the seatbelt and ensured it was fastened. I cradled her body to mine until emergency technicians arrived, and I kept her soul lit. I did everything it was in my power to do. You know the... terrible things we are forced to witness. How many men did you watch enter Riley Parra's bedroom? Did you count the times you ignored her pleas for help?"

Priest looked away.

"Sariel was right. You have let your human personality overwhelm your true self. If I had been as negligent as you claim, Gillian would have been tossed against the side of the van. The impact of her skull against the metal~"

"Stop."

"~would have broken her neck. The doctors would have endeavored to save her, but she would die on the table. She would have been buried in~"

"Shut up." Priest grabbed the collar of Cassiel's shirt and, after a moment, released it. She looked at her fingers and then dropped them to her side.

"Do you think of yourself as Zerachiel? Many of us have wondered, since you were reunited with your true self. You lived as a mortal for so long, and it can be tempting to fall~"

"I have not fallen."

"No. You've stepped right to the edge of falling, but you've stayed on the right side of the line. There was some tension not long ago, but fortunately that was artificial. That time."

Priest looked away, focusing on the children again.

Cassiel sighed and touched the glass. "So many people still having children in this world, in this battleground of a city. I don't know whether it's inspiring or heartbreaking." She dragged her fingers down the glass and stepped away. She stopped and, without turning, spoke again. "When you asked me to be with Riley as she died, I went. I made the passage easier for her. If anything happens to Gillian, I believe she will be more comforted by your presence than by mine. She knows you, and she loves you. If you'd be willing to watch over her during this crisis~"

"Yes."

"Thank you, Zerachiel."

Priest rested her forehead against the glass and looked at the babies.

Riley slept.

It was a deep, dreamless sleep that seemed more like a coma than actual slumber. She was stretched across two of the chairs in the waiting room outside the emergency room, her hair undone and piled under her head like a thin pillow. Her hands were folded over her stomach, fingers laced loosely so her hands wouldn't fall. Her feet were crossed at the ankles, and others who came to sit for a while before leaving didn't disturb her.

Joshua McKenna, Gillian's surgeon, gently touched her shoulder. "Mrs. Hunt?"

Riley was immediately awake, as Priest had assured her she would be. "Pardon?"

"I was told you were Gillian Hunt's wife."

Riley sat up and decided not to confuse the issue. "I am. What's, what, is she, the~"

He held up a hand to stop her. "The surgery was a success. Her spleen was ruptured, and we wanted to take care of that as soon as possible. We stopped the bleeding and we'll be observing her to see if it will heal on its own. If not, we'll have to remove it but we'll cross that bridge when we get to it. Right now, we're confident she'll pull through. She's resting comfortably at the moment, but you can see her soon if you'd like."

"Yeah, of course. Thank you, doctor."

He nodded and walked away and Riley dropped into her seat. She closed her eyes and pressed her face against her fists. "Thank you. If any of you are listening, thank you." She took a deep breath and took her phone out of her pocket. She had eighteen missed calls, including multiple attempts by Kenzie. Briggs had called twice, and everyone in their meager circle of friends had tried once.

She scrolled down until she found a number she'd never dialed, but had entered into her phone in case of an emergency. Somehow she never thought she would use it, despite where they lived. Maureen Spenser was Gillian's best friend from childhood and maid of honor at their wedding. She dialed the number and stood up, walking toward the fire exit so no one would gripe at her for using a cell phone in the hospital.

"Hello, this is Maureen."

"Maureen? This is Riley. Gillian's wife."

"Oh! Hey. What's up?"

Riley leaned against the wall and lowered her head. Saying the words was like a vice around her chest. "She's okay. She's going to be fine. But there was an accident..."

Riley was in the hospital lobby staring at the vending machine when Briggs showed up. Her arrival was the first indication that it was later than Riley thought, and she stared in confusion at the streetlights shining through the window. "Boss. Nice of you to come down." A nurse walked by in pastel-colored pants and a floral scrub top. Riley nodded at her and, when she was out of earshot, said, "What happened to the old white dresses and little caps? If Gillian has to be in a place like this, I at least want her to get some fantasy fuel out of the deal."

"The times they are a-changing, Detective." Briggs smiled and squeezed Riley's arm. "I thought I'd see how everyone was doing." She crossed her arms over her chest and glanced around. "Does Priest know anything about, uh, who did this?"

"It wasn't... it was just a random thing. N.D.I."

Briggs frowned. "What's that?"

"No Demons Involved."

"I'll have to remember that. How is she doing?"

Riley sighed. "It sounds worse to me than it probably is. Her doctors are all optimistic, but all I can hear is surgery and bleeding and ruptured." She looked at the change in her hand and then looked at the vending machine again. "She's in recovery right now. The doctor says I may be able to go in and see her soon."

"That's good."

"Yeah." She jingled the change. "And I know she's going to ask if I've eaten anything all day. I don't want to lie, so I came down here but the idea of food..."

Briggs took the money from Riley and fed it into the machine. She punched the buttons and retrieved a bag of Wheat Thins.

"Thanks, boss." She walked back to the elevators and Briggs followed. "How's the case going?"

"We assigned Timbale to it." Riley rolled her eyes. "I know. The replacement ME came in and determined the throat wound was self-inflicted. Right now Timbale's working on the theory it was a suicide that someone made to look like a murder. He was talking to the parents when I left. Are you okay?"

"Yeah. I'll be fine." She and Briggs stepped into the elevator. "Priest is helping out a lot. She gave me a dreamless nap a while ago that worked wonders."

"Wow. I could use one of those once a week."

Riley smiled and escorted Briggs back to the waiting room that had quickly become familiar to her. She resumed her seat and looked up at the television mounted on the wall. One game show had morphed into another, and Riley sat and opened her snack. Briggs sat in the chair across from her and sighed. "I can't believe it's just a stupid traffic accident. I spent all day thinking this was a gauntlet being thrown down. I was ready to put you on administrative leave just so you'd have time to deal with it."

"I appreciate that, boss. If you're offering leave~"

"Compassionate leave is granted. Don't even think about coming into work the next few days."

"Thanks. And I guess now that I'm thinking clearly, I don't..." She stared at the television and watched as letters were revealed to form a hidden phrase. She felt like tiles in her mind were turning over as well, pieces of a puzzle that formed a frightening thought. "Huh."

"What's wrong?"

Riley shook her head. "I don't know. Something I have to ask Priest." She forced herself to eat some of her snack, and the food reminded her stomach that it hadn't been fed in a while. She and Briggs sat in silence while Riley ate. The game show ended and a prime-time drama started. Priest appeared and greeted Briggs before taking a seat beside Riley.

"I didn't think you would be here, Briggs."

"I could go home to an empty apartment, but I'd rather be here. Dr. Hunt... Gillian... needs my support, and I can worry about her just as easily here as I can at home."

Riley nodded. "She'll appreciate you being here. Cait, can I talk to you alone? No offense, boss."

"No, it's fine."

Riley stood up and led Priest down one wide corridor that stretched off the waiting room. When she was sure they were out of earshot of anyone else, Riley guided Priest to the wall and stepped closer to her.

"You said you investigated to see if the demons were involved with this."

"Yes. I believe them when they said they weren't involved."

Riley shook her head. "Yeah, I have no problem with that. If they didn't take credit, then they definitely didn't do this. My question is *why*."

Priest furrowed her brow. "I don't understand. If a demon had been involved, then drastic countermeasures would have to be taken. We~"

"I'm not asking why you did it, I'm asking why you had to. Why did you even think it was possible a demon could have done this?" Priest still didn't understand. "Three years ago, you took me down to Georgia. I found Gillian, and we came to an agreement. I gave her part of my tattoo, and you said that it would protect her if she came back here. It's why she agreed to come back with me. But if the tattoo protected her, then why was demon involvement even a possibility? We both should have known they couldn't touch her. Unless you lied. *Again*."

Priest lowered her head. That was enough of a confession for Riley.

"Unbelievable." She turned and walked away, but she didn't go far. She kept her head down, hands on her hips as she tried to contain her anger.

"Like you said, Riley, the tattoo was the only reason Gillian felt safe coming home. So I told you that it would work."

"So this entire time~"

Priest said, "Do you remember when Gillian allowed the demon to take possession of her body during the siege of the precinct? She only did that because she had the confidence granted to her by the tattoo. It was the reason she was brave and strong enough to fight it. If I hadn't lied, she wouldn't even have come back. Would you have preferred I tell the truth? That she is vulnerable, that she's always been vulnerable?"

Riley slumped against the wall. "What if we tell her and she wants to leave again?"

"When she left, she was your girlfriend. Now she's your wife. She would never leave you, Riley."

"Yeah. That's kind of what I'm afraid of. What if she refuses to leave because of me and something happens to her? I'm the reason she's here. Anything that happens to her here is my fault." She looked down the hall as if she could see through the walls and into the recovery room.

Priest put her hand on Riley's shoulder. "Gillian nearly died today because of something mundane. It could have happened to her no matter where she lived."

"Is that supposed to make me feel better?"

"She's been safe here for three years, Riley. You've kept her safe for three years."

Riley scoffed. "Yeah. With a lie. I can't take this away from her,

Priest. It's a security blanket, but it's comforting to her. I know it is. If I tell her it doesn't really work, she might panic. But if I don't warn her that it doesn't work, how will I live with myself if something happens to her?"

"Nothing has changed, Riley."

"Yes, it has. Now I know, okay? Whatever happens now, it'll be a decision on my part. To tell her and take away the placebo, or to leave things as they are and risk something happening. Is there a way you can fix it? Make it so the tattoo works?"

Priest scratched the back of her neck. "Riley, the reason I didn't do it in the first place is because you can't just share the protection of your tattoo with someone. If I had given Gillian a part of the protection, then she would have become your successor as champion. And now that you've chosen Aissa, there's... nothing left to go around. You would be left entirely vulnerable. Just like Christine Lee."

Riley winced. "So I can choose to protect myself or to protect Gillian."

"Gillian doesn't need a tattoo to protect her from demons. She already has the best protection she can get; you. Me, Sariel. Just because she doesn't share your protection doesn't mean she's vulnerable, Riley."

Riley rubbed her face. "She's vulnerable. There's just jackshit I can do about it." She pushed away from the wall and walked away.

Priest waited until she was at the end of the hall before she said, "Riley. I have to know if you and I are okay."

Riley stopped, but she didn't turn around. "I'm in the same position you were in three years ago, Cait. You did the right thing. I would have lied, too. And your lie meant that Gillian came back to me. We're okay."

Priest leaned against the wall with relief and sadness for passing on her burden, and Riley continued on to wander the halls until the nurses said she was allowed to see Gillian.

"Parra and Priest are on this case." Nelson smiled at Gillian as they walked to the van. "You always brighten up when we get one of them. I think you have a little crush on Priest."

Gillian laughed. "You caught me. But that Detective Parra isn't bad, either."

"Either way, you might want to watch how chipper you are. People get freaked out when they see a happy medical examiner."

"Noted."

Nelson Holt was almost ten years younger than Gillian and a full six inches taller than her. She'd once teased him about if he'd ever played basketball and he'd scoffed. "Just because you're empirically tiny doesn't mean I'm objectively tall." From then on, he'd been her favorite of the assistants that tended to rotate through the medical examiners office. They went on to further schooling or to another assignment. Gillian hoped Nelson would stick around for a while.

Nelson held up a fist when they reached the van. "Paper rock scissors for shotgun?"

"Nope. I'm pulling seniority. You can take the front next time."

He shrugged and opened the back doors to climb into the back. Gillian wasn't sure why she had made such a fuss about riding up front. Usually she didn't mind the back, but the day was nice enough that she wanted to enjoy the scenery, such as it was. She fastened her seatbelt and the driver - a volunteer medical student she hadn't met before - pulled out of the garage.

It was a nice day, but she kept the window up despite thinking it would be nice to have the wind blowing in her hair. She was thinking about Riley and their interlude in the shower. The memory made her tingle and she tried to hide her smile. Sometimes it was bizarre to part ways with Riley at home only to reunite with her at a crime scene. It was also comforting. A dead body was present, but Riley was on the case. That was one of the reasons she had liked working on Riley's cases even before they became lovers; having Riley involved all but guaranteed the family would get closure.

Gillian glanced to her left and noticed movement beyond the driver. It was just a quick flash of green, a car where her mind assured her a car couldn't and shouldn't have been, and then everything went white. She felt like she had just blinked but, when she opened her eyes, she hurt everywhere. Something was taped to the side of her head. She heard beeping. Her eyes seemed to roll in her head rather than being moved by any conscious decision, and they focused on the form in the chair next to her.

Riley's leather jacket was draped over the back of the chair, and her bright-red shirt was rumpled from being slept in. Gillian stared at her and realized she wasn't frozen, she was asleep. She tried to say something, but her mouth was too dry. Instead she tried to figure out how she had gotten from the truck to here. What about the crime scene? There was a dead body she had to sign off on, and they couldn't move it until she gave the okay. The detectives needed her to okay moving the body. She had to get to work.

Something changed. She wasn't sitting up anymore and Riley

was out of her chair. A nurse was standing over her, checking one of the displays before noticing Gillian was awake. She smiled. "Hi, Dr. Hunt. I'd ask how you were feeling but I think that question is a little moot, huh? Let me just take care of some things before we take care of you."

"Okay." Her voice didn't sound familiar to her, and she reached up to touch her throat.

"Can I give her some ice chips?" That was Riley.

"She can actually have a little bit of water," the nurse said.

Gillian heard water pouring, and then Riley appeared on the side of the bed opposite the nurse. Gillian's eyes widened at the sight of her. "Hi, honey."

Riley smiled. "Hi. Want to take a little sip? I'll hold it for you."

The cup pressed against her bottom lip, and Riley tilted it up so a little poured into her mouth. It was like liquid sex, like the best drug she'd ever heard of. Riley pulled the cup away. Gillian wet her lips with a pass of her tongue and leaned back against the pillow.

"Thank you."

"My pleasure." She gently took Gillian's hand in both of hers.

Gillian chuckled weakly. "You shouldn't be here. You should be out fighting... demons and flying around with angels."

Riley looked at the nurse, who smirked knowingly. "It's all right. You wouldn't believe the stuff I've heard people say in here. It's just the morphine making her a little loopy."

Gillian's eyes widened. "I'm on feel-good drugs. Hey! Now we're even."

"Babe, I think you need to stop talking, okay?"

The nurse was still chuckling when she headed for the door. "I'll check back in on you soon, Dr. Hunt. Mrs. Hunt, don't stay very long."

"I won't," Riley said.

Gillian frowned at the closed door and then looked at Riley. "Mizzes Hunt?"

"I told them I was your wife when I got here. I didn't realize they'd made the assumption until they started calling me Mrs. Hunt, and I didn't care enough to correct them."

"Mm. You're too Parra to be Hunt."

Riley laughed. "Well, maybe you need to be Gillian Parra."

"Pair of what?"

"Parr-ah. Like my last name."

Gillian closed her eyes. "Hm, yes I do, I do."

Riley bent down and kissed Gillian's eyebrow. "I think you need to get some rest, sweetheart. You've been through a lot."

"No, I... wait. What happened?"

"You don't remember?"

Gillian had only opened one eye. "Demons?"

"No. Not this time. Just an idiot driver who was texting."

Gillian stuck out her tongue. "So cliche. I... I... I hope he's dead."

"Me too. Get some rest, Gillian."

Gillian groaned. "You always think I'm sleepy when I'm not sleepy."

"Yeah."

Gillian squeezed one of Riley's hands. "Don't go. 'Kay?"

"I'm not going anywhere."

"Good."

As she drifted off, she thought she saw a woman with red hair standing behind Riley. There was something vaguely familiar about her. Something about the hair and the freckles. Cassie. The only other red-haired girl in Georgia growing up. "Hey," she whispered. "You killed a spider for me."

Riley either didn't hear or chose to let the strange comment go by, and Gillian chuckled to herself as she went to sleep. She thought it was very nice of Cassie to come all this way just to make sure she was okay.

There was a couch in the waiting room and, when Riley was relatively sure no one was going to be joining her, she stretched out on it. The TV was still on, and she wondered if there were people who actually watched television at such odd hours. When she was a kid, she remembered test patterns, end-of-the-day Americana montages of flags and war memorials that eventually faded out to static. Now, even at three in the morning, it was easy to find something to watch if you were willing to search a little.

A nurse walked by with a doctor, nodding at something he was saying. "...if they're not being a nuisance or disturbing anyone, we'll just have to..." He paused and glanced at her. "Actually, Mrs. Hunt, you work with the police, don't you?"

Riley frowned. "Yeah... what's going on?"

"It could be nothing. And please, believe me that I wouldn't ask you to work at such a sensitive time~"

She was already standing. "No, really. Jill is asleep and I need something to keep me from going crazy. What's wrong?"

The nurse shook her head. "I'm not sure anything is wrong, per se. It's just unusual. Come with us and I'll show you."

The nurse and doctor led Riley down the hall to a window that overlooked the street outside the hospital. "There."

Riley looked and saw one of the Good Girls standing on the street corner. She was facing the hospital with her head bowed, the hood of her white robe pushed back to reveal thick black hair. The nurse scanned the sidewalk and pointed out a second and third Good Girl, all of them facing the building with their heads bowed in prayer.

"They aren't harassing people in the parking lot or at the main entrance so we can't call them a nuisance. I'm just wondering if we should be concerned."

"No," Riley said, trying to speak through the tightness in her chest. "I wouldn't be concerned. They're here to help."

The nurse looked skeptical, but she accepted Riley's reassurance and moved off with the doctor. Riley smiled down at the praying woman and knew that the Good Girls probably hadn't left their self-appointed rounds without a little nudge in the right direction. She had a pretty good idea who had done the nudging.

"Thanks, Aissa."

The next time Gillian woke, she was coherent enough to understand what Riley said about her accident. "What about Nelson?"

Riley rubbed her fist with the fingers of the other hand. "He broke both of his legs. The damage was pretty severe. The doctors aren't sure if he'll ever walk again."

"God. That poor kid." She shook her head and looked out the window and tried not to think of the kid's life as ruined. "That should have been me."

"Don't..."

"I'm five-five, he's over six feet. Maybe the thing that broke his legs would have just glanced off mine."

Riley said, "Or you would have been thrown around more and broken your neck. Priest..." She looked down at her hands. "Priest said your guardian angel guided you to the front seat to protect you. She said you were both where you needed to be."

"What about the driver? He was a medical student, I think. A volunteer."

"He'll be fine. The doctors aren't sure why, but he came through the whole thing with scrapes and bruises. I think he might have dislocated his shoulder or something, but other than that, he's in one piece. And before you ask, Priest went down to check him out. I guess he just got lucky."

"Lot of coincidences today. The world is just... random. Even here. Even to us." She blinked back tears. "Scary thought."

Riley stood up and took Gillian's hand again. "We can take whatever this world throws at us. Ordinary or supernatural."

Gillian smiled. "Everyone's probably so worried about the lady stretched out in bed, I bet no one's asked how you're doing."

"A couple of people have asked."

"And what lie did you tell them?"

Riley chuckled. "I told them I'm hanging in there. By a thread sometimes, but... hanging in there nonetheless."

"The truth?"

"Scared to death. Borderline crazy, Jill." She leaned down and hugged Gillian. "I thought I'd lost you."

Gillian held her. "I know. I've been there myself. You're not exactly the easiest person to be with, Riley Parra, Demon Fighter."

"Oh, so this is payback. Nice." Gillian kissed Riley's neck, and Riley sat up. She fixed Gillian's hair where the embrace had messed it up.

Gillian sighed. "I've been so out of it since the surgery. Who all do I owe thank-you cards? Who has been here to see me?"

"Who hasn't? Half the staff of the Medical Examiners Office came by to wish you well." She cleared her throat. "Leah Mason came by."

"Whoa. Were you civil to her?"

Riley smiled. "I wasn't here when she came by. I just saw the card. Lieutenant Briggs was here for a while the first night, but she had to go back to work. Kenzie and Chelsea stopped by. Kenzie bought you that owl."

Gillian looked at the stuffed owl sitting on the windowsill. "Yeah, did, um... did she explain why she bought me an owl?"

"It has your hair color."

Gillian laughed. "What about Priest? Sariel? Have I had any angels watching over me?"

"Neither of the usual two, no. Priest has been kind of wrecked about this whole thing. I'm not exactly sure where she went, but she hasn't been here in a couple of days. She... I think she feels guilty about something I dragged out of her."

"What?"

Riley sat on the edge of the bed. "Your tattoo, Jill. It doesn't... it's never protected you. Priest lied so that you would feel safe. I didn't know. I didn't know until this happened, and Priest went to investigate to see if demons were involved, and why would she do that if the tattoo was protecting you? I just didn't~"

Gillian gripped Riley's forearm. "I never needed the tattoo, Riley."

Riley stared at her.

"I ran away because this was all just so massive and monumental. Demons and angels, and the woman I just started sleeping with was the only human who could stand against them. I didn't know if you were worth the danger, Riley. I loved you, I did. I truly did. But I wasn't sure. Now, though? Riley, you're all I want. All I need. I don't care if Priest lied about the tattoo. I understand her reasoning. Back then... I needed the lie. But as soon as I was back here, with you, I knew that nothing would make me leave."

Riley smiled sadly.

"I love you. And I love who you are. Part of who you are means living in a demon-infested city where you put yourself in danger all the time. I decided a long time ago that you were worth it. You're worth everything I have to go through to stand by your side. Demons, car accidents, snoring..."

Riley groaned and closed her eyes. "I don't snore."

"Ask your guardian angel if you snore."

"Oh, *her*. She'd just lie."

Gillian grinned and pulled Riley to her for a kiss. "I love you, Riley. Whatever that entails, whatever that signs me up for, I'm in."

"Good." Riley rested her forehead against Gillian's. "Oh. I also called Maureen and your family again while you were sleeping. I gave them all updates on how you were doing."

"Thank you. But you really shouldn't be doting on me so much. You have other responsibilities, Riley. The city needs you."

Riley shook her head. "Marchosias can have the city for all I care. You're what's important to me. I'm staying right by your side until well after you're sick of seeing me. If something comes up, Priest or Sariel can handle it. Aissa or Kenzie or Chelsea... hell, I have an army at my beck and call, and you think I'm going to give up the most important assignment. I'm not going anywhere, Dr. Hunt."

Gillian smiled. "Well. As long as you're so determined, maybe you can get me some more Jell-O?"

Riley nodded. "Yes, ma'am, general." She bent down and kissed Gillian's lips. "I'll be right back. Don't go anywhere."

Gillian mock-saluted. "Get me blue-flavored if they happen to have it."

Riley was already halfway out the door. "Blue is not a flavor."

Gillian's smile faded slightly once she was alone. She didn't want Riley to know just how badly she was hurting, how terrified she was. She moved her hand along her left side and felt the bulge of bandages under her hospital gown. Her fingers trembled at the sensation, as if they had minds of their own and were scared of what the bandage represented. She traced the shape of it and closed her eyes.

So close.

She could easily imagine herself climbing into the back of the van, perched on the edge of the seat with no safety restraints whatsoever. When the car hit, she would have been thrown like a rag doll. She pictured the back of the van, wondering what she would have hit first. How many of the tools would have sliced her, how many hard surfaces would have she have impacted? She thought of Nelson Holt, hating herself for thinking herself fortunate when his entire life was now altered. She covered her eyes as she began to cry.

"I couldn't find... blue."

Riley dropped the Jell-O on the floor and closed the distance to the bed in one step. She gathered Gillian in her arms, kneeling on the edge of the bed.

"It's okay, sweetheart. I've got you."

Gillian pressed her face into Riley's shirt and let the tears flow.

The sun beat down on the barren ground, sending up swirling dust devils. Caitlin Priest stood on the concrete slab that she assumed made up the front porch. She wore a sleeveless white undershirt, her dress shirt removed with sleeves tied around her waist. She had never felt heat like this, and she was not a fan. She wondered how anyone mortal could stand it. A fence enclosed the concrete slab, and she saw a large barbeque pit at the back. She unlatched the gate and stepped into the enclosure.

Inside the mobile home, a dog began barking. Priest wasn't carrying her gun or sword, and she felt completely defenseless when the front door swung open and a man appeared. She froze halfway to the front steps. He was a broad-shouldered man with thinning black hair, his work shirt stained with sweat at the collar. The sleeves were rolled up to the middle of his forearm, as far as he could probably get them to go, and he squinted out into the sunlight at the uninvited guest on his property.

"Can I help you?"

"Are you Alvin Siler?"

The screen door protested loudly as he pushed it open. "You're an angel, aren't you? Tell whoever sent you that I'm done with all of that shit."

"I know. That's why I'm here. My name is Cai... My name is Zerachiel. I'm here because I'm the guardian angel for a champion in~"

"Ah, for cripes sake." He sighed and turned to go back into the house. "You want to talk, do it in here."

Priest crossed to the front door and paused on the wooden steps that led into the house. She could feel the lingering stench of evil on the place, the afterecho of his association with demons, but she pushed through it and stepped into his living room. A counter stretched out in front of her, separating the kitchen to the right and the living room to the left. In the living room was an armchair that faced a television and an oscillating fan and stacks of old newspapers and magazines. Alvin picked up an ashtray off the table by his chair, brushed past her to dump it outside, and then closed the door against the heat. He sighed and walked back into the living room and sat down in the chair.

Priest waited for him to speak, but he seemed far more interested in the TV. Finally she said, "I didn't come all this way just to watch you watch television. Will you help?"

Alvin grunted. "Everyone wants to break the rules, and they want to come to me and find out how. Maybe I broke the rules 'cause I wanted to be left alone. You ever think of that? But fine. I guess newbies go to Michael Jordan for tips on their jump shots. When you're the greatest, you have to deal with the wannabes. You want to know how I got free and retired as champion. Odds are you won't be willing to do what it takes."

"I'll never know unless you tell me."

He bent down and picked up a can of beer off the floor. He took a long drag, put it back down, and settled into his chair. "Okay. I flipped the game board."

Priest frowned. "You what?"

"You know when you're losing a board game and you flip the board so all the pieces fly everywhere?" He shrugged. "That's what I did. I got sick of the whole thing and decided I'd had enough. I convinced my demon to help me kill the other guy's angel, and then he was a sitting duck. I slit his throat. Then I used the knife, wet with the blood of a champion for good and an angel, and I stuck it in the gut of my demon handler. He died, and I was the last man standing." He smiled and held his hands out as if waiting for her to applaud. She didn't, so he dropped his hands.

"So everyone got to start from scratch. New angel, new demon, new champion for good... and since I'd already chosen my replacement, he got called up from the bench to take my place. I was put out to pasture, and I've never looked back." He took another drink of his beer, looked at the TV. "You figured it out yet? The thing Riley Parra has to do?"

Priest's eyes flashed with surprise and anger.

"Oh, don't look so surprised, Zerachiel. Even if I'm retired, I keep my ear to the ground. I hear about the big stuff. Riley Parra is protecting the Ladder. The *Ladder*. I'm fucking impressed. She dies, and you give up your wings to bring her back. Champions know about Riley Parra, and even us guys on the other side have to respect her. But that's not what I asked. Do you know what Riley has to do in order to retire like I did?"

Priest looked at the door. "Yes."

"She killed Gremory. Gail Finney died, and the demon in your neck of the woods... Markyotis or something like that... he's dragging his feet to pick a new one because there's someone sniffing around to take over. Riley picked her replacement, or so I've heard. So in order to retire there's just one more step she has to take." He lifted his hand but, instead of his beer, he brought up a Colt revolver. "You have to die."

Priest swallowed hard and Alvin smiled at her. He lined up the sight of his weapon on her head and closed one eye.

"Like I said. We heard all about you, even down here. I figured you'd be coming around before too long. This whole trailer is surrounded by flax. You can't get out of here unless I say." He stood up, keeping the gun on her as he moved. "I'll leave the choice up to you because I'm golden either way. Either I get to kill an angel, or you get to prove you're a selfish mortal rather than a sacrificing angel. Your little champion getting screwed over in the process is just a bonus.

"An angel would do anything to save her friend. But a human would pick herself every time. I heard rumors about you, Zerachiel. Or is it Priest? Sexual intercourse, eating, grooming... Nice haircut, by the way. It looks nice short. And your little girlfriend! I hear your notching up your bedpost quite nicely. Taking your~"

"Stop talking." Priest glared at Alvin, a wrinkle appearing between her eyebrows as she clenched and unclenched her jaw.

Alvin smirked. "You made your choice that quick?"

Priest nodded and closed her eyes. She held her hands out to the side, palm-up to show she was unarmed, and lifted her chin.

"Kill me."

TWO WITNESSES

Each morning upon waking, Aissa listened for the sound of the cloister bells to sound a call to morning prayers. The city wasn't silent, but the absence of the hollow chimes made it seem so. As always it took her a moment to remember she wasn't at home; she was at the Morton Avenue Shelter, the same place that gave her a purpose in this strange and dangerous city. She knelt beside her bed to say her morning prayers before going into her personal bathroom to take a quick shower. Hers was the only private room at the shelter, a luxury Eddie had insisted on when she refused to sleep on his and Anita's foldout couch. She liked the little room. It reminded her of the home she had left behind.

She dressed in blue jeans and two shirts, pulling on boots Anita had donated to her. She wore a hoodie under her leather jacket, because after a lifetime of wearing a hood, she felt naked without one.

It was still dark out when she left the shelter. She climbed the stairs to the elevated train station. As she waited, she took out her notebook and flipped it open to the last page with writing on it. She had filled almost half the book so far with tight handwriting so small even she had to squint to make out some of her own words. She double-checked what she had found out, making sure she could answer any questions that might come up, and then flipped the book shut as the train pulled into the station.

A man was standing in front of the train's doors, hands in the pockets of his jacket and his bald head down so she couldn't clearly see his face. He looked like a vulture perched on the inner windows, but the doors parted to reveal his lower body. He twisted sideways to disembark as quickly as possible, striding toward the stairs with a gait that would take him there in four steps.

In the second their eyes had met, Aissa read him with ease. She knew his heart and knew that he was intending to cause violence.

Aissa backed up and fell into step with him. When he turned to look at her, she kicked the side of his knee. The man cried out in surprise and went down. His right hand came out of his jacket and he thrust a pocketknife at her midsection. Aissa grabbed him just above the wrist and struck out against his hand, snatching the weapon away as she twisted his hand back. The wrist snapped and the man shrieked.

Someone pulled Aissa off of him and she pointed. "Check his left pocket."

As the train security officer bent to do as she said, someone in the train said, "My wallet is missing."

The security officer took a handful of wallets out of the thief's coat and turned to look at Aissa. She shrugged as people began to flow out onto the platform to retrieve their belongings. Aissa sat on one of the now-empty plastic seats and rested her head against the glass, waiting for the fervor to die down so the train could leave the station. Eventually the thief was led away in handcuffs and the train was allowed to continue on. As they pulled away, Aissa saw the security guard looking around, most likely for her, but the train soon turned a corner and he was left behind. She checked her watch, grateful she had left early. The delay meant that she would arrive just after breakfast.

Gillian woke in her own bed, sore but not as sore as she had been the past few weeks. She pressed a hand to her side as she rolled over, pausing before she sat up. Bacon was cooking in the kitchen, the smell wafting down the hall on a wave of freshly-brewed coffee aroma. She carefully climbed out of bed, put a robe over her nightgown, and shuffled carefully down the hall to find her new servant girl hard at work in the kitchen.

Riley had obviously heard Gillian coming and was filling a glass with milk. "Morning, hon."

"Wow. You really did turn this place into a bed and breakfast while I was away."

"The doctor said you should take it easy. You've made me enough breakfasts, so... sit down, take a load off."

Gillian took her usual seat and let Riley serve up her breakfast. "So, um... I was thinking about what we should do today."

"Uh-huh?" Riley said.

"It's not that I don't love~"

Her carefully orchestrated speech, which she had worked on last night while Riley was washing her hair in the bath, was interrupted by a knock on the door.

"I'll get it," Riley said. She swept out of the kitchen and around the couch, checking the peephole before unlocking the front door. "Aissa? What are you doing here?"

Gillian got to her feet and saw the girl standing in the doorway. "Riley. Dr. Hunt. I'm sorry, I'm interrupting your breakfast..."

"No, it's okay," Gillian said.

Riley stepped aside to let Aissa in. "What's going on? Is everyone okay?"

"Everything is fine at the shelter," Aissa said. "Today was actually supposed to be an update of sorts about what I've been doing since last we saw each other, and I also wanted to see how Dr. Hunt was doing." She smiled at Gillian. "You're looking very well."

"I'm feeling better every day, thank you. And thank your sisters for coming down to the hospital." She wasn't a strong advocate of the healing power of prayer, but she also knew it couldn't hurt. She wasn't about to discount the fact a group of nuns who dedicated their lives to praying for protection were praying for her in her speedy recovery. "And please, call me Gillian. Everyone who has seen me in my nightie calls me Gillian."

Aissa blushed and looked at Riley again. "I've been making my presence known throughout No Man's Land as much as possible while still keeping a low profile. I talk to people about injustices and things that could be fixed with a little elbow grease. I don't mean to give you more to do~"

Riley shook her head. "No, Aissa, that's... outstanding. With my reputation, I can't get within ten feet of those people without having them run the other way. Find anything interesting?"

"Yes. Um." She looked at Gillian.

"I can go back into the bedroom~"

"It's okay. Whatever you say to me, she'll end up hearing about it anyway. What did you find out?"

Aissa cleared her throat. "Five years ago, a woman was killed in a hit-and-run. Detectives tracked down the vehicle and arrested the driver who insisted he'd been home asleep the entire night. The case went to trial, at which the driver was revealed to be a blackout drunk. He was sent to prison for ten years. I spoke to someone who knew about the case and knew that it was a setup. The woman was targeted, and the man who went to prison was framed."

"Blackout drunk?" Riley said. "You're talking about Lisa Kennedy. Kara and I investigated this." She pointed at Gillian. "You remember the case. We're the ones who found the car, we... we arrested Drew Hartley."

Aissa nodded. "You arrested the wrong man, Riley."

Riley stepped back and sat heavily on the couch. Gillian moved into the living room and took Riley's hand. "Is that possible?" she asked. "Could you have arrested an innocent man?"

"Yeah." She shrugged. "We don't like advertising it, but sure. It happens." She looked at Aissa. "Who did you talk to?"

"One of the woman's coworkers. She's been fighting to get someone to listen to her for years. Her name is Annie Irving, and she had an internet thing called Lisa's Peace. I saw a flyer for it and sought her out. That's when I heard the whole story. I was hoping you might be willing to reopen the case."

Riley winced. "Normally, yeah. Of course I would. But with Gillian~"

"Ah," Gillian interrupted. "That actually was what I was trying to say when Aissa showed up." She knelt and took both of Riley's hands in hers. "You know I adore you, Riley, and you know that every second we spend together is a... gift. Especially now, after what just happened. But honest to God, if you don't get out of my hair, I'm going to strangle you."

Riley frowned. "What?"

Gillian kissed Riley's cheeks. "I love you. And I love that you're willing to spend your every waking hour either at work or tending to me. The baths and, and the foot rubs and the meals. And I love that you brought your paperwork from the office so you can work and take care of me at the same time. But it's been ten days since I got home from the hospital, Riley, and to be honest, I need some time to myself. I was going to ask you to take me down to the morgue so I could take care of some paperwork of my own just to have a little... me-time. Please don't take this the wrong way, Riley. I wish~"

"No." Riley kissed Gillian's lips. "I've been smothering you. I've been treating you like a kid. I knew what I was doing, but I couldn't stop myself. You were almost killed, and there was nothing I could do. I couldn't help you or get revenge, so I... I made sandwiches." She sighed. "But if what you need now is for me to be gone~"

"I really, really do."

Riley smiled. "Then I guess Aissa has pretty good timing."

Gillian scooted forward on her knees and hugged Riley. Riley carefully returned the hug and kissed Gillian's neck before pulling away. "I'll have my cell with me if you need anything. The three of us can ride to the station together. Unless you'd rather take a cab..."

Gillian slapped Riley's shoulder with the back of her hand. "I think I can handle one car ride."

Riley kissed the tip of Gillian's nose and stood up. "I'll help you to the car, though."

"I'd be sad if you didn't."

Aissa had smiled through their exchange. "Will we be picking up Detective Priest on the way?"

"Priest hasn't been around the past few days. I think she's still feeling guilty about Gillian's accident. I'm giving her some space."

Priest lay flat on her back in the middle of the space that once housed Alvin Siler's trailer. She blinked at the clear southwestern sky over her face and tried inhaling. It worked, so she exhaled. Her clothes were tatters. Her skin was blackened. Sariel's face appeared over hers and eclipsed the sun. "I hope you learned your lesson."

Priest turned her hands palm-down onto the concrete foundation and pushed herself up. Alvin Siler was lying a few feet away. She watched his chest rise and fall before she looked at Sariel. "Ouch."

Sariel held out her hand. "I couldn't enter the flax without becoming trapped myself. But I heard your idiotic request and knew I had to act."

Priest only remembered asking Siler to kill her. Then an immense flash. She took Sariel's hand, got to her feet, and looked at the damage all around her.

"You ignited the flax. You could have turned him into charcoal."

"The alternative was to see what happened when he shot you in the head. I doubt it would have killed you, but your body could have been permanently damaged. I don't imagine you'd be open to creating a new one." She brushed the ash from Priest's shoulders and back. "What were you thinking?"

"How much did you hear?"

"Enough to be concerned about your state of mind."

"Riley wants to be free. If granting that wish is within my power, isn't it my responsibility as her guardian angel to do whatever it takes?"

"Not at the cost of your own life. Alvin Siler asked if you were human or angel. Offering your life in place of Riley's was a very human thing to do, *Caitlin*."

Priest wasn't certain if that was meant as an insult or compliment, so she remained silent.

"Come with me. You're far too weak to return on your own." Sariel held out her arms and Priest embraced her. They disappeared in a blinding flash moments before Alvin Siler regained consciousness. His hands and legs jerked and then began patting his doughy flesh to make sure he was still in one piece. He scanned the open air around him, realized what had happened, and sneered.

"Damn angels."

Aissa stopped at the doorway and drank in the sight of the Homicide offices. The east-facing windows were glowing with the morning sunlight, and the room seemed divided into rumpled and exhausted men and women who were coming off the night shift, and the fresh-faced officers who had just started their day. Riley stopped when she realized Aissa wasn't following her. "Aissa? Everything okay?"

"I've never been up here before. It's a little daunting."

"It's not so bad once you get used to the smell of bad coffee." She led Aissa to her desk and pulled an empty chair away from Priest's desk.

Aissa sat and looked at the clutter in front of Riley's computer. "You have to understand, Detective Pa~ Riley. I've spent my entire life up to this point praying for this city's protector. I only knew your name. I didn't know what you looked like. And now I live a train ride away from your home. I've seen you barefoot in your pajamas. And now I get to see you at work. I hope you forgive me if I act a little awed."

"I'll try to keep my ego in check. And since we're investigating the idea I put an innocent man in jail, it shouldn't be too hard."

Aissa nodded and folded her hands in her lap. She may have

looked like a normal girl out for a walk, but her rigid posture and deferential nature identified her as a Good girl. "I'm certain you and Detective Sweet did everything in your power to ensure you had the right man."

Riley's mood darkened slightly. "Yeah. You didn't know me back then..."

2007

Riley hid her hangover behind a pair of aviator sunglasses, her hand curved along the side of the glasses to block the sun from getting around the edges as she got into the passenger seat. Sweet Kara, also known as Detective Kara Sweet, had her blonde curls tamed in a ponytail that looked like an explosion, and she pushed down her sunglasses with one finger to get a good look at Riley's current state of disarray. "Hope you at least got her phone number."

"What would I do with her phone number?" Riley's voice was rough, and she treated it with a swig from Kara's coffee cup. She grimaced but managed to force it down before she made a disgusted noise. "What the hell is that?"

"Non-alcoholic. You should try drinking more stuff like it now and then."

Riley pressed back against her seat and put her foot on the dashboard. "You know what shit they put in water these days? Heineken is healthier for you. They did a study."

"Uh huh." She gestured at the placement of Riley's foot. "And you know if the airbag goes off it's going to shoot your knee into your face and break your nose."

"So don't get into an accident."

Kara smiled as she reached over and pushed Riley's foot down. "So whose apartment was that? Honestly. I'm not teasing you anymore."

Riley shrugged. "Some woman."

"You hopeless romantic."

Riley flipped her off. "I get laid regularly, and I don't have to deal with the drama of a relationship. Tell me what I'm doing wrong."

"You mean you don't have to care."

"It's easier when you don't care."

Kara had stopped smiling. In her casual blouse and tight jeans, Kara looked like a college student driving her older sister around town. Riley looked like a haggard hitchhiker who had just rolled out of bed, which was uncomfortably close to the truth. Her hair was still wet from her quick shower, she was wearing yesterday's clothes, and her breath stank of booze. When they pulled up at the scene, Kara took out a container of breath strips.

"Here. In case Hathaway makes an appearance at the scene, you don't want her smelling what you did last night."

"Yeah." Riley obediently popped the strips into her mouth and hissed through her teeth as the flavor crystals did their work. She and Kara got out of the car at the same time, and Kara let Riley lead the way to the portion of sidewalk where everyone else had gathered. The ME was already on the scene and Riley checked her out as she ducked under the yellow crime scene tape. A nice ass and, due to her position kneeling over the body, she saw a hint of the good doctor's underwear.

"Dr. Hunt."

"Detective Parra." She looked Riley up and down. "Oh, good. The dead bodies are starting to come to me and save the gas money."

"Har-har. Like you've never had a bad night."

Gillian looked back at the body, but Riley thought she might have seen a smile before a curtain of chestnut hair fell over her cheek. "Not as bad as this young lady."

A uniformed officer approached with his notebook in hand. "Witness says she was crossing with the light, inside the crosswalk, by the book the whole way. Green car comes barreling down the street and slams into her."

"And she went airborne from the looks of it." Gillian indicated the scrapes where the woman... the girl, really... had hit the pavement. "Witness moved her out of the road so other people wouldn't hit her."

"Damn it. Considerate, but... still." Riley knelt and looked at the body. Her arm brushed Gillian's thigh. "Sorry," she murmured.

"S'okay."

"Any identification?"

Gillian picked up a billfold off the pavement. "Found it in her jacket pocket. Just a library card and a few dollars."

Riley flipped it open and looked at the library card. "Just a patron number. And you know the librarians are going to be super-helpful giving us her information."

Kara smiled. "Maybe you could work your magic on one of them, Riley. Flirt her into the back room while I check the records."

"Shut up, Kara," Riley said, harsher than she intended. She

stood up and looked up and down the street. There were a few businesses that, in the light of day, looked so poorly maintained she wasn't sure if they were still open. "Any of these places have security cameras?"

The officer shook his head. "Only the nearest two would answer when my partner knocked, and they both said they were deterrents. Duds, not hooked up to anything."

Kara sighed. "You know what a good deterrent is? Working security cameras."

Riley motioned for Kara to follow her. "All right. Looks like we're canvassing."

"Great." Kara followed Riley away from the crime scene. Once they were out of earshot, Kara slapped Riley's arm. "Cigarette."

"Are you still quitting?"

"As we speak."

Riley took Kara's pack out of her coat pocket, tapped one free, and handed it to her. Kara muttered a thanks as she held it between her lips, lighting it and returning the lighter to her back pocket. "Just to take the edge off before I talk to these skells."

"Detective!" Riley and Kara both turned to see Gillian waving at them.

Kara nudged Riley again. "You go. You've got seniority. Plus you want to fuck her."

Riley snatched the cigarette from Kara's lips and flicked it down the street. Kara called her a choice pair of curse words, words Riley wasn't sure went together, but she ignored it as she walked back to the medical examiner's truck.

"Find something already, Doc?"

Gillian held up a small plastic card holder. "This was in her shoe. A lot of women do that when they have to walk somewhere at night. They have a decoy for the pickpockets and muggers to find, but the real stuff is out of sight. We have credit cards and a state ID. Lisa Kennedy."

"Excellent work. I'll make a detective out of you yet."

"Thanks, but I'm happy right where I am. Go get 'em, Detective."

Riley waved as she walked back to Kara with the ID. "We caught a break. Let's go see if anyone is waiting at home for her."

2012

Five years later, Riley paused in her recounting of events. Lisa had lived with her boyfriend, and Riley lost the game of rock paper scissors for who would break the news. He was crushed, naturally. She could see Kara standing in the kitchen doorway, hands in her pockets, nervously shifting her weight as they watched the poor guy whose name she couldn't even remember sobbed. Afterward she gave the man her card - Ian. His name had been Ian something - and told him to call if he remembered anything.

She looked at Aissa again and saw she was waiting for the rest of the story. "The boyfriend told us she was probably walking home from work. She was a dancer at a club not far from where we found her body. So Kara and I went down there and..." Her mind was flooded with memories and flashes of sensations. "We questioned her coworkers."

Kara looked back at Riley as they entered. "Are you going to be able to restrain yourself?"

"Restraint is overrated." Riley smiled at a topless waitress who offered her a drink. She refused, but made a note of the woman's face for later. She followed Kara toward the bar, eyes on the girl currently on-stage. She was incredibly petite, dressed in a green brassiere and thong, with fairy wings hanging off her shoulders. She glanced at them as she curled her leg around the pole and swung her body in a wide arc that made it look like she was flying. When she came to a rest, the bra was gone and her small breasts were exposed to the room.

Kara was speaking to the bartender. "-talk to some of your girls?"

Riley nodded at the waitress. "I'd like to start with her, if I can pick and choose."

"How did that go?" Aissa prompted.

Riley cleared her throat and shifted uncomfortably in her chair. "Uh."

Riley took the shot glass from the waitress' cleavage and tilted her head back, downing the tequila before stretching to tease the lime from the stripper's mouth. They were in a curtained area, so no one could see what she was doing. One shot wouldn't affect her judgment. It might even help with the headache pounding behind her eyes. Hair of the dog and all that. She closed her mouth around the wedge and took it into her mouth, letting the woman kiss her as she reluctantly observed the no-touching rule.

When the lime was gone, the waitress plucked the rind from Riley's mouth and dropped it onto the table with a smile. "I thought you said you had some questions for me."

"I do have some questions for you. First and foremost, the no-touching rule. Does that apply for you touching me?"

"Oh, Detective. I think you'll like the answer to that."

Riley scratched her neck. "I wasn't exactly the consummate professional back then, but we did our jobs. Andrew Hartley took a car matching the witness description to a body repair shop to have some dents banged out of the hood. We went, we questioned him, and he admitted that he'd gotten blackout drunk the night before. He was a frequent customer at Lisa's club and some of the other strippers confirmed that... that~"

"You know, detective... we have special rules for cops."

"And what would those rules be, Sinamon?"

"You can touch us all you want. But we get to take off your clothes."

Riley slid her hand over the curve of the waitress' hip. "Well. Rules are rules."

She focused on the actual information she had gotten from the dancers she'd spoken to after her rendezvous in the private room. "The other women confirmed he liked her. He would spend hours in front of the stage waiting, and then he'd be riveted by her dance. He always left right after she finished her last set. So Kara and I figured he propositioned her, she said no, and he decided that if he couldn't have her, no one could. He admitted he couldn't remember, and the car was in his garage when he woke up in the morning. Case closed." She looked at Aissa. "Until now. What did you find?"

Aissa took out her notebook. "One of Lisa's coworkers, Annie Irving, never believed the official story. She said Hartley was obnoxious, but he would never hurt a fly. She thinks Lisa was killed by someone who had been stalking her for a while. She was scared of someone. The night she died, she asked some of the other dancers if they could take her home, but no one else was scheduled to get off at the same time."

"They never told us that." Riley knew it was a flimsy excuse. "You said Annie Irving had a website?"

"Lisa's Peace. It implies she won't rest in peace until her real killer is behind bars."

"But she has evidence that Hartley's not the right guy?"

Aissa said, "You have no reason to feel ashamed, Riley. You did your job. Hartley couldn't deny his actions. He was a viable suspect. Annie Irving only pursued the case because she was the last person Lisa asked to take her home, and Annie lied. She wanted to do some errands on the other side of town, so she told Lisa she couldn't help her. The next day she saw the news and felt responsible."

"Ah. That's a hell of a thing. Is Lisa willing to talk to me?"

"She was hoping you'd be willing to talk with her. I said I would either bring you by today or at least come by to tell her you'd passed on the meeting."

Riley stood up. "I'll let Briggs know we're reopening the case. I'm not going to sit back and hope I have the right guy. Either we right a wrong or we waste a day. I'm fine with either."

"Stop."

"You shouldn't be exhausted." Sariel's hair hung in her face, caught in her eyelashes and the sweat of her brow. She nipped at Priest's shoulder, growling as she pressed harder against her. Priest was on her hands and knees, naked and sweating, and Sariel was kneeling behind her. She had both arms around Priest's waist, one hand stretched down to cover Priest's sex. "Your mortal body is weary, but your angelic self..." She pressed harder and Priest cried out. "Your divinity is unflagging."

Priest pressed one hand against the headboard. Her eyes were closed and she bared her teeth as Sariel teased between her legs.

"Come for me, Zerachiel."

"I ca-can't."

Sariel bit Priest's neck, and Priest cried out in another orgasm. She had lost count of how many times she'd come; she was sore all over. She just wanted Sariel to stop touching her, she just wanted to rest. She dropped onto the mattress and Sariel pinned her there.

"Please."

"Say the words."

Priest whispered, "I'm human."

Sariel put her hand in the middle of Priest's back and pushed herself up. Priest's body jerked and twitched as the hand was taken from between her legs, and she buried her face into the pillow. Sariel rolled to one side, the sweat that had been dripping down her body evaporating as she leaned against the headboard.

"You may have regained your divinity, and Zerachiel may live on through you, but you're more mortal than angel."

Priest sat up, her legs folded under her and her hands in her lap. She took a breath and met Sariel's eye. "Get out of my apartment."

"I didn't make you say anything you didn't already know. Riley Parra has corrupted you. This city has corrupted you. I knew Zerachiel before she took your form. She was a very~"

"Is," Priest snapped. "Is, is, *is.*"

"Zerachiel *was* the strongest of us," Sariel said smoothly. "We shouldn't have been surprised she would make such a stubborn and headstrong host. You've fooled yourself into thinking you exist just because you drew breath without her. You're nothing but a suit, Caitlin Priest." She slipped off the bed and picked up the remains of the suit Priest had been wearing in Alvin Siler's trailer. "And like a suit, you'll be discarded when you're of no further use."

The crumbling material glowed slightly as Sariel's energy flowed into it. Pieces flaked off in disappearing cinders that vanished before they hit the floor. When the suit was gone, Sariel brushed a hand over her own chest and a red blouse and slacks appeared to cover her nudity. She eyed the row of suits in Priest's closet and made a small sound of judgment.

"Goodbye, Caitlin Priest."

Priest crossed her arms over her bent knees and pressed her face into the crook of her elbow. The apartment door closed with a crash, and Priest let her wings extend and close around her as she healed herself.

Driving into No Man's Land, Riley passed several Good Girls standing on street corners with their heads bowed in prayer. She watched Aissa out of the corner of her eye. As a former member of their ranks, Aissa paid attention as they passed, but she didn't seem morose or mourning. Riley cleared her throat before she spoke. "I guess you've been seeing them a lot, working in No Man's Land."

"Not as much as you would think. They tend to remain near the demarcation between the good part of town and the bad. Morton Avenue is too deep inside No Man's Land. Although I do occasionally see them during my wandering, yes."

"Must be hard."

Aissa shrugged. "They have their mission, and I have my new work. I'm too excited to feel I've lost anything." She wet her lips and tilted her head to the side. "My Sisters are born into prayer, and those who don't die or become exiled grow up to become Mothers. That path is set from the moment we're born. Sometimes it feels as if we're all merely waiting for something to happen. And something did happen to me." She smiled. "I'm very happy where I am, Riley, and I'm honored to be your successor."

Riley felt guilty. She was actively looking for a way to retire her position as champion, but doing so would call Aissa to take her place. How could she possibly shirk her responsibilities knowing it would condemn Aissa to take her place? She was just a kid. She grew up in a nunnery and now she was scouring No Man's Land for wrongs to right. When was she going to have a childhood?

She parked in front of a bar and put her badge on her hip where it could be easily seen. Aissa started for the door but Riley stopped her. "Whoa. How old are you?"

"Old enough to enter a bar."

Riley dropped her hand, chagrined. "Sorry."

Aissa smiled and held the door open, and Riley stepped inside. The room was dim even early in the morning, and the few people seated at the bar held up their hands to block the sun. Riley let the door swing shut behind her and paused on the threshold to let her eyes adjust to the darkness.

Riley finished her latest mug of beer, tapped the young guy on the shoulder, and stepped between him and his date when he turned toward her. She smiled drunkenly. "I want to fuck your girlfriend, so why don't you go ahead and take a hike so we can get to know each other better?"

She absently rubbed her jaw as the memory came rushing back. Not her proudest moment. Shamefully, it also wasn't her worst. Aissa noticed her hesitation. "Is everything okay?"

"Yeah. This case is just reminding me a lot about who I used to be."

Kara stood over her. Riley was sitting in the alley, lip busted and eye swelling shut. Kara crouched and touched Riley's cheek.

"Ow. That hurts."

Kara pressed harder.

"Ow!"

"How about this for a new rule," Kara said. "You hold my cigarettes for me, and I slap you in the face every time you want to go into a bar? It'll heal faster."

Riley grimaced. "She was into me. She kept eyeing me."

Kara stood up. "Sure. You want a ride, Casanova?"

Riley took Kara's hand and let herself be hauled up. "Slap me if you must, but not hard. I don't want to explain big red marks on my cheek to everyone."

"Who said anything about slapping your face?" Kara swatted Riley on the ass hard enough to make her yelp.

The bartender, a much-too-thin woman with glasses too big for her face, came around the bar. She was so focused on Aissa that she didn't notice Riley until she was almost in front of her. She stopped and pointed her finger. "You."

"Lotus."

The bartender bristled. "I go by Annie now." She looked at the barflies. "Mike. I'm going to take five."

A man came out of the pool room, and Annie led Riley and Aissa into the back. Cases of beer lined one side of a narrow corridor leading to a fire exit. "Why did you bring her?"

"I told you I was going to try bringing her."

"You said you'd bring someone named Detective Parra. You didn't say she was the one who screwed it all up in the first place."

Riley said, "I told you my name when I interviewed you."

"Yeah, well, then I guess neither of us was listening in that interview."

Aissa put up her hands for peace. "Riley is only interested in the truth."

"Five years too late."

"So you're willing to throw away the opportunity to get the truth out there just because you're pissed at me?" Riley stifled her anger. "I'm a different person than I was five years ago. If I made a mistake, give me a chance to make it right. Please."

Annie took a milk crate away from the wall and dropped down onto it. She looked up at Aissa. "You'll vouch for her?"

"Of course. I wouldn't trust anyone else, except maybe her partner."

"Okay." Annie pushed her hair back with both hands and leaned forward. "Okay. I've been begging cops to listen to me for five years, I'm not going to throw it away just because the wrong one showed up. Lisa was scared the night she died. She begged someone to take her home. And I was... a bitch. I lied because I didn't want to take an extra five minutes. I just wanted to go home and relax."

Riley nodded. She remembered this part, but she had originally heard it from a girl wearing a green thong and fairy wings.

"When I found out she was dead, that she'd been hit by some asshole drunk driver, I blamed myself. Never mind that ten other people had all refused to drive her home, I was her last chance. I went to her place to... hell, I don't know. To confess or to apologize to her boyfriend. When I showed up, there was a guy there with him. I heard them arguing before I knocked. Whoever the other guy was said that what happened to Lisa could easily happen again."

"Did you see the other guy?"

Annie took out her phone and brushed her thumb over the

screen. "Yep. I have a drawing of him up on the Lisa's Peace website. I told you about all of this when you interviewed me that night." She turned the phone around so Riley could see the drawing. The man had a lantern jaw, close-set eyes, and dark hair cut short. Riley didn't recognize him.

"The boyfriend never mentioned being threatened when my partner and I spoke with him."

"He was scared. You guys were so ready to believe it was an accident that he didn't want to stir the waters. If he had, would you have listened to him?"

"Back then, probably not," Riley admitted. "Drew Hartley knew Lisa, and he was a blackout drunk. Are you claiming this mysterious man just happened to steal his car, or are you saying there was a conspiracy to frame him in particular?"

"I'm saying it was no coincidence that it was Drew Hartley's car. Lisa was targeted, and he was as good a mark as any."

Riley found another milk crate and sat down. "Okay. I testified against Hartley in court and then I forgot the case. You've spent five years on it. Tell me what you have."

Annie looked up at Aissa, and then held out her phone. "Here's something I didn't tell you five years ago... Lisa's boyfriend Ian was a pimp. He would arrange Lisa's boyfriends for her and set up the 'dates.' Lisa went along with it because the money was good and she liked sex. It turned her on. But after a while it got more scary than sexy. Can you imagine coming home and your boyfriend says you have a date with some guy you've never even met? That's part of the reason I didn't want to drive her home. I didn't want Lisa thinking we were friends, because I was afraid she'd try to recruit me or something." She took off her glasses and rubbed her eyes. "I could have helped her. Not just saving her life by giving her a ride, I could have gotten her away from the douche bag."

"Or gotten yourself killed for your trouble," Riley said.

"Right. Well, I think Lisa was scared of a date that went wrong." She pointed at the sketch. "I think that's the guy."

Aissa shook her head. "If he wanted to date Lisa and she said no, then it would make sense for him to kill her. But why would he then threaten the boyfriend?"

Riley looked up at the girl. "You know what date means in this context, right?"

"Yes. They dined together."

Annie stared at Aissa and then looked at Riley. "Is she for real?"

"What?"

"Lisa was a prostitute, Aissa." Riley handed the phone back to Annie. "But her point stands. Once Lisa was dead, there was no point in threatening Ian. Have you spoken to him about the threat?"

Annie shook her head. "He won't talk to me. He's married now, and he says that it's part of his past and he'd rather just move on."

Riley tapped her badge with two fingers. "I have this. He'll talk with me one way or another."

The door swung open and Ian Dawson looked Aissa up and down before he spoke. He wore a white T-shirt and baggy white pants, his dark hair uncombed and bushy over his ears but thinning on top. He squinted at her and leaned heavily on the doorknob. "Yeah? Help you?"

"I heard you were the guy to talk to if my boyfriend and I wanted to have some fun. Someone mentioned your wife, but wasn't sure if she, um, catered to couples."

He straightened slightly and looked past her. His apartment was on the second floor, facing a railing that looked over the drained pool. "You heard? Who'd you hear from?"

"Once of the dancers down at the Shaded Glen. She said I should come here and talk to you. I really hope you can help us."

"Well. Joy prefers guys, you know, but I can talk some sense into her. If the price is, you know, appropriate. How much you looking to pay?"

"It's our anniversary so we've been saving up. We don't want to pay a lot, but I mean, you get what you pay for."

Ian nodded. "Couples are a little extra, o'course." He leaned against the doorframe. "Two hundred gets you an hour, but if you want the whole night, it's a grand."

"And what does that... I mean... I sound like an idiot. But two hundred is for, um..."

He smiled. "Basic touching, kissing, and oral. Your boyfriend gets penetration, front-door only. For an extra hundred, he can finish in her mouth. For an extra two hundred, she'll swallow."

"Swallow?" Aissa said. "Swallow what?"

Riley stepped around the corner, badge held at eye level. "That's okay, Aissa. I think we have enough."

Ian tensed like he was about to bolt, but all of the windows in his apartment faced either the walkway where Riley was standing or a fifteen foot drop. He groaned and then focused on her face.

"Hey. You're that detective who was here after what happened with Lisa."

"Detective Parra. I thought I'd drop by for a little reunion. How's that sound?"

He looked at Aissa. "Like entrapment."

"Look at you, with your big words. So I don't arrest you now. I go downstairs and wait for you to do something stupid and arrest you then. Or we go in here and have a nice chat about your former employee."

Ian frowned. "Lisa was my girlfriend."

"I've had girlfriends. Never rented any of them out by the hour." She stepped into the apartment and Ian was forced to retreat or get pushed out of the way. "You didn't tell me the whole story about what happened to Lisa."

He followed her into the living room. "Yeah, well, it was a hit and run, okay? No sense dragging out all our skeletons, right?"

"Hit and run," Riley muttered. "So who was the guy threatening you the day after she was killed?"

Ian froze. "I-I-I don't... I don't..." He closed his eyes and began to pace. "Oh, that bitch and her fucking website..."

"Who was he?"

"I don't know his name. Honest. After I found out about Lisa, he just showed up."

Riley laughed. "So your girlfriend dies and this guy uses it as an opportunity to just randomly threaten you? He wanted something. It's been five years."

"You think he's just forgotten about it? Silence for life."

"This guy can't be that powerful."

Ian laughed. "You want to know who he is? Look up. And then keep looking."

Riley didn't like the sound of that. She glanced at Aissa and realized that if one person had been threatened, another could have been paid off. "You told this guy about Hartley, didn't you? You set him up as a patsy. Whoever wanted you quiet stole Hartley's car and used it to kill Lisa. And Hartley's been sitting quietly in prison because someone paid him for these ten years. Who was it?"

"I told you, I don't know the guy." Ian sat on the coffee table, defeated. "But I know who he represents. Shit. I can't believe I'm about to say this."

"I'm all ears, pal."

"Dominic Leary."

Riley thought she felt the air sucking out of the room and looked at Aissa. Even she looked stunned. "The guy who threatened you, who killed Lisa..."

Ian nodded slowly, accepting his fate. "He was hired by the mayor. Mayor Leary was a real regular. He saw Lisa at the strip club and wanted her, so he... took her."

"And Lisa took pictures."

"Worse. Lisa took Tic-tacs instead of birth control pills. She used condoms with everyone else, but told Mr. Mayor she was on the pill."

Riley lowered herself into a nearby armchair. "And eventually she had something bigger than a photograph, didn't she?"

"Six pounds, three ounces. Little girl."

"What happened to her?"

"Shipped away. Adopted. I don't know. I never saw her again."

Riley sighed. Five years ago, Leary was starting his first term as mayor. A scandal of that magnitude would have destroyed his career. "Lisa was a stripper. How did she manage to hide her pregnancy?"

"She claimed she got sick. Took a few months off."

"All we have right now is your word on this. Are you willing to testify?"

Ian shrugged helplessly. "You're going to keep investigating anyway, and eventually he'll know I talked. So... if testifying means you'll keep me safe, then fine. I'll do it."

Riley stood up. "All right, come on. We're going to get you protective custody."

"What about Joy?"

"Don't worry. We'll make sure she's protected. And as far away from you as she can get."

Ian sighed and stood up, trudging toward the door. Riley wasn't inspired to make him move faster. Once Ian Dawson was taken care of, she would torpedo her career by confronting the mayor about the five-year-old murder of a stripper.

Drew Hartley listened as Riley explained her theories. His time in prison had taken at least twenty pounds off his frame, and his hair was receding away from his forehead. Briggs was in the room with her, but they'd asked the guards to step outside to give them privacy. Drew's hands were still cuffed, resting on the table between them, and his stony expression wavered as he listened to Riley's story. When she was done, he was covering his eyes with one hand.

"Does that sound about right, Mr. Hartley?"

"You don't understand," he said softly. "The money was... really good. And I couldn't be sure. I mean, the way I was back then? It was only a matter of time before I hit someone for real. So I figured this way... this way at least I come out on top when it's all over."

Briggs said, "You'll be charged with conspiracy and concealing evidence, but a judge can be convinced to sentence you to time served if you help us out. How's that for coming out on top?"

Hartley stared at them both and then looked at his hands.

"You liked Lisa didn't you, Drew? You had a little crush on her. Someone used that crush, used it to frame you, and now Lisa is dead. And the man who killed her isn't going to face justice. He's had five years of freedom. Isn't that enough?"

"I never saw his face. I only dealt with the man who came to the door, who told me what to say. He's the one who drove the car. Rollie Daniels."

Riley looked at Briggs, whose face was set and determined. "Mayor Leary's right-hand man. It's enough to get him down here and talking. Go find your partner and bring him in."

Riley let herself into Priest's apartment after knocking for five minutes with no response. "Cait? Come on, vacation's over. I know you're feeling bad about what happened to Gillian, but we're all in one piece." She scanned the kitchen and went down the hall to the bedroom. She knocked and the door swung open. "Caitlin? Are you in here?"

"Yes."

Riley stepped into the room and saw Priest on the floor. She was naked, her feet crossed in front of her and her knees pressed against her chest. Her closet was empty, everything taken off the hangers and dumped onto the bed.

"Having trouble deciding on an ensemble?"

"I'm mortal."

Riley furrowed her brow. "Again? What happened?"

"No, I'm..." She rubbed her face and stood up. "I'm still Zerachiel, but Sariel made me realize I was... I was... ruined."

Riley stepped closer and saw bruises on Priest's thighs. "Cait... what happened?"

"'Cait.' And Priest. You never call me Zerachiel. Why?"

"Because Zerachiel is the part of you that always pisses me off, and Caitlin has always been there for me through thick and thin." Her voice softened. "What's going on here?"

Priest sat on the edge of the bed. "I found a way for you to retire as champion. If every player but one is removed from the field of battle, and if that individual has chosen a successor, they are effectively retired. Sariel killed Gremory, Gail Finney killed herself, and you've chosen Aissa to take your place. The only thing remaining is to remove the final player."

Riley laughed. "You? Priest, you've got to be kidding me."

"It could free you. And if I wasn't so attached to being mortal, I would do the right thing and~"

Riley crouched in front of Priest and put a hand on her shoulder. "That's not the right thing, Priest. I don't want to just retire and ride off into the sunset. I want to retire so I can enjoy my life and my loved ones. That includes you. If there's one path to retirement, then there must be another. We'll keep looking for it, and we'll find it sooner or later."

Priest finally met Riley's eye. "I'm sorry."

"Don't be sorry. Just get dressed. We have to go somewhere and, as much fun as Aissa is, I'd rather have my guardian angel at my side."

"Where are we going?"

"We're going to arrest the mayor."

Priest stared and shook her head. "The one day I don't go to work..."

The mayor's office was located in the courthouse. Riley and Priest, both wearing bulletproof vests, led a squad of uniformed officers up the marble-and-tile staircase. When they reached the top floor, a contingent of security officers was waiting for them. One held up a hand, palm flat, to stop their advance. "I'm sorry, detective, but this is as far as you go."

Riley pressed the warrant against his palm as if she was high-fiving him, and continued past, bumping her shoulder against his in the process. "Feel free to read it out loud for your less-literate friends."

The security officers trailed behind her. "You can't just barrel through~"

"Sure I can. Warrant says I can. Stay back or I'll arrest you for obstruction."

He fell back as they reached the doors to the mayor's office. The mayor was standing behind the desk with his deputy, both of whom had obviously been alerted to the disturbance making its way to his office. Mayor Leary had the receiver of his desk phone in one hand, while Deputy Mayor Lark Siskin was speaking rapidly into her cell phone. Riley motioned for them both to hang up with forked fingers.

Leary was six-four and built like a linebacker. The sleeves of his shirt were rolled up to reveal thick, muscular forearms. His hair had been shaved down to snow-white peach fuzz. Lark, on the other hand, looked as if she could have been carved from marble. She let her gaze linger on the intruders as if sizing them up in preparation of a fight.

The mayor stared at Riley for a moment with cold, unblinking eyes, but then he carefully lowered the phone to the cradle and held his palms out.

"Dominic Leary, you're going to have to come with us, sir."

Lark stood stoically next to her boss, hands behind her back and chin raised defiantly. "I would advise you not to go anywhere with them, Mr. Mayor. We can handle this without the authorities getting involved."

"Another group of officers are taking Rollie Daniels into custody as we speak. How loyal do you think he is, in terms of a prison sentence?"

"Mr. Mayor..." Siskin warned.

"You can go downtown now, with me, or we can wait around until Mr. Daniels tells us what we all know he's going to tell us. And by that time, we'll have to walk you out of here past reporters. And even if we cover the handcuffs with a jacket, everyone knows what that means." She looked at Lark, daring her to intervene. "Your career ends today, Mr. Mayor. The only question is how much dignity you take with you when you go."

Leary took a deep breath and then looked at Lark "Hang up the phone."

"Sir..."

"Hang up the phone." He took his jacket off the back of his chair and stepped around the desk. "I'll go with the detective." He stopped in front of Riley and said, "Mr. Daniels has been a good friend, but when the noose is around his neck, I fear he will not be the loyal soldier I need. I surrender to you, Detective Parra."

"You remember me?"

"Of course. I gave you an award last year for stopping the Angel Maker."

Riley smiled. "Well. Maybe someone else will give me an award for this. Dominic Leary, you're under arrest for the murder of Lisa Kennedy, and a whole host of other charges we'll sort out at the station. But mainly... this is for Lisa. Put your hands behind your back, sir."

"I thought we could do this without all that."

Riley shrugged. "Lisa Kennedy's family expected to get justice five years ago. We all have disappointments we have to live with."

Gillian looked up when Riley darkened her doorway. She smiled and put down her pen. "Go in to work for a few hours. Just following up on an old case."

Riley shrugged and slumped against the doorframe. "You know me. If you're going to spend a day at work, make it count."

"How was your afternoon?"

"Unsettled. I kept bouncing from one interrogation room to the next to the next. Mayor Leary, Rollie Daniels, Ian Dawson, all of them telling different parts of the same story. We've managed to put most of it together. Mayor Leary likes strippers, and he liked Lisa more than the rest. She propositioned him and decided having a kid would put her on easy street. After she got pregnant and asked for money, Rollie Daniels explained why blackmail was a very, very bad idea. After she had the baby and gave it up to Daniels, he kept hanging around and watching her. She realized she was a loose end. Daniels told the mayor she was getting scared enough to start talking, so the mayor gave the okay to get her out of the picture."

"Where'd the baby go?"

"A woman on the mayor's staff had a baby who was stillborn. The timing wasn't exactly right, but it was close enough."

Gillian looked away. "The baby *happened* to be stillborn at a convenient time?"

"If the baby was born alive, they would have just added a second one and said they were fraternal twins. At least that's what I'll be telling myself to get to sleep tonight."

"Will you whisper it to me, too?"

"Depends. Where will you be?"

Gillian leaned back in her chair, momentarily cradling her side. "Oh, I'm sure I can find a woman willing to let me share her bed."

Riley sat on the edge of Gillian's desk. "Did you like me?"

"When? Just now?"

"No. When we first met. When I was working with Kara and I had... problems."

Gillian shrugged. "I only knew you from the morgue. You were lively enough that I guess I didn't mind the company. Why?"

"A lot of old memories came flooding back today. I drank too much, I slept around, I was rude and short-tempered."

"You were that way when we started sleeping together, too."

Riley frowned. "No. By then, I was..."

Gillian was shaking her head. "You drank a lot when we started dating, Riley. You were rude. You got angry over the smallest things. You would brood and sit quietly in my living room and it was torture getting you to say two words about your day. But I could tell that wasn't the real you. When I came back from Georgia, you had relaxed. I knew that I could be good for you, and that you could be good for me."

"So if not for you, I'd be that same hothead." Riley considered that as she toyed with her wedding ring. "I really didn't like her, Jill."

"You just didn't see her potential." She took Riley's hand, kissed the palm, and brushed the knuckles against her cheek. "She's matured into quite a fine lady."

"Lady?" She twisted and looked at the desk. "What kind of pain meds do they have you on?"

Gillian laughed. "Help me up. Take me home. Make gentle love to me."

Riley took Gillian's hand and helped her out of the chair. She might not exactly be a lady, but she had certainly learned how to follow orders.

Riley held up the newspaper as she joined Gillian in the kitchen. "MAYOR LEARY ARRESTED. Faces Murder, Conspiracy Charges." She dropped the paper on the table and went to refill her orange juice.

Gillian smiled. "It's always nice when my wife makes the news."

"I'm a very small part of the story. Footnote, practically."

Gillian picked up the paper and focused on the newspaper. "Who is that standing behind Mayor Leary as he's led out of the building? Why, I think I know that hand. I think that hand was inside of me twenty minutes ago."

Riley bent down to kiss the top of Gillian's head. "That was my right hand. My left hand is on his shoulder."

"Oh. My mistake." She put the paper down and sipped her coffee. "How is Priest?"

"Still reeling a little bit from the whole Sariel thing. She won't say what happened, but I can tell it was something big. Sariel's not exactly the type to make a subtle point."

"Hm."

"I'll talk to her today." Her phone buzz and she checked the display. The text was from dispatch and showed an address where a call had gone out for Homicide to step in. "And someone died last night. Do you want me to wait and drive you in?"

"No, that's okay. I won't be in the field today, so you'll get to play with one of my assistants."

"Oh, joy," Riley muttered. She kissed Gillian goodbye and took her jacket off the hook as she left the room. She called Priest as she headed downstairs.

Fifteen minutes later, she parked with the nose of her car in front of a strip of yellow crime scene tape. "Do Not Cross tape. Now there's a recession-proof business," Riley said. "How much crime scene tape have I ducked under? Miles and miles of it. Guys must be making billions."

Priest's smile was wan and Riley dropped it. She'd been trying to get something out of her the entire drive, and even a weak smile was better than sullen silence.

The first officers on the scene were standing in the middle of the alley facing a body on the far side of a dumpster. As Riley approached, she had a sudden, chilling premonition that she was about to see Annie Irving's body sprawled on the ground. She braced herself and nodded a greeting to the nearest officer. He moved to meet her halfway. When their paths crossed, he turned and started walking with her.

"What do we have here, Officer?"

"No ID, no trauma, no markings. Looks like she just sat down and went to sleep. Fully dressed, no wallet... could have been a robbery or could be she just wasn't carrying one."

"Did you check her shoe?"

"Pardon?"

"Never mind." She stepped around the dumpster expecting to see Annie, but the dead woman's identity hit her like a slap in the face. She recoiled and twisted to see Priest was almost on her. "Cait. Stay back."

Priest stopped. "What's wrong?"

"You recognize her, Detective?"

Riley looked again. "Yeah. I, uh..." She wiped her hand over her face. "Officer, could you and your partner start canvassing? Find out if anyone heard or saw anything in this alley."

"Yes, ma'am." He eyed her for a second before he gestured for his partner to lead the way. Riley stepped back from the corpse and faced Priest.

"Riley, you're frightening me. Who is it?"

"Sariel."

Priest blinked, pushed Riley out of the way, and stepped around the dumpster to see for herself. Sariel was barefoot, but otherwise dressed for work. Her hands were limp in her lap, palms turned up and fingers loosely curled around nothing. Her chin was down against her chest and Priest could see that her eyes were closed. She touched the former angel's cheek and then rubbed her thumb against the tips of her first two fingers.

"It's like wax. Not even cold or warm, just... there."

Riley cleared her throat. "Didn't you, ah, didn't you say angels create a shell and then just leave them behind when they... leave?"

"Yes." Priest's voice was flat. "Sariel is gone. This is Sara Elmore."

"Did she say anything about~"

"Not a word." Priest stood and looked down at the body. "Why would she do this?"

Riley massaged her neck where it met her shoulder. She turned and watched the Medical Examiner's van pull up behind her car. One of Gillian's assistant MEs get out of the cab and go to retrieve the body bag. "You said that yesterday she coerced you into admitting you were more human than angel. In the time she's been here, she's been following in your footsteps. She took on a mortal identity, she got a job, she's... she started a sexual relationship. Maybe she was afraid of going down the same road you did. Maybe she made such a big deal about your humanity because she saw it happening to herself."

"Maybe." Priest looked in the direction the policemen had gone. "We can't list her as a Jane Doe. We'll have to identify her as Sara Elmore in the official report."

"Great. Two reporters who wrote the same column end up dead in the space of a year, and I'm standing over both bodies. People are going to talk."

Priest actually smiled. "Yeah. They'll wonder why you're not targeting the food critic." Riley stared at her with wide eyes and Priest's smile wavered. "I'm sorry. That was in terribly poor taste..."

"It was gallows humor. It was a very cop thing to say, Cait. You're getting more human every day." She paused as they looked down at Sariel's discarded form. "I meant that as a compliment."

"I know," Priest said quietly. "I take it as one."

Riley patted her on the shoulder and nodded toward the ME that was coming toward them. The fallout of "Sara Elmore's" death was going to be at least as hectic as her arrest of the mayor, but Riley had little doubt she would be able to handle it. With Gillian at her side, and Priest at her back, she was confident she could take on whatever the demons threw at her.

HATCHING VAIN EMPIRES

Gillian was using a cane to get around, although it was hardly necessary. When Riley called to let her know about the "special guest" she was about to receive, she let the temporary coroner know that she was able to do the autopsy. The body was delivered to her and Gillian removed it from the stiff black bag to begin her work. Four years ago she had examined the shell of another angel. That one had been forcibly removed and, from what Riley and Priest said, it seemed Sariel had left her shell willingly. She touched Sariel's cheek and pressed her lips together in a passing moment of grief. Sariel wasn't really gone, but she still felt the loss.

She had removed the clothes and washed the body when Priest arrived.

"Caitlin." She glanced at Sariel's body. "I was just about to start-"

"I know. I was hoping I could... assist. Or just..." She furrowed her brow and shook her head slowly. "I'm not sure what I want. Sariel's last act on this plane was to make me admit I'm more human than angel. I guess I just want to see how different we really are when it comes down to it."

Gillian nodded. "Well. I could use an assistant in the know. Scrub up." Priest started for the prep room. "Caitlin?"

"Yes?"

"I've known you as a mortal, and I've known you as an angel. I don't think you're either one. I think you need both to make yourself whole. You can't just ignore one half of yourself and carry on. You're a package deal."

Priest considered that. "Like you and Riley."

Gillian smiled. "Yeah. If you want to consider it like that. You may not always get along with Zerachiel, but you shouldn't be at war with her, either. You need to find a harmonious balance between the two."

"Thank you, Gillian." Priest smiled. "That's... just..." She sighed. "Thank you."

Gillian nodded. "You can put on the apron you find in there, too. I'll finish preparing the body while you get ready."

Priest disappeared into the prep room and Gillian placed her cane against the wall before approaching the table again.

After the autopsy, Priest walked home alone. She could have flown, but the ache in her thighs and back helped her connect with her mortality. Once there she locked the door and rested her head against the chipped-white paint of the wood. She was exhausted, and the rooms of her home seemed hollow. The praise music drifting through the floor made her feel slightly more elated, but her depression was deep. She left the lights off in her living room and went into the bedroom, undressing in front of the full-length mirror on the back of her closet door. When she was naked, she ran her hands over her curves.

Sariel's body had been nearly identical to a regular mortal's, according to Gillian. There was a unique bundle of muscles between the shoulder blades and, concealed along either side of the spine, were contracted wings. Gillian asked her what should be done with them, and Priest assured her they would fade eventually. Within twelve hours, probably much less, the corpse would be indistinguishable from a mortal.

Sariel had called her "mortal," had made it an insult.

Riley said the same thing and said it was a compliment.

Zerachiel had assumed a mortal form in the past. She was a man in sixteenth century England, and she had abandoned the shell when her mission was over. She hadn't mourned, couldn't even remember the name she had used.

She was Caitlin Priest. She liked Italian food and guitar music. She enjoyed sex with women, although she was curious about trying it with a man. Cutting her hair had been an experiment, but she was pleased with the results. She liked to wear suits because she liked how she looked in them. It was pure aesthetic.

The question, then, wasn't if she had become mortal. She loved Caitlin Priest, and she was horrified of the thought of not being her anymore. That was mortality in a nutshell. The question now was whether she could accept the fact. She leaned closer to the mirror and examined her features.

It was now or never. She could leave the Priest shell behind, rejoin the choir invisible, and create a new body. Zerachiel could be male this time. She remembered her previous experiences as a male and thought of the things that would be different. Shaving, for one. And the genitalia. If she was a man - Calvin Pierce? - she would find Kenzie and Chelsea. Would they still be interested in her? Would they allow her into their~

Her eyes widened and she leaned back. She was mortal. She was Caitlin Priest. She smiled as the revelation settled on her mind.

"Sariel was right. I'm mortal."

You're more than mortal.

"Yes. I am. I'm both."

She went to the hamper and took out a shirt Sariel had once worn. She pressed the material to her face and breathed deeply before she put it on. She turned off the bedroom light and crawled into bed. She hugged the pillow, wishing it was Sariel, and closed her eyes.

You don't need to do this.

"No," she whispered to the voice in her head, "but it makes me feel better."

Suit yourself. Waste seven hours of your day in unconsciousness.

"I will." She smiled at the petulance in Zerachiel's voice.

For the next seven hours, she may have been unconscious but the time was far from wasted. For seven hours, Caitlin Priest dreamed as a mortal.

An entire section of the waterfront was taped off, with officers stationed every few feet to prevent the journalists and their cameras across the street from getting a closer look. It took Riley a moment to recognize the tune being whistled by the uniformed officer standing in front of the crime scene tape. "Technically another *two* have bitten the dust, Officer. At least that's what I heard from dispatch."

The officer shrugged with a chagrined smile. "Queen didn't sing about double homicides."

"No, but 'Bicycle Race' may have caused a few." She ducked under the tape and held it up for Priest. There was something different about her partner, but she couldn't put her finger on it. "Gillian said you, ah, attended the autopsy last night. How was it?"

"Sad. I think it helped me accept that she really was gone." She paused and pressed her lips together. "I'll miss her."

"Yeah? You seem a little lighter today."

Priest smiled. "I slept very well last night."

"Glad to hear it. Jill was worried about you." They had reached the shoreline, a muddy strip of land between low-tide of the water and the lichen-clad stones. Gillian, still using a cane and moving cautiously on the uneven shoreline, looked up and smiled. "Dr. Hunt. Nice to see you up and around."

"Detective Parra. We're definitely looking at two victims."

"I deal in facts, Doctor. How can you be so sure?"

Gillian gestured with two fingers. "You see how there are two skulls?"

"Yes."

"They usually come one per skeleton."

"Oh, you doctors."

Riley knelt and looked at the two skulls. They weren't as smooth as she expected them to be, and they were dirtier than skulls she'd seen on display in museums and the like.

"Any sign of the bodies these skulls came from?"

"The uniforms looking. I can tell you both bodies will be male judging from the size and shape of the jaw."

Riley smiled. "I love it when you talk sexual dimorphism to me."

Gillian winked. "We can get DNA from the teeth if we don't find the bodies." Something near street level caught her eye. "Although judging from the look of that officer, we won't have to go that far."

Riley and Priest turned and saw a uniformed officer standing on the inside of the tape. He waved and pointed down the waterfront.

"Looks like we have our secondary crime scene." She held out her hand, and Gillian hooked her little finger around Riley's. They pulled free with a snap and Riley straightened to walk back up the rocks. Priest followed, one hand in the small of Riley's back to help her keep balance. Riley looked over her shoulder. "What are you doing?"

"Being conscientious. And I am your guardian angel, lest you forget."

"I appreciate the assist."

The officer started shaking his head as soon as they approached, turning to face the water. "I found the bodies."

"Then why are you shaking your head?" Riley asked.

He shrugged helplessly. "Because the reporters are watching."

Riley started to smile, then ran a hand over her hair and tugged on her ponytail. She let her shoulders sag with defeat. "Good thinking. What did you find?"

"Two blocks north on the left side of the road." He gestured with his eyes. "Car parked in an alley and covered with a tarp. Someone wanted it found, but maybe not too quickly. It had a couple of bodies missing their heads in the front seat. I didn't open the car or snoop around; thought I'd leave that to you."

Riley raised her voice. "You didn't find *anything*? You're not being paid to walk around the block with your head up your ass." She lowered her voice, hands on her hips, and faced the water. "Sorry."

"No, it's okay. I, uh, got a little... sick... near the crime scene. A little behind the back tire. I tried to... aim."

"We can deal with that." Riley paced a few steps, shot him an angry look, and then glanced down to read his name. "Are you planning to take the detective's exam, Officer Lucas?"

"Yeah, actually."

Riley shook her head angrily. "Let me know if you need a recommendation." She spun on her heel and ducked under the tape. "Stay here! Useless piece of... with me, Priest."

She stormed away from the officer and down a side street. The reporters who noticed her didn't attempt to give chase; no one wanted to harass a grumpy detective. Once they were out of sight, the anger faded from Riley's face and she straightened her shoulders. She checked the alleys and immediately found the car.

"Officer Lucas will be a detective by Christmas."

The alley was just narrow enough that Riley could move sideways along the car's driver side while Priest walked on the passenger side. It sat like a small green hillock, just a part of the scenery unless someone was looking close enough. They lifted the tarp as one, lifting the sides like wings to peer underneath. The light filtered through blood-spattered windows to make the interior of the car look like a gory green aquarium.

Driver and passenger were placed like mannequins. Their heads had been removed with what seemed like a single swift strike. Blood had coursed down the front of their suits, making them look painted red-black. Riley bent her knees and closed one eye to sight along the cut. "Looks like the blade went through the driver's neck and then just kept going. That would take a hell of a blade, though. And even if he was sinking into the backseat... there's no way he could have enough room to maneuver."

Priest said, "If he was powerful enough, he could have done it with a smaller blade."

"Powerful. You mean demonic."

"I'm implying demonic, yes. It would also explain why the heads are completely flayed while the bodies seem to be freshly murdered."

Riley made a sound of irritation. "Okay. Careful of fingerprints, but open the door and see if you can find anything in the glove box."

Priest got the door open and carefully navigated around the passenger's corpse to open the compartment. She used the side of her small finger to search, and withdrew a long leather pamphlet. "Registration and insurance information." She opened it and read, and Riley saw her shoulders slump.

"Oh, that's always good. Go ahead, Cait. Ruin my day."

"The car belongs to Liam Burke."

"Of the Burke Family. So we can assume his passenger was his son Finn. Since you said demon involvement, we can probably also assume the killer was Danny Falco."

Priest looked down and said, "The passenger isn't a Burke. His skin is dark."

Riley hadn't noticed the hands, and the skin of the neck had been discolored by spilled blood, but the hands very obviously belonged to a black man. Riley looked at the freckles and fine red hairs on the back of Liam Burke's hands. "The head of the Burke family and... based on the suit~"

"Odds are good he was meeting with the head of the Rowland family. Theodore."

"The *head* of the family," Riley repeated. She was remembering her brief meeting with Theodore Rowland the year before while trying to clear Muse's name. "Falco is sending us a message. He's taken two more heads, and he has two more armies gathered under his banner."

Priest had her hands on her knees as she scanned the interior of the car. "Who does that leave?"

"Donald Pierce and... McGowan. I can't think of... William McGowan."

"He took out two at once. What does that mean?"

Riley grimaced. "It means he's getting ready to take on Marchosias once and for all."

Members of the Organized Crime Division were brought down to Homicide as members of a task force meant to deal with the Falco threat. Riley and Priest briefed the gathering about what they had found, then handed control of the meeting over to Lieutenant Briggs. "It's common knowledge that the crime in No Man's Land is generally funneled through the Five Families." She gestured at the photographs taped on the board. Underneath each photo was a list of names. "You all recognize these folks. The families are Burke, Rowland... Hyde, McGowan and Pierce. The heads of the Five Families are managed by a man named Alphonse Dupre whom Organized Crime believes is simply a middle manager. They think there's a single boss controlling it all, a mystery man who~" she paused to glance at Riley, "~whose identity has never been confirmed.

"In recent weeks, a man by the name of Daniel Falco has begun a coup. He insinuated himself into the Hyde family and, through his machinations, managed to get the head of the Hyde family arrested. He then took control of Hyde's men and resources. And as Detective Parra just informed us all, this morning he took Mr. Burke and Mr. Rowland out of the picture as well. Their forces will either align underneath him, or they'll scatter."

Riley said, "Either way, Falco just increased the size of his army. As it stands, No Man's Land is split down the middle between the two members of the Five Families still standing - McGowan and Pierce - and those now loyal to Falco."

Detective Delgado raised his hand. "This may just be a stupid question, but why are we trying to stop this guy? Let him take out the Five Families, consolidate or whatever he's doing, and then we take him out when he's done."

Briggs said, "Because when he's done, he'll command every criminal in No Man's Land like his own personal army. The Five

Families were associates, but they spent a good amount of time in-fighting. Simply put, we'd rather have the devil we know. Detective Parra has provided a sketch of Falco so you can be on the lookout for him."

Delgado's partner, Robert Lewis, raised his hand. "What's the plan, Lieutenant?"

"I know this isn't going to be popular, but stick with me. We're going to offer protection to Donald Pierce and William McGowan."

She paused for the murmur to pass through the room. "All right, people. Quiet down. I said it wouldn't be popular. This is an olive branch. We stop Falco's forward progress, and the two remaining families are in our debt. This could be very good for future relations. The word came down from on high, so take your complaints to the commissioner. Anyone? No? Didn't think so. You have your assignments. Detective Parra, Detective Priest, my office, please."

Riley and Priest waited for the rest of the detectives to leave before they joined Briggs in her office. She shut the door and sighed. "Now that we have the mundane battle plan under way, do we have anything planned for the more... fantastic angle? We can't exactly tell people Burke and Rowland were killed by a demon."

"Jill gave us a cover story for that. The killer talked Burke and Rowland into meeting and pulled into that alley. With a sharp enough sickle, a human could have taken off both men's heads even with the limited space."

Priest said, "I've read up on Falco. There's a chance he actually did use a weapon called a falx." She noticed their blank stares. "It's similar to a sickle or a scythe."

Riley shrugged. "The car had a sunroof, so the story will say the killer crawled out through that, took the heads, and cleaned off the flesh with some kind of industrial solvent. It's plausible enough. There are stories about the Five Families doing the same thing to some of their enemies back in the eighties."

Briggs nodded and sat down. "And Falco?"

"Priest and I will take care of him." She glanced at Priest and leaned forward. "I actually had an idea of how we might be able to do that."

"Pray tell."

"It will involve working with either Pierce or McGowan. Falco's already taken out three Family heads. Right now the two remaining are gearing for war, but it's not outside the realm of possibility that one of them might have a different reaction. We want one of them to extend an olive branch to Falco. He offers to lay down arms and hand control over to Falco in exchange for continued life."

"How does that help us?"

"We'll have someone on the inside."

Briggs leaned back. "And who do you suggest? Falco has met you and Priest, and I've been on the news enough that I wouldn't be much use undercover." Her eyes flashed with an idea that she immediately dismissed. "Kenzie is far too recognizable due to her scars. It would be too easy to look her up."

Riley looked at Priest, letting her take the ball.

"Yes. I had... an idea about that." She shifted in her seat. "There's someone we could send in who, even if she was recognized, has a true background that would plausibly make her a criminal. Chelsea Stanton."

Briggs smiled. "You want our eye on the inside to be a blind woman."

"She's not technically blind." Riley shrugged at Briggs' contemptuous look. "She can see shapes, light and darkness... But Priest has some ideas about that as well."

"It's recently come to my attention that I'm... mortal. I have my divinity, and it will always be a part of me, but I can be separated from it and survive. I can use a small part of it to temporarily give my sight to Chelsea."

Briggs leaned forward. "How long would that last?"

"Not long. It would never work permanently. But perhaps two days, three at the outside."

Riley said, "I think that would be long enough for Pierce or McGowan to set up a meeting with Falco. A meeting at a place of our choosing, where we can trap him. We'll lock him in the Cell and send him back where he came from."

Briggs whistled. "It's ballsy, I'll give you that." She considered it for a long moment before she looked at Riley. "We were both around back in the day, when Chelsea had her~"

"She's changed. I trust her."

"Then if she agrees, I'll give you the resources you need." Riley nodded and stood up. Briggs stopped her from leaving with an upraised hand. "Do you really agree this is the best course of action? Maybe Delgado has a point. Let Falco take out the heads of the Five Families and then we can focus on him and Marchosias. Take them both out."

Riley considered the question, but shook her head. "Having the Five Families was like being hit across the face with a flat hand. It hurts, but it's survivable. Wiping them out condenses all that power into a single point. It would be like a bullwhip across the cheek."

Briggs sighed. "I know. Wishful thinking."

"Wiping out all the bad guys at once really is tempting. But that leaves a vacuum to be filled by even worse villains. If Falco takes Marchosias' place, we have no idea if he would rule with an iron fist, or even play by the rules to the degree Marchosias has. There are better ways to take out our enemies."

"Blind leading the blind," Briggs said. She sighed and gestured for them to leave. "Let me know how it works out, Detective."

Chelsea carefully poured herself a cup of tea, returned the pot to the burner, and cradled the cup with both hands as she walked back to the living room. She saw the room and furnishings as vague shapes, hazy outlines that she couldn't bring into full focus. The couch was a large white area directly in front of her, and the blue-and-red person sitting upon it was Riley Parra. Caitlin Priest was...

Chelsea had never told anyone how she saw Priest. Part of her was uncomfortable about bringing it up, and another part of her thought they would think she was making it up, especially after she learned Priest really was an angel. But when she looked at Priest, she saw a bright glow spreading out all around her. Sometimes, like now, that glow took the shape of wings and a halo. She couldn't have said what color Priest's clothes were, or the color of her eyes, but she was unmistakable.

It was late, and Kenzie was working a case downtown, so they were alone. The streetlight on the corner was already shining through the living room window. Chelsea sat down and crossed one leg over the other, letting the steam from her tea rise into her face. She let the silence stretch out as she considered what they had come to say. Finally she spoke. "That's quite a plan you have there, Riley."

"It wouldn't be permanent. You should know that immediately. I don't want to give you false hope."

Chelsea smiled. "I wouldn't ask that of you, Caitlin. It means the world to me that you're offering me this gift. And Riley... you would be comfortable with me in such a vital position?"

"You were always a good cop, Chelsea. You made a lot of bad decisions, but that doesn't change who you were. Or who you've become since. I'd trust you with a badge."

"Wow." Chelsea looked down and closed her eyes. "There's a chance it won't work at all."

"Yes. But I spoke with Gillian about your injury. Your optic nerve was the part damaged by the bullet. I can make a... sort of... bridge. If I tried to do it permanently~" She hesitated. "I wouldn't want to risk it in something as delicate as the human brain."

"I understand." She took a drink of her tea and leaned forward, resting it on the edge of the table. She saw Riley move to take it and smiled. "I know my way around my own home, Riley."

"Right. Sorry."

"It's okay." She sat up and turned toward Priest. "I'd like to try it. When?"

"We can do it right now if you're ready."

Riley said, "Should you talk this over with Kenzie first?"

"No. I don't want to get her hopes up in case it doesn't work. I can't do that to her. And besides, it's temporary. A gift. A gift for her, too. Whenever you're ready, Caitlin." Priest knelt beside Chelsea's seat and lifted a hand to her forehead. Chelsea leaned away just before she made contact. "Will it hurt?"

"No. You won't feel anything. But you should probably close your eyes."

Chelsea closed her eyes, and Priest lightly brushed a finger over her temple. She imagined the last thing she remembered seeing clearly; a swaying green tree across the street from the prison. She had seen the tree countless times in her dreams, and the scene had become washed-out at the edges. The sky was more brilliantly blue than it could possibly have been, and the leaves looked like liquid shards of stained glass. She focused on the tree as she felt an odd but not unwelcome warmth spreading through her head, and she gasped as she realized it reminded her of Caitlin.

The glow faded.

"Well?"

Chelsea held her breath and opened her eyes.

Two women in dark blue police uniforms were waiting at the elevator when Chelsea approached. The doors opened and all three stepped inside. "Floor?" the Hispanic-looking one asked.

"Fourth."

"Come on, Riley, you knew that," the other one chided. She smiled at Chelsea. "We're, ah, big fans of you."

Chelsea watched the doors close. "Uh-huh."

"I'm Mackenzie Crowe, this is my partner, Riley Parra."

Riley raised two fingers in the bare-minimum of greeting. Chelsea pressed her lips together in response and nodded once. Kenzie stood between them. The doors parted and Chelsea took a step forward.

"If you're ever up for a threesome, come find us," Kenzie said.

Chelsea spun on her heel, shock and indignation crowding in next to intrigue. Riley was jabbing the "Door Close" button while Kenzie was giving her a shit-eating grin. She winked as the doors closed on her face, and Chelsea allowed herself a quick, disbelieving laugh. She ran her hand through her hair and walked into the bullpen.

Chelsea walked slowly down the aisles of her greenhouse, spraying her white roses and leaning in to watch the beads of water roll over the petals. She held them up to the light and smiled at how beautiful they were. Riley and Priest left an hour earlier, assuring her that tomorrow morning would be an early enough start on the undercover assignment. Riley claimed the delay was so Chelsea could adjust to having her eyesight back, but her knowing smile - and how wonderful was it to have *seen* that smile? - gave away her true intentions.

Chelsea was near the back door when it opened and Kenzie blustered in. Her black leather jacket was draped over one shoulder, and she wore a dark blue blouse and jeans. Her stakeout clothes, she called them. She walked past Chelsea without seeing her, moving straight for the office entrance. "Chels? Is everything okay? You sounded weird on the phone."

"I'm right here."

Kenzie stopped and turned. "Oh. I saw the light on, but I figured..." She looked at the roses. "What are you doing in here so late?"

"Just admiring the beauty." She plucked one of the roses and advanced carefully on Kenzie. Kenzie looked at the rose, then focused on Chelsea's face. A line appeared between her eyebrows. "Chelsea? Your eyes..."

Chelsea smiled sadly. How many times had she lovingly stared into Kenzie's cheek, or just over her shoulder? How many times had she said "I love you" while gazing at an eyebrow or an errant strand of hair? Now she was locked on to Kenzie's face, steady eye contact, and it was obviously strange enough that Kenzie was concerned.

"It's okay, sweetheart. Priest and Riley came by earlier. They have a plan, but they need someone who could conceivably be working with some bad people. I'm their top choice, but there was one thing that didn't work." She brushed Kenzie's hair back, exposing the right side of her face, and tucked the flower behind her ear. Once it was secured, she ran two fingers down the tangled scar tissue of Kenzie's cheek. "I needed to be able to see."

Kenzie stared. "You can see me?"

"Very clearly."

Kenzie recoiled, turning away as she brought one hand up to her scars. "Fuck, Chels."

Chelsea pushed Kenzie's hands away. "I've kissed your scars, Kenzie. They're just a part of you~"

"Yeah. But you hadn't..." She turned her face away. "You had a picture of me in your mind. You saw me when I was a young cop, before I went away, before I got... hurt."

"I did create a picture in my head. But you are more beautiful today than I ever imagined, Mackenzie. When I saw you just now, I was amazed at how wrong I was. How if I had known just how beautiful you'd become, I never would have tried to be with you. Because you are. You are so gorgeous, Mackenzie. My Kenzie." She cupped Kenzie's cheek.

Kenzie turned her head and pressed her lips against Chelsea's palm.

"I love you. And seeing your face... seeing how you truly look... Kenzie, it makes me love you even more."

Kenzie moved Chelsea's hand from her mouth to the scars that covered the right side of her face. She tensed, but then opened her eyes and met Chelsea's gaze.

"Your eyes are the strangest shade of brown," Chelsea said softly.

"Strange good?" Kenzie asked, her voice breaking.

"Strange beautiful." Their lips met in a tender, glancing kiss, but then became hungrier.

Kenzie curled her fists in the collar of Chelsea's blouse and pulled back, kissing her closed eyelids.

"How long?"

"A few days."

"And when do you have to meet up with Riley?"

Chelsea smiled. "Tomorrow morning."

"Then I'm sorry."

Chelsea raised an eyebrow.

"You're going to be really tired for your first day back at work."

Chelsea grinned and let Kenzie lead her out of the greenhouse, laughing as she was practically dragged up the stairs to their apartment. Once there, Kenzie pulled away to turn on every light she could find. When she returned to Chelsea and lowered her onto the bed, the entire room was bathed in the brilliant yellow glow of four sixty-watt bulbs. They had one night to store up a lifetime of visual memories, and Kenzie wasn't going to waste a second of it in shadows.

They decided to shower at midnight, giving themselves a clean slate for the rest of the night. Chelsea came out of the bathroom to find Kenzie standing at the bedroom window. She was nude, and the moon was bright enough to paint her blue. Chelsea hesitated in the doorway long enough to store the image in her mind before crossing the room and putting her arms around Kenzie's waist. Kenzie leaned back against her and turned to kiss Chelsea's lips.

"I wish we had time to plan. I'd buy us plane tickets. Show you Paris..."

"Paris is overrated." She ran her hand over Kenzie's stomach. "It's just a lot of museums filled with pale variations on a work of art I can find in my own bed. Perfection." She kissed Kenzie's neck and moved her hands lower. "And it doesn't matter where I am, as long as I have you. And the stars." She looked up. "People talk about sunrise and sunset. Blinding displays of color. I don't get it. But the stars. I could look at the stars for an eternity."

Kenzie smiled. "How about me?"

"You?" Chelsea kissed the shell of Kenzie's ear and pressed a hand between her legs. "I could look at you for an eternity and two minutes."

Kenzie turned in Chelsea's arms and kissed her. "We have six hours before Riley shows up. That's not enough time for Paris or museums or stars, but it's enough time for you to examine me from head to toe."

Chelsea shrugged as she walked Kenzie back toward the bed. "I disagree. But six hours is definitely a very good start."

Priest spent the night on Riley and Gillian's couch, accepting the fact she may have a few issues during the first night of blindness. She woke twice, terrified at the complete darkness until she remembered where she was, settling back onto the cushions before she cried out. She welcomed the infirmity, grasping it as a chance to fully embrace her mortal side. Angels didn't require eyes and they had no optic nerve. If she wanted to, she could rise slightly out of her Caitlin Priest shell and see more than anyone else in the room. But she remained.

Occasionally she experienced shared-sight with Chelsea and she blushed at some of the things she saw her doing with Kenzie. She smiled, fondly remembering their time together until sleep finally claimed her.

In the morning, Gillian helped Priest dress and they ate a very early breakfast before Priest and Riley went to pick up Chelsea. She was waiting on the stoop, dressed in bright colors with her hair braided and hidden under a cap. She smiled when she saw Riley's car and climbed into the backseat as soon as they stopped.

"Good morning."

"Where's Kenzie?"

"Asleep," Chelsea said. "She wanted to come, but she was worried about me. She wanted to sleep through it, if at all possible. Plus I'm sort of to blame... she had a long night."

Riley smiled in the rearview mirror. "Good girl. How are you handling the... change?"

"I watched Kenzie sleep. I saw the sun rise. Whatever you need from me, you've more than earned it." She leaned forward and put her hand on Priest's shoulder. "Thank you, Caitlin. This is the most amazing thing anyone's ever done for me."

Priest smiled and covered Chelsea's hand with her own. "I love you and Kenzie both. I'm glad I could help. I only regret the gift's impermanence."

"For now it will more than suffice. Thank you." She looked at Riley. "What is the plan?"

Riley had called Briggs for her own update on the drive over. "During the night, Detective Delgado convinced Donald Pierce to work with us in return for certain considerations. If we manage to take down Falco, he and McGowan will agree to a more 'jovial relationship with law enforcement,' whatever that means. He called Falco early this morning and they've set up a meeting this afternoon. We sweep in, arrest Falco, Priest and I take him to the Cell where we lock him up until we can figure out what to do next."

Priest shook her head. "I still don't think Marchosias or Dupre will like the fact their men are working with us. They may kill Pierce and McGowan on principle and just replace the Five Families entirely."

"Right now we have Marchosias backed into a corner. We're

hacking away at his forces. He doesn't have a champion, he's down to two families..."

"But taking down Falco will just free up the families he's already taken," Chelsea said. "Those people will just latch on to either Pierce of McGowan."

"Who are now, for better or worse, tied to us." She shrugged. "I'm not saying it's the ideal situation, but right now we have one of Marchosias' top agents agreeing to work with us."

Priest made a noise and Riley glared at her.

"What?" Chelsea looked between them. "What's going on?"

Riley sighed. "She's convinced it's a trap."

"I think Pierce is just pretending to work with us. He'll arrange the meeting with Falco, but not for our benefit. He'll wait until the opportune moment and then hand Riley over as a peace offering. Even if that isn't the end game, I'm wary. The Pierce family has worked for Marchosias for over one hundred years."

"They work for Marchosias. They might not be willing to see him knocked down."

Priest said, "You're basing that on a belief demons are loyal."

"Even a dog can shake hands."

Chelsea said, "And there's no honor among thieves. Riley, Caitlin's right. I'll be surrounded by police, so there's no reason for you to be nearby. If Pierce honors the arrangement, everything will be fine. If it's a ruse to draw you out, then you'll make it impossible for him to turn on you."

Riley drummed her fingers on the steering wheel as she waited at a stop light. Chelsea watched her and, thanks to Priest's gift of sight, saw that she was drumming with her right hand. Her left was resting on the steering wheel, and it was that hand she was staring at. Specifically the ring on the third finger of it.

"All right. Briggs will be in charge anyway, and I'd just be another body at the scene. I'll be at the Cell getting things ready for Falco's internment." She looked at Priest. "Satisfied?"

Priest smiled. "Very. Thank you."

Riley twisted to look at Chelsea. "Are you prepared for what we're about to do?"

Chelsea said, "Con a demon? As ready as I can be for something like that."

"Not that. I'm taking you to a room that's operating as task force headquarters. It'll be filled with cops from both Homicide and Organized Crime. Cops with very long memories. The people in charge will be the very people~"

"I'm ready," Chelsea said. "Like I said. As ready as I can be for something like that."

Riley nodded. "Okay. Off we go."

Chelsea leaned back in the seat and watched the city pass by the window. The decay in their neighborhood had advanced to an alarming degree; it was the first time she wished she couldn't see details. As they passed an intersection, she saw women in hooded robes standing under a streetlamp with their hands folded in prayer.

"The Good Girls," she murmured.

Riley glanced over as she passed them. "Yeah. Wow. I barely even notice them anymore. They're just part of the landscape, I guess."

Chelsea smiled ruefully. "The landscape is pretty much all new to me."

"Right. Sorry."

"Don't be."

Riley drove into No Man's Land, turning north into territory ran by the Pierce family. They passed sentries standing idly on street corners, casual except for the eyes that locked onto Riley's car with laser-like precision as it passed them.

"Very peculiar," Chelsea murmured.

"Yeah. Not used to being an invited guest in these parts. But I guess fighting demons makes for strange bedfellows, huh?"

They parked, as instructed, in the teacher's parking lot of an elementary school. With Priest's hand on her shoulder, Riley led the way across the lot and down a cracked sidewalk to Donald Pierce's grand Victorian home half a block away. There was no visible police presence but Riley knew spotters were watching from the houses on either side. The trio climbed onto the porch and knocked, and one of the younger Pierce men answered. His brown hair was thin, barely covering his large skull, and his eyes were buggy and impossibly wide on either side of his large nose. Riley took a step back from the odd-looking man, but he was obviously expecting her.

"Detective Parosh?"

"Parra. And Priest. This is Chelsea Stanton."

He motioned them in with two fingers. "I'm Joshua. Pop's in here." He led them down a short entryway into a large parlor. The furniture had been moved to the back wall to make room for folding tables currently covered with an assortment of computers and monitoring devices. It always amazed Riley how quickly the tech guys could set up their gear. A few officers looked up and tensed when they saw Chelsea, and she heard their whispers circulating around the room. She refused to look away and accepted their judging glares as Briggs and Sergeant Vogt from Organized Crime approached.

Vogt was a brutish man with curly black hair and weasel-reminiscent eyes. He glared at Chelsea but spoke to Riley. "I don't know what the hell trick you're trying to pull here, Parra, but last I heard, *she* was blind, and blind people don't make very good undercover detectives."

Chelsea reached out and plucked some lint off his shoulder. "Call it divine inspiration."

Vogt pointed at her. "What the f... if I find out you've been faking the injury to get public sympathy, so help me, I will be your worst enemy."

"It's a temporary reprieve," Riley said. "Former Detective Stanton is experiencing a short-lived window of sight, and she's using it to help us with this case. You should be thanking her for being selfless instead of using every minute of it with her girlfriend. God knows I would have made a different choice."

Vogt sneered and started to turn away, but Riley spoke again.

"I said you should be thanking her, Sergeant Vogt."

He glared at Riley, the first time he'd acknowledged her visually, and then glared at Chelsea. "Thank you for your assistance in this case, Former Detective Stanton."

"It's the least I could do."

Briggs intervened before Vogt could say anything else. "All right. Mr. Pierce is getting wired as we speak. We're going to be listening in, so if anything goes south, we'll be there."

"Change of plans, boss," Riley said. "I'll be getting Falco's lodgings ready for him."

Briggs frowned. "Everything okay?"

"I'll just be in the way."

Briggs nodded slowly, sure there was a reason that couldn't be shared in mixed company. "All right. But even without Riley there, we'll have more than enough people to keep you safe. Regardless of what anyone in this room thinks of the person you used to be, or how we might feel about working with scum like Pierce, there is a greater evil. Falco is the only enemy any of us should be worried about right now. Agreed?"

Vogt muttered an acknowledgement, and a few of the other

cops in earshot did as well.

"Okay. Let's go over the plan carefully. I don't want any surprises out there."

Donald Pierce's head was as large as his son's, giving the impression of an egg balanced on a teacup. His hair was pure white, and he had a slate-gray mustache that concealed his mouth when he spoke. Large eyebrows knit together over his slender, relatively small nose, and his eyes glared at out the windshield as he was driven to the meeting.

Chelsea was reluctant to take her eyes off the road. She still wasn't comfortable behind the wheel, even though her eyesight was pristine. In extreme, emergency cases she could drive without catastrophe, but on the whole she preferred to let Kenzie drive. She was feeling the anxiety now, the rush that came with being behind the wheel of a car. It could go from mode of transportation to deadly weapon with one twist of the wheel. She focused on the tense man seated beside her. "Are you okay, Mr. Pierce?"

"Okay?" He sighed and shifted nervously. "My house is full of police officers. In order to protect myself, I've aligned myself with people who would love nothing more than to put me and my children away for the rest of our lives. Three men I have worked with and fought with all my life are dead, slaughtered by the man we're about to meet. I may not always have gotten along with Theodore or the others, but by God we respected each other. So no, Detective, I am not okay. Nor will I be okay any time soon."

Chelsea didn't correct him on her official position with the police. "Everything will be fine, Mr. Pierce. I've worked with Detectives Parra and Priest enough to trust them implicitly. If they say a plan will work, either it will work... or they'll come up with something on the fly."

"Hmph. This is my life we're dealing with. I don't trust~"

"Riley Parra saved my partner. I trust her with the life of the woman I love, and my life. If she said she wanted my gun so she could shoot me in the kneecap, I would assume she had a good reason and hand it over. Don't trust me, and don't trust cops. Trust Riley Parra and just ignore the fact she's wearing a badge on her hip."

Pierce was silent for almost five blocks before he spoke again. "We've all heard of this Riley Parra. She's not just a police officer, is she? She's something more. Just like the man we're going to meet is something more than just a criminal."

Chelsea kept her eyes forward. "I know a lot about this town, Mr. Pierce. I know exactly what Riley is facing, and I still trust her. You're not the only one being sent into the firing line today."

"True. True." He turned to look out the window, drumming his fingers on his thighs. "If this fails, I'm handing myself over to a man who has already killed three of our number. William McGowan, the coward, won't be able to stand. He'll fold, and this *vlakas* prick Falco will win. So either way this is going to end today."

"I concur. Like I said, trust Riley."

Pierce grunted again and said nothing else for the rest of the trip. They reached the destination prearranged with one of Falco's men, and Chelsea parked. Falco had agreed to meet in a courtyard formed by a group of parking garages that rose up on three sides like battlements. Chelsea didn't like it; there were way too many vantage points where a shooter could get a bead on them and disappear without a trace. A button on the collar of Pierce's jacket would relay their conversation once it was activated. It was currently disabled in case Falco did a sweep, but Chelsea could turn it on with a switch disguised to look like a car security fob on her keychain.

They got out and walked into the courtyard. The air was preternaturally still, silent enough that Chelsea thought she would be able to hear a footstep from a block away. She was braced for the echo of a gunshot as she crossed the ankle-high grass.

They had barely reached the center of the courtyard when Falco's voice echoed out into the open air.

"I thought I told you to come alone, Donny."

Pierce shrugged with his hands held out as he looked around for the source of the voice. "If I leave her alone, my boys fight over which one gets to seduce her away from me. You understand."

"No," Falco said, still out of sight, "but then again I rule my people with an iron fist. They wouldn't dare cross me."

The echo faded from his voice and Chelsea turned to see Falco standing within arm's reach. He wore a grey three-piece suit, his dirty blonde hair lying flat in the back but spiked away from his forehead like a crown of thorns. He smiled and looked at Chelsea. "Hello, Miss Stanton. How's Riley? And the angel... are you still fucking the angel?"

Chelsea bristled. Pierce glanced at her with a raised eyebrow. Falco put his hands behind his back and pursed his lips.

"Strange. Very strange. You're here, and you can *see*. That made me curious enough to walk into such an obvious set-up. But now that I'm here, I'm going to change a few rules. First..." He pressed all four fingertips against his thumb, pointed them at Pierce, and flashed out with his fingers in a mimic of fireworks going off. He pursed his lips and said, "Pft."

Donald Pierce exploded.

Chelsea screamed and jumped away from the surge of gore, but Falco grabbed hold of her arm. It felt as if his fingers were breaking the skin, tearing the muscle, and she dropped to her knees as Falco towered over her.

"Second..." He tapped her forehead with the knuckle of his free hand. "The angel is the one giving you sight, yes? Sharing her divinity with you? Angels. Always willing to expose their soft underbellies. Because now that I have her sight, I can do this." He pushed Chelsea's eyelids down with his thumb and forefinger with exaggerated tenderness. There was a sudden pressure and then he pulled his hand back and shoved her onto the dirt.

In the Mobile Police Unit, while the technicians were waiting for Chelsea to activate their bug, Priest suddenly pressed the heels of her hands against her eyes. "Ah..."

Briggs turned to look at her. "Detective Priest? Are you~"

Priest screamed and stood up so fast that her chair slammed against the opposite wall. The scream was loud enough that every person in the room recoiled from it, and Priest dropped to her knees with a wail of utter agony. "Stop, stop... don't make me see that... no..." Her vision, until then a field of blurry objects and strange shapes, had suddenly snapped into focus like a film projector had been switched on. The images were all inside her head, and they ran on a screen just behind her eyelids so she couldn't hide from them.

Riley.

Bloody death.

Carnage and destruction.

She was aware of hands on her shoulders, voices calling for assistance, but she ignored them all. It was taking everything she had to keep herself from screaming, to save herself from going inside from the horrific slideshow. Only one thought penetrated the frenzied insanity.

Something just went horribly wrong.

Falco unbuttoned his jacket and swept the two halves aside to rest his hands on his hips. "Now, Chelsea Stanton. Where's Detective Parra? I assume this clusterfuck was her idea. Odd of her not to take part in it. Strange of her to be hiding." He crouched in front of her. "Where's Riley? This is her game."

Chelsea glared up at him. "Riley's far away from here."

"Well. I guess I'll just have to give her an incentive to come to me then, huh?" He grabbed a handful of Chelsea's hair and reached for her throat.

"Wait..."

Falco stopped, stared at her, and then grunted with frustration. "Seriously? Oh, for..." He tossed her and straightened. "Such bullshit. I go out of my way, I wait *all morning* for a little torture, and you cave immediately? That is so unfair." He looked at the spray of blood and gore that had once been Donald Pierce. "I should have taken my time with him. At least he had balls." He sighed at what could have been and walked back to her. "Okay. Make your deal. Take me to Riley because you think Riley will be tough enough to take me out. Is that what you were going to say? Am I stepping on your big moment?" He sneered at her. "How does it feel?"

Chelsea groaned. She had just gotten her ass handed to her by a demon who was now taking the time to pout.

"She'll stop you. If not today, then~"

"The next day or next year, blah blah blah. I'm not as nice as Marchosias. He let Parra have these piddling little victories that, in the long run, mean nothing. Let her fight me for a while, sweetcheeks. Then we'll see how cocky she is." He winked and hauled her up. "Come on, Judas. Take me to your friend."

Priest was speaking through her tears. The horrific images of Riley being flayed alive had stopped, but she was still shaking from the experience. She and Briggs were outside the surveillance truck, speaking low so they wouldn't be overheard. "Falco has her. Whatever happened, this whole thing has gone wrong."

"What will he do to Stanton?" Briggs asked.

Priest thought for a moment. "Chelsea will think fast. Riley is at the Cell. It's a fortified building, designed to hold demons at bay. Chelsea will offer to take Falco to her, and he won't be able to resist that. They're going to the Cell."

"Then so are we." Briggs looked to make sure none of the other members of the task force had come out before she ushered Priest toward her car.

The right side of Chelsea's outfit, the side Pierce had been standing beside when he was killed, was splattered with his blood. Falco was sitting beside her in the seat so recently occupied by the now-dead man. He didn't threaten her, didn't even keep a hand on her to make sure she complied with his orders. She knew he was dangerous, and constantly threatening her was unnecessary. The second she tried to run, she would end up as dead as Pierce.

She parked in front of the Cell and Falco whistled. "Impressive. At least Detective Parra hides in style. Come on."

Chelsea got out of the car and, after a momentary fantasy of running, led him across the lawn. She wanted to warn Riley somehow, to alert her of what was about to happen, but she was wary of Falco's reaction. She was furious at her fear, almost willing to sacrifice herself if it meant Riley would get the upper hand if even for a second. She could only think of Kenzie, and her courage faltered.

They walked to the back of the building where Riley's car was parked. The wooden storm doors extended from the side of the building at a steep angle, the handles gleaming silver in the sunlight. A padlock was lying on the grass next to the doors, and Chelsea knelt to pull one side open. Stone stairs led straight down, and Falco leaned in to look. "Ah, the Cell. I've heard of this. Quite a few demons in this town are actually frightened of it." He smiled and gestured. "You first."

Chelsea reluctantly went down, followed by Falco. He took the time to close the cellar door behind him and followed her down. Their steps echoed. When they were nearly to the bottom, Falco roughly jabbed Chelsea's arm and mouthed, "Call her."

"Riley? A-are you there?"

"Chelsea? What are you doing here?"

She glanced at Falco. "Things got... pear-shaped, Riley. I'm so sorry."

"Eh, don't worry about it. Best-laid plans and all that. Come on down. I want to show you something."

Falco narrowed his eyes and prodded her to continue. She reached the bottom of the stairs and saw Riley aiming a gun at her. Her eyes widened and she ducked to one side. Falco looked at her, looked at the gun, and pressed his lips together in a tight smirk. "Well, well, well. Look who got the jump on me after all."

Riley smiled. "You shouldn't have hurt Priest. She knew something had happened, so she flew here to warn me. Even without eyes, it wasn't too hard... a guardian angel can always find her ward."

"So where is she?"

"Outside."

Falco shrugged. "I didn't see her."

"You wouldn't have. She stayed out of sight. Couldn't let you know she had extended the Cell's perimeter before you walked inside."

Falco tensed. "What did you do?"

His question was drowned out by a sudden thrum of power coursing through the walls and floor of the old church. Falco looked up at the ceiling, eyes wide with panic, and then looked at Riley again. "You... bitch."

"Chelsea, are you okay? The blood..."

"It's Pierce's. Falco killed him."

Riley kept her gun trained on Falco. "Shame. Keep your hands up, Falco. This might not hurt you, but in here it'll leave a mark. You're not exactly yourself right now, remember? All that power at your fingertips... but you just can't summon it. Must be like a dying battery in your Walkman. Weak."

Falco smiled. "Weak. Heh." He walked forward but stayed well away from Riley. "I'm not trying to grab you, Detective. I don't want you to get all trigger-finger-y. I'm just conceding. You win." He stepped into the circle carved in the concrete floor and held his hands up. "You outplayed me. My cockiness was my downfall. If I hadn't taunted Zerachiel, she wouldn't have known to warn you. Best laid plans and all that."

Chelsea suddenly hissed in pain and touched her temple.

Riley tensed. "What are you doing to her?"

Falco shrugged. "You said it yourself. I can't do anything."

"It's my eyes, Riley." She cried out and dropped to one knee. "Oh. God. I think Caitlin was optimistic about how long this would last."

Priest appeared at the base of the stairs. She had one hand cupped next to her eyes, squinting into the room. "Chelsea?"

"I'm here. I think it's~"

"I'm so sorry. I overestimated how long this would~"

As they went to each other, Riley was distracted by Falco. His eyes rolled back in his head and he dropped like a sandbag. She checked to make sure Chelsea and Priest were relatively okay before she moved closer to the ring. Falco was sprawled in a horribly twisted fashion, uncomfortable for human and demon alike. His eyes were focused on the ceiling, unseeing, and his fingers twitched like dying creatures.

Chelsea touched Priest's face. "Thank you, Caitlin. For this gift."

"I only wish it could last longer."

Chelsea kissed Priest's lips and then cried out. Priest groaned at the same time and they rocked away from each other. When Priest opened her eyes, she could see. She blinked and saw Chelsea waving her fingers in front of her face with a stricken expression.

"It's gone."

Priest's heart broke. "I'm so sorry."

"Don't be... just he-help me up."

Priest got to her feet and they gripped each other's forearms. Priest pulled, and Chelsea rose and leaned against her side. Priest stroked her hair. "I'll reinforce the barriers around the church. We shouldn't take any chances with..." Her voice trailed off when she looked at Riley, who was looking at the ground. Falco was inside the circle, apparently dead, but his entire body was twitching.

Priest understood in an instant.

"He tricked us."

Riley turned. "What?"

"This is what he wanted. Riley... we have to go."

Riley pulled her arm away and pointed at Chelsea. Priest understood; Chelsea was far more vulnerable than Riley, and she would require more help to escape. Priest hooked her hands under Chelsea's arms and half-carried her out of the room. The angel side of her protested leaving Riley behind, but it couldn't be avoided. She ascended the stairs faster than human legs could have taken her, the soles of her shoes barely touching the stone as she rose toward daylight. She deposited Chelsea on the ground, turned, and looked into the stairwell that had become a pit. She was trembling as she waited for Riley. Seconds passed before Riley appeared on the bottom step. She was still looking behind her.

"Riley, *run*! I can't come get you. I can't... I-I can't go down there if~"

There was an inhuman howl. Priest's teeth were clenched so tightly that her jaw ached as she grabbed the door and slammed it shut. She threw her weight down on it, adding Zerachiel's muscle to keep it shut as the howl grew in timbre. It was a godawful sound, nauseating and hateful, and Chelsea clasped both hands over her ears.

As the waves battered the door, Priest cried. Falco's entire gambit was to end up here, inside the Cell, with Riley Parra standing in front of him. Killing the Five Families was just a means to an end. Seconds passed, but it felt like days. When the energy finally dissipated, Priest pushed herself up on weak arms and looked at the chipped white paint of the cellar doors. Tears dripped from her chin onto the weathered wood.

Chelsea uncovered her ears and lifted her head. "Caitlin? What... happened? Did Riley make it out?"

Priest closed her eyes as someone began to knock on the other side of the cellar door.

"Priest? You out there? Open the door."

She stepped back and lifted the door. Riley was standing as high as she could on the stairs, squinting up into the sunlight. Priest glared at her.

"What the hell was that all about? Slamming the door in my face?"

Priest's voice was flat, almost unrecognizable. "You never would have outrun it, Riley. Why don't you come on out?"

Riley looked at the cellar door. "Why..."

"If you can. Come out."

Riley's face hardened and she looked up at Priest. "Why don't you help me out here, Priest?"

Chelsea was standing now. "I'm confused. What's wrong?"

"When the shell of an angel dies, its divinity spreads outward in a surge of light. When a demon dies, its darkness floods the air around it like a bad smell. I was in the room when Selaphiel died. He released Zerachiel, and his divinity brought her back to life. Restored me. I became an angel again.

"Riley was just in the room when Falco killed himself. His darkness, his energy, filled the Cell like gas."

"Caitlin, no. Riley..."

Riley's eyes were nearly black now, and her smile contained not a shred of humor. "You gotta admit," Riley said, "it was a hell of a plan."

"What plan?" Chelsea demanded.

"This was Falco's plan from the start. He never wanted to dethrone Marchosias, he wanted this moment. He's turned Riley into a demon."

Priest lifted the heavy wooden door and shut it on the abomination of Riley's death's-head grin. As she fumbled to lock the doors again, Riley began to laugh.

THE DEVIL YOU KNOW

Quiet. But not silent.

Breathing. A heartbeat drumming. Blood rushing.

Riley Jacqueline Parra. She looked down at her hands, palms cupped and fingers splayed. She breathed deeply and closed her eyes. Oh, it felt strange. Good. But bizarre. She felt like she could do anything. She felt like she was standing in front of a tide of power and all she had to do was direct it. A flick of her wrist would tear down the walls, a twitch of her eyebrow would create a chasm that would close after swallowing her enemies. She could tear down No Man's Land and rebuild it as a shining beacon of light and hope and still make it home in time for supper.

She thought of people with power comparing themselves to God. But that was inaccurate. God wasn't the highest because God still had to follow the rules. For real power, you had to become the Devil.

Of course, to use even a fraction of her power, she had to escape the infernal Cell. She helped to choose the location, and she'd picked it specifically for the challenges it would present to a demon. Consecrated ground, surrounded by sacred markings... oh, yes, she and Priest had done an excellent job. Sariel had fortified it further, so it was one newborn demon versus the power of two angels. Riley flexed her arms, rolled her neck, and held her hands out in front of her to test her strength.

Strange. She could feel the energy coming off the walls. The secondary barrier she, the mortal she, had instructed Priest to erect was like a steel shell. There was no way she would get past that on her own. Fortunately she had been outside of the circle carved on the floor when she became a demon, but she was still trapped in the basement.

All that power and no way to tap it. Tantalus. Cursed forever to stand in water he couldn't reach. True torment. She lowered her hands and looked up at the ceiling. Very strange. She felt very strange indeed. Her gun was heavy in the shoulder holster and she took it out and peered at its polished body. She turned it around, pressed the barrel against her side, and used her thumb to pull the trigger.

She stumbled and pushed out her left hand to stop herself from falling. Pain caused her mind to whiteout, her senses blank for half a second before she realized it was already subsiding. She straightened slowly and looked down at the hole in her shirt. It was still smoking and she could see the wound within, but the flesh was knitting together. She watched the blood flow without concern, saw it stop like a clogged faucet, and then the blazing red scar tissue turned purple, red, pink, and then skin tone. There wasn't even a scar or a hint of evidence.

Daniel Falco's body was lying nearby, and Riley walked to it. She put her hand in the center of his chest. Her feelings about it were odd. Like an old suit that didn't fit anymore. She had absolutely no use for it, but she was still... sentimental. She put her hand on its chest and checked her new reserves of power. Hm. Not a lot. Barely any, really. But enough for a simple immolation. She directed it into Falco's corpse, and it was reduced to cinders and ash in a matter of seconds.

"Ha! Oh, that could come in handy." She looked at her palm and thought of the possibilities. The next time someone pulled a gun on her, the next time Detective Timbale said something misogynistic or racist, the next time someone cut her off in traffic... she would offer to settle everything with a simple, peaceful handshake and then...

"Poof," she whispered.

Riley smiled as the door to the surface crashed open. She glanced toward the foot of the stairs and aimed her gun where Priest's head would appear. The footsteps stopped just short of the door, and Riley smiled. "Knew you would be too smart for that, Zerachiel."

"What's your name?"

"You know my name." She holstered her weapon. "Same as it's always been. Riley Jacqueline Parra."

"No. That's not who you are anymore."

"The demon in Falco didn't possess me, Cait. That was never their plan. When Marchosias kidnapped me a while back, he said I would play on his side one way or the other. He said turning me into one of his followers was the easy way. I guess Falco was Plan B." She cupped her left hand inside her right and began to pace slowly around the edge of the room. When she got to the point where she could see Priest standing on the stairs, she tilted her head to the side and wagged her fingers.

"Hello, angel. Why don't you come down here so we can talk all civilized? Like real people." She smiled. "Although I guess neither of us are really people at the moment, right?"

Priest came down into the doorway of the basement. Riley smiled at her.

"So what were you doing up there while I got used to my new tricks? Did you call in the SWAT team? Is Chelsea setting up barricades so the big bad Riley Monster doesn't get out?"

"Kenzie and the Good Girls are on their way."

Riley rolled her eyes. "Great. You know, demons aren't actually affected by prayer, we just find them *so tedious*. And hymns? Don't get me started on those. Trite and untrue." She cracked her knuckles and nodded toward the door. "So... go ahead and knock down the barrier outside."

Priest furrowed her brow. "Why in the world would I do that?"

"So I can leave." When Priest still didn't react, Riley stepped toward her. Priest stepped to one side, avoiding Riley but at least entering the basement. "Priest, this is the holy hand grenade of Antioch, okay? The past three and a half years, I've been a mortal woman going up against demons. I didn't stand a chance without the tattoo. But now there's a level playing field. Now I can give back whatever they throw at me, and then some. We can go on the offensive."

"We? I can't... and won't... work alongside a demon."

"But it's me, Priest. It's really me. The tattoo... I can feel it working."

Priest shook her head. "No. You feel the tattoo, your shield, fighting the demon. But it will lose. The power will fade, and it will crumble. Then you will be truly lost to us. The tattoo is the only reason there's still a chance to save Riley."

"To save *me*, you mean?"

"No. I've known Riley Parra her entire life. I've held Riley in her sorrow, and I've listened to Riley while she slept. I know when I'm talking to Riley, and I know when Riley is standing in front of me. You wear her face, but you are not her."

Riley held her hands out. "We can change the rules, Priest. You were supposed to be dead last year, remember? Zerachiel flew the coop and you were just a shell. But you and I fought that. I kept you alive, and now you're an angel again. But you're also mortal. I can see it when you think I'm not watching you. The sad tilt of your head. You're not the angel you once were. But that makes you better. Don't you see? You have your angel and mortal sides, and I have my demon side. We can learn to control it."

Priest smiled without humor. "We can't do anything. If you're a demon, I can't have anything to do with you. Demons don't get guardian angels."

"But we can still be partners."

Priest sighed. "I suppose it would be possible, but I wouldn't want to be around you. You're evil, and that is disgusting to me. I can barely stand to be in the same room with you."

Riley sneered. "I can't believe you're not seeing the opportunity here. Falco and Marchosias screwed up, Priest. They screwed up big time by giving me this power. Half the Five Families are gone, and there's a power vacuum in No Man's Land. All I have to do is waltz in and organize it all under my banner and then I'll take down Marchosias. If demons have to be represented in No Man's Land, then why not let me sit in the big chair? You can keep watch over the rest of the city and we'll keep it safe together."

"How does your tattoo feel?"

Riley had been ignoring the pain. It felt as if something sharp had been pressed into the muscle under her tattoo and was being twisted. A spiral of heat spread out from the initial contact point and radiated across her shoulder.

"That's the power of your protection fighting the demon. It can't hold out forever. It will succumb. Do you remember the demons in Marchosias' hotel, the first time you ever encountered them? They nearly tore you to shreds." She said something else after that, but the words slipped out of Riley's mind. "A concentrated attack can get through even your protections. Having a demon inside you is not survivable. The tattoo may be winning small battles, but it will lose the war. And you will become a corrupt, vile demon that wears the face of my friend. And that I cannot abide."

"Are you saying you'll kill me?"

Priest nodded without hesitation. "When it's clear to me that the woman I knew and loved is dead, I will murder the demon who took over her body."

"I would like to see you try."

Priest tilted her head to the side. "And who was that speaking? Because it certainly didn't sound like Riley."

Riley put the heels of her hands against her temples and rubbed in slow circles. "You're pissing me off, Zerachiel."

"You can't even decide what name to call me. Am I an angel? Your friend? Your partner? Which is it? You've called me all three. Priest, Zerachiel, Cait. Which is it?"

"I always call you all three, you dumb feathered bitch." Riley tightened her lips, hiding her teeth again as she turned and walked back toward the corner. "How am I supposed to know who you are? You don't even know? Guardian angel, cop, lesbian, bisexual, angel, mortal. What are you, Caitlin? Don't use my confusion against me until you've figured it out for yourself."

"I'm all of those things."

"Yeah?" Riley turned. The pain had faded slightly. "Not much of a guardian angel. You saw what was about to happen. You understood Falco's plan, and you ran out of the room with Chelsea. You left your ward behind. Odd behavior for a guardian angel, don't you think?"

"Riley told me to take her out. The only odd thing is that you don't remember it." The demon snorted. "And it was the right decision to make, a calculated choice. Chelsea was once again visually impaired and had no chance of getting out on her own. Had Falco's energy hit her, she would have become a demon with no hope of redemption. You, on the other hand, have the tattoo as protection. There was a chance you could be saved." Her face darkened. "I should have considered your stubbornness and the appeal of absolute power."

Riley said, "I think you're right. It was a calculated choice, but not the one you thought. The angel side of you understood the possibilities of having a demon working for good. That's why you abandoned me. Zerachiel made you, just like when she decided to help the Angel Maker and when she abandoned me for the trial. The difference is that I *want* this. I never considered it, but now that it's happened, let's embrace it! Let's not look a gift horse in the mouth."

The pain in her shoulder was now almost intolerable, a fireplace poker pushing into the muscle. She resisted the urge to massage the pain away; she wouldn't give Priest the satisfaction. She narrowed her eyes.

"That's it. You don't want me to be this powerful because then I wouldn't need you anymore." She smiled, then laughed. "Now that I'm as powerful as you... well, more powerful than you, probably... you're useless. Poor Priest. Left behind, discarded like yesterday's waste. And you've been tainted by your time as a mortal, so you probably won't be allowed back upstairs. So what's left? Staying down here with the rabble? Quite a ways to fall for an angel like Zerachiel.

"Would you grow old and gray? Would you die?" She tilted her head to the side. "Huh. What's to become of the poor half-mortal wing girl? Doomed to wander the Earth forever because she was a human for a day or two. Heck of a punishment." She stepped closer and lowered her voice. "But oh... there are other possibilities, Priest. You've lived as an angel, and as a mortal, but there's one flavor you haven't tried yet. I could make it happen. I could be your in, get a few of my old friends together and see if one of them wants to make history. Angel. Mortal. Demon. We'd have to think of a new name for you. Caitlin's the mortal, Zerachiel's the angel, and your demon would be~"

"Silence." Priest barked the word and immediately looked away. "I'm sorry. But listening to such blasphemy is~"

Riley scoffed. "Blasphemy. What's blasphemy? Just someone trying to ignore stuff they don't want to hear. Come on, Caitlin. A little dab'll do ya."

"You have two options now. Here they are, laid out before you." Priest kept her voice steady. "If you remain a demon, even if you claim you're still in control, you will no longer be the champion. The protection of your tattoo will vanish and you'll be completely taken over by the demon. At that point, I will join forces with Aissa, Kenzie, Chelsea, and," she said something else but Riley forgot it, "and we will stop at nothing to destroy you. If you think they'll hesitate... they won't. Because they'll only see you as the beast wearing the skin of a loved one who was taken away from them.

And they will kill you."

Riley growled, "I'd like to see them try."

"You would kill them?"

Riley held up her hand. "I would rip Aissa's head from her scrawny neck. Do you think she'd honestly pose a challenge after everything I've done and seen? I'd tear her limb from limb. I'd take a torch to Kenzie's face so at least she would be symmetrical when they buried her~"

Priest's voice was choked. "Do you even hear what you're saying?"

"Yes." She hissed through her teeth and clutched her shoulder. "I'm just... frustrated. I, obviously, I would never do that. You're just... you call me stubborn, but will you stop and think about how this could be a *good* thing?"

"No. Because nothing good can come from demons. It's their nature to cause mayhem and strife. They feed on destruction and dismay."

"Said the angel. You know, demons have some ideas about angels. I bet they would be surprised to discover you and Sariel were lovers. Angels would never do something as base as making love. Fornication? Perish forbid."

Priest ignored the provocation. She began to pace along the perimeter of the room with her hands behind her back. "I said you had two options; here is the other. I need your help to save you. I need you to push when I pull, and together we can free you from the demon's grasp. It has to be soon... it has to be before it completely ensnares you. The tattoo is holding it back, and it's buying us time. But it's time that's measured in minutes, not hours. The chance to free you without permanent damage to your body is slipping away from us. Do you remember when Gillian showed us what happens to a body that has played host to a demon?"

"This is different. I'm not a host."

"But your body is still suffering under tremendous strain. A demon is worming its way into you, and your body is fighting it tooth and nail. The longer your tattoo holds it off without winning, the weaker you'll become. If it takes me an hour to free you from the demon's grasp, you won't survive. You'll go to the hospital with complete organ failure. You will die."

Riley smiled. "So there's a time limit. All I have to do is wait an hour, and *your* choice will be letting me live as a demon or watching me die tonight."

"I'll let you die as yourself than live as... this. So would..."

Riley didn't know why Priest suddenly trailed off, but it didn't matter. She rolled her shoulders. The pain was ebbing and flowing. She wished the tattoo was in a more convenient place, somewhere she could get at it with her fingernails. Maybe if she could scratch around the edge, she could rip it off her skin like a bumper sticker. The demon would heal her just like it had healed the bullet wound. She looked down and saw blood drying on her shirt and pants. That trick alone was worth being a demon.

"Neither of us is going to back down. So why don't we just save each other some trouble and end this now." Riley took out her gun and aimed it as Priest. "An angel and a demon walk into a Cell. Only one can leave alive. Is that how it is?"

"You don't want that. I've been an angel much longer than you've been a demon."

"So?"

Priest feinted right. Riley was distracted enough to move her weapon in that direction as Priest lifted into the air. Her wings flashed out to either side and caught a breeze Riley couldn't feel, carrying her farther than any human could jump. She closed her hand around Riley's and plucked the gun away, breaking her grip along with all four fingers on Riley's right hand. Riley cried out in surprise, and Priest twisted. Riley's forearm snapped and her weapon was taken from her. Priest landed lightly on the ground behind Riley, removed the gun's clip, and tossed the pieces to opposite sides of the room.

Riley chuckled and worked her muscles, warming them up for the fight to come. "Something familiar about this. I seem to remember I kicked your ass when we were high on U4IC. Care to try for round two?"

Before Riley could answer, Priest launched herself up until she touched the ceiling, then dived with her right fist extended. The punch connected with Riley's chin and her head was knocked violently to the side. She knew her jaw was disconnected, and she flopped weakly to the floor on her broken arm.

"Best three out of four?"

"Get off of me."

Priest walked away, recreating the space between them. She crossed her arms over her chest as Riley twisted and propped herself up, and felt her body beginning to mend. Priest was eyeing the ground, and Riley saw the moisture of tears shining on her cheeks.

She scoffed and, when her jaw was healed enough to speak, she said, "Pathetic. You really believe you could kill me if you weep because you caused me pain?"

"If I have to, yes. I'm glad I'm weeping. It means that Riley is still somewhere inside of you. I could feel myself hurting her, and it hurt me."

Riley flexed her fingers. The middle one was a little cockeyed, so she broke it again so it would heal right. She got up onto one knee and looked at Priest.

"How long are we going to do this, Zerachiel? City's falling apart out there. Marchosias could choose a new champion while we're down here having a pissing contest. 'My deity can kick your dark lord's butt.' It's childish. Things aren't black and white in the real world. Never. There is an excuse for anything under the sun."

"Child abuse?"

"Cycle of violence." Riley rolled her shoulder. Her hand and jaw were better, but the damned tattoo was still like a million bee stings. "Go back far enough, you can find a reason for anything. Angels aren't all good, demons aren't all bad, and ninety percent of the bad things that happen to people are caused by other people. Angels and demons don't come into it. Some guy hits his wife because he had a shitty day at work, because his boss was stressed because his boss is breathing down his neck. Ask me, we oughta just wipe out the whole lot of them."

Priest said something, and then continued, "You have to know how that sounds, Riley. That's the demon talking."

"Then maybe your dear sweet Riley isn't so much in control anymore. Maybe she welcomed the chance to give in and hand over control to someone stronger for a change." She smiled, showing her teeth. "You think of that? Maybe you give your little champion a little too much credit." She realized she was insulting herself, but that didn't stop her. She felt like it was true. She wanted to say it. So if~

No.

She was just trying to stir Priest up enough so she would end this ridiculous standoff and drop the barrier.

"Let me out of here, Zerachiel. I'll show you what we can do together. Forget just protecting this city. We can be so much more than what we've been. We can change everything. We don't have to be detectives. We can just be partners."

"Rule together." Priest's voice was flat.

Riley smiled. "Yes. No more angels, no more demons, there would just be us and them. Good needs evil to exist, and vice versa. We can balance each other out. Between us we can keep everybody else in line."

Priest shook her head sadly. "The Riley I knew would never want to rule. She would want peace~"

"I'm offering peace! I'm offering unity. No angel would ever trust a demon, and a demon would never willingly join with an angel. Until now. You and me, Cait. We can change... everything. Because you love me, and I trust you. Demon, angel, it doesn't matter. What matters is that we're together, and we have the power to make people do what we want."

Priest nodded slowly, sadly. "And if they don't do what we want?"

Riley growled, "Then we burn them to the ground and spread the ashes to the wind."

"How's your tattoo?"

"Will you forget the goddamn tattoo?" Riley pushed her hands into her hair and pulled. The pain distracted her from the burning in her shoulder. "I don't need you. I can rule it all alone." She closed her eyes and began to pace in a tight circle.

Priest stepped closer. "We're running out of time. The tattoo won't stem the tide forever. Soon the demon will overpower it and you'll be left with a scar on your shoulder. Not that you'll mind, because by that point you'll be a completely different entity. It's destroying you from the inside out, and that tattoo is the only thing holding it back. Choosing to let the demon win is not a sane choice. It's not the choice Riley would have made."

"You're not calling me Riley. Since you've come down here, you haven't referred to me by... anything."

Priest shook her head. "I won't tarnish her name by using it to refer to a demon."

Riley straightened her shoulders. "Get used to it. From here on, I'm the only Riley you have. And you're wrong. This is *exactly* the choice I would make. To have this level of power? As a mortal, I was weak. I was a victim who put on a badge and carried a gun because I was terrified of what was in the shadows. It gave me a fighting chance against the monsters. How many men came into my bedroom when I was a defenseless girl? Do you know how many times I prayed for help? For strength?"

"You said nineteen hundred and forty-two prayers. Eighty-five of them were out loud. Six hundred of them were muttered and barely understandable. Three hundred were just a single word. Nineteen hundred and forty-two exactly."

Riley blinked. "What?"

"Who do you think heard those prayers?" Priest's voice was tight. "Who do you think begged for a chance to intervene and was told to stand down? I heard your prayers, Riley. Every nineteen hundred and forty-two prayers for someone to do something. And all I could do was grant you sleep when it was over, and what forgetfulness was possible. I've lied to you in the past, Riley. Everyone does get a guardian angel, but I was assigned to you because of how loudly you prayed. I couldn't help you every time, but your prayers didn't go unanswered."

The walls darkened behind Priest, and Riley saw a street in No Man's Land stretching out behind her. She stepped around Priest and into the sepia-toned memory. Only a few things seemed real, seemed static, and she watched as a slender Hispanic teen dropped from a fire escape and brushed off the legs of her torn and faded jeans. Priest stepped forward to stand beside Riley and directed her attention to the convenience store on the corner.

Two young teenagers were lounging on the sidewalk. One spotted the younger Riley and nudged his friend. He communicated without speaking what he was thinking and started to rise up. He watched Riley start down a blind alley before he started walking. His friend unbent and followed without a word.

Priest spoke quietly. "Their intent was robbery, but I'm sure you would have fought. The bigger one, the leader, eventually went to prison for breaking someone's skull with a brick. They had sixty dollars in their wallet but he was hoping for eighty. Little disappointments. The little one is a pervert who works in a shoe store and does unspeakable things to their shoes. You never bought any there because it always gave you an uneasy feeling. You thought the store was dirty, but you could never quite explain where the feeling came from. Me. It came from me."

The boys were almost to the alley.

"You would have fought, and the big one would have hurt you. Badly. He would have held you down so the little one could do whatever he wanted. And he had ideas. Wicked ideas."

A police car turned the corner. The leader stopped and turned, signaling his partner with a slight shake of his head. They walked away. In the alley, Riley saw herself scale a fence and drop to the other side as the car slowly rolled on. Riley and Priest stepped out of its way, although Riley knew it wasn't really there.

"He wasn't looking for anything or anyone in particular. He was sent out on patrol, and he decided to check out this neighborhood on a whim. 'Haven't been down this way in a while. Might as well see what's going on.' I whispered in his ear, because I knew what those boys had planned for you. You focus on the times I wasn't there for you because you don't know about all the times I was."

Riley turned to face Priest. They were back in the Cell, closed in by inscribed stone walls. Riley could feel their hold even stronger now, and she reached to scratch at her tattoo through her clothes. Priest saw her and dropped her hand to her side. She sneered and turned away.

"Bad things happen to good people. Deep. But I'm not a people anymore. Bad things don't have to happen to me anymore. I'm going to stay like this, Priest. You can either accept that things have changed, or you can become my enemy."

"Oh, you don't want me as your enemy."

Riley turned. "Try me."

"I broke your jaw, your arm, and your fingers. What else would you like me to break? Or maybe..." She faked a jab. Riley ducked, but that was Priest's intention. She lifted up on her toes, guided Riley past her, and slapped her palm down on Riley's shoulder over her tattoo. She extended her wings as she wrestled Riley to the floor and pinned her to the concrete. The space between Priest's hand and Riley's tattoo glowed with holy light, and infernal smoke began to rise through her fingers. Riley howled.

"How does your tattoo *feel?*" Priest growled.

"Get off of me!"

Riley could feel the intense heat spreading through her body, and some vestige of her brain reminded her that fevers came from the body fighting off an infection. A fever, heat, was a sign of healing. Riley howled and tried to buck Priest off, but the angel suddenly seemed to weigh twice as much as before. She forced Riley's head down against the pavement as the holy light washed through her body, pushing back the tide of demonic energy.

"Bitch! You'll pay for this, angel whore!"

"I love you, Riley. If you're in there somewhere, know that I'm doing this for you."

Riley's lips were pulled back to expose her teeth, showing her gums as she flattened her hands to the concrete and shoved up with all her strength. To her surprise, it was enough to topple Priest. The searing pain coming from her tattoo faded to a more manageable level, and Riley turned to face Priest.

"I will slaughter you, angel."

Priest, sprawled a few feet away on the concrete, sat up and flexed her wings. "Now we're getting somewhere." She stood up and said, "What shall I call you?"

"Call me what you like."

They circled each other, keeping the prison in the center of the room between them.

"It doesn't work like that. But I know names are power to a demon, so you'll want to keep yours close to the vest. I refuse to call you by Riley's name. How about I call you Contrariel?"

Riley laughed. "Whatever pleases you, milady."

The door above opened and Riley cringed. She turned her head away from the stairs and made quiet, almost unintelligible noises of irritation until the doors were shut.

"Good Girls are here," she grunted.

By the time she straightened up, Aissa had reached the bottom of the stairs. She wore a hooded sweatshirt over a rust-colored T shirt, a black skirt, and charcoal-colored stockings. Her curly blonde hair was loose, and a scarf was loosely draped over her shoulders to hang down in front of her. Riley ran her eyes up and down the girl before her lips curled into a smile.

"Kicked the habit and decided to slut it up a little, eh? You've got the body for it. Are you still a virgin, or have you gotten a little experience?"

Priest ignored Riley and focused on Aissa. "You shouldn't be here."

"She's my mentor. I should be here if this is when she falls."

"How sweet. C'mere and give me a kiss."

Aissa backed up a step and Riley laughed.

Priest put a hand on Aissa's shoulder. "I admire the strength it took for you to come here, Aissa. To face her. But this is not your challenge. It's not your fight." She looked at Riley again and said, "The Good Girls are praying for Riley. Can you feel it, Contrariel?"

Riley walked away. "They're wasting their breath."

Aissa frowned. "She wants to remain like this?"

"Why wouldn't I?" Riley said. "These past four years I've been fighting the demons with my hands tied behind my back. The only way I would ever win was if I got lucky. Well..." She gestured at herself and stepped closer to Aissa. "I got lucky. You know, I could do the same for you. All you have to do is let me in. I know you're thinking it's a bad thing now. This morning I would have said the same thing. But until you feel the power for yourself you just can't know." She held out her hand. She was just barely out of reach. "Let me show you."

Aissa took Riley's hand. Riley smiled, then hissed as the blade concealed by Aissa's fingers sliced through her palm.

"Little fucking sprite!" Her face became red, her eyes wide and spittle flying as she spoke. "I'll tear your goddamn head off for that."

Priest stepped between Riley and Aissa. Her uppercut glanced off Riley's chin, and Riley's feet were lifted off the ground before she landed in a heap.

"That was unwise, Aissa," Priest said. "But nicely done."

"The blade was dipped in holy water."

Priest nodded. "Go. Add your prayers to the others'."

"Are you sure you're all right alone?"

"I'll be fine. Go. Now, please."

Aissa looked at Riley. "If you kill Riley Parra, I won't rest until I've hunted you down and killed you."

Riley was still lying on her back, arms spread out to either side. "Good. I look forward to the rematch. Hide all the blades you want, little mouse. You have no idea what horrors *I* can hide. Run away, run away and pray."

Aissa backed away, not taking her eyes off Riley until she reached the stairs. Priest listened to her sneakers slapping the stone, waiting for the door to slam shut before she began to pace again. Riley's hand was dripping blood, healing slowly.

"How does that holy blood feel, Demon? Aissa believes in the sacraments, so she can use that sort of thing. Not like you."

Riley laughed. It was a hollow sound, echoed off the stones. "Such a heathen, right?"

"This world is full of heathens. It matters not how low you've fallen, so long as you keep your face turned toward Heaven."

Riley rolled onto her stomach. "Yeah, but if you're always looking up, you make it real easy for people to slit your throat. Trust is weakness."

Priest shook her head. "Trust is strength. When all else has failed you, when you can count on nothing else, you have to trust others. You trust me. You trust Kenzie. When the chips are down, the only weapon you have is the knowledge someone is watching your back. Are you really prepared to throw that away?"

"I don't need it anymore. I don't need anyone in my corner."

Priest said, "What about Gillian? Are you going to just throw her aside?"

Riley brushed the wound in her palm. "I'll do just fine on my own."

"Answer my question."

Riley looked up and frowned. "What question?"

"I'm willing to accept you're ready to turn your back on me, Kenzie, Chelsea, even Aissa. But Gillian? How can you do that to her? How can you forget the love you have for her?" Riley looked down at her palm again. "Demons can't love."

"What?" She looked up as if startled. "What does that have to do with anything?"

Priest furrowed her brow. "Are you questioning Gillian's importance?"

Riley laughed and shook her head. "I had no idea it would be so easy. You're not even trying now. Say *something*, Zerachiel."

"I... I've been..." Priest recalled several other instances where she'd mentioned Gillian's name, but the thing inside Riley had never acknowledged it. "I want to try something. Word association."

"Oh, for the love of..."

"Humor me."

Riley growled and motioned for Priest to get on with it.

Priest said, "Love."

"Weakness."

"Strength."

Riley rolled her shoulders back. "*Me*."

Priest ignored the posing. "Amusement."

Riley grinned. "You."

"Aissa."

"Child. No, victim."

Priest said, "Gillian."

"Are we done?"

"Briggs."

"Crooked."

"Orgasm."

Riley laughed. "Fun."

"Gillian."

Riley looked at the wall over Priest's shoulder, then looked down at her hands. Priest stepped closer. "Gillian." Riley brushed her thumb over her knuckles.

"Romance."

Riley looked up. "Oh, what is the point of this?" She waved her hand dismissively. "Fine, romance. Uh, distraction."

"Marriage."

Riley rolled her eyes. "Convenience. This is~"

"What about the ring?"

"A-ding-ding."

Priest said, "We're not playing now. I mean your ring, on your hand."

Riley looked at her right hand and raised her eyebrow, as if to imply Priest had lost her mind. Priest grabbed Riley's left hand, lifting it so Riley could see the gold ring on the third finger. "Your ring. Your wedding ring with~"

Riley snatched her hand away. "Don't touch me, angel."

Priest grabbed Riley's head with both hands and forced eye contact. "Gillian Hunt. Your wife. Acknowledge her, demon."

Riley cried out in pain and pulled away, punching Priest until she was released. She turned, nearly fell, and caught her hand against the wall to stay upright. "No. I... it's not... no. It's not important."

"Not important?" Priest backed up again, giving Riley room to pace. She was furious with herself for not following this thread earlier. "Gillian Hunt is the single most important person in Riley's life. They exchanged a vow to one another, life and death and sickness and health. But this travesty will break that. If you turn Riley into something else, you'll break that bond. Their marriage will shatter. Do you hear me, Riley? Can you hear me through whatever veil this demon is using on you?" She watched Riley closely for a reaction. "Your marriage will be destroyed, and Gillian will once again be free. With a heart as big as hers, as deeply as she feels love, do you believe she will remain single for very long? She'll find someone else."

Riley spun on Priest. "Stop it." Her face was a dangerous shade of purple, and spit flew when she spoke. The voice was barely recognizable. "Stop talking now, angel, or I shall pluck your wings apart one feather at a time."

"She will find love. And someone else will hold her at night. Someone else will kiss her lips. Another person will make love to her. And when Gillian's heart feels love, it will be for someone else.

Riley will just be her first wife. A memory that she mourns. For a while, anyway."

Sweat poured down Riley's face and she swiped at it with her sleeve. "It won't work. Fine. Let her find someone else. Probably... safer in the long run."

"It won't happen like that." Priest began to move in a circle. "This demonic force has tainted Riley Parra, but you were right. It's not a possession; it's a mingling of energies. The demon is overwhelming Riley, and it will win, but the shell will still be Riley's. The demon will have her thoughts and her needs and her love. Riley is tainting the demon with mortality, just like I was tainted with the idea of Caitlin Priest, a human who had been formed out of whole cloth. Imagine how much worse the taint will be with a living, breathing human being..."

Riley was almost panting now. Sweat dripped off her chin as she tracked Priest with her eyes.

"The demon will win. And when it wins, the little part of Riley that is left behind will go to Gillian."

"No."

"And when Gillian rejects this abomination, the demon will have no other recourse but to murder her to keep her from moving on."

Riley screamed wordlessly.

"Unless you stop it. Right now. Unless you fight it, Riley. Fight this God damned thing."

Riley opened her eyes and turned toward Priest. "Cait..."

Priest braced herself for another onslaught. "Yes?"

"Tell... me how... to stop... it." Each word was forced, erupting from her mouth like bullets. She wobbled a bit, almost dropping before she corrected herself. Her face was a dangerous shade of violet, and her eyes rolled back as she finally hit her knees. Priest knelt in front of her, hands shaking, and cupped the back of Riley's head with both hands.

"You'll feel the demon fighting when I begin to pull. Imagine an ocean with an oil slick. When the oil begins to recede, you need to keep it from flowing back in. Can you do that?"

Riley closed her eyes.

"Riley! You have to answer me, Riley."

"Yeah-huh. Uh-huh." She pressed her lips together and nodded. "Hurry."

Priest spread her wings to their full span. Each feather was spread apart from the others, and light glowed from each vein. The room filled with light, and Riley shrunk in on herself with a weak whimper of pain.

"Hold, Riley."

"Glah..." Riley choked on the sound and shook her head. "Mine. Eyes. Have seen. The... glory of... the... coming..." She cried out in pain before she could voice the next words. "The Lord. He... is... dun duh dun... duh duh... grapes of wrath are... stored."

"What are you doing?"

"Praise... makes you stronger." She growled and thrashed her head from side to side. "Need you strong. Glory. Glory..."

"Battle Hymn," Priest said. "Apt."

Riley smiled weakly. "Be better if I knew the words."

"Focus on the chorus."

Riley grimaced. "His truth is... march...ing... on... Glory, glory, hallelujah."

As Riley sang, her voice became stronger. Sweat flowed down either side of her face, and then she suddenly pushed away from Priest.

"No!" She fell onto her back, and Priest retreated.

Riley's body was shrouded in the only darkness that remained in the otherwise shining basement. She rolled onto her front and crawled on her elbows to the trap painted in the middle of the space. She recoiled but continued on until she was entirely inside. Priest stood and guided her divinity into the barrier to reinforce its strength. It snapped up, and Riley convulsed in pain. She held her stomach and began to shake, and Priest's eyes filled with tears as she watched Riley writhe.

"Fight it," Priest whispered. "You're stronger than it is, Riley. You always have been."

Dust began raining down from the ceiling and Priest looked up. The Good Girls had increased their prayers, and they rained down on the ensnared evil like a cyclone.

"Demon. Leave my friend. Return to the depths from which you were spawned. You will not have her soul today, nor will you ever hold her in your sway. *Egressens necessos victavi voceramus empto exerrimum.*" She pushed her hand against the barrier, as solid to her as if it was brick, and concentrated her power through it. Priest's eyes darkened. "Get the fuck out of my friend."

Riley howled, the veins in her neck standing out as she directed her shouts at the ceiling. Her voice slowly faded to a croak, and she clutched an arm to her stomach as she crumpled inside the barrier. She was still panting when Priest lowered her hand. The barrier was still up.

"Riley... crawl out."

"I can't."

"Yes, you can. Crawl out."

Riley lifted her head to gauge the distance and shook her head in denial of her abilities, but she began to crawl. Her hand passed through the barrier, and Priest took it in hers. She pulled, and Riley crawled the rest of the way through the barrier. It sizzled slightly as she passed through. Priest looked past Riley and saw a shimmering shroud of darkness remained behind her. It was all that remained of Falco's essence, his demonic energy reduced to a haze.

"Be gone."

The air inside the trap flared golden-white and, when it faded, the barrier collapsed. There was no more threat. Priest sat down on the concrete floor and pulled Riley onto her lap. She cradled her friend's head, brushed the hair out of her face, and smiled at the familiar person looking back at her.

"Riley. Nice to see you again."

"Hi." She grunted and looked down at her hand. The knife wound was still there, ugly and red, and Priest took off her tie to wrap it.

"How is your tattoo?"

"Feels fine, now." Riley looked at her left hand. "I kept grabbing for my ring. Trying to hold onto it. I think it and the tattoo both played a part in keeping me around."

"I wouldn't be surprised." Riley's eyelids dropped and then snapped open. "You must be exhausted."

"I... it's..."

Riley's voice cut off as she went limp, and Priest tightened her grip to prevent her from slumping to the floor. She held Riley tight and twisted to look toward the stairs. "Aissa! Chelsea, Kenzie, I need help." She looked down at Riley, confirmed she was just sleeping, and smiled when she heard them descending the stone steps to help her carry Riley home.

Gillian was waiting at the top of the stairs when they got Riley home. She was leaning on her cane, but she let it drop and took Kenzie's position under Riley's right arm. With Priest on the other side, they ushered the semi-conscious Riley into the apartment.

Gillian put her hand on Riley's stomach and looked at Priest for an explanation. Priest exhaled and shook her head. "It's an incredibly long story. Which I will tell you after you have bathed Riley and put her to bed. If you don't mind, of course."

"Mind?" Gillian said. "Help me get her into the bathroom. Is she okay?"

"She's been fighting hard all day. Her body has been forced to do things a mortal body isn't equipped for. She's strong, though, and I helped where I could. She just needs sleep."

They took her into the bathroom and Gillian sat her on the edge of the tub. Priest excused herself to get food, and shut the door behind her. Gillian knelt in front of Riley, who had again dozed off. She brushed Riley's cheek, and her eyes opened. She smiled weakly.

"Hey."

Gillian smiled. "Hi, there. I'm trying not to be offended by the fact you're falling asleep while I'm undressing you."

"I'll try to pay closer attention."

"That's all I ask." She looked at Riley's shirt once she had it off. She slipped her finger through a ragged tear, then looked at the corresponding smear of blood on her abdomen. She could smell a slight hint of burnt gunpowder, and the edges of the tear were scorched. A contact burn. She looked up at Riley without condemnation. "This looks like a bullet hole. I've seen a couple of them in this particular area. Usually they're on corpses I'm autopsying."

"I'm a little livelier than that."

"Barely." She put aside the shirt and helped Riley out of her bloodstained pants. She refused to ask any questions. Riley was in no shape to be interrogated, and she knew Priest would fill her in after she finished. She helped Riley into the tub and let it finish filling with water. She took a sponge and began to wash away the more obvious bloodstains. She scanned Riley's arms and legs, her torso and face. Her relief at finding no wounds other than the cut on her palm was overwhelmed by her curiosity.

"Usually when you come home like this, I have to change bandages for a week or two."

"The thing I was fighting healed my wounds."

Gillian raised an eyebrow. "Really. Well, that's a nice enemy."

"It wanted my body."

"I can't really fault him for that." She ran the sponge over Riley's chest and squeezed. Water followed the shape of her breasts and Riley murmured in approval. Though her physical wounds were minor, there were bags under her eyes. She looked more exhausted than Gillian was comfortable with. "Are you sure you're okay?"

"I will be. Thanks to Priest. She saved my life. Again."

"Then I owe her a nice bottle of wine." She finished washing Riley and gestured for her right hand. "Let me clean that for you." The bloody tie was undone, and Gillian hissed through her teeth at the sight of it. "God. The thing you were fighting didn't heal this one?"

"Aissa did that."

Gillian narrowed her eyes. "Aissa? Why...?"

Riley shook her head. "It was good. I was glad she did it. Made me proud of her."

Gillian washed away the dried blood and briefly left the bathroom to get the first-aid kit from the kitchen. When she returned, she cleaned and dressed the wound in a way that allowed Riley the use of her hand.

"Can you at least tell me who you were fighting?"

"Priest."

"And Aissa?"

"She was Priest's backup."

Gillian glanced toward the closed door. "Is it... safe with her here?"

Riley nodded without hesitation. "She saved my life."

Gillian sighed. "This had better be one hell of an explanation."

"Heh." Riley coughed and sank lower in the tub. She furrowed her brow as if the cough hurt her, then turned her head and looked at Gillian. "Hey. Get in here with me."

Gillian grinned. "This is not the time, Detective Parra."

"I don't want sex. I just want you as close as possible."

Gillian looked for signs Riley was being prurient and found none. She put the sponge on the side of the tub and stood up. She was already barefoot, so she slipped out of her jeans and underwear. She draped her sweater over the towel rod, but left her undershirt and bra on as she stepped into the water. She lowered herself, her knees under Riley's arms, and Riley crossed her wrists under Gillian's shirt. The hem of the shirt floated around her waist like a water lily.

"Sure you're okay?"

Riley smiled and nodded. "I'll survive. It was a close thing. I'm not even going to lie about it. If Priest hadn't been there, and if she hadn't done everything in her power, I wouldn't be here right now."

"I'm really glad you have her back. Would Sariel have gone~"

"No. Sariel wouldn't even have fought." She ran her wet hands down Gillian's back and cupped her ass with both hands. "The woman I work with is now definitely more Priest than Zerachiel. She traded up. The power of an angel with the heart of a mortal. It's a really good trade as far as I'm concerned."

Gillian nodded. "Me too." She bent down and kissed Riley, then retrieved the sponge and resumed her bath. When she was finished, Riley felt strong enough to walk to the bedroom under her own power. Gillian stayed by her side as a crutch, both of them dressed in robes for the short walk from the bathroom to the bed. Riley went down without a protest, allowed Gillian to tuck her in, and drifted off quickly.

Gillian dressed in a pair of old jeans and a T shirt before she went to rejoin the group in the kitchen. Kenzie, Chelsea and Priest were at the kitchen table, and Aissa was sitting on the counter with her feet dangling. Gillian snapped her fingers and pointed at the floor, and Aissa hopped down with an apology. A pizza box was standing open on the table. Everyone had paper towels with slices on them, but no one seemed interested in eating.

Priest stood up as Gillian joined them. Gillian crossed her arms over her chest, her relief and gratitude at finding Riley in one piece replaced by anger and confusion.

"Someone... start talking. Now."

"We were wrong about Falco's master plan," Priest said, indicating Gillian should take her seat.

By the time Priest finished talking, all but two slices of the pizza had been consumed. Gillian had no appetite, and the others were only picking at their food. Finally Gillian leaned back and, despite not eating much, took the time to wipe her hands and lips with a napkin. Priest was leaning against the counter between the stove and fridge, and Aissa had sunk down to sit cross-legged on the floor. Kenzie and Chelsea were holding hands. Gillian watched them, knowing that despite their concern for Riley, they were still recovering from the brief gift of sight Priest had bestowed on them.

Priest said, "I didn't anticipate how far Falco and Marchosias were willing to go in order to get Riley in their pocket. The Five Families have been all but wiped out, and there's a power vacuum in No Man's Land. Marchosias is now most likely going to focus on filling those positions with new and improved acolytes. And now that Riley's slipped out of his grip for a second time, he's going to stop going after her as his new champion."

Kenzie said, "Well, that's a good thing, right?"

Priest shrugged. "In the short run, of course. But our brief peace will most likely be at an end. Marchosias will choose a new champion, one who is more likely to accept his terms than Riley was. Riley's going to have a new enemy within the month. Maybe even within the next two weeks." She had been avoiding Gillian's gaze. "I'm sorry, Gillian. I should have been thinking long term, I should have looked~"

"Shut up." Gillian pushed her chair back, the legs scraping on the tile as she stood up and stepped around the table. Priest straightened and braced to be struck, but Gillian embraced her. Priest relaxed and returned the hug. "Thank you, Caitlin. You keep bringing her back to me."

"It's my job."

"No, it's not. Not exactly. And that's why I'm grateful." She stepped back and rubbed Priest's shoulders, then looked at Kenzie and Chelsea. "Will you two take this woman home and fuck her until she can't stand up straight?"

Kenzie grinned. "I think that could be arranged."

Priest blushed and squeezed Gillian's arm. "Are you certain Riley is okay?"

"She's in one piece. She's in her own bed. She's about to be cuddled by me all night. I think she'll be okay."

Chelsea said, "With the two of you in her corner, there's nothing she can't overcome." She stood up. "Cait, Kenzie and I didn't have a chance to properly thank you for the gift you gave us. I think we'll take Gillian's suggestion if you'd like to come home with us. Riley's not the only one who had a tough day today."

Priest's weary smile made her look more human than she had since she was reunited with Zerachiel. "I think that would be very nice. Thank you." She kissed Gillian's cheek. "Let me know if you need anything else tonight."

"I think you've gone above and beyond today, Caitlin. Go home. Reap the benefits of being good on the mortal plane."

She nodded. Kenzie and Chelsea led the way out, with Kenzie slipping an arm around Priest's waist as they left the apartment. Aissa stood, and Gillian smiled at her.

"Do you need a ride somewhere?"

"No... you should stay with Riley. Thank you, though." She

glanced toward the bedroom, and for a brief moment Gillian was reminded of how painfully young the girl was. Too young to deal with the reality of the job she had been recruited for.

"Do you want to talk?"

Aissa looked at her and looked ready to refuse, but then looked down at her feet. "How can she do this to you?"

Gillian was thrown by the question. "Pardon?"

"How could she marry you, knowing that she'll constantly be in danger?" She looked at Gillian. "It's selfish."

Gillian said, "She loves me."

"If she really loved you, she would keep you as far away from Marchosias and his minions as possible."

"That's wrong. Being the champion doesn't make you a machine, Aissa. It doesn't shut down your heart. And if it did... if it did, it would make you a lesser person. You would just be a weapon waiting for the next time you needed to be implemented. Riley needs a real life. She needs a home. She needs something to come back to. She needs someone to fight for. It's what makes her so formidable. And when she does come home, and she's been beaten and battered, she needs someone to hold her, which is what I'm going to do tonight. When she has nightmares about what that damned demon was doing in her brain, I'll be there to tell her it's all right. Priest and the tattoo keep her alive. I keep her sane."

Aissa looked down at her shoes.

"Don't pass up on... anything... just because of that tattoo Riley gave you. Don't pass up love or friendship just because you're worried about the one day you don't come home. You'll be glad they are every single night you do make it home." She looked into the living room and gestured with her chin. "You can crash on the couch if you want. I have blankets and a pillow..."

Aissa shook her head. "No, thank you. I'll walk. I've been out of No Man's Land all afternoon, and I'm getting anxious." She smiled apologetically. "I shouldn't have said anything about you and Riley's marriage..."

"I'm glad you did. I've been thinking those things for a while now, but saying them out loud makes them more real to me." She looked at the remaining pizza and picked up the paper towel roll. She wrapped the leftovers and handed them over. "Here... I'm not going to send you out into the night empty handed."

"Thank you, Dr. Hunt."

"Gillian. And don't be afraid to ask me whatever you want."

"I'll keep that in mind."

Gillian walked her to the door. "Are you sure you're okay getting home on your own?"

"Oh, yeah. I'm really starting to learn the streets." She looked back at the bedroom. "Apologize to Riley for the knife, please?"

"She said that made her proud."

Aissa smiled and looked at her feet. "She said that?"

"Riley's never doubted making you her successor. But I think what you did today showed her that she definitely made the right choice."

"Well." She shuffled her feet shyly. "I should go. They'll be expecting me at the shelter."

"Okay." Gillian fought down the urge to tell Aissa to call when she got there so they wouldn't worry. "Have a good night, Aissa."

"You too, Dr. Hunt."

Gillian considered correcting her again, but she let it drop. Aissa turned and Gillian closed the door. It was still relatively early, but she wasn't going to stay up while Riley was alone. She took the time to toss the greasy paper towels and turn off the lights, and she undressed except for her T shirt before she joined Riley under the blankets. Riley murmured and rolled onto her back, and Gillian embraced her.

"Sh. Go back to sleep. It's me."

Riley turned toward Gillian and burrowed against her. Gillian stroked Riley's hair, which was damp from sweat due to some nightmare. Gillian kissed Riley's temple and resigned herself to not getting much sleep. She didn't stay up all night very often, but she still technically had convalescent leave coming up so she could sleep late. Besides, a little weariness was a small price to pay to be awake when Riley needed her. Riley had her fights, and Gillian had hers. She was happy to do her part.

She settled in for a long night.

Kenzie left Chelsea panting on the bed, wrapped herself in a sheet, and went in search of their errant third member. Priest was sitting on the window seat, naked with her knees pulled up to her chest, bathed in moonlight that made her sweat sparkle. She heard Kenzie's bare feet on the hardwood floor and turned, smiled, and swept her hair behind her ear before looking out the window again.

"There you are. You're not tired already, are you?"

"No. Is Chelsea...?"

"She's spent for now. I was hoping you and I could entice her to go another round." The sheet fell off Kenzie's shoulder, nearly exposing one nipple. She tilted her head and noticed how melancholy Priest seemed. "You okay?"

"Oh, I'm fine. I forgot how lovely you two were." She smiled. "And how insatiable."

"Well, we're ladies of taste and refinement. You can't expect us to be happy with some quick wham-bam." She stood near the edge of the window seat and stroked Priest's hair. "What's wrong, little angel?"

Priest angled her head into Kenzie's embrace, her eyes closed like a cat being petted. "I'm concerned about Riley."

"Well, she has Gillian. She's home, and she's safe."

"Right. But today I saved Riley from becoming a demon by reminding her that Gillian as at home waiting for her. I tried everything else in my power, I tried coercion and arguing, I tried physical violence, and none of it worked. Gillian was the key, and only Gillian was strong enough to break the demon's hold and make Riley fight."

Kenzie was confused. "That's a good thing, right?"

"I suppose. I don't know." She looked out the window. "It concerns me. Gillian has been possessed by demons twice, and she once left town for a year without any of us knowing when or if she would return. That accident in the ambulance could have been far more tragic than it was. Gillian is Riley's heart and soul, and she's an anchor that keeps Riley grounded. If anything ever does happen and she loses Gillian... I'm afraid that not even I will be powerful enough to save Riley from the darkness."

Kenzie put her arms around Priest's shoulders, and Priest rested her head against Kenzie's chest as she sat in the moonlight and worried.

HAMMERS & NAILS

Lauderdale-by-the-Sea, Florida

The black sedan was parked to face a bike path, angled so the man behind the wheel could see the water. He wore a lightweight suit the color of cream, a baby blue shirt open at the collar, and he was waiting to see the sun rise over the water. His hair was a mixture of gray and white, cut short on the sides and a little longer on top. Twin creases ran down either side of his face, framing a mouth that only a select few had ever seen turned up in a smile. One hand rested on top of the steering wheel, angled so he could see the face of his watch.

When the first rays of the sun peeked over the horizon, he slipped a pair of sunglasses over eyes so light blue that they matched his shirt. He dropped his hand, delighted in his own way at the sight before him. He'd never watched the sunrise over water before. It was beautiful. The sky changed colors, and the night melted away. Twelve minutes later, with the sun firmly in its throne, a blue Volkswagen panel van backed into the spot next to him. Also precisely on schedule, he was pleased to discover.

Roland Knox stepped out of his car and walked to the van as its driver and passenger climbed out. The passenger was young and Cuban, the driver a surfer type with spiked blonde hair and no T-shirt under his unbuttoned Tommy Bahama. They were local boys, trustworthy and reliable, and he greeted them with quick nods as the trio moved to the back of the van.

"Did he give you any trouble?"

The driver smiled as he unlatched the back door. "No more than they usually do. We can handle it."

He opened the door and stepped back so Roland could see their cargo. The man lying in the back of the truck was stripped to a pair of boxers, his hands chained to opposite sides of the van. He hung in the center of the space, arms stretched out to either side, and weakly lifted his head as the new sun's light poured into the dark space. Fresh bruises bloomed on his face. His jaw and right eye both looked swollen, and his lips were so bloody that it looked like a child's attempt at playing with makeup. Roland took hold of the door and hauled himself up and inside.

"Good morning, Mr. Van Owen. Do you know what you're doing here?"

"No... please. These maniacs grabbed me out of my home in the middle of the night, beat the shit out of me, chained me in this goddamn rape mobile~"

Roland smiled. "Rest assured, Mr. Van Owen, my men weren't hired to rape you." Behind him, he could hear the driver and passenger laughing. He ignored it. "That's more the sort of thing *you* hire people for, hm? Rape and extortion, that's just the sort of thing Clyde Van Owen gets out of bed for. Bobby, how lucrative have Mr. Van Owen's endeavors been for him?"

"Sweet-ass house, boss. Three cars. Julio says he saw a maid coming in while we were scoping the place out this past week."

"Cuban?" Roland asked.

"*Sí.*" Julio had been born in America, but he liked playing up his heritage when surrounded by white men.

Roland sighed and looked at Van Owen again. "How little did you pay her? How much more would you have paid a white woman to do the same job? No, better question... how much would you have wanted to be paid for doing the same job? I bet the discrepancy would have at least doubled the poor woman's income. Thieves always seem so much stingier with their ill-gotten gains than those who actually work for it. Strange."

Van Owen swallowed hard. "I-is this because... I mean... are you guys, like, the maid Better Business Bureau or something?"

"Would you like something to drink?" He reached into his jacket and took out a flask. "You've had a hard morning."

"Yeah. Yes, please..."

Roland unscrewed the cap. Van Owen tilted his chin back and Roland dribbled some water over his lips. Van Owen swallowed once, then convulsed. He coughed violently, and Roland stepped back before any blood could mar his nice pale suit. Van Owen finished coughing and hung from the chains looking even weaker than before. He lifted his ashen face, eyes sunken into black pits, and bared blood-smeared teeth.

"What the hell did you give me?"

"Holy water, Mr. Van Owen." Roland's voice was chipper. He returned the cap to the holy water and took a piece of chalk from another pocket. He stepped forward and began drawing symbols on the metal floor where Van Owen was kneeling. "You can drop the poor confused victim act. It won't make us feel sorry for you no matter how pathetic you make yourself appear."

Van Owen rolled his shoulders and narrowed his eyes. "All right. So you have parlor tricks. What do you want? A cut of the proceeds?"

"You don't know who I am, do you?"

"Some ass in a suit. I don't know. What should I care?"

Roland smiled. "Oh, you should care very much, Clyde. Because I represent the good people of this town. Do you think their prayers would go unanswered just because it's a small community? Did you think you could operate with impunity because the angels were too busy focusing on the big cities like New York and London? Those cities get someone permanent to watch over them because they're important. Small towns like this one, well, unfortunately they have to wait until someone can come down here and clean house. I'm a champion, Mr. Van Owen, and I have been sent to stop you from further victimizing these fine folks."

"No..." Some of the bravado had gone out of him, but it wasn't the simpering put-on that he'd been playing earlier. The demon wearing Clyde Van Owen's body was scared. "I'll leave. I'll go somewhere else..."

Roland's smile faded. "And I'd follow you. I don't protect a city, or a geographic region. I cover the blind spots, Mr. Van Owen. I make sure Hellheads like you don't fly under the radar. So wherever you go, you can be damn sure I would follow you."

"Hey, boss? You got a visitor."

Roland raised an eyebrow without turning around. "Hm. Bobby... you've been itching to do one of these yourself. Why don't you give it a shot?"

"Yeah?"

"The apprentice must learn eventually." He straightened and brushed his hands together. The van sagged under Bobby's weight as he climbed inside. "Don't do it too quickly. Exorcise the beast slowly so you can be certain you're doing it right."

Van Owen's eyes widened. "No! That will be torture."

"That's the *idea*, idiot." Bobby cleared his throat and began reciting the Latin phrases he'd spent the last six months memorizing. Van Owen began screaming almost immediately, and Roland jumped from the back of the van so Julio could close the doors. The sound immediately cut off; their soundproofing worked wonders. Roland adjusted the collar of his shirt and looked at Julio, who nodded toward the edge of the parking lot. Roland looked and saw a surprisingly tall, dangerously slender bald man in a baggy tank top and swim trunks that reached past his knees. He walked over and stood beside the new arrival.

"What in Heaven's name are you wearing?"

Phanuel looked down at his clothes. "I'm blending in."

"No. You're not." He smiled and shook his head as he joined the angel in watching the tide. "We've got the guy who has been running around this place."

"Yes, I heard. Well done. I have a new assignment for you."

Roland laughed. "You mean that email I got? You were serious?" The angel didn't respond. "I don't work in the big towns, especially not ones that already have a champion."

"This is an unusual situation, Agent Knox. The champion *is* the reason we're sending you there. We need some boots on the ground, a fresh set of human eyes to let us know just exactly what is happening."

"Something big going on with the Ladder?"

Phanuel hesitated. "No... not yet. Although He tells us to be prepared for something of great importance regarding the Ladder. It would appear that the local champion was present when a demon perished. The energy went into her, and she became one of them."

Roland tensed. "God in Heaven." He dipped his chin and said a quick prayer. "Okay. You don't have to say anymore. I'll get up there and take care of her."

"That... won't be necessary. She is mortal again."

"She can't be."

"She is. Her guardian angel stood beside her and, when they

emerged from the room, the champion was whole once again." Phanuel looked at Roland. "We need to understand exactly what has occurred so we can trust the champion and her angel in the future. We believe trusting them will become of vital importance soon."

Roland shook his head. "All right. I'll go."

Phanuel nodded and looked at the water again. "Do you believe these conditions are appropriate for surfing?"

Roland couldn't stop himself from laughing. "Ask Bobby when he's done with our guest. He might even loan you a board. Just watch out for sharks." He turned and strolled back to his car. He took out his phone and scrolled to the message he'd gotten a few hours earlier, but he saw that the other champion wasn't mentioned by name in the request. "Phanuel. This champion I'm supposed to check out. What's her name?"

"Riley. Stop fidgeting." Gillian moved her hand from Riley's shoulder to the back of her neck. She squeezed with two fingers and her thumb, massaging in gentle circles that made Riley close her eyes. They were sitting in the back pew, near the door "in case of escape," Riley had joked when they first arrived. Now she wasn't entirely certain she had been joking. The opening prayers felt maudlin, and the readings were endless. She felt like everyone was somehow staring at her without turning their heads. Mirrors, maybe.

It didn't help that she felt like she was undercover. She was wearing a skirt, a gray pleated skirt that draped over her knees, and uncomfortable heels. Her arms were bare, but the shoulder straps of her blouse were wide enough to hide her tattoo. Her hair was down, and she kept reaching up to tuck it behind her ears.

Gillian, on the other hand, looked resplendent in a pale green dress. Riley reached over and squeezed her thigh, and Gillian covered Riley's fingers with her own.

Riley was still having trouble believing church was her idea. After the incident with Falco a few days earlier, she decided she needed all the goodness she could get. Sitting through a sermon for one morning seemed like it would do the trick and maybe solidify her as being one of the good guys again.

She'd entered the church without hesitation, even dipped her fingers in the font of holy water just to make sure it didn't burn. She held the hymnal and the Bible without burning. But after only a few minutes of the Gospel she was starting to feel like the walls are closing in. She reached for her hair again.

Gillian's hand tightened on the back of Riley's neck. "Stop. Fidgeting."

"Yes, mother."

Gillian leaned in, her lips brushing Riley's ear. "If you're going to call me that, I prefer mommy."

Riley shivered and inwardly cursed the fact they were in church. She leaned back against Gillian's hand. Gillian began to move her fingers again, and the massage got her through the rest of the sermon. After standing for one more sing-along, which Riley only mouthed along with so she could hear Gillian's beautiful voice, they were set free. Gillian slipped an arm around Riley's and let herself be carried out, pausing only briefly to greet people before they were finally out of the church and back in the sunlight.

"You did well in there," Gillian said.

"Good to know. So I'm officially not a demon?"

Gillian smiled. "As far as I'm concerned, you've passed with flying colors. Priest has been convinced since you guys left the Cell."

Riley stopped halfway across the parking lot and turned to face her. "I don't care what Priest thinks. I only care that you know, I mean really know, that I'm one hundred percent me. After what you've been through, I don't want a shred of doubt in your mind."

"Thank you, sweetie." She lightly kissed Riley's lips. "You're you. I have no doubt whatsoever. And the fact you were willing to sit through the most boring church service I've ever seen just for my peace of mind - in a skirt, no less - means the world to me." She slipped her hand down Riley's arm until their palms were lined up. She laced their fingers together and walked to the car. "Want to pick up some lunch on the way home?"

"Sure. You pick; I'm not hungry for anything in particular."

"Chicken?"

"Sounds good."

"Want to pick up Priest on the way?"

"Ah..." She shook her head and let her voice trail off, but Gillian glanced sideways at her, prompting her to go on. "No. Priest has gotten very in tune with her mortal side lately, but Zerachiel gets the same thrill from worship as always. So when the two combine, she's, ah..." She cleared her throat and looked to make sure no one was close enough to overhear. "She masturbates herself into a stupor on Sunday mornings and then spends the rest of the day recovering."

Gillian laughed. "Whoa. Go, Cait. So maybe we won't interrupt her for chicken."

"Yeah, I'm thinking."

When they were in the car, Riley took off her heels as Gillian started the car and maneuvered out of the parking lot. An hour in a church, some mediocre songs, all capped by a quick kiss on the lips from Gillian Hunt. Riley smiled and stretched out her toes. There was an infinite number of worse ways to spend a Sunday morning.

Riley was out of her skirt as soon as she was back in the apartment, shedding clothes on her way to the bedroom. She changed into a pair of track pants and an old T-shirt and felt comfortable for the first time since she woke up that morning. They ate on the couch and watched an old movie on TV. Gillian took a nap with her head on Riley's shoulder, and Riley tried to stay as still as possible so she wouldn't be disturbed. The day felt fragile; the fact they were both off duty and neither of them had any obligations meant they could spend the entire day together. She stroked her wife's hair, watched the people moving around on the TV in the hopes it would coalesce into some kind of plot she could follow, and let herself relax.

The next morning, Briggs woke Riley five minutes before her alarm with a call to come in early. Riley hung up and twisted to see Gillian was also awake, so she bent over to kiss her good morning. "Duty calls."

"Keep the streets safe."

"Will do. Go back to sleep." She tucked the blankets tighter around Gillian's shoulders and got out of bed. She dressed blind, not wanting to further disturb Gillian's sleep. She checked in the living room to make sure her outfit wasn't too atrocious before she left the apartment, a Pop Tart caught between her lips as she shrugged into her jacket on the way downstairs. The sun was just starting to reflect off the windows in No Man's Land, casting a golden glow down onto the streets as she drove to the office.

Priest was already at her desk and stood when she saw Riley approaching. "Good morning. You look rested."

"Sunday, day of rest," Riley said. "What does the boss want? Were you here when she called?"

"I was. She's been in her office with someone for a while. He looked very official. There's something..." She narrowed her eyes and thrust her chin forward, shaking her head as if giving up on hope of finishing the sentence.

"What? Is he a bad guy?"

"Not necessarily. He just feels different from everyone else. I can't figure out why. I'm not alarmed by his presence in any way. I feel if something bad happened, he would stand alongside us to stop it and protect innocent people."

"Well, super." Riley knocked on Briggs' office door as she stepped inside. Briggs was at her desk, and a man in a cream-colored suit was standing in front of her. He turned when the door opened. He looked to be in his mid-sixties, his gray hair slicked back. His eyes wrinkled when he smiled, and he offered Riley a weather-beaten hand. She took it and was gratified that he didn't feel the need to crush her fingers in the grip. She offered him a polite squeeze.

"You must be Detective Parra. People have told me good things about you."

"Then they must have left out the interesting bits." Riley glanced at Briggs for the official introduction.

"Riley Parra, Caitlin Priest. This is Special Agent Roland Knox with the FBI. He requested your help on a case he's been following."

He nodded once, his expression instantly becoming grave. He picked up a file and looked at Priest. "Were you working with Detective Parra during the Angel Maker investigation?"

Riley and Priest exchanged a look. Priest nodded slowly. "For the vast majority of it. Yes, sir."

Knox smiled again. "No need for that. You can just call me Knox or Rollie. I'm not picky." He opened the file and handed Riley a crime-scene photograph. The photograph showed a man standing upright against a wooden stake, his arms stretched out to either side and strapped to a crossbar. His head hung down against his chest, and the amount of blood on his shirt left little doubt as to the cause of death.

"Two nights ago, an officer in your precinct found this body in an alley off Wallace Street. It was assigned to your Detective, ah... Delgado. It set off an alert with us in Washington; the display of the body matched a killer we've been calling the Scarecrow." He smiled and shrugged almost apologetically. "A few agents had a more religious name for how the body was left, but some people took offense. Scarecrow is more accurate anyway. We thought, what with this being your neck of the woods and your recent success with the Angel Maker, we would avail ourselves of your services."

"Detective Delgado is okay with handing the case over?"

Briggs nodded. "He wasn't too keen about working with the FBI."

Riley looked back at Knox and caught him staring hard at her. For a moment she felt as if he was examining her, watching for some kind of tell. She furrowed her brow as his face relaxed and became jovial once more. She nodded.

"Okay. I'll get the file from him and we'll see where we stand."

Knox said, "Fantastic. We need to speak with the victim's roommate. Ah, perhaps Detective Priest could get the file and she could give us both an update before we speak to the roommate. I was hoping I could speak to Detective Parra one-on-one before we began investigating. There is a bit of sensitive minutiae I have to go over before we can officially combine forces."

Riley glanced at Priest and raised her eyebrows. *You sure about this guy?* she asked without asking.

Priest answered with a shrug and a subtle nod.

"All right. Cait, you don't mind driving yourself?"

"No. I enjoy driving." She smiled and walked out of the office.

Briggs cleared her throat and pointed after Priest. "Has she... passed...?"

"We're working on it," Riley said. "She'll be fine. Come on, Agent Knox. I'll show you the way out."

She walked him to the elevator and waited for two people to disembark before stepping into the empty car. Knox joined her and stood in front of the buttons as Riley pressed Lobby. The doors closed and the car smoothly went into motion. They were halfway between the first and second floors when Knox's right hand shot out like a gunslinger's quick draw. He jabbed the Emergency Stop with two fingers and pivoted to face Riley.

"We don't have much time, Detective Parra, so I suggest you listen closely. I need you to get rid of your partner so we're able to speak freely for the duration of my stay."

Riley had drawn her gun while he was speaking and pressed it against his chest. "How about you restart this elevator and rethink the definition of cooperation?"

Knox rolled his eyes and reached for his shirt collar. Riley furrowed her brow as he pushed his tie aside and began undoing the buttons.

"What the hell are you doing?"

"Just trust me, Detective." He reached inside and tugged up his undershirt, baring a muscular and smooth chest that would be the envy of a man half his age. In the center of his chest, just below his collarbone, was a tattoo of ornate flames dancing inside a half-circle. Riley let her gun lower a bit, and he took that as an invitation to explain. "If I'm not mistaken, your tattoo is a pair of torches joined at the base, on your right shoulder. It's a symbol of protection from your guardian angel and marks your status as champion for good. It is anathema to demons and you can draw strength from it. It allows you to resist demonic energy to a certain degree."

"Who are you?"

He tugged down his shirt and began working the buttons again. "Everything you know about me is the truth, Detective. My name is Roland Knox and I am an agent with the Federal Bureau of Investigation. But I am also a champion, like you. The difference is I'm a little higher on the payroll. I have been doing this for a very long time, so I've been entrusted with the job of making certain you're completely... intact... following your recent flirtation with the dark side."

Riley holstered her gun. "Great. Why didn't~"

Something landed on top of the elevator car and they both looked up. The access hatch was pulled up, and Priest jumped down into the car. She flipped in the air, grabbed Knox by the collar, and slammed him against the wall hard enough to make the entire car rattle. Riley grabbed her by the shoulders. "Whoa, Cait. Cool off a little..."

"What are you doing? Why did the elevator stop?"

"He just wanted to talk to me about my little episode the other day. Apparently the higher-ups are worried I'm not looking out for the company's best interests anymore."

Knox frowned. "She... knows?"

"Of course she knows. She's my partner. And my angel."

"Your..." He looked even more confused now. "What is your name?"

"Detective Caitlin Priest. Zerachiel."

Knox shook his head slowly. "You're her angel? And you also work as her partner? That is... that's unheard of!"

"We seem to do all right," Riley said. "Priest, lay off him a little, would ya?"

Priest let go of Knox's suit and stepped back, but she kept her eyes locked on him.

Riley stood between the two of them. She doubted Priest would attack him again, but she felt more comfortable with them separated. "Okay, so you're here to give me a performance evaluation, right? That's the general idea?"

Knox smoothed down his clothes. "Yes. I'll observe how you work, how you interact with your associates, and I'll give my report to... well, the people to whom we answer."

Priest said, "Why didn't they just ask me for my opinion?"

"No offense, Zerachiel, but you were down in that basement, too. What is it called, the Cell? Besides, our friends would prefer an outside opinion of the situation."

"And the case? This Scarecrow business was just a happy coincidence?"

"Ah. No, actually. Everything you saw in the file was manufactured by me last night. Your Detective Delgado's case is authentic, of course. I just hacked into your files, found something suitably unusual, and created a serial killer who matched the modus operandi. We'll solve the case and I will declare it's not the work of the Scarecrow. It's not exactly a lie."

"Nice line you've drawn," Riley muttered. "What happens if you decide I'm a risk? Or if you can't fully clear me?"

Knox shrugged. "Then you get your wish, Detective." He smiled and looked at Priest. "Word among us is that you've been looking for a way out. You want a chance to resign your position as champion to hand the mantle to your protege. If I declare you unfit for your duties, I'll just suggest redaction. You'll return to the private sector and this, ah... Alicia Good will take over for you."

Riley was too stunned to correct him on Aissa's name. The elevator reached the lobby, although she didn't remember anyone restarting the elevator, and Riley stood with her back to the open doors for a long moment. Knox stepped around her to exit the car. "Well, Detective Parra? Come along. We do have one very real murder to investigate."

They rode together in Riley's car, since there was no reason for secrecy, and Priest filled them in on the case file. The victim, Robert March, was a twenty-eight year old convenience store clerk. He worked the overnight shift, was already divorced, and lived with a roommate in a third-floor walkup just off Jefferson. His body had been found in an alley two nights earlier by a garbage collector who thought it was a bunch of rags someone had dumped some rags out the window and it got hung up on a chain link fence. Delgado had spoken with the victim's friends, coworkers, and the man who found the body. No one had any motives, but the roommate was out of town. He'd returned that morning, so Riley wanted to have a word with him.

Riley led the way up the stairs with Knox behind her and Priest bringing up the rear. He looked back a few times, eyeing her with something she couldn't quite identify. Suspicion? Just curiosity? It was difficult to say. Priest was determined to give the man room to observe Riley, so long as he didn't get in her way.

Riley found March's apartment and knocked as she checked her phone for the notes she'd taken from the files. "Dennis Cook? Detectives Parra and Priest, RCPD. We'd like to have a word with you about your roommate."

The chain was removed, and the door opened a crack. Dennis Cook, the victim's roommate, was a short man with a receding hairline and the smooth, round face that made Riley think of the man in the moon. At first Riley thought he had been crying, but she quickly took into account the smell wafting out behind him and deciding he was dealing with his grief with pharmaceuticals.

"Dennis Cook?"

"The landlord said someone was talking to everyone in the building, but he said it was a cop named..." He seemed to think for a very long time. "De-glade-o."

"Delgado," Riley corrected. "We've taken over the case from him. Can we come in?"

His eyes widened slightly. "Um."

"We don't care about your recreational activities, Mr. Cook. We just want to know what happened to your roommate."

"Okay. Uh. Sure. Whatever."

They stepped inside and he stooped down to begin clearing away takeout containers. The apartment looked ransacked, torn apart and sloppily put back together. Clothes littered the couch and coffee table. Cook scanned the place as if seeing it for the first time.

"Uhhh. I've been cleaning up a little this morning. You know. Getting rid of Robbie's shit. People are gonna be coming over to look at the room." He scratched the back of his head and turned to look at them as if surprised they had followed him inside. "That's not... I mean, I got rent due at the beginning of the month. I'm not being insensitive or, like, suspicious. I didn't kill him."

Priest said, "According to Detective Delgado, you were visiting your parents in New Mexico when the body was discovered, correct? Didn't get back until a few hours ago"

"Yah-huh."

"Then I'm fairly certain you have a good alibi."

He seemed to relax. "Sorry. I guess I'm a little paranoid."

Knox's smile was too big to be authentic. "Recreational activities will do that to you."

"Mr. Cook, do you know of anyone who would want to hurt your roommate?"

Cook laughed. "Robbie? No. The guy was... he was really awesome, you know. He didn't smoke, but he didn't mind the smell, you know? So he didn't make me go out on the fire escape like my last roommate did. As long as I paid my part of the rent, he was pretty casual about everything." He seemed to have a sudden insight. "Hey. Is there, like, a... grievance period or something? Maybe I could get a month free on my rent until I find someone to take over Robbie's half. You think?"

Riley shrugged. "Couldn't hurt to ask the landlord. Maybe you'll get lucky."

He grinned. "Awesome. That would be cool." His eyes drifted to Riley's chest. "Uh. You lookin' for a place to live?"

"My wife's apartment is just fine with me."

"Oh. Oh, that's cool. That's really cool. No on Prop 8, right? Unless... wait. Was Prop 8 good for you or bad?"

"It was in California, so it's not really applicable to me. Why don't we focus on your roommate?"

"Right." He ran his eyes down her body again and Riley resisted the urge to punch him. "So, uh, what? Robbie. No one wanted to hurt Robbie. I mean, when I heard he was dead, I just figured it was a robbery at his store. He worked overnight. Dangerous. Not that, you know, it's not just as... uh. Dangerous. All the time. Right? Dangerous city we live in." He sniffed and looked at the three of them again. "Hey. You only said two names. Why are there three of you?" He blinked. "There are, right?"

"This is Mr. Knox. He's... observing."

"Nice to meet you," Cook said, very formally.

Riley said, "What do you do for a living, Mr. Cook?"

Cook inhaled, squinted, rolled his shoulders back, and then widened his eyes. "Oh! I'm a delivery boy."

"Pizza?"

"Uh-huh. I mean, no. I deliver packages. UPS on a bike. Mercurial Delivery." He pronounced the name slowly, as if his tongue was tripping over the syllables. "I mean, I used to. I got fired. That's why I had time to visit my parents, you know? Time off." He looked around the apartment. "I need to find a new job, huh? If I got to pay for this place myself..."

Riley took a card from her pocket. "Okay, Mr. Cook. This is my card. I want you to call me if you think of anything once your head clears. Can you remember that?"

"Par-ra," he said, reading the card. "Okay."

They showed themselves out, and Knox whistled. "Kid's gonna be lucky if he can tie his shoes when he's fifty. Brain cells don't grow back."

"This part of town, he could eat salads every meal and still die at thirty because he was standing on the wrong corner. Might as well enjoy the time he has while he has it."

"That's a very bleak outlook, Detective Parra."

Riley turned on the second floor landing to face him. "Look, Agent Knox, I'm doing everything in my power to make this city a safer place for Cook and people like him. But I'm not naive enough to think it's just going to magically happen overnight. It's going to be a slow process. I'm probably not going to be around to see it, as much as it pains me to say. So I'm not going to act like this place we're living is just one parade away from being a shining city on a hill. Forgive me if I'm a little bleak now and again."

Knox nodded slowly. "My apologies, Detective Parra."

Riley continued down the stairs with Knox and Priest following behind her. They reached the sidewalk just as a hooded Good Girl slowly passed by, her chin lowered to look at her hands as she walked.

Knox watched her back as she continued on and then followed Riley and Priest down the street. "Heard about those ladies. Trying to keep the peace until Marchosias picks a new champion to go against you. Are they really being left alone by the, ah, riffraff?"

"You should see what the Good Girls are capable of," Riley said. "I'm more worried about the riffraff." She stepped off the sidewalk to look down the street. A red-and-yellow awning advertised the nearby convenience store as selling *Coffee - Soda - Beer - Cigarettes*. She didn't see a name, so she pointed. "Is that where March worked?"

"According to the file, yes." Priest touched Riley's arm and then pointed to an alleyway. "That was where the body was discovered."

"Halfway between the store and the apartment. Someone grabbed him after his shift, when he was walking home."

Priest nodded. They stopped at the car and Riley took the file out of the backseat where Priest had left it. She opened it on the trunk where Priest could see it, and Knox stood to one side with his hands in his pockets.

Riley scanned the file, lifting one page to read the next. Notes of interviews, small snippets of information that she knew would be expanded upon in the official report. "Delgado already interviewed the manager and coworkers, right? What did they have to say about March's performance?"

Priest said, "He was an exemplary employee. No complaints. There was a robbery during his shift about six months ago; the thief got away with almost six hundred dollars and has never been apprehended."

Riley scoffed and shook her head. "Tell me a convenience store's been robbed in No Man's Land, I'll tell you that water is wet. It's most likely not connected, but keep it in mind."

Priest nodded and noticed Knox was watching her. "Yes?"

"I don't mean to stare. I just find this situation extremely unusual. You're Riley's guardian angel, but you... work alongside her. You accept a subordinate position to her. She is the senior partner on the force..." He shook his head.

"That's not how you do it?" Riley said.

"My angel is named Phanuel. He acts as a sort of... handler. He delivers messages to me, hands out assignments, generally watches over me in case I need assistance. But I see him once, maybe twice a week. I've never seen a champion-angel relationship as involved as yours."

"Priest is my friend."

Knox pointed. "That's another thing. Caitlin Priest. You think of her as a person before an angel." He looked at her. "How often do you think of yourself by your true name?"

"Very rarely." She kept her eyes on the file. "You must understand, Agent Knox. I spent the better part of a year as a mortal. I made my peace with that part of me. Now, even though I've been reunited with Zerachiel, my identity is closer to Caitlin Priest than Zerachiel."

He shook his head slowly. "Unbelievable. It's truly amazing."

Riley said, "How long was he out of town?" Priest and Knox

both looked at her, and she tapped the file. "Sorry, I'm still working the case. Is that okay with you two?"

Knox cleared his throat, and Priest said, "The roommate? He was out of town for close to three weeks."

"Visiting his parents for three weeks in New Mexico." She looked toward the convenience store and then turned to look up at the apartment. "So for three weeks, it must have looked a lot like March lived alone."

Knox tilted his head to the side. "I suppose."

Riley closed the file and handed it to Priest. She walked around the car, forcing Knox and Priest to follow her into the alley. The crime scene tape was still up, but naturally the body and the boards to which it had been strapped were long gone. Riley scanned the area and then tilted her head back to look at the buildings on either side of where the murder had happened. Windows on the apartment side were either completely blocked from the inside or painted shut. The business on the opposite side had covered the windows with brick a long time ago.

"Nice quiet place to kill someone," Riley said.

"What are you thinking?"

Riley rubbed her thumb over her bottom lip and looked at Knox. "I think Robert March died for no reason. Priest, you have your phone with the GPS map thing?" Priest handed it over, and Knox stared in wonder at an angel with a smartphone, but he kept quiet as Riley punched in a name. She read the address and handed it back.

"Where are we going?" Knox asked as they got back into the car.

"Delgado checked into all of March's people. His coworkers and his manager, everyone. The only person he didn't check up on was Dennis Cook."

"He was out of town. He just got back this morning."

"Right," Riley said. "So we're going to Mercurial Delivery to ask about him."

Priest frowned. "His alibi seems pretty solid."

Knox was smiling. "Maybe too solid. Delivery boy loses his job and then splurges on a three week vacation with his parents? He couldn't have come up with a more solid alibi if he tried. So Detective Parra wants to see if that was exactly what Mr. Cook was doing."

Riley smiled. "Who said the FBI didn't know how to put a

puzzle together?"

Mercurial Delivery was a sliver of a storefront in an old brick building. It was one glass-fronted shop in a row of identical other shops, none of which appeared to be doing very brisk business. Riley parked and turned to Priest, nodding for her to go around to the alley and watch the back door. Priest disappeared, leaving Riley and Knox to go in from the front. Knox watched Priest go before he spoke.

"It's such a highly unusual situation."

"You keep saying that. But it's the only one I know. You might be surprised how handy it is to have an angel watching your back. From what I gather, champions don't really last long in this business without a little help from their winged friends."

Knox said, "I've been a champion for forty-three years." Riley looked at him, surprised, and he shrugged. "But I see your point. I'm one of very few who make it to this age. Maybe if more of us had a more congenial relationship with our angels, we would survive more of what the demons threw at us." Riley opened the door of Mercurial as Knox said, "You and your wife aren't intimate with her, are you?"

Riley stared at him for a long moment before she angrily gestured him inside with her head. She followed him in, putting a lid on her emotions as her eyes adjusted to the relative dimness of the room. A counter ran from one wall to the other with only a narrow break for employees to pass through, leaving only a small waiting area for their customers to wait. The wall behind the counter was covered with maps of the city and a chart showing what they charged. A door was standing slightly ajar to reveal metal shelving that held boxes and clear plastic bins filled with manila envelopes.

A freckled blonde in a bright red polo shirt smiled from behind the counter. "Hi. I'm Tammy. When do you need it there?"

Riley showed her badge. "I'm Detective Riley Parra. This is Mr. Knox. Is your manager around? We'd like to talk to him, if we could."

Tammy blinked and her head tilted just slightly to the left, like a robot switching from one program to another. Her smile didn't falter. "And what is this in reference to?"

"A former employee."

"Just a moment, please." She picked up a phone and pressed

one button. "Mr. Burton? There is a police woman here to speak with you. A former employee." She looked up. "No, she didn't say. Okay." She hung up and resumed her customer service smile. "He'll be right with you."

Riley stepped through the opening on the desk and Tammy shuffled quickly to intercept her.

"Oh! You're not allowed back here."

"Sure I am," Riley said. "He agreed to meet with us. I'm just saving him the trouble of walking all the way out here." She put her hands on Tammy's shoulders and gently guided her to one side. Tammy stuttered and stammered in impotent frustration as Knox walked past her as well. He smiled politely and nodded hello to her as he followed Riley into the back room. Riley took one of the boxes off the shelf and looked at it as she walked.

"This came from Bruce Banner at 123 Green Street. Well, points for the reference." The manager came out of his office and stopped when he saw Riley walking toward him. He was slightly overweight, with a ring of dark black hair that had been dyed to cover gray if his beard was any indication. Riley smiled, trying to look friendly. "Mr. Burton, I presume? Riley Parra. I'd like to ask you a few questions."

Burton turned and ran.

Knox said, "Why the hell is he running?"

"I have no idea. Let's find out." She put the box for the Incredible Hulk back on the shelf and casually followed. Knox turned and went back the way they had come, and she knew he was making sure Tammy didn't slip away. Riley reached the back exit just as it swung shut again, and she pushed it open and went out into the alley. Priest had Burton against the wall, his right arm pinned up between his shoulder blades. His face was bright red, and a vein was throbbing above his right eyebrow.

"Mr. Burton, if you had just answered our questions, we would have left. We didn't have anything to arrest you on. But now, running from the police... that's highly suspicious behavior. We're going to have to take you down to the station to have a more official conversation." She turned at the sound of the back door opening. Knox looked at Burton and then said, "I have the girl. She's in Burton's office."

"She doesn't know anything. She's just the receptionist. She takes orders, and she... she doesn't know anything."

"You want us to go easy on her?" Riley patted him on the

shoulder. "I think we could work out a deal that keeps her out of trouble."

Burton faced the wall again and knocked his head gently against the brick.

"What's your first name, Mr. Burton?"

"George."

Riley took out her cuffs. "George Burton, you are under arrest. Anything you say can and will be used against you..."

Tammy and Burton were both taken back to the station, but Tammy was allowed to sit with Priest at her desk while Riley and Knox spoke with Burton in the interrogation room. He seemed to relax once he was assured Tammy was going to be treated as a witness rather than accessory, and he agreed to answer their questions. Riley had a crime scene unit sent to Mercurial Delivery to start opening boxes.

Riley and Knox didn't have to prompt Burton to start talking. He folded his hands on the table and stared at the interlocked fingers and confessed. "The business hasn't ever done so hot. Rent on the office space was killing me, and we were barely breaking even most months. So one day this guy came to me and said he needed something time-sensitive delivered. He said he would do it himself, but he didn't want to be seen near the drop-off. He said he wanted to make sure our people could be trusted, and I told him they were good kids. He... paid extra. A lot extra.

"He would call for a pick-up, and we'd go get it. Or sometimes he would drop off a bunch of stuff at the beginning of the week and he'd call us to deliver it at a later date. He never put his own return address on the packages in case one of our cyclists got caught. And if they did get caught, we had plausible deniability."

"What was the man's name, Mr. Burton?"

"He called himself Rush. That's the only name I know him by, I swear. I never knew what was in the packages we were delivering, even the normal stuff. That's the client's business, not ours."

"But you suspected," Riley said.

Burton's shoulders sagged. "With what he was paying, I didn't suspect jack shit."

"What happened with Dennis Cook?"

"Him." Burton wrinkled his nose and shook his head like he'd caught a bad scent. "He suspected. He was curious. He thought that if we were going to be hauling drugs and guns - his words, not mine

- we ought to be making more of a profit. I told him to keep his mouth shut and do his job. I offered him a raise, but he kept making a fuss. Finally, I just had to fire him. Good riddance to bad rubbish."

"And then what happened, Mr. Burton?"

He looked at Riley and then shrugged, focusing on his hands again as he sank back against his seat.

"Something happened between the time he was fired and when his roommate's body showed up. Rush came back, and he wanted information. Did you give it to him, or did you just leave the office so he could find it for himself? You might be less culpable that way, if he found it on his own."

Burton swallowed hard and closed his eyes. "I may have left him alone in the office. For a little bit."

"When?"

"About a week ago."

Riley pushed her chair back and stood up. "Stay here, Mr. Burton." She and Knox left the room, and Riley found a uniformed officer and stationed him at the door. "We need to get a protective detail to Dennis Cook's apartment in case whoever killed Robert March find out they killed the wrong man."

Priest saw them and came over to join them. "Crime scene just called. They've started opening the packages and found some very interesting items."

"Guns or drugs?"

"Both. Tammy didn't know anything about it."

Knox said, "What do you think happened?"

"I think Cook decided he wanted a cut of the profits for being the courier. You saw how much stuff they had lying around waiting to be delivered. He took some of the packages for himself when he was fired, and I think whoever Burton's boss is found out about it. Maybe he noticed deliveries didn't get made, maybe Cook called and tried to arrange a deal. Whatever happened, he went to Burton and got Cook's address."

Priest said, "But Cook knew someone would come looking, so he ran."

Riley nodded. "The killer probably watched the apartment and only saw one guy going in and out. He thought March was Cook. March was killed for something he probably knew nothing about." She thought back to the mess in Cook's apartment and started for the door. "The apartment was searched, most likely after March was already dead. If the killer found evidence of a roommate, if he found out he had killed the wrong person~"

"He would have staged the body to make it look unusual," Knox said.

"Yeah. To throw us off. He didn't want us to know Dennis Cook was the real target so we wouldn't protect him." Riley had her phone out as they started downstairs, calling for any available units to get their eyes on Dennis Cook.

Muse put his hands on top of the car and leaned down to look in the driver's side window. "Hey, no. What happened to your beautiful blonde partner, Detective Parra? You had a good thing going with that one."

"Priest is keeping an eye on someone. This is Agent Roland Knox. FBI."

"Oh, good. For a second I thought he was someone in law enforcement."

"Federal Bureau of Investigation," Knox clarified.

Muse smiled. "Right. Glad you're not in law enforcement. At least not effectively."

Knox grinned and shook his head, turning to look out the passenger window.

"Muse, I need to know about someone named Rush."

Muse whistled. "No, you don't."

Riley smiled. "Humor me. We're kind of in a time crunch here. We think he's planning to kill someone that crossed him."

Muse nodded. "That's his knee-jerk reaction, sure." He rubbed his cheek and then said, "All right. His name's not Rush, it's Reyes. Jerome, Jason, something like that. People don't cross Rush. He's like, uh, like Mother Teresa. You need a gun can't be traced, or you just need to refill your stock of..." He looked at Knox. "Your stock of marketable goods, you can go to Rush and he'll get it to you without your folks getting wind of it. People go to him for care packages."

"Yeah. I need to know where he operates. The delivery company he was using had a pick-up address, but that's not where he's headquartered. We need to know where he hangs his hat when he's not filling the streets with drugs and bullets."

Muse clicked his tongue and drummed his fingers on the roof of the car. "Sorry, Riley, no can do. Not this time. Rush is big, okay? I'm not getting on his bad side. But just for my own safety, don't go anywhere near Madison, okay? Down by the docks, the big building with the Co'Cola ad painted on the brick wall of it. Don't even go near that place, Riley, 'cause people might think that I sent you there."

Riley drew a cross over her chest. "Thanks, Muse."

"Thanks for nothing. I didn't give you a thing." He pressed two fingers to his lips and held it out to her. Riley winked and blew him a kiss as he backed away from the car. He waved and said, "Goodbye, desk jockey! Maybe one day you'll get yourself a real job."

Riley smirked as she pulled away from the curb. "Don't pay much attention to him. He puts on a good show, but he's a solid informant. I helped him out of a jam a while back and acting like a goofball is easier for him than acknowledging he owes me. I prefer it this way."

"Are you kidding? I love that guy." He twisted to look out the back window. "I have a couple of informants like him in various cities. Unfortunately most aren't as clever as he is, slipping you the information that way." He straightened his jacket. "Does he know about...?"

"Angels and demons? No. I've kept him in the dark for his own benefit."

"How many people are, ah, clued in?"

Riley thought the number was low until she started thinking of the list. "Gillian and Priest, Lieutenant Briggs~"

"You told your lieutenant?"

"At the time a demon was trying to assassinate her. I figured she should know exactly what she was dealing with. Besides, Gillian is the one who spilled the beans to her. I just approved of it. There's also Kenzie and Chelsea. Mackenzie Crowe and Chelsea Stanton."

He thought for a moment. "They weren't mentioned in your file. Who are they?"

"Kenzie is my former partner. She left the force to join the Army, got hurt by an IED. Chelsea is a former cop who was sent to prison for drug charges. She's trying to redeem herself now. Aissa Good knows about us, too, obviously."

"Hm," Knox said.

"Hm what? Is that a demerit on my permanent record? I put too many innocent people at risk, let too many people let in on the secret?"

Knox shook his head. "On the contrary, Detective. No one is expected to do this job on their own. We have informants, confidants, partners... we have people we need to rely on. My last job was in Florida, and I availed the services of a surfer and a local pastry chef. The 'hm' was simply an expression of how impressed I was at the sort of people you've surrounded yourself with. Police, soldiers... It's little wonder you were able to fight off a demon's energy."

Riley felt a surge of pride. "So you're going to give me a positive report?"

He laughed. "I'll consider it. You know, Detective, I chose this case for a reason. A brutal murder with religious overtones... any champion would have been forgiven for making the leap to demonic involvement. You took the evidence at face value and very rapidly made connections that revealed the truly... mundane... circumstances surrounding Mr. March's death."

Knox paused for a long time, watching the city roll by. When he spoke again, his voice was hard. "I was twenty when I was recruited. I wanted to sign up for the Air Force but my night vision is terrible. The recruiter took me aside and told me about my town's champion. Told me to give him a call if I really wanted to fight a war right here at home. So I talked to him. I became an apprentice and, on my twentieth birthday, he tattooed me. Four years later, he was decapitated by a demon. The head was sent to me in a box. The note said 'You're Up, Kid.'

"I fought for ten years. It cost me a wife, and she took our daughter with her when she left. After that, I went through the motions. Killing demons, stopping them from doing whatever they were up to, and tried to clean up my city as much as I could. But I didn't care anymore." He sighed. "You're not being punished for trying to find a way out, Riley. If anything, that just proves how human you still are. But we wanted to be sure you were still a good champion, that you were dedicated to the cause."

Riley frowned. "And I proved that by *not* looking for demons?"

Knox's smile returned. "To a carpenter, every problem is a nail. I wanted to make sure you were still open-minded enough to see all the possibilities. Being a champion might make you a hammer, Riley, but your mind is definitely open. I don't care if you spent a week as a demon. I'm going to tell Phanuel that his fears are unfounded."

"Wow. Mixed feelings," Riley said. "I was kind of looking forward to retirement."

"That's what you get for being competent and good at your job."

Riley shook her head. "Damn."

They rode in silence until Riley spotted the Coca-Cola ad. She parked and called for a SWAT backup team and waited for their arrival to make her move. Normally she wouldn't have thought twice about going in herself, taking Priest as backup to stop the guy in his tracks. But she was behaving for Agent Knox. He may have already told her she was safe, but he could always change his mind in the official report.

"There is a light at the end of the tunnel, Riley. Champions are assigned for life, but there's a future. One day you might be allowed to take on a lot more responsibilities—"

"Wonderful."

He held up a hand to stop her. "I've been doing this for four decades. I don't have a city to watch over. I'm sent where I'm needed, I do what needs to be done, and then I'm free for the rest of my time." He twisted in his seat to take out his wallet and flipped it open to the plastic-protected pictures. "This is Anna. She's my daughter. Her mother still doesn't like me too much, but she lets me see Anna. We're making amends."

Riley smiled. "She's beautiful."

"Survive, Riley," he said. "Survive, and one day you'll get a call. This city won't be your problem any longer, and your wife will have the partner she deserves. All you have to do is survive. And what I've seen of Zerachiel, that won't be as much of a challenge as it would be to some champions."

"Thanks, Knox."

He nodded toward the Coca-Cola building. "And by taking this guy down, you're taking steps to make this city a much safer place."

"Well. We can hope that. But the fact is, someone else will fill the void."

"But that will take time. Even if it's just an hour, you'll have made a difference. Don't look at the big picture, Riley. Don't expect huge sweeping changes. They don't exist. The only thing we're able to do is chip away at it and hope we're around long enough to step back and see what we've helped create. You might be surprised by the results."

Riley nodded. "I'll keep that in mind."

An unmarked black van pulled up behind Riley's car. Knox and Riley got out and she opened the trunk to retrieve her bulletproof vest. Knox borrowed one from the SWAT team.

"How does this work?"

"You don't do raids in the FBI?"

He smiled. "Actually, I don't. Not in my particular division. But I was actually referring to Zerachiel, or Detective Priest. Your guardian angel is across town watching over Dennis Cook while you're about to go into a dangerous situation. Shouldn't she be here to watch over you?"

"I can handle myself. It's not her job to jump in front of a bullet for me, or mess up the bad guy's shots. Guardian angels often have to stand by and let bad stuff happen. So if I'm supposed to die here, there's nothing Priest could do anyway. Being across town makes it easier for her."

"And what if you're not supposed to die here? What if there's a ricochet that~"

Riley stopped him. "I don't second guess anymore. Just because I know my guardian angel's name doesn't mean I need her to hold my hand every minute of every day. And just to answer your wholly inappropriate question from earlier, no. Gillian and I are monogamous."

Knox nodded. "I apologize for crossing any lines. I still find your relationship with Zerachiel very fascinating." He checked his gun and holstered it, then looked at the building. He smiled. "I am looking forward to this very much. I haven't done anything quite so... mundane... in a very long time."

"Then by all means, Agent Knox, lead the way."

He raised an eyebrow and motioned for the SWAT team to join them. Riley waited until he was looking away from her before she smiled. She had been planning to hate this son of a bitch, but he'd won her over. She checked to make sure the team was locked and loaded before she set off after Knox to take down Rush and whoever else was unlucky enough to be in the building with him.

Two drug dealers were lying on tables in Gillian's morgue. She looked up as Riley entered, her yawn hidden behind one hand as she waved. Gillian waved back and fought the urge to yawn as well. She looked down at the first body and said, "Hispanic male, twenty to twenty-five years of age, shot once in the chest. A clean shot. Obviously the work of a highly-trained professional badass detective who spends too much time at the gun range and smells like disgusting gunpowder afterward."

Riley scoffed. "I resent that. I've been using that soap you bought me."

"Yes, you have. Where is Agent Knox?"

"Tying up loose ends with Briggs. Confirming that this murder was not the work of his fictional serial killer. Although we did take down one of the biggest weapon suppliers in No Man's Land, so he's suggesting the police commissioner gives me a commendation."

"Ooh, fancy pants."

"Oh, shut up."

Gillian grinned. "Priest told me he was here to evaluate you for..." She gestured vaguely at the ceiling. "What did he decide?"

"I'm stuck with the job. For now."

Gillian considered the news, and then nodded. "Good."

"Yeah?"

"Yeah. You make a difference, Riley. You made a big dent in Marchosias' empire by taking down Jerome Reyes. Drugs were flowing into the city and you plugged the leak. You changed a lot of lives today. And you saved Dennis Cook."

"That was just being a cop. Even if I got out of being the champion, I'm still going to be a cop."

"I know. And you know way too much about what's really happening in No Man's Land to just ignore it. So if you have to be a cop, and you have to be burdened with the knowledge of the truth, then I would just as soon have angels watching over you when you're on duty. I know it was my idea for you to start looking into this, and I love you for going as far as you did. But I think it's time for both of us to accept you're going to be champion for a long time."

"You'd be okay with that?"

Gillian considered the question. "I will be."

Riley walked around the table and put her arms around Gillian's waist. "But one day, when I get my pension and we're both old and gray, I'm going to resign both my jobs. And we're going to move to a cabin in the country. And I am going to be your silly doting wife who keeps bugging you when you try to do the gardening."

"I can't wait." She turned her head and kissed Riley's nose. "Now get away. I don't like associating your hug with two dead bodies."

Riley backed away with her hands up. "I'm going to crash in the on-call room upstairs. Come find me when you're ready to go."

"It may be a while."

"I don't mind waiting." She winked. "I love you, Gillian."

"I love you, too."

Riley left the morgue, and Gillian took a moment to slip back into her professional mindset before beginning the tape. "Medical Examiner Gillian Hunt's autopsy report, six forty-three PM..."

Deputy Mayor Lark Siskin ran the water until it was nearly too hot to bear, using her left thumb to work the blood out of the lines of her right palm. Her blonde hair was pulled back into a tight bun, the color as pale as her skin so that it gave her an unfortunate death's-head appearance. She reveled in that comparison. She enjoyed the wariness she saw in people's eyes when they looked at her. She looked at her reflection in the private bathroom's mirror and smiled. It was a horrible expression, and she backed up a step to examine her business suit for spots of blood.

Something thudded out in the office. She went out and watched as Abby and Emily finished securing the corpse. The women had red hair cut identically, and wore suits tailored perfectly to their body so they looked even more identical. They weren't twins, but much expense had gone into making them appear so.

Lark snapped her fingers. Green and blue eyes looked up toward her. "Be careful with him. We wouldn't want any unusual lividity confusing the poor medical examiner."

A man stepped out of the shadows across from her. He appeared young, with a charming smile and dirty-blonde hair. In his tailored suit, he appeared like a young lawyer on his way to court for his first case. He brought a hand up and stroked his jaw before he chuckled and looked at Lark with respect.

"Well. That was... alarmingly enthusiastic."

Lark straightened her blazer. "It's been a long time coming. So what happens now?"

Marchosias shrugged, palms out. "The body will be discovered tomorrow, the crime will go cold - I've arranged for the proper detective to be assigned to the case. It's always nice having the ear of the commissioner. In the meantime, you will ascend to the mayor's job that has been so rudely withheld from you all these years. When the election rolls around, the position will be made official."

"Hm. I suppose that's acceptable if there's no faster route."

Marchosias laughed. "Patience. The job will be yours in no time at all. But now that I've fulfilled my part of the bargain..."

"Yes. Is there a procedure?"

"You'll have to be tattooed. The design can be your choice."

She nodded once. "Very well." She held out her hand. "I'll serve you well, Master."

Marchosias took her hand and squeezed tightly. "Mayor and champion... I wonder which position is more powerful."

Lark finally smiled. "It's not the position that's powerful; it's the one who holds the position that produces the power. And I swear to be a very powerful champion for you, my Lord."

Marchosias bent down and kissed her knuckles. "Then let's get to work. We have a lot of ground to cover before morning."

The twins took the previous mayor's body out of the office, and Lark took her seat as Marchosias began to tell her about their next moves.

THE GOOD GIRLS

At midnight, two Good Girl handmaidens sat down in a greasy spoon for their mid-evening meal. They had hamburgers with pickles, onions, big leaves of lettuce, lots of mustard, and French fries washed down with chocolate milk. Their Mother didn't approve of how their diets had suffered since coming to the city, but she stopped short of forbidding them from partaking. Several restaurants knew who the Good Girls were and offered the food free of charge. They had gained quite a reputation throughout the city as being peacemakers. People just seemed much calmer when a Good Girl was around.

Cerys and Annora were sitting on the same side of the booth. Cerys had her hand on the vinyl between them, and Annora occasionally dropped her hand to trace lines over the upturned palm. This *was* expressly forbidden by their Mother. Physical relationships of any kind were against their oath, even relationships between Sisters. So far they hadn't explored beyond kissing and light touches, but Annora was eager for more. She slipped her fingers between Cerys' and squeezed.

Cerys whispered, "Nora..."

"I'm sorry. I can't help myself." She put her hands back on the table and picked up her napkin to dab at the grease on her lips. They looked similar enough to really be sisters; they had the same black hair, the same high cheekbones. Cerys was slightly older, but they didn't keep track of ages in the sect. There could have been ten years between them. Annora didn't care how much older than her Cerys was; her love had grown to something more intimate since before they relocated to what Mother called "this heathen city." Cerys felt it too, she knew, but she needed more time to accept it. The fact she had kept her hand still during Annora's touching spoke the volumes about everything she was too afraid to say aloud.

Annora was finished with her meal and pushed her plate aside. "I will see you in the morning, Cerys. Peaceful night."

"To you as well."

Annora started to slide out of the booth, but Cerys gripped the collar of her robe. Annora turned, and Cerys surprised her with a quick closed-mouth kiss. Annora's heart soared, and she smiled when they parted.

"Thank you, Sister."

Cerys was blushing, and she turned back to her plate. Annora reached out and brushed the back of her fingers over Cerys' cheek, then rose from the seat.

"I will see you in the morning. Perhaps we can find housing together."

Cerys didn't look up, but she nodded.

Annora grinned as she bid farewell to the woman behind the cash register. She stepped outside and pulled her hood up over her dark hair. She could feel her heart as a separate entity in her body, a warm and glowing presence that had been awakened by the touch of Cerys' lips. She folded her hands, closed her eyes, and centered her soul. She found the peace within her and began walking.

Good Girls had no predetermined routes for their nightly wandering. They simply went to where they were drawn. Annora liked the waterfront, loved the smell off the water despite the awful things that were surely hidden beneath the waves. She paused for a moment on the corner to look at the water, wondering at the lights in the buildings across the way. The city was alive at all hours, conscious and progressing forward. Some might say it was even more active during the night hours than when the sun was high and everyone stood exposed in its light.

She turned and walked to the north. A woman was standing against a brick wall, her arms crossed over her stomach and her head bowed. Annora approached slowly, tilting her head to the side to see past the veil of hair that obscured the woman's face.

"Are you injured?"

The woman looked up and blinked large green eyes. Tears had made her cheeks shine. Her bottom lip trembled and she scanned the street before ducking her head again. She sobbed, and Annora rested a hand on her shoulder.

"Would you like me to pray with you?"

The woman's right arm shot out before Annora's training could respond to the move. Her eyes widened as she felt the pain in her abdomen, a tearing sensation that spread as the woman cut her again. Annora bent double, trying to protect her midsection as the woman continued to slash and cut, thrusting her arm until the front of Annora's robe was soaked red. The woman shoved her, and Annora didn't have the strength to remain upright. Her hands trembled over her stomach as the blood throbbed from her wounds.

The redhead stepped over Annora's body and stood with one foot on either side of Annora. She bent at the waist, their faces level, and examined her in a clinical manner. The tears had stopped and her eyes were cold and emotionless. Her face was still wet, the tears remaining behind like a mask. Annora felt tears on her own cheeks now. Her stomach was so cold, so unbearably cold, and she could feel the warm blood staining her hands. Her blood.

The woman pressed her blade against Annora's throat.

No. Cerys kissed me. You can't do this. Not tonight.

"You should have saved some prayers for yourself." The woman's voice was as cold as her stare. Her arm tensed, and she began to apply pressure to her weapon.

Annora was aware of being unable to draw breath. Lights seemed to swarm behind her killer's head, flashing ever brighter with each painful throb of her heart. Her lips tried to form another word, but she lacked the strength and oxygen to make it heard.

Cerys...

"Let's make this quick, okay?"

"Like you know any other way, Mike." Detective Wanda Kane pushed away from the wall and followed Michael Sherman through the club. She was dressed conservatively compared to some of the other people on the dance floor, but she still felt overexposed. Her gun was in her clutch, and it had been too risky to wear a wire. Her partner was outside waiting for her to give the signal with the panic button built into her bracelet, but she didn't see how he would arrive in time to help if something bad did go down.

Sherman knocked on a door marked Invitation Only. After a moment it was opened and a woman with amazingly red hair answered. She wore a club T-shirt and a skirt tight enough to reveal she wasn't wearing anything underneath. She looked at Sherman, looked at Wanda, and nodded for them to come inside. The office was small and smelled of smoke, but it was soundproofed enough that the music of the club was reduced to a dull drumbeat in the walls.

Wanda looked at the redhead. "Is this the customer?"

Sherman walked behind the desk and sat down, brushing his hands over the thighs of his pants before he looked at her. "No, actually."

"Look, I don't have time for games. You want to hire me, then hire me. Don't play these games. My time is money." She turned toward the door, but the redhead moved into her way. "Sweetie, I don't usually shoot for free, but in your case I might make an exception."

Sherman said, "I've been reading some very interesting reports, Wanda. Reports about you and your list of accomplishments. Eight kills in the past year."

Wanda kept her eyes locked on the redhead's bright blues, unwilling to break the staring contest. "I don't like using the word 'kill.' Never know who might be listening."

"That is very true. Ms. Ketch, I have received some very concerning reports that I'm hoping you can counter. I'm hoping you can prove that they're incorrect so I won't have to do something I regret. Will you please take a look at these photographs?"

She reluctantly looked away from the redhead. Sherman had lined up three pictures on the desk. They were turned so they would be right-side up for her. She was the subject of each picture, and the building in the background was very familiar to her. It was the 410 Precinct, her base of operations. She had only been there three times in the past month, and it seemed as if someone had taken a picture of each visit.

"I'm going to get penalized because the cops can't hold onto me?" She smiled as if she pitied Sherman's paranoia. "I cover my tracks, but every now and then I get caught up in a sweep. I'm good at what I do, Mr. Sherman, and I convince them to let me go."

He smiled. "Well, it's a balance between you being a good liar and the cops being incompetent."

Wanda laughed. "Six of one, half a dozen of the other like they say, right?" She picked up one of the pictures. "I like this angle, though. Can I have these for my website? Nothing sells a rep like a picture of a hired gun walking out of a police station scot-free."

Sherman seemed to relax. "No nonsense. I like that, Ms. Ketch. No tells. But here's the thing. The person who brought this to my attention didn't just snap a few photographs. She went above and beyond."

Wanda turned to look at the redhead, who was still standing stoic by the door. When she looked back, Sherman had another picture lying on top of the other three. Once again, she was the focus of the picture. It was a professional shot, showing her head and shoulders and a flag behind her. She recognized the curly afro (why had she ever gotten rid of it?) but was more concerned about the police uniform she was wearing in the shot.

Sherman stared at her expectantly, waiting for the lie she would tell to get out of this one. Wanda fumbled for the panic button hid in her bracelet, but her fingers slipped mindlessly, usefully over the metal. It was like someone was in her head, screwing up her motor functions. She forced herself to focus.

"Where did you think I learned how to shoot? How to get past cops? I learned from the masters and then turned it back on 'em."

"I actually want to believe you. You have me doubting myself. It takes a lot to get me to doubt myself, so I want to applaud you for a valiant effort. But we've reached the end of our business arrangement."

Wanda turned, ready to body slam the little firecracker to get out the door. To her surprise, when she turned she was looking down the barrel of a gun that seemed impossibly enormous. The beat of the music out in the club faded to nothing, the room seemed utterly still and silent. The redhead smiled.

"Anything to say?"

"Kill a cop, and they'll hunt you down no matter where you hide."

"You missed the point. We're not hiding anymore. This is our debut."

Wanda brought one hand up to grab the weapon as the girl pulled the trigger.

Riley remembered it all. The darkness split by a sudden knife's-edge of light from the main room of the apartment. The comforting weight of her blanket being pulled away to expose her young body.

Of course, in the dream, she was an adult. She didn't remember faces; they were always either in the darkness or backlit by the doorway. Rough hands touched her cheeks and her face and then... lower. She learned early on that fighting made it worse. She could kick and claw and bite, but they were always stronger. It hurt less to just let them do whatever they wanted and get it over with.

A hand touched her cheek and Riley realized she could move. "Don't you touch me," she shouted, propelling herself backward and off the bed. Something sharp poked into her left shoulder and then she was on the ground, her legs still on the bed as whoever had touched her reared up in the darkness.

"Baby!"

Riley's mind cleared away the last cobwebs of the dream. Gillian's voice, their apartment, their marriage bed. Her heart was pounding loud enough that the neighbors would complain, and she was drenched with sweat. She turned her hips and dropped her feet to the floor. Gillian scrambled over and joined her on the floor, hands on Riley's shoulder and head.

"It was a nightmare," she said. "You're okay. You're with me."

Riley ran her hands over Gillian's arms. "Did I hurt you?"

"No, baby. Are you okay?"

"My back... I hit it on the nightstand when I fell."

Gillian guided Riley forward, and Riley put her head on Gillian's shoulder as she examined the injury. "You're bleeding. Let me go get the first aid kit." She paused and said, "Can I let you go?"

"Yeah. Just hurry back."

"I will."

Gillian stood and went into the bathroom, and Riley drew her knees up to rest her elbows against them. She pushed her hands into her hair and closed her eyes, trying to dispel the last remnants of the nightmare. It had been months since her mind had thrown one of those memories at her; she didn't want to think about why it was surfacing now. Gillian left the bathroom light on when she came back with the first-aid kit, and the soft glow turned the bedroom back into a safe haven.

"Shirt off," Gillian said. Riley was too tired to even make an innuendo as she took off her sleeveless undershirt and twisted toward the bed.

"How bad is it?"

"Just a scrape. This will sting." She sprayed something on it and Riley hissed, lowering her head to her arms. "Sorry."

"It's okay. You're not used to working on live people."

Gillian chuckled and put a bandage over the wound. "That may have been true before I fell in love with you, but you've given me lots of training. Lots and lots."

Riley closed her eyes. "Say that again."

"Hm?"

"That you love me."

Gillian sighed happily and slipped her arms around Riley's waist. "I love you, love you, love you." She kissed the back of Riley's neck and shifted her legs. Riley moved, bending her knees and sitting on her feet as Gillian hugged her from behind. Her lips moved down the curve of Riley's shoulder. Riley stretched her arms out in front of her, palms flat on the mattress, and settled her weight against Gillian's lap.

"You sure?" Gillian whispered.

"Yeah."

Gillian rearranged herself. "Okay. Hold on." She guided Riley to a better position, grunted quietly, and eased her hands under the elastic of Riley's shorts. She cupped Riley's mound with one hand and let the other explore lower, massaging as she kissed Riley's neck through her hair and began to move her fingers in a slow rhythm. She kissed her way up to Riley's ear and began to whisper to her. The word "love" was repeated several times, along with terms of endearment to "my love, my wife, my heart."

Riley's fingers curled in the sheets, her head turned to silence her moans against her bicep. She could feel Gillian's whole body pressed against her from behind, Gillian's fingers easily moving inside her, and she worked the skin with her teeth as sex was pulled from the realm of nightmares and turned into something beautiful and real.

Riley came quietly and leaned back, angling herself to kiss Gillian's lips as Gillian kept hold on her. Riley slipped her tongue over Gillian's and turned her head, their cheeks brushing together as they reluctantly separated.

"You okay?"

"You do very well with live patients, if I say so myself." She stood up and got back into bed, and Gillian crawled over her to get to her side of the bed. They faced each other on top of the blankets, Gillian's arm tucked under the blankets and their foreheads almost touching. Riley wet her fingers and reached down, easing her hand between Gillian's legs. She lifted the hem of her nightie and Gillian gasped quietly.

"Why on earth are you giving me first aid, Detective Parra? I wasn't hurt." Gillian's voice was breathless, making her sound like a teenager.

"Preventative medicine, Dr. Hunt."

"Oh." Gillian's eyes closed and she moaned. She circled Riley's wrist with her fingers. "Oh, Riley."

The bed squeaked quietly with the gentle movement of Riley's arm. Riley kept her eyes open, watching Gillian closely for signs of impending climax. When she thought she saw the evidence, she changed position. She kissed Gillian's breasts through the sheer material of her nightie, kissed her stomach, and eased her legs apart just enough to get her head to where her hand was. After a few seconds, both of Gillian's hands were on the back of Riley's head and her hips were moving in almost imperceptible circles as she gasped her wife's name.

Riley kissed both of Gillian's thighs when she finally went boneless. She kissed the soft red hair between Gillian's legs and then slid up her body. Gillian demurely tugged her nightie back into place and cradled Riley against her, kissing her cheeks and lips as they settled in the shape of each other's bodies.

"You okay?"

"Yeah. Thanks for taking my mind off it."

Gillian smiled. "My pleasure."

They had both just about managed to fall asleep when Riley's cell phone went off. She grunted. "Damn it."

Gillian's cell phone joined the chorus, and they looked at each other. Riley checked the clock and saw it was only a few minutes past three in the morning. Whatever had happened, it was bad enough to wake both a homicide detective and the medical examiner. Riley reached for her phone with a sense of dread.

Before she could answer it, someone began frantically knocking on the apartment's front door. Gillian looked at Riley, eyes wide, and they climbed out of opposite sides of bed to see what the hell was happening.

The message was the same on the phone and at the door: "one of ours was murdered." Gillian dressed in scrubs and a sweater, pausing only long enough to kiss Riley and put on a pot of coffee before she ran out the door. She didn't even bother with contacts, wearing her horn-rimmed glasses instead. Detective Wanda Kane's body had been dumped outside the police station with a large portion of her head missing.

Riley tried to process that information as she drove into work with a very shaken Aissa Good in the passenger seat. Aissa had come to tell Riley that one of her sisters, Annora Good, had been murdered by the waterfront. Gillian was on her way to examine both bodies. Riley could at least comprehend how an undercover detective wound up with a bullet in her skull, but a Good Girl? Riley had seen Aissa fight. She'd gone to bed thinking the Good Girls were the most dangerous group in the city, even if they did only fight in self-defense.

Lieutenant Briggs was dealing with a swarm of activity when Riley arrived. She looked visibly relieved when Riley walked in, so glad to have her head detective on-site that she didn't even seem to notice the girl Riley had in tow. Briggs seemed to be wearing pale pink pajamas underneath a buttoned blazer, and she was wearing two different tennis shoes, both lefties. She took the time to put her hair in a ponytail as she explained what they knew so far.

"About half an hour ago, someone dumped Wanda Kane's body on our doorstep. Whoever it was didn't stick around long enough for us to see their license plate. Probably wouldn't have done much good anyway. She was investigating a murder-for-hire ring, pretending to be a sniper offering her services to a man named Michael Sherman, owner of a club called Speakeasy. Her partner was stationed outside, but she didn't think she would get away with wearing a wire. So he didn't even know she was in danger until he got the call about an officer being found dead. He's crucifying himself downstairs."

"Poor man," Aissa said.

Riley looked at the flurry of activity. "What about the other murder?"

"John Doe. Hands and head are both missing. Gruesome."

"No, a woman. There was a stabbing victim on the~"

"Waterfront. Right." She pinched the bridge of her nose. "Sorry. Right. One of the Good Girls. It's the first time we've seen anything bad happen to one of them. Dr. Hunt is~ well. You know where Dr. Hunt is going. We'll know more once she has a chance to examine the body, but Riley, priority~"

Riley nodded. "Wanda's first. I know." She looked at Aissa, who nodded her understanding. "What can I do?"

"SWAT is being rounded up right now. Get to the bar and get

Sherman down here if you have to drag him by his ears."

"Yes, boss. Have you seen Caitlin?"

"We called her, but I haven't seen her yet."

Someone else caught Briggs' eye and she went to deal with them. Riley went to her desk and opened the drawer, lifting a plastic tub and taking out a black elastic strap. She fitted it over her badge and hooked it back on her belt before motioning to Aissa to follow her to the stairs. "We're going to multitask, okay? Every cop in this city is going to be looking for Wanda's killer. I'm not going to forget Annora."

"Thank you, Riley."

She nodded and took out her cell phone. "Kenzie. Were you asleep? Sorry. We're having a hell of a night over here. Thought you and Chelsea might be able to lend a hand. A cop was shot, and..." She smiled. "Thanks, Kenzie, but that's not why I was calling. We have another murder we need to look into, and I can't even find Caitlin." She paused. "She's not there is she? Sorry. I had to check. I'm heading to Speakeasy; why don't you head to Priest's apartment and see if you can find her. See you soon." She hung up. "I don't like this. A cop and a Good Girl... maybe whoever did this took out an angel, too."

"Do you think they..." Aissa furrowed her brow. "I mean, how could they?"

"I don't know. They don't necessarily have to kill her. They just have to keep her out of the fight. There are ways to neutralize an angel."

Outside, an unseasonable drizzle had started. Riley and Aissa jogged to her car. Aissa sat on her hands to warm them and watched the rain streak over the glass as Riley drove.

"Did you know her well? The officer who died?"

Riley shook her head. "Not well. I went undercover last year, and she was a lifeline for me then. Getting messages to Jill, dropping off reports to get them back to Briggs... she kept me connected. But no. I didn't really know her very well."

"I'm sorry for your loss, regardless."

"Thank you. Me too." She tensed her hands on the steering wheel. "Do you have any idea what is going on tonight? Any... vibrations?"

"I'm sorry, no. Maybe if I was still with my Sisters, but I'm too far removed from them." She straightened in her seat. "I should go to them. They'll need to speak with someone from the outside, and

I can make that easier for them."

"Good. Thank you. Let me know where to drop you off. Make it close... I don't want you out running around in this rain."

Aissa directed her to a covered alleyway near the waterfront and Riley parked. She twisted into the backseat and came back with a rainslicker and an umbrella. "Take them. I'll feel better about dropping you off."

"Thank you, Riley." She kissed Riley on the cheek. "I was worried about trying to survive without my Mother. But you've been like a mother to me."

"Watch your mouth. I'm not that much older than you."

Aissa smiled. "I'll call you if they know anything. Be safe, Riley."

"You too."

She watched Aissa disappear down the alley and then reluctantly pulled away from the curb. She got a text from Briggs and held the phone against the steering wheel to read it. "SWAT ready two blocks from location. Meet w/ them there 1st. You give the OK."

Riley snapped the phone shut and tossed it onto the passenger seat. The SWAT van was two blocks away from Speakeasy. She got out of the car as the SWAT leader got out of the back of the van. He was a tall, lanky man whose body armor made him look like a Ninja Turtle. She forced the comparison out of her mind when he spoke. "Detective Parra? Sergeant Dillon. We've got nothing from inside. No one's come in or out since we arrived."

"Maybe they're getting ready to close for the night." She secured her vest and looked at her watch. Almost four. A little early for this part of town, but not unheard of. "Your boys ready?"

"Bastard took out a cop. Just tell 'em where to point their guns."

Riley introduced herself to the SWAT team and led them down the street. The drizzle had picked up a little, but Riley barely noticed it due to the heat coming off her skin. The armor was heavy, and the street was a surreal kaleidoscope of lights reflected in the rain. She stopped by the front door of Speakeasy and looked at her watch again. One hour and twelve minutes ago, Gillian's fingers had been inside of her. It was too easy to imagine this was just some bizarre dream, that she'd wake up and everything would be fine. She shook off the thought and turned her face to the sky. Raindrops ricocheted off the bridge of her nose into the well of her eye and she blinked the water away.

The SWAT team was lined up behind her. She held up two fingers and a thumb, counted down, and then dropped her first.

"Go, go, go, go!" Dillon barked. His men moved as one entity, moving like a sentient shadow and breaking down the gaudy purple front doors of the club. Once they were all inside, Riley followed with her gun drawn. She brought the gun up to sweep the room and then immediately lowered it.

"What the hell?"

Dillon and his men were standing along the inside wall, weapons still ready but wavering with nothing to aim at. Dillon himself pushed up the visor of his helmet and looked at Riley with confusion. She shook his head and moved deeper into the room.

The dance floor was covered with corpses. Their clothes were drenched with blood. Riley went past the bodies around the bar to a room marked Invitation Only. She pushed it open and saw a man seated with his head on the desk like he was taking a nap in the middle of the work day. The hair at his temple was matted with blood, and streaks of it ran down and around his sightless eyes. His mouth was open slightly, as if the final blow had been a complete shock to him. It probably had been.

She glanced at the wall and tensed. A spray of blood, brain matter, and a bullet hole. Her chest was tight, and she had to struggle past the urge to throw up at the sight. Wanda had died in this office, and then... whoever had done it decided Sherman had outlived his purpose. The others in the club were just collateral damage.

She left the office and took a breath of the sickening, but relatively fresh compared to the office, air of the main room. Dillon approached and stopped himself from saying anything when he saw the expression on her face.

"Get forensics. No one goes in that room until they've gone over every inch of it."

He tapped his ear. "We're getting word about one of those nuns getting killed near here. Detective, all due respect, but what the hell is going on in this town?"

Riley suddenly knew, but it was nothing she could tell Dillon. She muttered something about being as confused as he was and passed through the abattoir to the entrance of the building. She went outside and stood on the sidewalk, breathing in a lungful of cold, wet air. The drizzle washed over her face, cooling her down, and she clutched her right shoulder.

She'd been dismissing the pain as aggravation of the wound she'd gotten from falling out of bed, but that was her left shoulder. Her right shoulder hurt because her tattoo was thrumming with energy. The Good Girls were allowed to operate in the city, to walk the streets and pray for protection, because evil had no champion. But now a Good Girl had died.

Marchosias had a new champion. And whoever he'd chosen was making their name known in a big, bloody way.

The three newest residents of Gillian's morgue lay like broken statues underneath the harsh light. Two women and a man, only one of them with a fully intact head. Gillian's assistant Lydia was working on the John Doe, while a medical student named Zach worked on the Good Girl. Gillian had assigned the fallen detective to herself. She had known Wanda Kane, had liked her. She didn't often visit the morgue, but they had passed in the hall. Gillian hesitated in her vocal report, speaking quietly so her voice wouldn't transfer to Zach and Lydia's recording devices, and took a moment to reflect.

A detective had fallen in the line of duty. How easily it could have been Riley.

"Dr. Hunt?" Lydia, sounding confused. "Could you take a look at this?"

Gillian pivoted and took one step to stand beside her assistant. She started to ask what the problem was when she saw for herself. The John Doe's head and hands were both missing, most likely to deter identification, but the killer likely hadn't known what would be found when he was opened. Gillian bent closer and examined the abdominal cavity where the heart should have been. "I've only seen this in textbooks. *Situs inversus.* All the organs are swapped, reversed."

"So this was natural?"

"Yes. He was born like this. Might not even have known about it until he needed another medical procedure." She took off her gloves and went to her office, standing over the laptop as she logged on. Lydia had followed her and stood in the doorway. "We just have to see if there have been any cases of *situs inversus* in the city and we should have our John Doe's identity." She did a quick search and smiled. "Here we go, patient is..." Her smile faded and she straightened slowly. "Shit."

"Doctor?"

"This day just got a lot longer."

Riley parked in front of the station and felt at least a portion of her stress evaporate when she saw Priest standing on the front steps. She wore a black coat with the collar turned up, and she hunched her shoulders against the rain as she hurried down the steps to meet Riley on the sidewalk. Riley greeted her with a quick hug. "I'm glad you're okay. No one could find you."

"I was in No Man's Land. I had to follow up on something. Riley, it's happened~"

"Marchosias has a new champion."

Priest stared at her as they walked into the surreal warmth and dryness of the building. The windows appeared supernaturally dark due to the rain, and every light was glowing. It still felt like the middle of the night even though it was technically closer to daybreak. Riley shed her coat as she led Priest toward the stairs.

"How long have you known?"

Priest said, "I started feeling something three or four days ago, but I assumed it was due to Roland Knox's presence in town. I thought he was the other force I felt. But then he left, and the sensation only grew stronger. I wanted to be certain before I alerted you. How did you know?"

"It's been a busy night." Her phone rang and she pulled it from her pocket. "It's Jill. Hey, hon. Yeah. We're right by there. We'll detour." She hung up and directed Priest to the third floor landing. They went to the morgue where Gillian and her two assistants were gathered around a table holding a male body. Riley looked at the bodies of Wanda and Annora Good. "John Doe has taken precedence, so I assume you identified him."

Gillian still looked stunned. "You've actually met him, Riley. You arrested him not too long ago. Meet Mayor Dominic Leary."

Riley went cold. The rain was still dripping from her coat, and it seemed like the impact of the droplets on the tile was the only sound in the room.

"You're sure?" she finally said.

"He had a rare condition, so the odds are something like one in ten thousand. The body type, age, height, everything else matches. It's him, Riley."

Priest said, "He should still be in prison."

"He was out on bail. House arrest." Riley remembered cursing at the breakfast table when she heard the news. "There should be officers watching him."

Gillian shrugged. "All I know is his identity."

Riley sighed and looked at the other tables. "The mayor, a detective, and a Good Girl. Someone is trying to make a statement."

Riley met her eye. They couldn't talk freely with the two assistants in the room, but she nodded and Gillian's shoulders sagged.

"I should go report to Briggs."

"Yeah. There's going to be a press circus over this." She glanced at Lydia and Zach. "You might want to call in some reinforcements, if you can. You're going to get a call about a lot more bodies. We found the site where Wanda was killed, and it's a bloodbath."

Gillian sighed. "Well. Lydia..."

The girl was already moving toward the phone. "I'll call."

"Thank you. I'm going upstairs to tell Briggs about what's going on. The commissioner will have to be involved too, I'm sure."

Riley nodded. "I'll walk you up. I have a report of my own to give."

When they were out of the morgue, Gillian looked at Priest. "There's a new champion for the other guys, I guess."

Priest nodded. "Yes. And from her introduction, I would say she's going to make Gail Finney look like a cakewalk. This is senseless violence. Brutality and murder for its own sake. Marchosias has picked someone as evil as he is."

Gillian closed her eyes and slipped her hand into Riley's. "Well... that's just wonderful."

The church was just under a hundred years old, but it had been built to mimic the style of older churches in England. The rain brought the stone walls and wooden framework to life, and the interior of the church smelled timeless and untouched by the forward march of the world. There were ten Good Girls present, offered the space by the deacon who had given them shelter and food in the past. Their Mother, the Paladin and commander of their sect, stood at the pulpit, her speech interrupted by the doors squeaking open and a rain-soaked waif stumbling into the sanctuary. She flipped back the hood of her slicker and revealed frizzy blonde hair, her eyes wide and lips parted as she scanned the people present before she locked eyes with the Mother.

Adira was the first one off her pew, lifting the hem of her robe so she didn't trip as she ran to Aissa. She grabbed her, ignoring the wetness that transferred to her pristine robes as she embraced her lost sister. Soon the others were on their feet and Aissa was surrounded. Some hugged her, but others could only touch her hand or her hair. Aissa closed her eyes and let herself be crushed.

The Mother came down off the pulpit and moved slowly down the aisle, giving the younger handmaidens time to greet their prodigal Sister before she cleared her throat. The throng dispersed, but remained surrounding Aissa as she stepped forward and bowed her head.

"Mother."

"Sister Aissa. You look very well." Her gray eyes wrinkled when she smiled. "We have been frightened for you since you left our flock."

Someone took Aissa's hand and squeezed. Another touched the back of her shoulder. Aissa said, "I've missed you all. But I've found a place where I belong. It was my fate to be exiled so I could continue serving. Thank you, Mother, for sending me away."

The Mother blinked back tears, smiling wide enough to reveal small white teeth. Her blonde hair was parted in the middle and tied in twin braids that hung over her shoulders. Aissa knew how difficult it was for a mother to follow the sect's guidelines and cut loose one of her Daughters. She stepped out of the crowd and took her Mother's hand. She brought it to her lips and kissed the knuckles.

"You know why I've returned tonight of all nights."

"Annora."

Aissa nodded. "She was murdered. The champion is investigating the crime, but it should not have been possible."

"The fact it was possible is a sign to us," the Mother said. "The demons have chosen someone to stand for them. This city is no longer a safe place for our prayers, and the new champion has made that known. We are leaving today."

Aissa's heart shattered. It was one thing to be cut away from the flock but still know they were nearby. But now they were leaving. Without her.

"I will... see to it that Annora's murderer doesn't go unpunished. And I will see to her funeral myself."

"No." Cerys was standing at the back of the crowd, but she stepped forward as she spoke. "I will take care of her. I'm not leaving."

Mother's face was stone, but traces of emotion slipped through.

"If that is what you wish, Cerys."

"It's what Annora would have wanted," she said softly. "It's what I must do."

"Then I will grant you leave, Daughter. Aissa..."

"I'll watch over her, Mother."

The Mother smiled. "I am not your mother any longer, and you are not my child. You are more." She touched Aissa's cheek. "You have become a source of pride for me, Aissa."

Aissa blushed and dipped her chin.

"We are not leaving for several hours. The man who presides over this church has granted it to us for the day, so you are welcome to remain with us to say goodbye to your former Sisters if you wish."

Aissa knew Riley would need her help with the investigation, but she would never forgive herself if she walked away without a proper farewell. She nodded and said, "I will stay." The other Good Girls surrounded her again, and Aissa closed her eyes as they closed ranks around her.

By seven that morning, the sidewalk in front of the station was covered by the myriad of cameras and reporters who had each brought their own ponchos. Equipment was draped by a protective canopy of plastic, so a swath of concrete directly in front of the steps was practically dry by the time Commissioner Preston Benedict emerged to give his statement. Lieutenant Briggs was at his side, and they both stood in the rain without benefit of umbrellas as they reported what they knew.

An undercover detective had been murdered by persons unknown at the club known as Speakeasy. That very club was also the sight of a mass killing which resulted in twenty-two more bodies that were currently filling up the morgue freezer.

A Good Girl had been brutally attacked with a knife, her throat slit before she could succumb to her abdominal injuries.

But the story that had drawn the press out on such a dreary morning was the brutal killing of Dominic Leary. Recently arrested for the murder of a stripper, disgraced and removed from his position as mayor, and now dismembered. Commissioner Benedict mentioned the other deaths as a matter of ceremony before he delved into the information about the former mayor's murder.

"The Medical Examiner determined Mayor Leary suffered a brutal beating before his death and dismemberment. After his death, his hands and head were removed in what we believe to be an attempt to conceal his identity for as long as possible. The body was dumped outside of an all-night service station. The owner could not identify the vehicle that left the body except to say it was a large black SUV."

Once he finished the prepared statement, he opened the floor to questions.

"How was the body identified?"

"We're not releasing that information at this time. The Medical Examiner, in the course of performing her duties, found undeniable evidence that the body was that of Dominic Leary. It has since been confirmed by blood type, and a DNA test will be forthcoming to completely settle all doubt. Yes?"

"Surely the police department had officers watching Mayor Leary in the event he tried to run. Where were they?"

"We're not commenting on that at this time. There were officers watching the Leary residence, but until they've been fully debriefed, we're not going to reveal anything publicly."

"Do you believe these murders are connected?"

"It's unlikely, but we're not discounting anything at this point. The fact that they were all different methods of killing seems to point toward unconnected killers."

"Are the other Good Girls in danger?"

"Our officers have been out all night searching for other members of this religion, but they seem to have all vanished overnight. Whether this is a good sign or bad, we're not certain yet." He pointed at another reporter.

"Due to her experience with such high-profile cases, will Detective Riley Parra be involved in these investigations?"

"Detective Parra has been assigned the Wanda Kane investigation. I've personally assigned Detective Benjamin Harding to the mayor's case."

The questions went on until Commissioner Benedict declared it had run its course. He brusquely thanked the press for their time and turned, disappearing back into the building so quickly that no one could think to stop him with any further questions. Briggs followed him, and they took a moment to shed their rain gear before moving deeper into the building. Briggs took the brief time they had on their own to broach an uncomfortable subject.

"Sir, I believe Detectives Parra and Priest would be a beneficial presence on all three cases."

"Unless they each split in two, I'm not going to spread them so thin. Parra can handle Wanda Kane's murder. Her partner can handle the Good Girl murder, if they're willing to work apart. We're going to need all hands on deck for this, Zoe. You have more than one team in your division. Don't make the mistake of relying too heavily on them."

Briggs winced. She couldn't tell him that her real reasons were because Riley and Priest knew to look for demonic influence in the murders. Detective Harding was a good enough cop, but he was in the dark. If Mayor Leary was killed by Marchosias, or someone working for Marchosias, true justice would never be achieved. She had no valid arguments, so she simply agreed with Benedict's assignments and went upstairs to tell Riley.

Detective Timbale said she had gone into the on-call room to get something to eat from the fridge. Briggs went in and found Riley sitting at the small card table that served as a dining room for the Homicide Division, head down on her hands, fast asleep. She nearly let her sleep, but decided Riley would be irritated if she did.

"Detective?"

Riley sat up quickly and grunted, rubbing her face with both hands before she focused on Briggs. "Sorry, boss."

"Don't apologize." She pulled out the chair next to Riley and sat down. "You're heading Wanda's case and Priest is working the Good Girl's death, but Commissioner Benedict wouldn't budge on the mayor. He assigned Detective Harding."

"Ugh, that guy bugs me."

"Who *doesn't* bug you?"

Riley said, "You've been okay lately."

Briggs chuckled wearily and rested both elbows on the table, pushing her hair out of her eyes with both hands.

"Twenty-five dead bodies in a single night. Even for this town, that might be a record."

"We still don't have the patrol numbers from No Man's Land. Could be higher."

Briggs groaned. "You're a real miserable person, Riley."

"Sorry, boss."

Briggs stood up and pushed the chair back in. Riley started to stand as well, but Briggs waved her back down. "I found you and told you all of that fifteen minutes from now. You deserve a rest. In fact, I insist on it. No one here wants you making any mistakes because you're sleep deprived. We may have the guy who shot Wanda on a slab down in the morgue, but we still need to know who was pulling his strings. Something bad happened in that club. You need to be on top of your game to find out what it was."

"Okay. Thanks."

Briggs nodded and walked away as Riley put her head back down. At the door, Briggs turned off the light and looked back to where Riley seemed to already be asleep again. She said a silent prayer that she hoped would bring luck, then left to let Riley nap in peace. If any of them could be said to have any peace in this city. She sighed and went to her office to see what other fires needed her attention.

At home, the Good Girls slept in dormitories, so bunking on the pews was hardly new to them. Aissa sat on the stage with her Mother, talking quietly to her about what she had done and seen since her exile from the order. Mother touched Aissa's shoulder, her hair, her hands and, although Aissa normally hated to be fussed over, she allowed the contact. When she was finished, Mother looked at the pews that kept her from seeing her girls.

"Perhaps we have all been tainted by this town. We've done things... experienced things that would cause us all to be exiled. And with Annora's loss, and Cerys deciding to remain as well..." She pressed her lips together and looked down at her feet. "Come home, Aissa."

Aissa's brain refused to hear the words until it turned them over a few times. "I killed. I've injured people. Good Girls..."

"The Grand-Mother has forgotten what the world is like, and she has never experienced No Man's Land. What good is our training if we don't use it? To exile a Daughter like you is wrong. I will support your return, and I will fight Grand-Mother myself if she refuses. The things we have all done and seen in this city can make us stronger... but not if we turn our backs on those who actually experience the evil this world can breed. Come home, Aissa. Come back to us, and teach us to be better."

Aissa was crying. She covered her mouth with her hands, overjoyed at hearing the words she'd never even fantasized about hearing. She wiped at her cheeks, sniffled, and turned to hug Mother tightly. She pressed her face against her Mother's neck.

"No."

Mother pulled back. "Aissa, please. You~"

She shook her head. "I can't, Mother. Thank you so much for the offer. It means the world to me, but it just... it makes this my choice." She clutched Mother's upper arms and kept her voice steady. "I've made a promise to someone. She rescued me after I was cut loose, and I gave her my oath. I will be this city's champion when her time has ended. Even if I could back out of my promise, I don't want to. Please understand, Mother."

"Of course I understand." She leaned in and kissed Aissa between the eyebrows. "It will be an honor to give our prayers to someone we already know and love. Our prayers will shake the walls of Heaven with their strength."

Aissa laughed. "Thank you, Mother."

"No. You're not my daughter any more, champion."

Aissa felt pride swelling her chest and she looked down to swallow the lump in her throat. "Thank you... Isolde."

Isolde smiled and kissed the crown of Aissa's head, holding her hands and squeezing the fingers. They held each other for a long moment before Isolde turned her head to whisper in Aissa's ear. Aissa listened, nodded, and kissed her former Mother's cheek before she stood up and walked down the center aisle of the church toward the exit. She looked at the sleeping women she had once called Sisters and pulled her sweatshirt's hood up over her hair and stuck her hands into the pockets of her borrowed windbreaker. She hadn't realized how far she had already come from her Family until she sat in a room with them and understood she didn't belong.

She knelt next to the pew where Cerys was lying down but not sleeping. She touched Cerys' leg and gently nodded for her to follow. Cerys picked up the rucksack containing her meager belongings and stepped out into the aisle. Isolde was on the stage and blew a kiss goodbye, and Cerys blew one back.

They walked out of the church together. Cerys put her hood up against the rain and Aissa pressed against her as they hurried to the protection of the el station. They sat together on the cold bench, and Cerys looked at the world around her like she had been transported to a completely different universe. Aissa squeezed her shoulder.

"It's the same place you've spent the last few months. It's not different."

"It is different. I get to hurt them now... the people who killed Annora."

Aissa smiled. "Yeah. We're going to find them together. We'll make them pay."

Cerys put her head down on Aissa's shoulder. "I loved her. I should have told her."

"I'm sorry."

Cerys began to cry softly, and Aissa stroked her arm as they waited for the train.

Priest woke Riley and followed her back out to their desks. Riley brainstormed a strategy as they walked through the room. "We'll coordinate on both murders. We know the Good Girl was murdered as a statement, and Wanda's death was probably the same. Marchosias wanted to make sure we knew there was a new champion in town. Now we're going to focus on finding who it is."

"What about the mayor's death?"

Riley glanced toward Benjamin Harding's desk. "I don't know, but we're out in the cold on that one whatever the cause. I'll keep in touch with Benji and see what he knows. If it looks like it's turning into one of our kind of cases I'll offer to lend him a hand with the investigation." She sat down and turned her chair to face Priest's desk. "We need the security cameras from both locations. Wanda was killed in the club district, so there have to be at least three security cameras covering that block. Parking garages, other clubs, liquor stores. Annora was killed on the waterfront, so there won't be as many cameras aimed just right, but we could get lucky."

Priest was marking down notes when Briggs came out of her office. She stopped by Riley's desk and said, "Hope you have something to report, because we're about to get called in front of the principal." She looked across the room. "Benji. Could you come here, please?"

Benjamin Harding was a young and cocky detective, wearing three days worth of stubble. When he moved, he seemed to navigate the obstacles in his path with a sharp grace of a boxer. He settled between Riley and Priest's desks, nodding a greeting to them before he focused on Briggs. "What's up, boss?"

"We're about to have an esteemed guest who would like updates on the three major cases that came in today. The acting mayor, Lark Siskin, is on her way up. I've told her that it's still extremely early in the investigation, but she insisted on meeting the three of you. Just give her a quick review of what you're planning. She can't honestly expect results within an hour of the press conference, but she's just establishing her new position."

Benji nodded. "No problem. I'm already following a few leads on the mayor's finances. Apparently the office wasn't as clean as he claimed during his last campaign."

Briggs said, "You may not want to mention that lead when Siskin arrives. She *was* his deputy, after all." The elevator bell chimed and Briggs sighed. "Here we go."

The doors parted and Lark Siskin stepped into the bullpen like a dictator surveying a sweatshop. Her chin was held high and her shoulders were back, and every head in the room turned to follow her progress to where Briggs was standing. She wore a charcoal black dress suit over a blood red blouse that was fastened at the collar by an ivory cameo. Trailing behind her in identical black suits were two aides who, for all intents and purposes, were exact copies of each other. One had her red hair tied back in a ponytail while the other wore it loose.

Lark reached Briggs and offered a polite smile. "Lieutenant Briggs. It's nice to see you again, despite the circumstances." She turned and looked at the trio of detectives, focusing on Riley. "And you must be the famous Riley Parra. The mayor was quite a fan of your heroics during the Angel Maker case. You're making quite a name for yourself in this town."

Riley took the manicured hand offered to her. She was magnanimous and attributed the cold skin to the fact Lark had just come in out of the rain, but she withdrew her hand as quickly as she could manage without being impolitic. Lark turned to introduce the women behind her. "These are my aides; Abby Shepherd and Emily Simon."

Riley shook Emily's hand. When she moved to do the same with Abby, the woman apologized and held up her right hand as a silent explanation. A long narrow cut ran along the meaty part of her palm.

"That's quite a slice," Riley said.

Lark smiled. "Culinary incident. She was cutting a bagel when we received the news about Mayor Leary. Such a tragic fall from grace."

Riley nodded and watched as Abby put her hand behind her back. Briggs continued with the introductions.

"This is Detective Benjamin Harding... he'll be investigating the murder of your predecessor." Benji nodded, surprising Riley that he wasn't trying to make an impression. Briggs continued, "And this is Detective Caitlin Priest."

Priest stood up. "Detective Parra is aware of my progress on the case. She can fill you in. I have to go get some warrants." She turned without waiting to be dismissed and weaved between the desks until she reached the stairs.

Briggs furrowed her brow and said, "She's usually a bit friendlier than that."

Lark didn't seem offended. "We're all under a great deal of stress. It's been a very trying day for us all, but for you especially. I won't keep you from your duties any more than necessary. I just wanted to let you all know that you'll have the full power of the mayor's office at your disposal. Whatever you need, we'll cover your back. Don't worry about the press or backlash. Just solve these... heinous crimes."

"Thank you. That's very much appreciated."

Lark nodded. "I will leave you to your jobs, Detectives. Anything you need, you have a friend in the mayor's office."

She smiled at Benji, held Riley's gaze a bit longer than necessary before she turned and motioned for Abby and Emily to follow her. Riley stood up once Lark's back was turned. Benji drifted off toward his desk, and Briggs touched Riley's arm to keep her from running off. Once the acting mayor and her aides were in the elevator and Benji was out of earshot, she spoke.

"What was that about, with Priest?"

"I have a suspicion. Let me go confirm it." She touched Briggs' arm before she crossed the office and went to the stairs. Priest was standing on the next landing down, her back to the wall and her arms crossed over her chest. She looked up at the sound of Riley's footsteps and pushed away from the wall. Riley spoke before she could. "It's her, isn't it? She's Marchosias' new champion."

Priest nodded. "She's evil, Riley. I can't explain it so you'd understand, but she has... something wrong with her. She was born wrong. She's kept it hidden from sight for a very long time, but Marchosias has just given her an outlet for it to grow and flourish."

"Looks like Marky's moved up from Gail Finney. Did you see the cut on Abby's hand?"

"Yes. Do you think she was involved in Annora's death?"

Riley nodded. "Not only that, but the wound was been treated. It had been bandaged, but the bandage was removed before she arrived. Mayor Siskin wanted me to see it. She wanted me to know. That was the whole point of the meet-and-greet."

Priest said, "So what do we do?"

Riley gestured up the stairs with her head. "We go get those warrants, we scour the security cameras, and we arrest the killers."

Priest wet her lips and nodded as she followed Riley back up the stairs.

Lark poured herself a glass of wine. Abby and Emily were standing across from her, on either side of the devil seated in the single visitor's seat. Lark made him wait as she sniffed the wine, closed her eyes, and tossed her head back to take it all in a single swallow. She touched the corner of her mouth with her pinkie and put the glass back down on the blotter. She fixed Marchosias with eyes so blue they were almost like ice.

He smiled at her. "Don't expect me to reproach you. You deserve a celebration. We've had a remarkable day."

She took her seat and leaned back. "We had a good day. It hasn't achieved remarkable. Not yet. My plan has one more step before I'll consider myself satisfied."

Marchosias' smile faded slightly, but he retained a look of bemused satisfaction. "We've been over this, Lark. The plan was bold, but the final part was a step too far."

"I'm stunned by your cowardice."

He finally let his amusement fade completely and leaned forward. "I would watch my tongue if I were you, Lark. Let's not turn this into a civil war. We won today. Riley is looking into the security footage just like we knew she would, and she'll find the damning evidence. She'll arrest our patsy and a big flashy 'Cop-Killer' trial will ensue. We'll wait for the opportune moment and exonerate her suspect with incontrovertible evidence of his innocence. When all is said and done, Riley Parra will be a curse word among police officers. Her reputation will be ruined."

"In a year's time, or two years? We have Riley Parra on her knees now, so what better time to deliver the crushing blow?" Lark leaned forward as well, her elbows on the edge of her desk. "Retreating is for the weak. We crush Riley Parra and take our victory."

Marchosias shook his head. "There are rules in place, Lark. Rules that protect us as well as the other team. We must abide by them."

"Why?"

"Because no matter how many battles we win, no matter how many bodies we put in the ground, in an unfair fight, the forces of good will always triumph over us. The rules give us a fighting chance."

"The rules hold us back. The rules restrain us when we should be spreading our wings and flying. You chose me to be your champion, Marchosias. You will not stand in the way of my victory."

He rose and put his hands on her desk. The wood steamed where his skin made contact with it, and his voice dropped to a low growl. "You are not the commander in this army, Lark. You will follow my orders. Is that understood?"

She returned his stare without blinking.

"I asked you a question, Mayor Siskin."

"I understand your position, Marchosias."

He lifted his hands and straightened his suit jacket. "Good. Excellent. Sorry for the display, but you must understand... I've been doing this a lot longer than you can even imagine. Riley will orchestrate her own downfall. We simply have to provide her with enough rope to hang herself, and she will do everything else for us." He looked at Abby and Emily, smiled at a private thought, and dipped his head to her as he walked to the office door. "Big things will happen in this city, Lark. Riley Parra won't know what hit her."

Lark reclined in her chair, fingers steepled, and held her smile until the door slammed shut behind Marchosias. She turned her eyes toward Abby and Emily. "When one makes a literal deal with a devil, one does so hope that devil isn't a coward. Marchosias is disappointing. To say the least."

"So what do we do now?" Emily asked.

"Now." Lark said the word softly and eyed the burnt palm-prints on her desk. "Now we continue as planned."

Abby frowned. "But Marchosias~"

"Marchosias is a weak, pathetic excuse of a devil who has already allowed Riley Parra to defeat him once. The war was started anew because of her. She is unafraid of him because she has no reason to be. He is weak. Fortunately, he has chosen the right champion to assure victory this time. We're continuing with my plan as it was written. Ignore Marchosias' warnings."

Emily nodded, although she still looked lost. "Yes, but... how? He made everything possible, ma'am."

"Go into No Man's Land and find a demon who isn't as... cautious... as our tin-pot leader. There are bound to be a few. Find one and give him his instructions. I want news of Gillian Hunt's death before this time tomorrow, or I will squeeze the life from her myself."

Abby and Emily nodded and muttered assurances that it would

be done as they turned to leave the office.

Lark turned toward the window and smiled. The early-morning rain had moved on, leaving the city gleaming in its wake.

It really was shaping up to be a most beautiful day.

HELL BREAKS LOOSE

Author's note: The following story contains scenes of rape, torture, graphic violence, and death. The rape isn't shown graphically, but reader discretion is advised.

"A little while we tarry up on earth,
Then we are yours forever and forever
But I seek one who came to you too soon."
~ Orpheus and Eurydice

Riley woke when Gillian came out of the bathroom, freshly scrubbed and ready for another long day in the morgue. She was still making her way through the bodies from Speakeasy, taking the time to give each one a proper examination rather than reducing them to a number. She bent down and kissed Riley's cheek in farewell, bidding her to go back to sleep until her alarm went off. She left a wake of apple-scented shampoo in her wake, and Riley closed her eyes and focused on that smell as she drifted back to sleep. She dreamt of green apples falling from a tree in an orchard. She was nearly asleep when she realized they hadn't said goodbye to each other.

The rain had moved on, and the early morning sky was a

brilliant shade of velvet. Stars were out in legion, and Gillian tilted her head up as she walked from the parking structure to the front door of the building. The desk sergeant returned her greeting with subdued emotion; everyone in the building was on edge following Wanda's murder. Every badge she saw was interrupted by a single black ribbon. Gillian wasn't a member of the police force, but she knew enough of them and was respected enough that she felt like part of their grief.

She liked arriving at the morgue early. It never actually closed, since people died at all sorts of hours, but between four and five in the morning it was frequently still and dark. She turned on the overhead lights and they flickered to life along the length of the room. The metal faces of the drawers and the tables in the middle of the room sparkled.

Gillian felt a brief, overwhelming sense of déjà vu when she stepped forward, her sneakers squeaking on the tile. She pushed the feeling aside and shook her head. She'd faced down that phobia. She had been attacked and locked in a drawer by demons when "demons are real" was still a new phenomenon to her. The fear had driven her away, but love brought her back. She overcame her fears and the morgue was once again her kingdom.

In her office she booted up her computer and put a lab jacket over her scrubs. She read the overnight coroner's report as she pinned her hair up and went out into the main room. She was humming under her breath when she realized someone was singing the lyrics to the same song. She stopped humming and the voice ceased as well. She walked to one of the tables and picked up the circular bone saw she used for cutting through ribcages.

"Is someone there?"

"Dr. Hunt?"

She admitted she jumped, but shook her head at her own silliness. "Zach? What are you doing here so early?"

"I thought we could get a jump on the day."

Gillian turned toward the voice. It was coming from the dark corridor that led to the service elevator, the one the bodies rode in. "I like your initiative." She kept the saw in her hand as she moved toward the shadows. "Why didn't you turn on the lights?"

A pause. Too long of a pause. "I just got here."

So you crossed a room in the dark? She didn't say anything out loud, however. She stepped around the corner. A dark shape loomed in the hallway a few feet in front of her, like a piece of night cut out and dropped into the lesser shadows. It was too big to be Zach. Gillian switched on the saw and its reassuring buzz filled the room, echoing off the metal and tile until it sounded like a swarm of bees had been let loose.

Gillian stood her ground. "Leave this place."

"Or what?" His voice had changed, the need for subterfuge gone. "You'll call down one of your angel friends?"

"On the contrary. I'd like to see how much damage I can do before you're forced to give up that body."

The demon stepped forward, his eyes remaining shadowed. "What a coincidence. That's what we were going to do with you."

She barely had time to register the "we" before the saw stopped buzzing. The cord went slack, and Gillian turned to run. The demons were between her and the two exits, and she screamed as powerful arms wrapped around her from behind and wrestled her to the floor.

The clerk put Riley's change down on the counter next to her order, and she swept it into her other palm before taking the two cups. Priest was waiting by the door and followed Riley out into the pre-dawn street. Their shift didn't technically begin until eight, but hardly anyone with a badge was adhering to strict shifts. Riley knew the warrants for security cameras from several businesses were coming in; she hoped to spend the morning reviewing the footage to spot the killer leaving Speakeasy.

"It doesn't necessarily bug me," she said in reply to Priest's earlier question. "I'm happy to share the workload. But it's a little frustrating not to know how the mayor's case is going. I feel like Benji should be keeping us in the loop a little more. I mean, hell, I was the one who arrested him. I'm pissed off I didn't get a chance to see him in court."

Priest smiled. "Well. As long as you aren't bugged."

"Hopefully Gillian can give us some information on the mayor's death, which we can then provide to Benji, and we'll have a way into his investigation."

"Sneaky."

Riley shrugged. "I do what I can. It *does* bug me that Lark Siskin is the new champion, and she seems to have gotten the job the same night her boss was brutally murdered. She must have had something to do with it. Not to mention Annora, Wanda, the whole scene at Speakeasy... she wanted to make sure her first day was as bloody as possible."

"I think she succeeded," Priest said.

"Yeah." She let Priest hold the coffees while she drove to the station. The sun was just beginning to color the sky, but it hadn't quite made an appearance yet even by the time they arrived outside the station.

Priest handed the coffees back to Riley when they were inside. "Is the coffee part of a bribe to get Gillian to share information?"

Riley grinned. "It's a bribe to make sure Gillian appreciates being with me. I can't rely on my good looks forever. So I'm setting it up that I'm the lady who brings her coffee in the morning. It's a long game, but I'm dedicated."

Priest laughed. "Gillian does indeed love coffee."

"See? I'm diabolical."

They rode up to the morgue. Priest tensed slightly during the elevator ride, and slumped against the door. "Oh..." She put a hand to her temple and closed her eyes.

"You okay?"

"I... don't know." She pressed her lips together and worked her neck back forth. "I'm not sure what I'm feeling. Something is masked. Something dark and evil, but it's been obscured so I can't see the shape of it. Like... ah... like..."

"Like that sickly sweet air freshener crap they use in the gym locker room?"

Priest nodded. "Yes. I can still get a sense of an evil presence, but it's dispersed by something else. I think I'm going to be ill."

They stepped out of the elevator and Priest doubled over, clutching her stomach. Riley put the coffee down on a gurney and touched Priest's shoulder. "Want me to get Jill?"

"No." She breathed in deeply and grimaced at something Riley couldn't smell. Her face was red, and a vein throbbed between her right eyebrow and her hairline. "No," she said with more conviction. She swallowed and straightened up. "I think perhaps Lark Siskin or one of her cohorts may have visited the station last night. Their presence... lingered."

"Let me know if you need to take a breather. Gillian gets mad if people throw up in her morgue."

Priest chuckled weakly and picked up the coffees. She handed them to Riley and motioned for her to continue on. Riley led the way and pushed through the morgue's swinging doors with her shoulder.

"Hey, Jill. We were hoping you could~"

Gillian wore white Keds sneakers and baby blue surgical scrubs. Someone wearing shoes like Gillian's was lying on the floor on the other side of the farthest examination table. Baby blue surgical scrubs were bunched around her ankles, along with a pair of purple and black panties that Riley recognized all too well. She dropped the coffee and was across the room before they hit the floor, rounding the table and confirming what her mind refused to believe.

Gillian's scrub top was torn open, her skin raked and bloody in several places. Blood also stained her thighs and the tile floor around her.

Riley dropped, a dull pain shooting up through her thighs as her knees hit the floor with a sharp crack. Her face felt hot; her throat was closed to sound and air, and she placed a trembling hand on Gillian's cheek. Gillian's lips were slightly parted and Riley could see pink stains on her teeth. Her eyes were wide and staring blankly at the ceiling. The right eye was slightly off-center, looking to the left rather than lining up with its partner. Gillian's chest rose with a single, trembling breath and then sank again.

She was alive. A sheet dropped down and covered Gillian from shoulder to thigh, and Riley nodded a quick thank you to Priest without taking her eyes off her wife.

"Help her." Riley cupped Gillian's face and brushed a thumb over the dry tears on her cheeks. "Help her. Caitlin. Help her."

"I can't. Oh, Riley."

"No you help... her. Help her now, please, you have to," Riley whispered. Her voice wasn't angry; it was far too desperate to be angry. "Help her. You brought me back to life, you can help her."

Priest lightly touched the back of Riley's neck. "This is different, Riley. What has been done to her is atrocious. It's what I felt in the elevator. The violence that was done to her body was only the first part of this torture. The demons who... did this to her..." Priest's voice broke into a sob, and she fought to control herself so she could finish. "They raped her mind as well. They broke her so that she will constantly relive everything that happened to her this morning. There will be no relief. It will continue until her body finally surrenders and allows her to die. At that point it... will be a mercy."

"How long?"

"I don't know. Days."

Riley felt like someone had set her entire body on fire. Gillian seemed to be looking at her now, and Riley moved so that their faces were lined up better.

"Baby?"

Gillian made a weak sound in her throat and tears welled in her eyes.

"Can she see me?"

"Yes. The memory is an underlying thread. She sees and hears us, but her mind is telling her that she's still being assaulted."

Riley said, "Then stop it."

"I can't. Not without destroying her mind in the process. It's a darkness that has been seated deep in her brain, and it spreads throughout the organ. To destroy even a part of it would be fatal to the Gillian you once knew. I cannot undo it."

"Help."

The word was spoken so quietly that Riley almost thought she imagined it. "Jill?"

Gillian whined and closed her eyes, rolling her head on her shoulders as her feet gently kicked against the tile floor. Riley cried out in impotent rage and turned to Priest.

"Days? She has to survive like this for *days*?"

Priest had backed off, one arm across her stomach and the other hand covering her mouth. She lowered her head prayerfully. "I can offer her peace. It would be a mercy."

Riley looked at Gillian again and saw her eyes had opened. She made a slight move of her head, either a twitch or a nod. A lock of hair had fallen across her face and Riley pushed it out of the way, tucked it behind her ear, and cupped Gillian's head with a trembling hand. She felt the tears on her own cheeks now and wondered how long she'd been crying.

"I can do it."

"No." Riley slid closer to Gillian. "Baby. Look at me, Gillian."

Gillian seemed to focus a little and the pain... Riley thought maybe it was just in her head, but she looked less pained when they were making eye contact. Riley was clutching Gillian's hand, and she felt the sharp shape of her wedding ring against her palm. It reminded her of Gillian's favorite word, and she smiled.

"You are about to see something so opalescent."

Gillian's lips curled slightly in what Riley took as an attempt to smile.

"I love you, Gillian. I've always loved you. I will always love you." She bent down and kissed Gillian's lips, eyes closed, lips lingering on the heated skin before she sat up and did what she had to do. She slid her left hand over Gillian's mouth, then pinched her nose between her thumb and forefinger. Gillian kept her eyes on Riley's, and Riley refused to look away even when the sobs threatening to break free made her eyes burn.

After a moment, Gillian stiffened. Her body briefly fought for air, the heels of her Keds kicked the tile in a slow staccato rhythm, and then fell silent. Gillian's hands, which had been twisted into claws went slack and fell to the side. Riley slipped her hand away and dropped back, horrified at what she had just done. Priest knelt next to Gillian and put a hand over her chest. She whispered a few words before she lovingly covered Gillian's face with the sheet.

"She's at peace now."

"Lucky her." Riley's voice was raw, and she wiped a hand down her face, blurring the tears. "So now what?"

Priest looked away from Gillian's shroud. "Pardon?"

"What do we do to fix this?"

Priest crossed to where Riley was sitting and knelt in front of her. "We don't, Riley. We can't. What's been done to her is... done."

"Use your divinity to bring her back."

"If that was possible, I would. But her mind has been shattered. Zerachiel could only heal her body. She would reawaken to her torture and begin it anew. We can't fix this, Riley."

Riley closed her eyes and became unnaturally still. She breathed slowly, flexing her fists and then extending her fingers. Time slowed and all Riley heard was the rushing of blood in her ears. Her head swirled around a single point: Gillian was gone. In an instant, the world became a place she didn't want to live in, let alone save. Nothing mattered. She felt it slipping away, like all the colors were being erased from everything. Her pain spread like tendrils, crossing everything else. No hope. No joy. Only Gillian's broken body (*because of me*). The one bright thing in the world had been tarnished simply because Riley was connected to her. Riley felt the darkness close in on her and felt an unnerving calmness wash over her.

Nothing mattered.

Nothing counted.

The world had just ended, and all that remained was dealing with the corpse. She opened her eyes and moved forward to touch Gillian's cheek, spreading her fingers so that they framed Gillian's left eye. Riley bent down and kissed her wife between the eyebrows.

"Okay. Help me get her up onto the table."

"What?"

"The table."

Priest followed her. "We can't disturb the crime scene, Riley."

"Fuck that. Get her on the table, Cait."

Priest hesitated but, when it became clear Riley was going to try to do it alone, she bent down and lifted Gillian's feet. They put her on the empty table and Riley searched the nearby carts for something. "Tools. I need a... the hair clipper. She said sometimes she has to cut people's hair to get... to clean head wounds. There should be clippers." She tossed aside trays that didn't hold what she was looking for, sterilized equipment clattering to the ground in a cacophony of metal and tile. Priest winced at the sound, but Riley seemed not to hear.

"Aha."

She plugged it in, pulled down the sheet, and pressed the vibrating blade against Gillian's temple. She pushed it up, and the hair fell away from her head in waves.

"What in the Father's name are you doing?" Priest asked. "This is obscene, Riley."

Riley inhaled slowly and let the breath out. She continued running the razor along the curves of Gillian's head, her hand steady as she cut another swath. "I need it."

"For *what*?"

Riley shook her head as she continued to cut. "Holy relics. I don't believe in holy water or, or crosses or any of that. But my badge worked when I melted it down because I believed in it." She took a deep breath. "I believe in Gillian." Priest started to speak, but Riley turned on her. "Will it work? Just tell me that."

Priest looked at the hair that had fallen around Gillian's head. She thought about lying, but the damage had already been done. "Yes. It will work."

Riley turned away and went back to cutting.

"What are we going to tell Briggs? There will have to be an investigation."

"We'll work around that."

Priest's voice was a disbelieving hiss. "You would lie... about *this*?"

Riley stopped the clippers and turned to face Priest. "What would be the point of trying to get justice? No one is going to jail for this, Cait. No one is going to stand trial for Gillian's death. At least..." She looked back at her wife and her face trembled with barely controlled emotion. "I'll get justice. I'm the only one who can." She cupped Gillian's cheek and bent down. Her lips brushed over Gillian's and she almost recoiled at how wrong it felt. She closed her eyes and her tear dripped down onto the bridge of Gillian's nose.

"You don't have to help me."

"Of course I'll help you," Priest said. She put her hand on Riley's shoulder and squeezed. "It's my job to watch over you."

"Yeah. Her angel didn't do such a good job, did she? Where was she this time?"

Priest didn't have an answer, so she remained silent. Riley wiped her tears with the cuff of her sleeve and picked up the clipper again to continue cutting her hair. After a moment Priest stepped away and returned with a plastic bag. She began taking the hair that had fallen and placing it in the bag for Riley. Riley watched her take the first few handfuls, nodded her thanks, and stepped around to get the other side of Gillian's head.

As the last strands fell away, Riley had the basic elements of a plan forming in her mind. It would be a hell of a risk, and the odds were against it working at all, but if she tried and succeeded, it might make all the difference. If she tried and failed, then it would just mean her death and she wasn't as terrified by that prospect as she had been an hour earlier.

Funny how things could change so quickly.

"God knows she doesn't look at me anymore. I'm sorry." The client pressed a handkerchief against her right eye and kept her head down until she had herself under control. When she looked up again, her makeup was slightly smudged. "I just want to know. If I know, then I can confront her without looking like I'm just being jealous. And we can talk about it. Work through it. That's all I want. I don't want to make an accusation if it's unfounded."

"I understand." Kenzie Crowe leaned forward and linked her fingers together. "We can watch your wife for you, but the detail of the report is going to depend on how much we find and how much you want to know. Now~"

The door opened and a haggard Riley Parra walked in. She looked like she hadn't slept for a week, and instead had spent the nighttime hours running marathons.

"Riley? I'm with a client."

"That's okay. She can leave."

Kenzie stood up. "Riley, I don't know what you're problem is~"

"Gillian's dead. She was raped and killed this morning." She looked at the client. "Sorry I don't feel like waiting."

Kenzie was still stunned by the first two words of Riley's outburst, slowly absorbing the rest. Finally she remembered the client. "I'm... so sorry, but~"

"No. God, of course." She stood up and looked at Riley with real compassion. "I'm so sorry for your loss."

Riley ignored the woman as she walked out, and Kenzie came around the desk. Riley didn't seem to notice when she was enclosed in the hug, but she didn't pull away. Kenzie put her hands on Riley's shoulders and looked at her.

"Where's Priest?"

"With Jill. At the station. Talking to Briggs." She furrowed her brow. "They think I went to the bathroom. I just... kept walking until I came here."

Footsteps on the stairs. Chelsea said, "I heard the door. Are you already finished with Mrs. Mendoza?"

"Chelsea, it's Riley. Riley has... she..." Kenzie was crying now. "Gillian was killed."

"What?" Chelsea came down the rest of the way and blindly sought Riley's arm. She found it and squeezed. "What happened?"

"That's not important. Not right now. I wanted to come to tell you about Gillian's, uh, wishes. She... after Priest did the..." She gestured at her own eyes, furrowing her brow with the effort of organizing her thoughts. "Gillian was an organ donor. She did some research and she discovered your optic nerve was damaged by the bullet when you were shot. That's why you can only see blurry objects. And she found out that someone could donate that nerve, so she wanted you to have hers in case anything ever happened to her. And now it has. So I thought you should know."

Kenzie touched Riley's brow with the back of her hand. "Riley, you're burning up. Did you walk here from the station?"

"Uh huh." Riley suddenly weakened, but Chelsea and Kenzie held her up. Kenzie slipped Riley's arm around her shoulders and carried her to the couch in the corner of the office. She lowered her, and Chelsea said, "I'll call Caitlin and let her know... I'm sure she already knows. But I'll call anyway."

Riley pinched the bridge of her nose. "Priest said there's no way to fix it. Said it's gotta stand." She rolled onto her back and Kenzie squeezed her hand. "She said she can't undo it. They broke Gillian's mind and her body both, so Zerachiel can't just put it back together."

"I'm so sorry, Riley. I'm so, so sorry." She picked up Riley's hand and kissed her knuckles. Riley had never been happier than she was with Gillian. She'd initially been jealous of the fact that some doctor had gotten in the way of resuming their romantic relationship when she got back from serving, but then she saw them together. Gillian was who Riley was supposed to be with. Every other relationship had just been killing time. Kenzie heard Riley sniffle and looked at her face to see that she was grinned.

"Riley...?"

"I shouldn't laugh."

"No. You shouldn't. What the hell, Riley?"

Riley put her hand over her eyes. "I'm going to fix it."

"You just said... if Zerachiel can't do anything, I think you have to accept it, sweetie." She touched Riley's hair gently. "Chelsea and I, and Aissa, and Briggs, we're all going to be here for you. We'll help you get through this."

"No. I can't just back down. I can't just let it happen." She sat up so suddenly that Kenzie nearly fell backwards to avoid knocking their heads together. "If I give up and let this stand, that means they win. The demons will have won. I can't let them think that. I have to hit them back hard and I have to do it fast. Then I can focus on saving Gillian."

Kenzie started to reply, but she was interrupted by Chelsea's return. Priest was following behind her and Kenzie was surprised to see her despite the fact traveling across town wasn't exactly strenuous for the angel. She looked exhausted, and relief flooded her face when she saw Riley. "Are you okay?"

Riley ignored the question. "What did Briggs say?"

"We debated what story to tell the media. Since an arrest or trial is unlikely, we've decided to say she died of an aneurysm."

Kenzie shook her head slowly. "That's wrong. Someone should be held accountable. The demon that killed Gillian can't just walk away."

Riley said, "Oh. The demon didn't kill her. I did."

Kenzie tensed and slowly looked at her again. "What?"

Priest said, "It's complicated. Riley acted mercifully. The demon left Gillian's mind in tatters. She was being shown horrors, forced to relive awful things."

Riley said, "It's not important." She put a hand to her temple and moved two fingers in slow circles. "We're going to fix it."

Kenzie stood up and moved closer to Priest. "She keeps saying that. Riley, if we fix it, then Gillian can't donate her optic nerve to Chelsea. You can't have it both ways."

Chelsea spoke softly from her desk. "I would rather have Gillian back, if it's up to me."

"No. It'll be okay. It'll all work out. It always does. I just need some time to think. To strategize." She stood up and Priest moved to stand in her way. "Excuse me. I need to walk, to clear my head."

"I think you've walked enough, Riley."

"No, I need to wa~"

Priest lightly touched Riley's temple. Riley stopped speaking in the middle of her word, eyes rolling back in her head, and her entire body went limp. Priest caught her easily, bending at the knee to scoop Riley up into her arms.

Kenzie stepped forward and stroked Riley's hair like she would a child. "Is she going to be okay?"

"Yes. She's only sleeping. She needs time."

"No, I mean." She wet her lips. "How is she going to get through this, Caitlin? How can they hurt Gillian? That's... beyond the pale."

Priest nodded, but said nothing. She didn't have an answer. Finally, she said, "She needs someplace to rest. I don't... think she needs to be home just yet."

Chelsea stood up. "Upstairs. She can stay here as long as she needs. If you need anything, or if Riley needs anything, we're here. We're going to clear our schedule. We'll be available for whatever you need."

"Thank you. Riley will appreciate that once the shock wears off. For now, there isn't anything we can do."

Kenzie shook her head. "Riley's right. We can't just let this happen. We can't let Marchosias get away with this kind of bullshit."

Priest shook her head. "We won't. Marchosias broke the rules that both sides have abided for years. That won't stand. There is nothing we can do to save Gillian. She is gone." Her voice broke and she took a moment to compose herself before continuing. "But the demons in this town have signed their death warrants. Gillian will be avenged. I vow it."

When Riley woke in Kenzie and Chelsea's bed, she felt calm.

She undressed and took a steaming hot shower, waiting until she was afraid her skin would blister before she finally shut off the water and toweled off. Her mind was empty of anything but the most basic things. Dress, step, breathe, stand up. She opened the dresser drawers and found a pair of Kenzie's slacks that would fit her, and also borrowed a pale blue T-shirt. Her own clothes were missing, probably a good thing. She didn't remember if they had Gillian's blood on them or not. She found her things on top of the dresser. She picked up her phone and wallet, hooked the holster for her gun on the side of her belt, and picked up her badge. She stared at it, at how the light caught the gold and glinted off of it.

She dropped it in the garbage as she left the bedroom.

She went barefoot downstairs, where Priest seemed to have gathered the troops. The quiet conversation ceased when she appeared.

Priest stood up. "Riley."

"Kenz, I borrowed some of your clothes."

"Okay. Riley..."

"I'm going out. Does anyone want anything? Coffee? I could get some lunch."

Priest and Kenzie exchanged a look. "Riley, I think you need to take it easy."

"No. I'm just going to get a breath of fresh air. I'll be back in a half hour or so. Stop worrying about me. Get to the hospital, Chelsea. I don't know the procedures for getting someone's brain tissue, but I figure there's a pretty small window. Uh, I'm going to have Gillian cremated. Caitlin, could you set that up for me?"

"Yes. Riley~"

"See you soon." She waved and walked out of the building. She was nearly to the corner when she heard the door open behind her. She was scanning the street when Kenzie reached her. "Do you know where I parked?"

"I think you said you walked."

"Oh. Right." She pushed her hands into her hair and started walking again.

Kenzie fell into step beside her. "Riley? You're scaring everyone."

"Don't be afraid. Just get Chelsea to the hospital and have the operation. Everything else will sort itself out while you're taking care of her."

Kenzie put her hand on Riley's shoulder to stop her from

continuing. "You need to take care of yourself, Riley."

"I am. I'm getting food. I'm exercising. Gillian would be proud of me." She patted Kenzie's arm. "Go on. Go back to your girlfriend. I'll be fine, Kenzie. I swear."

Kenzie hesitated, but then stepped back. "We're not going away, Riley. You'll need us, and we'll be here."

"Thanks. I appreciate it. Are you sure you guys don't want any lunch? I'm paying."

"You slept for a while, Riley. It's almost dinner time."

Riley looked at the sky. "Oh. I thought the sun was rising... never mind. The offer still stands."

"No. We're fine."

Riley smiled. "Great. Tell Priest not to worry. Give me some time to breathe, and to get my head on straight. I had kind of a rough morning." She winked, which seemed to terrify Kenzie in a way that insensate rage wouldn't have. "See you soon."

She felt Kenzie's eyes on her back as she walked away, but she ignored it until she turned a corner. She put her hands in her pockets and noticed Kenzie's jeans were a little tight on her. They'd once been similar sizes. Maybe she had gotten a little plump since marrying Gillian. Didn't really matter. She was still in shape, she just relaxed more. She had gotten plump, not soft. There was a difference.

It didn't matter now. She'd been lean before Gillian, and now she had no reason not to be lean again.

She took her car keys from her pocket, and also found a few strands of the hair she'd taken from Gillian's body. She wrapped the hair around the keys, catching the strands on the teeth before putting them back into her pocket.

It was almost full dark before she reached her destination. She'd heard of the bar, but never had any real reason to visit. The interior lighting was similar to the dusk, so she didn't have to give her eyes time to adjust as she crossed the floor to the bar. It wasn't crowded due to the early hour, but there were enough drinkers around for her to feel the room go still when she entered. She lowered herself onto a stool, and the man beside her moved one seat further down to get away from her.

"Rude," she muttered. She knocked her knuckle on the bar. "Barkeep. I'll take whatever's on tap."

He eyed her from a distance. "You won't like what we have on tap. There are other bars that are probably more your style."

"What, because I'm gay?" She looked over her shoulder. A few patrons had adjusted their weight to stand more quickly. "Because I'm a cop?"

She heard the scraping of a chair and knew one of the men in her blind spot was now standing. She faced the bartender again.

"Oh! You probably mean because I'm the champion for good, and this is a demon bar."

The demon who had moved away from her held out his hands. "Just go away, all right? None of us are in the mood for this, Detective. So just forget you walked in here and we'll all go home happy tonight."

Riley shrugged and rose from the bar. "Sheesh. Never thought demons would be so discriminatory." She walked away, but not toward the door. She went to the jukebox and rested one hand on the glass as she examined the selection. Someone stepped up next to her, in her personal space, and she felt the presence of someone else directly behind her. They crowded her silently as she flipped through the CDs.

"Are these albums just randomly selected, or is there some significance to U2 being played in a demon bar? I always thought it was suspicious Bono wore those shades everywhere."

"You were asked to leave."

"Fuck that. I want to hear music."

The demon behind her but his arm around her neck and pulled her away from the jukebox. Her feet nearly left the floor, the toes of her shoes skidding on the hardwood as she was spun around and half-carried to the exit.

"You were asked to leave," the other demon said politely. "This is our place, and you really don't want to cause trouble here."

"Oh, I *really* do..." She had taken out her keys just before the demon picked her up. She held them in her fist, one hair-wrapped key extending between her index and middle fingers. When she was almost to the door, she punched over her shoulder and stabbed the demon in the eye. He howled and let her go, and Riley spun toward the one that had spoken to her from the jukebox. She slashed at him with her keys and he caught the edge on his knuckles. He recoiled and looked down at the wound.

"What the hell?"

"Holy relics. I believed in my wife Gillian Eleanor Hunt, and this morning she was murdered by a demon."

She stepped to the bar and used the stool to climb on top of it.

She threw herself at the bartender, who had just revealed a shotgun from beneath the bar. She slammed into him and pressed her keys into the side of his neck. He released his grip on the shotgun and Riley wrenched it away from him. A demon landed on top of her and she aimed the gun under her arm. She felt it press against a soft stomach before she made the bartender's finger squeeze the trigger. The demon's blood splattered on her back, and Riley bucked him off so she could stand up. She brought the gun with her and aimed it across the bar at the other patrons of the bar.

"This isn't because I'm a champion," she said as she lined up a shot and blew out one of the demon's knees. "This isn't because it's my job to take out scum like you." One of the demons reached for the weapon and lost his hand. "This is because a demon killed the only truly good person in this damn town." She shot one of the demons in the head. "Right now, I'm just a pissed off woman with four years of experience fighting you fuckers. And I'm going to put it to good use."

Once the demons in the bar were all down and bleeding, Riley grabbed a bottle of whisky off the bottom shelf and poured it onto the bar. She repeated the move, walking back and forth until liquor was dripping off both ends of the bar. She checked to make sure the bartender was down, then walked out into the main room among the groaning and wounded patrons.

"If any of you survive this, spread the word. One of your kind made a terrible... fucking... mistake."

She bent down to search the pockets of the dead or dying demons until she found a book of matches. She tucked the shotgun under her arm and walked to the door before she scraped it across the striking surface, then tucked it into the book so that it lay across the igniters of the other matches.

"I've got a new plan. And it involves killing as many of your kind as I can find."

She turned and tossed the time bomb toward the bar. It landed, and flames erupted to either side atop the surface of the poured alcohol. Riley left the bar and hurried across the street, breaking into a dead run moments before the front of the bar erupted in flames. She stepped into an alley and pressed her shoulder to the bricks as she watched it burn. No one came out, at least through the front, and she retreated further out of sight when the first responders showed up.

As she walked back to Kenzie and Chelsea's, taking the back

ways since she was covered with blood, she tried to remember how many demons had been in the bar. Ten? An even dozen? There might have been more in the back who were hiding, cowardly, during the melee. So maybe sixteen in total.

It was a good start.

Kenzie looked up to see a small white cup of water being held to her, and she smiled as she took it. "Thanks."

Zoe Briggs nodded and sat down next to her. "How are you holding up?"

Kenzie shrugged, but her mind was running at world record speeds. Chelsea had been to the doctor about the donation, and he confirmed that everything that needed to match did. The surgery was scheduled immediately, and they only had one night in which to debate whether or not it was the best way to go. Kenzie was worried about appearing too eager, horrified of giving the impression that she thought of Chelsea as anything less than whole. And then there was the whole minefield of the fact her partner was going to get her eyesight back because her best friend's wife had been brutally slaughtered...

"I hate how good I feel," she finally said. "Especially considering what Riley's going through right now. I feel sick. And dirty."

Zoe nodded. "There's no good way to feel right now. But at least some good can come out of Gillian's death."

"Silver lining," Kenzie murmured. "How is Riley holding up? I haven't seen her since she came back to the office covered in blood."

"She insists she's okay, but Priest has been following her. She's acting like a vigilante. If the demons weren't already covering up the fires and car accidents on their own, I would have to create a task force to go after her. But as it stands, everything is the result of a series of unusual accidents. Gas leaks, improperly aligned brakes, guns misfiring..."

"She's trying to get herself killed."

Zoe didn't respond to that. They sat in silence until a short Indian man in blue scrubs approached. "Mrs. Stanton?"

Kenzie said, "Uh, Kenzie Crowe. Chelsea's not my wife yet." Zoe looked up at that, but Kenzie ignored her. "Was there a problem with the surgery?"

He smiled and gestured out of the waiting area. "Could we speak privately? I assure you everything is fine, but there are some issues we need to resolve."

"Oh. Okay..." She glanced at Briggs and then followed the doctor around the corner. His name tag identified him as Isaac Marabathina when he turned to face her. "Is Chelsea okay?"

"Yes, she's fine. I checked in on the surgery before I came to find you because I knew you would think the worst, but Dr. Shaffer is very skilled at this manner of operation. They're in the home stretch now, and it's pretty much all over except for dotting a few Is and crossing some Ts. She'll be moved into recovery soon."

Kenzie felt the relief flooding through her like a physical sensation. "Thank God."

"What I wanted to speak to you about was..." He reached out and touched her arm just above the elbow, and suddenly her entire body felt cold. She tried to ask him to pull back, but she couldn't move. His thick eyebrows knit together as if he was searching for the proper thing to say, and then he focused on her again. "The demon that killed Riley Parra's spouse did so without proper authority. Marchosias was appalled. He was literally minutes away from attempting to set things right when Riley Parra took matters into her own hands. She has now murdered thirty-four of us. That cannot go unnoticed."

Kenzie managed to ball her left hand into a fist, but the effort of lifting it to strike him was far beyond her capabilities at the moment.

"Riley Parra has shattered the authority of the rules. She has crossed lines that were never meant to be crossed. Yes, in response to someone from our side crossing the line, but that violation resulted in a single death. And Riley is now using the death of her partner to benefit another. The scales must be balanced, Ms. Crowe. It's too late for me to alter the results of your girlfriend's operation, but I have a contingency plan. I am very sorry."

He held up his free hand with the index finger and pinky extended. Kenzie tried to pull away from him as the tips of the fingers began to burn, and a weak whistle emerged from her throat as he pressed the fingers against her eyes. The paralysis broke with her first scream, and he pulled back his hand as Kenzie hit the ground. Briggs came around the corner at a run, but Dr. Marabathina slammed into her hard enough to change her direction. She slammed into the wall and then hit the floor, dazed and too sore to get back to her feet.

Kenzie, hunched over in the middle of the corridor, clutched at her eyes and howled in pain as her eyes continued to burn.

Priest quietly closed the door and turned to face Riley. "She's sleeping. Although more technically, I suppose a doctor would call it a coma. The pain is too great for medicine to do any good."

Riley was leaning against the wall across from the bedroom. Her arms were crossed over her chest, and she was staring at the floor without seeing it. Priest could see her jaw clenching and unclenching before she finally looked up. When she spoke, her voice was a flat monotone. "What did it do to her?"

"It touched her eyes with Infernal Fire. They'll burn endlessly." She swallowed. "They'll have to be removed."

Riley stepped forward, drew her fist back, and drove it forward with enough force to crack the drywall. She hissed and flexed her fingers, but her ring finger didn't want to cooperate with the others. She touched the knuckle and her hand jerked away from her finger. Broken, most likely. She growled at her own idiocy and looked at Priest.

"What now?"

"Marchosias has balanced the damage you've done... I think now... things return to normal. As much as they can."

"They raped Gillian. They made me put her out of her misery. And then they blind Kenzie, and you're telling me it's even?"

Priest pled with her eyes. "Yes. Please, Riley. Any retaliation will just make Marchosias retaliate. Any attempt to~" Riley turned and walked away from her. Priest pursued. "Stop this, Riley. You're playing right into their hands. You're doing everything they want. You're not a champion anymore because you are doing more to destroy this city than Marchosias ever~"

Riley spun on her so fast that Priest backed up a step. Riley grabbed Priest's shirt with her still-working hand, shoved her back, and pressed her against the wall.

"I don't care. You're not an angel, they're not demons, and this isn't about Heaven or Hell anymore. They're the people who killed Gillian. I don't care what they do to the town. I'm going to make them pay for it."

"What if they attack Aissa next? Or Zoe? You're not thinking about your friends, Riley."

Riley let Priest go and started for the door again. "No. I'm thinking about Gillian."

"Riley!" Priest's voice reverberated more than any human voice had a right to. Riley stopped in the doorway. "Do not force me to stop you."

Riley didn't turn around. "Don't come after me, Priest. I've killed angels before." She slammed the door behind her as she left, and Priest heard quiet whimpering coming from the bedroom where she'd left Kenzie. The fight had woken her, so Priest went to take care of her before the moans turned into full-fledged wails of pain.

The clinic seemed to have been placed in her way like divine intervention, so Riley went inside and had the doctor X-ray her hand and set the finger in a splint. Fortunately it was her left hand, so she wouldn't be crippled for what needed to be done. The doctor recognized Riley from the newspapers, so he didn't question how she had gotten hurt. As he tenderly wrapped her wounded hand, she asked him a question that made him pause momentarily and eye her with suspicion. She held his gaze until finally, haltingly, he answered her.

She thanked him, paid with a credit card she was pretty sure wouldn't cover the charge, and went back to her mission.

Her gun was tucked in the back of her belt, and she moved it to the front where it would be seen as she walked into City Hall. Most of the people in the lobby were leftovers from the previous administration, not yet replaced with minions from Marchosias' stable. Riley ignored the receptionist's repeated, "Ma'am? Excuse me, ma'am?" as she walked to the stairs and headed up. The woman fluttered just to one side as Riley continued up, ignoring her. The woman didn't have the authority to physically restrain Riley, so eventually she turned and retreated to find a security officer. Riley didn't plan to be around long enough to be taken away.

The carbon copy duo who had visited the police station with acting-Mayor Siskin was positioned at either side of the office door. One of them stepped forward and lifted her hand to stop Riley's forward progress. Riley reached up and grabbed her hand, twisting the wrist just to the point of breaking as she spun and shot her leg out. The other twin, who had been coming to help her clone, ran into the outstretched foot and doubled over in pain. Riley released the captive wrist and shoved the standing twin back against the wall. She hit with enough impact that her entire body tensed, and Riley was through the door before either of them recovered.

She pulled her gun and aimed it at the blonde woman behind the desk. Lark Siskin glanced up calmly, took in the gun, and then leaned to one side to check on the state of her guards. Finally she straightened in her seat and laced her hands over her stomach.

"Well, Detective Parra. You could have just called to make an appointment."

"Detective Parra, stop."

She didn't have to turn to see who had joined them in the room; Marchosias had a very distinctive voice. He moved around the perimeter of the room so Riley could see him, but she never took her eyes off her target.

"The past few days have been extremely... wrong. Ill-advised." He looked pointedly at Lark, who ignored him just as pointedly. "Gillian was never supposed to die. She was fair game for torture, for possession, but we would never... what was done to her was an affront. I have survived in this city for a very long time because of the rules set down when the first champion was chosen. I've had a good life, Riley. This isn't about good or evil. It's a *game*.

"Remember when you defeated Gail? You sacrificed Gillian. Who rewrote history so that you could make a different decision? I don't believe in love or decency, but I do love the game. I love my life. So why don't we just calm down, and we can find a way to settle this in a way that doesn't leave the streets boiling. We'll call a truce. The hostilities can end right now, and we can all work together to set things right. Now, I can't undo what's been done~"

Riley shot Lark in the head.

She rolled her shoulder and looked at Marchosias, whose eyes had widened to an almost comical degree.

"Sorry. You were just going on and on, and I'd heard all I needed to hear. You can't bring Gillian back? We're done talking."

"What have you done?" he hissed.

"She'll live. I asked the doctor who fixed my hand, and he said she could be saved. She'll be in a vegetative state, and she'll shit herself and eat through a tube, but she'll still technically be alive."

Marchosias rounded the desk and gingerly touched Lark's chin. Ruby-red blood ran down the right side of her face, dripping onto her shirt. He glared at Riley. "You should have just shot her in the forehead. Killed her right out. I could have replaced her with someone more... manageable."

"That's the thing, Marky Mark. I don't want things to go back to normal. Normal doesn't exist anymore." She turned and walked out of the office, sweeping her gun from one twin to the other so they wouldn't try to attack her. They barely acknowledged her, too focused on their former benefactor bleeding in the office. Security officers moved to stop her, but upon recognizing her they became uncertain in their stances.

"Your boss is upstairs bleeding. I would call 911 if I were you."

In the ensuing panic, she strolled out of the building. Marchosias was waiting for her on the sidewalk outside. His face was darker, his eyes looking like craters.

"You don't want to play me without the rules, Detective Parra. You won't like the outcome."

"That's your problem, Marchosias. You think I'm still concerned about how this all ends. You think I'm still concerned with anything. You took my wife. You blinded my friend."

He was wide-eyed, panicked, and she'd never seen him look more human. "Lark... broke a covenant. She went outside~"

"Shut the fuck up, Marchosias. You want a real war? You've got one. I'm abandoning my protection as champion, as of right now. Your demons want me? They know where to find me. This city isn't a prize anymore. It's our battleground."

Marchosias drew a deep breath. "Be careful, Riley."

"I'm done being careful. I'm living on borrowed time. My life ended when Gillian's did. As long as I'm here, and as long as I'm capable, I'm going to spend every waking minute taking down as many of your kind as possible. Now *run*."

Marchosias shook his head sadly. "You won't survive the onslaught, Riley." He disappeared while Riley was blinking, leaving her alone on the sidewalk.

She stuck her gun back into her belt and looked up and down the street. She could hear the wail of the ambulance siren, and probably a few of her fellow officers, responding to the second mayoral death in less than a month.

"Who says I want to survive?" Riley murmured. She looked down at her broken hand, turned her back to the sirens, and walked away.

two years later

Caitlin Priest shook a pill into her cupped palm and popped it into her mouth. She swallowed it dry and moved away from the window. The barricade near the stairs had been moved, and she told one of the recruits to put it back into place. He hurried off to comply. Priest wore a police jacket over a bulky bulletproof vest, an unnecessary precaution but it would have raised eyebrows if she declined to wear one. Most of the people in the room knew she was an angel, but there were some new arrivals that weren't trustworthy yet.

Not that it really mattered one way or the other. She sat down behind her desk and looked at the map she'd left there earlier. The morning update. Overnight No Man's Land had advanced three blocks, Marchosias' forces extending their barricades from Warren Street to East Avenue. On the south side of the city, fires were burning in empty tenements. Firemen were reluctant to approach for fear it was another trap. They'd lost eighteen men in the last one and they were embracing caution. Priest didn't blame them.

Michael and the other angels had been forced into action, so Heavenly and Hellish armies were marching in the streets. Priest could hear their battle raging, and she felt the part of her that she kept mashed down deep inside aching to join them. She clenched her jaw, her teeth grating against each other as she fought back the Divine presence. She needed to be here. The humans needed someone capable of fighting back in charge. If she let Zerachiel free, she knew she would run to her brothers and sisters without looking back.

She popped another pill and grimaced at the taste. She hadn't slept in eight days. As long as she was awake, she could hold on to Caitlin Priest and she could ignore the angel clawing to get out.

Priest rubbed her temples and wondered if migraine meds would react badly with her uppers. She was twitchy. She watched her hand as it lay on the desk, but it wasn't still. The fingers shook and danced against the wood until she folded them against the palm and dropped them to her lap. She took a deep breath and let it out slowly as she looked around the room.

The police department was a thing of the past. Now there were just former cops and hastily trained volunteers who looked like thugs in riot gear. Zoe Briggs came out of her office and caught Priest's eye and crossed the room to her.

"A squad car was just flipped over outside Trailblazer's restaurant. The two officers managed to get out, but someone was waiting on a nearby rooftop with a sniper rifle."

Priest winced. "Demon?"

"We don't know yet."

Humans were being humans. Those with a tendency toward violence and anarchy were thriving in the new world order. In addition to people who knew and understood exactly what was at stake, they had to deal with those who were causing trouble just to be destructive. Looters, arsonists, muggers, rapists... Priest was getting her fill of the worst in humanity. She rubbed her face and stood up, looking around her at the options.

"Who is available to take? Where is Alamo?"

Briggs' expression softened. "Alamo... he was killed this morning, Caitlin. I told you that."

"Oh. Right." She flexed and clenched her fingers until they stopped shaking. Briggs put a hand on Priest's arm and stepped into her personal space. Priest closed her eyes and, a moment later, felt the soft press of lips against hers. Priest returned the kiss and brushed Briggs' hair back. "I'm fine, Zoe."

"Are you?"

Priest opened her eyes and finally nodded. "I will be."

Briggs kissed her again, and this time Priest let herself truly enjoy it. It was hard to say which of them had been more surprised by their leap from coworkers to lovers. Briggs was only nominally attracted to women, but Priest was an exception to the rule. She was something solid, something trustworthy, and something real in a world gone completely insane.

"Be careful."

"Always."

They squeezed each other's hands before Priest stepped away from her desk. She let the recruits move aside the barricade again and slipped through, waiting for it to be replaced before she started descending. Outside, the day was dark. Buildings were on fire in No Man's Land, and it tinted the sky at the horizon with blood-red and sulfurous clouds. The sun seemed reluctant to even try brightening the streets, causing it to cast long shadows along the pavement that only served to enhance just how bleak everything was.

Priest took out her weapon as soon as she was on the street. It was standard practice for the handful of officers who still officially carried a badge; never be seen without a fully-loaded weapon you're prepared to discharge. A gang of five or six kids were moving down the street opposite, and Priest eyed them as they neared. They saw her gun, her vest, and her unwavering expression and decided she was too much of a threat. They moved on, but Priest knew they would find a victim before long.

She was almost to her car, an armored former-SWAT vehicle that she had taken control of when its original owner was killed, when she heard someone calling her name. She turned and saw a recruit rushing toward her, red-faced and panting. She backed up, meeting him halfway.

"Detective Priest. We have a sighting of Riley Parra."

Priest's face felt cold as the blood left it, but she kept her gaze steady. "Where?"

"The waterfront. Someone saw her messing with one of the discharge pipes about five minutes ago. I don't know which~"

"I think I do. Thank you, recruit." She turned and started back to the car, but it was suddenly staying grounded was too much to ask. She closed her eyes and directed her inner voice to Zerachiel.

If I let you out, promise me you'll behave.

She unfurled her wings and took two running steps before she bent her knees to launch herself into the air. She felt Zerachiel's presence at the back of her mind, a pressure like fog closing over the back of her brain. She pushed it back and arced over the city, avoiding the areas of higher violence to focus on the long and slender line of the waterfront. She came in for a landing, her shoes making deceptively quiet taps on the pavement as she transitioned from flying to jogging. Her wings retracted and she smoothed down her jacket as she stepped off the road and over the barrier.

"Riley?"

She was kneeling in front of the drainage pipe, elbows on her knees and face turned toward the emptiness. Priest approached cautiously; last time she tried talking to Riley she was rewarded with a bullet in her stomach. Without Zerachiel's help, that had taken a long time to heal. Riley glanced at her incuriously and then stood up. Priest braced herself, but Riley shook her head and smiled.

"Relax. I'm not going to shoot you again."

"Forgive me if I don't take that on faith."

Riley looked at her. "Faithless. Just like the rest of us. That's a shame."

"I'm not faithless, Riley. I'm just cautious. Do you blame me?"

"Nah." She gestured at the pipe. "I thought... if I came here... I thought there would be something."

Priest looked at the pipe. "This is where Ridwan's body was found?"

Riley nodded. "I've been all over, looking for the place where it started. I found the intersection where Christine Lee died. I found the spot where I was thrown off a building by Marchosias. I even rode that runaway train you stopped. I can't find it, Cait. I can't find the beginning."

"What would that do? If you found the beginning?"

"I don't know. It has to mean something, right? It has to be important. If I go there, maybe I can end it."

Priest quietly took stock of Riley's injuries. The fingers of her left hand were still skewed, the result of a broken hand that had been re-crushed before it could fully heal. A burn on Riley's neck was mostly concealed by the high collar of her shirt. Three long cuts ran down her right arm, from elbow to wrist, and Riley's right hand was wrapped with gauze that had become soiled with dirt and grit from crawling around the muddy waterfront.

"How?"

"I don't know, Cait. I thought I would know by now, but I don't."

Priest was saddened by the defeat in Riley's voice, but by now she was used to it. "Riley, you have to stand up and fight. You have to make amends for what has happened here. I know how badly you must feel the loss of Gillian because I still feel it. I can't imagine what it must be like for you."

"It's what you felt like when Zerachiel left," Riley said. "Unfinished. Partial. Like the best part of you was just... gone." She looked down. "I saw Kenzie. I'm glad she finally got out of that mental institution."

Priest tensed. "Yes. We were all worried for a time."

Kenzie had been committed to a local institution following the surgery to remove her eyes. It was originally meant as a therapeutic placement, a way to teach her to cope with her new blindness, but Kenzie's mental faculties deteriorated after Chelsea abandoned her. Newly sighted, Chelsea had crumbled under the weight of her guilt, certain that Kenzie's situation was her fault. When the doctor refused to take Chelsea's eyes and give them to Kenzie, Chelsea walked away. No one had seen her since. Kenzie, however, had finally checked herself out of the hospital and rejoined the battle in a new capacity.

"Riley. You must come back."

"No, I don't. I have to find a way to fix it."

"Gillian has been dead for two years, Riley. Her body was cremated. Anything that could have been done... it's too late."

Riley said, "I can't accept that."

"You have to, Riley."

"No. I'll find a way to fix it, and it will undo all of this. I can't be distracted by fighting a war that will never happen."

Priest stepped in front of Riley. "And if you fail?"

"Then I'll die, and none of this will matter anyway. Nothing matters, Cait. Either I succeed and get her back, or I die trying. Either way, none of this is important."

"What about everyone else who losing their lovers? Their children? Are you going to tell them that those losses don't matter?"

Riley turned and walked away. Priest pursued her. "If I undo it, then this war doesn't happen and it reverses all those deaths. This whole sequence of events will be erased. So by saving Gillian, I save more people than I could just running around putting out fires."

"So none of this matters?"

"None of it."

"Muse is dead."

Riley stopped walking. Priest caught up and moved in front of her again. "He was trying to save some people when the empty apartment building they were squatting in caught fire. He got a few of them out, but the smoke overwhelmed him."

"That fire won't happen if~"

Priest slapped Riley across the face, doing it again before Riley could recover. Riley backed up, one hand to her cheek as she stared at Priest in shock.

"Shut up. Just shut up about fixing it, about making amends. You can't do it, Riley. It's impossible, okay? Gillian is dead, she's gone, and you're not doing anybody any favors by holding onto it. You're killing yourself and letting this city go to Hell. You're a child, Riley. And if you're willing to let your friends, and your loved ones, pay the consequences while you go off on this fool's errand, then you're not the woman I thought you were. And you were never worthy to be the champion."

Riley blinked at her and turned around to face the skyline. "I was wrong," Riley said softly.

Priest's voice softened as well. She stepped forward and put a hand on Riley's shoulders. "I know. Gillian would have been proud about how hard you fought to save her. But she has to be released, Riley."

"No, not about that. I was wrong about shooting you again." She turned and pressed her gun against the soft, exposed skin beneath the edge of Priest's vest. She pulled the trigger twice, and Priest dropped to her knees with her eyes wide and lips parted in shock. Riley guided her down to the ground and whispered, "Don't come near me again, you fucking traitor. Gillian would be appalled at how easily you gave up."

Riley stepped over Priest and started toward the barrier. She was about to step over when Priest managed to get her gun out of the holster. She lined up the shot and pulled the trigger. Riley grunted in surprise, her balance upset by straddling the barrier, and she twisted as she fell. Her eyes were wide as she dropped, looking back toward Priest with a look of total and abject betrayal. Priest would never forget the fury in those eyes.

She dropped her gun, left arm extended. Her fingers went slack, and the gun clattered to the stones of the waterfront. She looked at the clouds overhead, trying to determine if they were storm clouds or smoke from the fires. She coughed and felt blood trickling from the corner of her mouth. That couldn't be good.

Zerachiel... save me.

Zerachiel's laugh echoed in her head, and Priest closed her eyes.

Marchosias was singing.

Riley inhaled sharply, going from unconscious to instantly awake in the space of that one breath. Her shoulder felt like it had been nailed to the ground with an iron spike, and she cried out when she tried to sit up. Marchosias stopped mid-verse and she heard the shuffle of his shoes on tile before he appeared over her. He smiled beneficently.

"Good morning, Detective Parra. You look like shit."

"That's how you talk to girls? You're never gonna get a date to the prom." She reached up and touched her side, knowing she had felt Priest's bullet go in. "So. Dr. Devil. Am I ever going to play the piano again?"

Marchosias smiled and took Riley's left hand. His touch was surprisingly gentle, but she tensed nonetheless as he examined the broken finger. "I could fix that."

"What would it cost me?"

"Your eternal soul." He chuckled and put her hand down. "Just kidding. We demons tend to ask for more concrete payment these days. Humans have gotten so good at destroying their own souls that there's really not a lot for us to do."

Riley touched her side just below and behind her armpit, where Priest's bullet had gone in. "Bandages? Stitches? You didn't just hoodoo your voodoo on me?"

"It wasn't necessary. The wound wasn't life-threatening."

"And Priest?"

Marchosias shrugged. "I arrived quickly, but she was already gone. And if you're going to ask how I knew where you were... you shot your guardian angel. Things like that resonate on a certain sphere. A sphere to which I happen to be very sensitive. I had hoped to collect both of you, but I'll make due with a half measure of success."

"That would have been a nice dinner. You, me, and an angel. The bloodshed would have started before the appetizers were cold."

Marchosias' face grew hard. "And that, my dear Riley, is why I hoped to scoop Zerachiel up when I grabbed you."

"Kill us both?"

"On the contrary. I hope to broker peace between you."

Riley laughed and then winced. "Yeah, that's you all over, Mark. The Peacemaker."

"This isn't what I wanted, Riley. I wanted a clean battle. This is anarchy."

"You guys *love* anarchy."

Marchosias walked away from the table and approached a sink. He began washing his hands as he spoke. "There is no honor in a melee. People die by accident or from ricochet, there's no victory. Even if every good-hearted person in this city dies tomorrow, it will be attributed to mayhem. Not because of something I did. I want to *win*, I don't want to be victor by default. I never..." He inhaled and then turned to face Riley so she could see his eyes when he spoke. "I refused the plan that killed Dr. Hunt. I feel it's important for you to know I had a line. Murdering her was a step too far."

"Oh, bullshit. You've gone after Gillian before. You had one of your minions possess her. You threatened me with her damn stuffed bunny when this whole mess started. You planted a bomb in the police station where we work. Don't tell me you have standards."

"What did all of those things have in common, Riley? You saved her. Each time, Gillian survived. And the bunny? The bunny is proof that I have standards. I *threatened* her with the rabbit, and she left town to remain safe. The bomb was planted, and you were given an opportunity to disarm it. Gillian was possessed by the Duchess, and you retrieved her intact. You were given a chance to save her. The playing ground was level, and you succeeded each time. Gillian was assaulted with no provocation. You weren't given a chance to save her."

"And you feel guilty? Don't." She slipped off the table and looked down at herself. She was wearing a white T-shirt, spattered with blood. "Where are the rest of my clothes?"

"Destroyed. I have someone going to get you more. It may take a while... this was a bad neighborhood to begin with."

"Screw it." She put her hand against her side to help with the pain as she shuffled toward the door. "Thanks for patching me up, Mark. Next time I see you, I'll yell a warning before I put a bullet through your eye."

"How far would you go?"

Riley stopped walking.

"What would you give up for a chance to put things right?"

Riley looked down at herself and thought about the losses and failures of the past two years. She was weary, and she felt like she was being pulled into a permanent fall. She could feel the vertigo at the edges of her vision and she couldn't correct herself or find her equilibrium. She shook her head and set off another wave of dizziness.

"It can't be set right. I've talked to angels, and Zerachiel tried to convince me of the truth way back when we were still being civil to one another. I can't... it's been too long. Gillian can't be saved." A tear she hadn't felt fall rolled down her cheek. "Right now I'm just trying to end things as painfully as possible."

"Martyring yourself for someone who is already gone?"

"Something like that."

Marchosias said, "There's a way. But the cost would be great."

Riley smiled. "Is now when you ask for my eternal soul?"

"I honestly don't know. I'm not the one who sets the toll." She heard his soft footsteps as he crossed the room. "Lark Siskin was a bad choice for my champion. She defied me. Cost me a victory I was rightfully due. That pisses me off enough to work with you to put things right."

"The city is as gone as Gillian."

"It doesn't have to be. You can still save it."

Riley turned and looked at him. "You didn't take off my shirt to operate, did you?"

Marchosias tilted his head to the side in confusion. "Sorry. You're not exactly my type."

"So you didn't see. You should have known anyway, but..." Riley gripped the hem of her shirt and turned her back to him again. She lifted it and showed him her tattooed shoulder. The twin-torch image that had so long ago been inked by Christine Lee was gone, replaced by a horrid burn that spread from Riley's neck down to her upper arm.

"I scorched it off. Nearly immolated myself in the process, but it's gone. You want a champion, you want someone to save the city, you don't need me. You need Aissa Good. She's the one in charge now." She walked out of the room, leaving Marchosias dumbfounded behind her. "I'm not a champion anymore," Riley called to him. "I'm just somebody who is waiting for one of your guys to get lucky."

Zerachiel opened her eyes and looked down at her body. She was topless, in a brassiere, and her abdomen was covered with blood. The flesh beneath was unmarred, however. She pushed herself up and looked around the room. A row of dirty windows let in tarnished brown light, and she could see a table covered with armaments, knives and guns that looked heavily used but well cared for. Strings of ammunition, like brass Christmas decorations, draped everything. She swung her legs over the edge of the table and stood up. She heard movement in the next room and turned her head as Aissa entered.

"Angel or mortal?"

"I am Zerachiel."

Aissa nodded and walked to one of the tables. Her hair was cut short, only a few curls remaining to cover her ears like a nun's wimple. She wore at least two shirts that Zerachiel could see, as well as a bulky army jacket. A framework enclosed her right leg, brackets pinching her cargo pants in order to hold the metal to her body. The stirrup clanked against the floor as she moved. Zerachiel observed the young woman's movement before she spoke.

"How is your leg?"

"I can still use it. That's enough for now. Do you want anything to drink?"

"It's not necessary." She found her shirt, the hem now ringed with dried blood, and chose against putting it on. "Did Riley survive her injuries?"

Aissa turned, her brows knit together in a frown. "Riley was here?"

"No, she was the one who shot me. You didn't find her when you picked me up?"

"No one picked you up. You came here, half-dead, bleeding all over yourself... we hoped you could fill in the blanks when you woke up... if you woke up. We weren't entirely sure that would be a foregone conclusion. So Riley is the one who shot you?"

"Yes. We had a disagreement."

"So who shot Riley?"

"Priest did." Aissa narrowed her eyes. "She was using the drugs that keep me docile, so I was barely conscious, but I know what I saw."

Aissa began limping back to the door. "Where was this?"

"The waterfront where Ridwan's body was found." Zerachiel followed her into the main room of the warehouse. The woman once known as Kenzie Crowe was sitting at a desk typing, her right ear plugged with an earphone. Her fingers moved over the keys, and she occasionally paused as the computer or some program spoke to her. She wore her typical uniform of fatigues, a white-gray-black camouflage outfit designed for urban environs. Her hair was carefully braided, and her face was concealed behind a teardrop-shaped mask that covered her burns. The mask had no eye holes, but left her mouth and nose exposed.

"Tiresias." Kenzie turned toward her. "I need to know any demonic activity near the waterfront around the time Wings here showed up."

Kenzie's fingers moved over the keyboard. She was hacked into the city's security mainframe, which an angel technician had helped upgrade to detect demons.

"So I guess Priest is asleep?" the woman once known as Kenzie Crowe said.

Zerachiel said, "I'm not sure. I don't hear her."

Tiresias stopped typing. "You mean she might be dead?"

"Caitlin Priest never existed. She is a consciousness that should never have existed. This body is a shell I constructed~"

Tiresias held up a hand. "You know what, shut the fuck up. I have what you're looking for. Apparently there was a demon there." She listened again. "Considering the vibrations he left on the spiritual plane, it was a heavy hitter."

"Marchosias?"

"If not him, someone just as big and nasty."

Aissa sighed. "Well, let's hope it's the devil we know."

Tiresias said, "So we're hoping that Riley is in the hands of Marchosias, the demon who has been waging war on us for the past two years?"

"Yep." Aissa sighed. "Strange days."

Zerachiel rolled her shoulders and inhaled sharply. "Caitlin

Priest isn't dead. But she's far too weak to take over. Aissa, will you do me a favor?"

"If I can."

"Convince Caitlin to cease her attempts to control me. This body was never hers. If need be, I can abandon it and she will die. I understand her loyalty to Riley. Believe me, I do. But she is not helping Riley as much as she thinks she is. Protecting Riley is my job, and I've been doing it a hell of a lot longer than she has."

Aissa shrugged. "Don't get angry at me. I don't even have a guardian angel." She looked at Tiresias. "At least I didn't when I was a Good Girl." She touched the back of Tiresias' neck, and Tiresias smiled before shying away. "Riley and Priest are partners, Z. Priest may have been born to be a shell, but you have to admit she's evolved."

Tiresias said, "No, she doesn't. Their kind doesn't believe in evolution."

Aissa hid her smile behind her hand, glancing at Tiresias' computer. "The demonic presence that apparently picked up Riley. Can you figure out where it went after retrieving her?"

"I can do a sweep of the general area and see what I pick up. It'll just be a matter of following the ripples he's making. It's like~"

"Like tracking a submarine by watching the wake it creates on the water on top of it."

"It's Bugs Bunny tunneling through a field. You just have to look for the disturbance." Her fingers moved across the keyboard again. Before losing her eyes, she had been a mediocre typist at best. Now it was as if the keyboard was an extension of her hands. "Got him." The corner of her mouth ticked up, and she tilted her head slightly to the left. "East. He crossed Davenport and then... I have to find him again. Sector one, clear. Sector two... gotcha. On Hughes, he cut south."

Aissa took out her cell phone. "I'll head out. You call me when you have a direction."

Tiresias nodded. "Be careful, Aissa."

"Always. Zerachiel, think about what I said about Riley and Priest. If you two weren't spending half your time fighting each other, you could both do Riley a lot more good than you are now." She took her guns off the wall next to the door and slipped them into their holsters as she stepped out into the sunshine. She hauled the door shut behind her, leaving Zerachiel and Tiresias alone together.

Tiresias turned in her chair and looked toward Zerachiel. Even without sight, it was easy for her to tell where the angel was standing.

"So. Just you and me." She drummed her hands on her thighs and pressed her lips together.

Zerachiel grimaced. "Caitlin Priest is the one you fornicate with, not me."

"I still know my way around the body."

Zerachiel shook her head and walked away, and Tiresias snickered to herself. She really had just wanted the angel to stop lurking. Zerachiel was darker, angrier since Gillian's death. Of course it wasn't like she should point fingers when it came to people changing. She reached up and stroked the smooth surface of the mask before turning back to her computer to continue the search for Marchosias and their missing former champion.

The hovel Riley called home had the bare minimum necessary for life. A bare mattress, a scavenged chair, a hot plate in the corner, and a sheet hung over the window to keep the sunlight out. Demons did most of their damage during the night, so Riley slept during the day. It was also easier to sleep during the day. The nightmares had to work harder to find her. She was so exhausted that it took her a moment to realize the entire room had been redecorated since she'd last seen it that morning. She stared at the ornate furniture, the plush carpet, and the marble statue of Hercules standing in the far corner.

Marchosias came out of the kitchen in a frilled apron, stirring the pot he was carrying in his other hand.

"Honey! You're home. I was just about to finish dinner. Kick your shoes off, relax..."

"Get out of my apartment."

Marchosias looked around. "Does this *look* like your apartment?"

Riley closed the door. "Good point. What the hell are you... am I..." She closed her eyes. "What's the point, Marchosias? I just want to sleep. I already told you to stop messing with me. I'm too tired and your bullshit is just exhausting."

"You shouldn't have burnt off your tattoo, Riley. It's complicated matters. I need a champion, so now we'll have to involve Aissa."

"Involve her in what?"

Marchosias put down the pot. Color seemed to bleed from it and, within moments, Riley was standing in her hovel again. Marchosias wore a charcoal suit over a black shirt.

"Your precious angel couldn't help you get Gillian back. There's not a demon or a seraphim in this town with that kind of power. Even I can't do it. But there is a... higher power to which you can appeal. Think of it like the Supreme Court. Have you ever read the myth of Orpheus?"

Riley shrugged. "I don't know. Has Spielberg made it into a movie yet?"

"Orpheus was a musician. Brilliant, talented, beloved by the gods. Then one day his... girlfriend, wife... someone like that, was bitten by a snake. She died, and Orpheus was devastated. Couldn't play anymore. So he decided to go down to Hades and beg for the life of his lover. Persephone, and that's a whole 'nother story altogether, was so moved by his appeal that she granted his wish."

Riley whistled and gently lowered herself to the mattress. The wound in her side was aching. "Boy, Mark, when you tell somebody 'go to Hell,' you really make an evening of it. So you want me to skip on down to Hades—"

"The story isn't *true*. It's just something the ancient Greeks wrote down to explain why my kind and the angels were hanging around. They were fun. I liked Aeneas." He waved his hand to clarify his thoughts. "Anyway. My point is that Orpheus found a cave and went to a different plane to appeal to the higher powers. You already know where that cave is."

Riley laughed and put her arm across her eyes. "Right. We have a ton of caves in the city. You mean the Underground, right? Or maybe you—" She sat up so suddenly that it felt like someone had pressed a spike into her side. "Ahh!"

"Now you've got it."

"The Ladder?"

Marchosias nodded. "It was created to connect the Pure and the Profane with this realm. It still exists. The blood of a champion can open it. I was hoping that would be you, but now we have to add someone else into the matter. Can your girl be trusted?"

Riley stood up and advanced on him. "What the hell good is it to open the Ladder? You're just trying to play me. Trying to win—"

Marchosias shouted to interrupt her. When she stopped talking, he said, "I can't win! Not like this, no matter what happens. Everything that has happened the past two years has been because of *her*. She wants my position. Gail Finney wanted to be a demon, but Siskin wants to be Satan. And you know, even comatose with a goddamn bullet in her head, I'm not going to count her out. There must be a change. A drastic, fundamental change to this city. Bringing Gillian Hunt back to life, returning you to your sanity, is what I need. And it's what you need. So we have, in a sense, become bedfellows. I need you, and you need me. We can work together to open the Ladder, and I will safely guide you through."

"What will happen when I go through?"

"I haven't the foggiest. I've never known anyone brave or reckless enough to try it. It was created for angels or demons. But a champion, or former champion, might have a chance to survive it. Look at it this way, Detective... what do you have to lose?"

Riley stared at him, looking for any sign of deceit despite the fact the demon was almost incapable of giving himself away.

"I want this town fixed when I take control of it, Riley. I want to stand proud and earn my victory, and I can only do that with your help. Please."

It was the politeness that finally convinced her. She worked her jaw, narrowed her eyes, and then said, "I think I can get Aissa to meet us somewhere."

Aissa was waiting on the front steps of the old 410 precinct. The windows had long ago been boarded up, and the bricks around them were darkened by swirls of smoke damage from the fire. The original doors were long gone, replaced by steel doors held together by a sturdy lock. The police who still worked upstairs under the auspices of Zerachiel and Caitlin Priest's peacekeeper regime had other, secret entrances they used.

A meager rain had started falling, so she turned up the hood of the sweater underneath her leather jacket.

Zerachiel was pacing on the sidewalk at the base of the steps, so she saw Riley's approach first. She sensed it, like a tickle at the back of her throat, and she turned before the secondary sensation had time to register. She bristled and moved up to where Aissa was standing to block her from any assault. "It's a trick."

"What?" Aissa stepped to one side. Riley was approaching them, but there was someone with her. "Is that Marchosias?"

Zerachiel's face was dark. The shadows around her eyes seemed to grow as she watched Riley approach with the devil. Riley was moving stiffly, favoring her uninjured side as she stopped in front of the stairs and looked up. "Aissa. Smart of you to bring a bodyguard. Zerachiel. Haven't seen you since I shot the woman who shares your body. How is she?"

"She is none of your concern. Why have you brought *that?*"

Marchosias hissed. "Ouch. Why do we have to resort to rudeness?"

Zerachiel came down one step. "You've crossed yet another line, Riley. Another one."

"Since when do you care? You're so pissed that Caitlin Priest took over your body that you haven't exactly been fulfilling your job as my guardian, have you?"

"There were others who needed me. Aissa, Tiresias~"

Riley said, "Who the hell is Tiresias?"

"Kenzie," Aissa said.

Riley looked at her, tilted her head to the side in confusion, but then dropped the subject. "Marchosias is here because he wants to help us put things right. He seems to think I've gone insane~"

Marchosias held up one finger. "Something I'm sure that Zerachiel could agree with me on, which means we may not be as different as she might think."

Zerachiel glared at him until Marchosias grimaced and touched his temples. Riley could see that Priest was radiating with energy, and she was concentrating it at Marchosias. Riley stepped between them. "Cut it out."

"Protecting a demon, Detective?"

"Protecting a chance to fix this."

Aissa said, "Riley, what are you proposing? Just tell us and we'll hear you out."

"He wants to open the Ladder."

Zerachiel laughed. "You're right, demon. I do agree with you."

"I want Aissa there to make sure he closes it once I'm through."

Zerachiel's laughter faded. "Through?"

"I'm going into the Ladder. I'm going to beg whoever I find on the other side to let Gillian come back. If I have her, then I can get to work on~"

"I should kill you now," Aissa said softly. There were tears in her eyes. "You're so far gone, Riley. I should have killed you when this all started, but I hoped... I kept hoping you would find your way back to us. It would have saved this city so much grief."

Marchosias coughed and turned toward Riley. Sotto voce, he said, "She's not wrong, you know..."

"Shut up. This is it, okay? This is my last ditch effort to make things better. If I can bring Gillian back, then maybe I can come back, too. Maybe I can be who you need me to be."

Aissa said, "And if you don't come back?"

"Then I'm out of your way. No more insane raids on demon strongholds. No more retaliation. Either way, your tomorrow looks brighter. But it all starts with the Ladder, and that's why I need you."

"Why me?"

Zerachiel said, "Because the Ladder requires the blood of a champion to unlock it."

Aissa said, "Oh. Well... why me? You could have taken as much blood as you needed from Lark Siskin. It's not like she'd miss it."

Marchosias' eyes widened. "Huh. I actually didn't think about that~"

Zerachiel was watching Riley. "You thought of it though. Didn't you, Riley?"

Riley didn't answer.

"You forced yourself to ask Aissa, knowing she would bring me, knowing how I would react. You wanted someone to try to stop you."

Riley shook her head. "I have to do this. I have to open the Ladder and go through."

"You'll fail," Zerachiel said softly.

"Then what does this mean? If someone like Gillian can just be taken away like that, and we can't do anything to fix it, then why the hell bother fighting? I'm tired. And I'm done. I just want to try one more Hail Mary pass. And if it kills me... well. At least I go out trying."

Aissa said, "You're asking me to help you kill yourself."

"Better than forcing one of you to kill me. I mean, that's where this is heading, right? I'm rogue. I burned off my tattoo, threw out my badge. You guys don't trust me anymore. Hell, I didn't even know Kenzie had changed her name. I'm making this city worse. I'm the bad guy. Sooner or later, you or Priest or Briggs will have to put me down for the greater good. Do you really think you'll be able to do that? Any of you?"

Aissa looked at Zerachiel, who had averted her gaze.

"Come on, Zerachiel. You've sat back and watched me go through a ton of bad things because you had to. Now I'm asking you to let something bad happen to me. And who knows? Maybe it'll work out. Maybe I'll bring Gillian home. I don't want to die without at least trying."

Zerachiel straightened her back and looked at Marchosias. "I don't want you there."

"Tough titty, said the kitty." Marchosias shrugged. "It's my plan."

"Why?"

Marchosias rolled his eyes. "Again? Fine. I hate what Lark Siskin did, and if there's any way I can fix that and get back to some good old-fashioned warring, I'm all for it. I want to win this fight, Zerachiel. I'm willing to do whatever it takes, even if that means working with Ms. Parra here, however briefly."

Aissa said, "Then why are we wasting time? Let's go."

Zerachiel and Marchosias worked together to access Bethel Luz. They weren't aware what, if any, defenses the building still had, but both angel and demon felt it was best that they work as a team to avoid any shenanigans. Riley remembered all too clearly the pain of broken bones she'd received within these walls, and she doubted Zerachiel or any of her brethren would give her a magic healing touch if she was hurt this time.

Zerachiel and Marchosias led the way downstairs, Aissa following and Riley bringing up the rear. As they descended, the air seemed to become darker and more oppressive than could be explained by the building's walls. It felt like the air was full of darkness and they were moving through it like water. Aissa was watching the floor and turned back to Riley, her face visible despite the apparent darkness.

"No spider webs. No rats, or signs of scavengers. Nothing's squatting in this building."

Riley felt a chill and nodded. The building was certainly creepy, but the fact it housed a supernatural portal that was opened at the dawn of time... she shouldn't have been too surprised. They reached the winding underground tunnel that led to the brick wall that hid the Ladder from prying eyes, and Marchosias turned to Aissa.

"All right, little lady. Your blood, if you please."

Aissa was tense, but she took out a small pocketknife and opened it. She lowered the blade to her palm and bit her bottom lip as she pressed down. Blood welled around the point, and Riley felt a surge of fear at the sight.

"Wait. Aissa, I can't ask you to do this..."

"It's done." Aissa stepped forward, blood pooling in her cupped hand. "Now what? I just... touch the wall?"

"Yes."

She turned her hand around and pressed it to the bricks. The floor underneath their feet seemed to inhale, rising and then slowly falling like the bedrock was just a plank on a becalmed sea. Aissa's shoulders hunched and she dropped her head. "I can't... move."

The mortar holding the bricks together began to glow, and Zerachiel put her arms around Aissa's waist. She forced her away from the wall, and Aissa cried out as her hand was forced away from the brick. Riley saw that the entire surface of her palm was bloody, and the palm-print she'd left behind on the wall was pulsing with life. The bricks began to fall, and Light poured from the other side.

"This is it," Marchosias said. "Are you prepared, Detective?"

Riley breathed deeply, nodded, and stepped forward. There was just enough room for her to slip through, and she paused at the threshold. Bricks continued to fall around her as she turned to face the odd trio behind her. Zerachiel stood and... her face softened. She looked human, and she looked terrified.

"Caitlin. Nice to see you one more time." She squinted into the light coming from the hole in the wall. "I know what you're going to suggest, but it won't work. It would tear you apart."

"Riley..."

"I know. I love you, too. Thanks for looking out for me all these years. I wouldn't have lasted this long without you."

Priest began crying. Marchosias looked away. Riley felt warm, and then she felt herself being drawn backward. She imagined herself on a cliff and letting gravity tug at her hands and shoulders. She closed her eyes and let the Light take her. No. That's not accurate. It enveloped her. It filled the space between her cells, entering through her pores, making her part of it. Her wounds became hollow points that were filled with light and made whole again. The press of air all around her and the weight of gravity pushing down on her faded, and she

fell

down

and opened her eyes. She was in a forest of evergreens, their bows turned blue in the darkness. It was the dark of a moonless night, tinted by the lights hidden by each trees trunk. The trees were evenly spaced, far too uniform to be natural. She looked down at herself and saw that her clothes had been replaced by a formless tunic and baggy trousers that hid the shape of her legs. She lifted her hands and was staring at them when the man stepped out of the trees behind her.

She somehow saw him without turning, looked up and suddenly realized she was facing the opposite direction. She fought the vertigo and focused on the new arrival.

He was naked, but his body was smooth and formless. He was neither handsome nor ugly, nothing at all remarkable about him. He stared at her, as if she had knocked on the door and he was waiting to see what she was selling.

"Hi."

He smiled slightly. "Hello."

"Are you God?"

His smile widened a little. "No."

"Where is this place?"

"Home."

"Can you say more than one word at a time?"

"Yes."

Riley laughed. It had been a long time since she'd done it, and the muscles felt odd to her as they moved. "Well, that's good to know, Ken Doll. Am I dead?"

"No."

"But I'm not alive."

He considered it and then shook his head. "No."

"Purgatory?"

"If you like."

"Hey, now we're getting somewhere." She stepped forward. "I'm here to make a deal."

His smile was solid, unmoving, as if it had been carved onto his face. As a matter of fact, he looked a little wooden. If she hadn't seen his lips move when he spoke, she would have thought he was a marionette.

She had seen his lips move... right? Of course she had...

"You have nothing with which to barter. What could you offer to anyone on this plane? Everything you have is granted to you by us."

"I don't know. I'll give whatever you want in exchange~"

"For Gillian Hunt."

Riley nodded. "She didn't... she shouldn't have died the way she did."

Ken Doll began to walk, and Riley followed him. "A woman with three children looks at her cellular phone a moment before stepping off a curb, and she is killed by a man who was drowsing behind the wheel of his vehicle. Does she deserve to die in that manner? Does the man deserve the guilt of knowing he has killed a fellow human being? A light has been extinguished. Is Gillian more important than the mother?"

"Yes. To me, yes."

"What do you have to offer in return?"

"This again. I get a chance to end the war, but it costs me Gillian. Now I have to ask what I'd be willing to give up to have her back? Anything."

Ken Doll tilted his head to the side. "Suppose the price I ask is steep."

"She's worth it."

"The city you've called your home since birth, where you were raped and violated in so many countless ways. Would you have it wiped off the map, and everyone residing there killed with it, if you and Gillian Hunt were allowed to return to the land of life?"

"No. If that's the price, then just let me die. I'll find her on this side."

He stared at her for another moment and then nodded. "One life is not worth a city. But there must be balance." He stepped around a tree and looked up toward the peak. "Each tree represents a life. The branches are lives touched by the person whose life gives the tree formed. Gillian Hunt had a wide and vast tree. Yours, Riley... yours put it to shame. You have touched so many lives, changed the course of so many events. Do you know how many people are alive today who would have died without your intervention?"

Riley shrugged.

"Four million, eight hundred twenty-one thousand, four hundred and twenty-seven."

"That's... not possible."

"A life touches a life, touches a life... you're a police officer and a champion. It's a bit on the high side, to be sure. But you have caused many ripples and those ripples have made waves. Through your action or inaction, unbeknownst to you or them, you have altered the course of many lives. Do you know how many lives you have ended?"

"Don't."

He took pity on her. "I can't bring Gillian back. She was destined to die that day. The circumstances don't allow any leniency. No one with foreknowledge was willing to step in and change the course of events. With the course of history set, there is no way for Gillian to survive that day. But perhaps if the events of the day were changed..."

Riley tensed. "Changed how?"

"Someone with the knowledge of what was to happen and the will to change it. If someone like that had been there, Gillian may well have had a chance."

"Can you do that? Can you... give me the information? Send it to me in a dream, or~"

He smiled. "No. But I can do something more. I can give you that day back. Time folds, and I can deposit you on that day with full knowledge of what is to come. Your present-time self will still be there, so you should proceed cautiously~"

"Yes. Send me back. Just give me a chance to be there."

He held up a hand, showing her the unlined palm. "Balance is necessary, Riley Parra. If Gillian survives, if you change the course of her destiny, there will be unrest. Balance must be preserved at all costs."

Riley closed her eyes and took a deep breath. When she opened her eyes again, she made a deal.

Riley stopped walking.

Where was she walking to? Or from, for that matter? She stood in the middle of the street and turned in a slow circle, trying to get her bearings. She smelled the air and discovered it was clean. The air was fresh for the first time in... two years. The realization dawned on her just as she saw the El rumbled along tracks overhead. The train was running. The tracks were still standing, and the fires were out. Her heart crashed against her ribs as if it was trying to escape, and she fumbled in her pockets. She needed a gun, a knife, a phone, anything she could use. She came up empty. Her hands were fixed, however, and she felt better than she had in ages. The wound in her side was gone, and she wore a plain white T-shirt over blue jeans. Her shoes looked like they were about to fall apart, and she realized she had been dressed by the angel-demon-ghost or whatever it had been.

She started running. She had no idea how much time she had, but she could sense it was running out. How? The word bounced around her brain, the only syllable worth focusing on. How could she save Gillian? She'd wasted two years hoping for this exact moment, but now that it was here, she had no idea how to go about it. She felt nauseated, but she forced herself to keep moving. Her mind filled with people she could call for help, but she discarded them all immediately. Kenzie and Chelsea would ask too many questions. Priest would help, but Riley wanted to keep her out of it. She didn't want anyone to know what was happening, what had been averted. She didn't want Gillian to know how close to death she had come, afraid it would make her flee again even if she did survive.

That left one option.

There was something ominous about the glow coming from the windows of Marchosias' building. Sickly and yellow, it looked like an oven on its last legs, boiling and unevenly burning everything inside until they were inedible black husks. Riley felt the eyes of demons on her as she entered the foyer, and the demons themselves appeared as she crossed toward the stairs.

She'd nearly died here, eons ago.

She climbed the stairs, hounded by demons that snarled and stretched for her without actually making contact. They could have swarmed her; she was on their territory. She was willing to take the risk they would be too stunned by her appearance to do much of anything, and she was rewarded by their curiosity.

Marchosias was in his office, apparently waiting for her. He turned away from the window as if she was late to an appointment. He waved off someone behind her; Riley didn't bother to see what it had been. He stopped in front of her, arms crossing his chest, and he stared into her eyes for a long moment.

"Something happened."

"Yes."

"Something very bad."

Riley swallowed. "Lark Siskin is going to take matters into her own hands and kill Gillian."

Marchosias shook his head. "That was her plan, but I amended it."

"She let you think she agreed. She's sent a demon to kill Gillian in..." She scanned for a clock and spotted it on the mantle. "In two hours."

He tightened his jaw. "No. I made it clear~"

"Your host is named Anthony Pollock."

For the first time, she saw true fear and confusion on his face. The name had come up randomly as they were walking to the precinct for their rendezvous with Aissa.

"I used to walk down here all the time. Well, not me. My host."

"You remember stuff from his life?"

"Of course. It's all there, it's just dull for the most part. I'm Anthony Pollock, I like baseball and baked beans. I swear, my girlfriend likes it when I hit her. You know. Blah, blah, blah. Same old story every time."

"Who told you that name?"

"You did. Two years from now. You want to win, Marchosias. You don't want to crush us because Siskin killed Gillian. That's why you helped us open the Ladder."

Marchosias bared his teeth and turned away from her.

"Come on, Mark. You know she's a loose cannon. You know what I'm saying is the truth. Why the hell would I come here if it wasn't? I'm smarter than that. I'd come up with a better story if I was trying to fool you."

He walked to the fireplace, then turned and walked back to her. "What do you need from me? What do you possibly expect me to do?"

"I just need you to show Lark Siskin which one of you is in charge. I know where Gillian was... where she's *going to be* attacked, and I can get there to stop her. But I need you to call me with the details. Who, when..."

Marchosias rubbed his eyes. "I can't believe I'm even contemplating this..."

"Believe it, Marchosias. You're my last chance at saving my wife. And this is your last chance to fight the war you want."

"If I help you, I can never call in the favor. I can never hold it over your head that I helped you in this hour of need."

"No."

"So you expect me to do this out of the kindness of my heart."

Riley's hopes sank. She was prepared to offer him whatever he wanted when he turned and walked back to his desk.

"Go. I'll call you when I have the information."

"You'll help?" She actually couldn't believe it was happening.

"Go."

"Marchosias... I..."

He spun on her. "You talked me into it, and you're damn close to talking me out of it again. Leave. Now."

Riley left the office. Demons lined the stairs and whispered to her as she passed, but she had no time to waste on them. She rushed past the snarling creatures and out into the pre-dawn air. She heard sirens, trash trucks, evidence of life going on as it had before, and she started running. She could feel her heartbeat in her temples, in her throat, and she felt like it was going to explode. Warnings flashed in her mind, telling her to take a rest, but she couldn't.

Here, at this moment, Gillian was alive.

She had to make sure she stayed that way.

The police station was never really closed, but there were slow periods when it was hard to tell the difference. Riley felt like she was walking through a waking dream, passing rooms full of people and standing in well-lit hallways. People passed her and offered greetings, or expressed surprise at seeing her so early in the morning, and she accepted their comments with terse replies and quick nods of her head. She didn't have time for pleasantries. She took the stairs to the morgue and let herself in. She hadn't been back since Gillian's death, and she wouldn't let herself look at the table where, if she failed, the body would be laid out. Instead, she went into the office and emptied the drawers of ink pens, markers, Sharpies... anything that could make marks.

She started at the doors. She had made thousands of devil's traps in the past two years, a skill she learned with The Cell and honed on the battlefield of her own making. She surrounded the doors with small marks, spreading them out so they would have maximum efficiency. Sweat dripped down the sides of her face, and she felt it in the small of her back as she stood on a chair to draw across the top of the door frame.

Both entrances were covered when the office phone rang. She ran to it and answered with an exhaled, "This is Riley Parra."

"The demons sent for Dr. Hunt are named Alastor and Saleos. They will arrive at the morgue in twelve minutes." Riley looked at the clock on the wall. "Our cooperation ends here, Detective Parra."

"Yes. Marchosias... thank you."

She heard silence on the other end and assumed he had hung up, but then he said, "The killer responsible for your sister officer's death will be brought to justice later today. Siskin needed to be punished."

"Thank you."

"I don't know what you're talking about." The phone clicked in her ear, and Riley looked at the clock again. Twelve minutes. Eleven now... She looked at her marks. The trap was done. All she had to do was wait. She had time to kill. She looked at the phone and dialed a number before she could talk herself out of it. She pressed the receiver to her ear hard enough to hurt as she heard the familiar buzz.

"Hello?"

"It's me."

"Riley?" A pause. "That's... I thought the call was coming from work."

"Oh. I... c-called there, because I thought you might already be there. So they must have forwarded the call to your cell."

"Oh." Her tone turned playful. "Well, either way, I thought I told you to go back to bed."

Riley closed her eyes. Just hearing her voice made everything worth it. The pain and anguish she'd gone through over the last two years. She pressed her hand against her eyes and, when she spoke, her voice cracked. "Gillian."

"Hon? Everything okay?"

"Yeah. I just... wanted... to..."

"Riley, you sound really odd."

"I'm just still half-asleep. That's all." She wiped her eyes. "I realized we didn't say goodbye. When you left this morning, I didn't say goodbye to you. I couldn't sleep."

Gillian laughed. "Aw, you romantic. But... to be honest, Riley... I don't like saying goodbye to you. When we say goodbye, it's like closing a door. Ending a chapter. When we're apart, it's like we're still together in a way. Silly, huh?"

"No. You were always with me."

"When?"

"Nothing. It's..." She shook her head. "Where are you?"

"Just a few blocks away. I could come back home..."

Riley blinked back the tears. "You know what? Please. Come home. Crawl into bed, wake me up, and make love to me. Make sure I treat you right. Just don't... don't go into work today, okay?"

Gillian laughed, and Riley heard the squeal of the el train's brakes in the background. "As amazing as that sounds, babe, there is just too much work to put off. We have all those bodies from the club murder~"

"Right. I know." She inhaled and looked at the clock. "How about this? Bring me breakfast. We'll have a proper morning together."

"What brought all this on?"

Riley considered lies, and then said, "I had a dream you died. That I lost you, and I woke up and you were gone. I just need to see you. I need to hold you, and tell you I love you."

"Baby." It was soft, whispered, and it reminded Riley of when Gillian whispered it just after climax. She choked back a sob, but Gillian still heard it. "I'm coming home."

"I love you, Jill."

"I love you, too, Riley."

She hung up without saying goodbye, but she felt like a weight had been lifted off her shoulders. She walked back into the morgue and stood among the stainless steel surfaces. The clock on the wall ticked, painfully slow, counting down. Down.

She heard footsteps in the hall and moved to where she couldn't be seen from the door. Seconds later, the doors opened and someone cautiously scanned the room.

"Hello-o-o. Anybody in here?" He waited. "Coast is clear. Come on."

Two men entered. They were taller than Riley, broader in the shoulder, and wore military style linen shirts with khakis. They looked like refugees from a GAP ad. The one in the lead stopped and turned his head slightly. "Hold up. Something isn't right..."

"Which one of you is Alice, and which one is Sally?"

They spun to face her. "The name is Alastor," the big blonde one said.

"I like Alice better." She picked up the bone saw and waved the circular blade at them. "Which one of you was going to hold down my wife, and which one was going to rape her?"

The smaller black-haired demon turned and ran for the door. He reached it only to be thrown backward off his feet. He hit the ground hard enough to break bones in a normal person, tumbling ass over head until he came to a stop against the back wall. Riley tossed the bone saw to her other hand, teasing the switch with her thumb.

"I've spent the past two years coming up with all kinds of great ways to trap and kill demons. Some of them are more fun than others. I call this one the Roach Motel. Demons come in, but they can't get out."

"You're making a mistake, bitch."

Riley shook her head. "No, you made the mistake. I'm just making things right."

The demon drew first blood, but it was a mosquito bite compared to Riley's reprisal. She swung the spinning blade and took a chunk out of his arm. The demon howled and shouted for his friend to join the fray. Rather than retreating, Riley threw her weight against her attacker and threw him off balance. They went down together, and Riley let her arm swing to one side with the bone saw as ballast. When they were horizontal, she brought it back up and let the blade tear into the meaty part of his side.

"You know what the best part of the roach motel is? Poison." She looked into his enraged eyes and spoke in a sing-song voice. "*Illos eccerat vostrum...*"

The demon thrown by the security at the door, Sally, suddenly began to howl. Alice, the demon on top of her, snarled and tightened closed his fist around her throat. "Stop... speaking..."

"*Puteramus excelleo. Sanctistis an praecisti vostrumi.*" She could hear Sally screaming, and the air to her right was a mist of black fog and smoke. It wasn't an exorcism; it was nothing that kind. She had found a way to make human flesh poisonous to a demon's presence while making it impossible for the demon to expel itself from the host. He was becoming allergic to his own skin.

Alice's eyes were bloody, and smoke rose from his mouth when he spoke. "Stop it. Reverse it. Now." The last word was a growl like stone against stone, inhuman.

Riley pressed the bone saw against him, burying it deeper into his skin. He howled and she saw blood on his gums. He focused on her again, his face losing what was left of its humanity as he looked down at her.

"You think you're the only one with traps? We've known how to kill your kind for eons." He put his hand over her chest and she felt it penetrating the cloth and skin. "Reverse it."

Riley pulled the saw back and shoved him away from her. He fell to the side, bloody and trembling with the force of her curse. She moved the saw to her other hand and dropped down, thrusting it forward like a sword. He tried to avoid it, but the saw hit the front of his pants and destroyed everything underneath.

"Rapist bastard," she growled.

Sally pounced on her from behind, howling like an animal. He couldn't have had much sense left, but he had enough. He shoved his hand into Riley's side and she cried out in agony as he grabbed whatever was convenient and pulled it out of her. Riley hit her knees, blood pouring from her side as she turned and weakly thrust the saw up under Sally's chin. Demon blood sprayed, and he collapsed to one side.

Riley looked at the organ he'd pulled out of her but, try as she might, she couldn't identify it. She was woozy, but she took the time to check both demons to make sure they were dead. Husks. Like charcoal shaped into human bodies. She knew she was in shock, but she found the gauze and wrapped it around herself to close the wound and stop the bleeding. She didn't want Gillian to walk in and find her dead on the ground. Even if the real Riley, the Riley from this timeline, was still alive, the sight would be too horrible.

The walk to the back stairs seemed to take days. Her mind was unfocused. She weaved from one side of the staircase to the other, and she left bloody splotches on the paint in her wake. She was dripping. Her body was pitched forward when she reached the bottom of the stairs, and she lost her balance. The sidewalk came up at her quickly and she braced for impact... but it never came. She opened her eyes and stared at it, then followed the arms up to the woman who had caught her.

"Oh. You."

Priest said, "Who are you?"

Riley understood. Guardian angels always knew where their charge was. Priest probably woke up and realized there were two Rileys in town. One was safe in bed, the other... She smiled and let Priest support her.

"I'm Riley. I need... to tell you something very important, Cait. But I think the demon hurt me too badly."

"Demon? What demon?"

"I called him Sally." Riley snorted and then cried out at the pain in her side. "I don't need you... to fix me... completely. Just... fifteen minutes. Just give me fifteen minutes, Caitlin. It's important. I have to tell you. You have to warn her."

Priest put her hand over Riley's side, and there was an instant sense of warmth and relief from the spot. Riley inhaled and sighed. The pain was by no means obliterated, but it was enough of a balm that she could speak without pain.

"Thank you. We need to go somewhere private. I have a story that's... pretty... long. But you have to hear it."

Priest nodded. "Okay. I'll take you somewhere, Riley."

Riley slumped against Priest. "Wake me when we get there." She felt unbelievably weak, and she hoped she was able to say everything that needed to be said before she died.

"So... are you *complaining?*"

Riley laughed. "God, no. I just wish I remembered making the phone call."

Gillian sat up and kissed her wife. They were both still sweaty from the impromptu lovemaking that had taken precedence over breakfast. Riley brushed both hands through Gillian's hair, still amazed at how strange the morning had been. Gillian rushes back in, pale with worry, holding Riley and telling her that it was all okay and it had just been a dream. Then realizing that Riley had been fast asleep and had no idea what she was talking about.

"I think we can just chalk it up to the fact we live in a very weird city and leave it at that. Maybe I was sending you psychic communications."

"Hmm. Maybe." She kissed Riley and pushed herself up. She sat on her feet, hands on her thighs, the blankets wrapped around her waist. "So you don't want me to stay and cuddle with you all day?"

"Want? Hell yes. But I know you need to be at work. And so do I." She sighed. "We need to bring down Siskin's people. I know that one aide of hers was involved, I just have to prove it."

"You will." She stroked Riley's hair. "You defeated Gail Finney. You won the war once, you can do it again."

Riley smiled. "Confidence. I like that in a woman."

Gillian leaned in and kissed both corners of Riley's mouth. "I'll always come running when you call me. You know that. Right?"

"I do. Go on... shower. I'll make some coffee."

Gillian clambered out of bed, twisting her leg to get it free from the blankets. "Not bad, for a do-over."

"Do-over?"

"Yeah. I got out of bed, showered, and left, and then I came back. It's like I got a chance to start the day over."

Riley said, "Want to try best out of three? My legs are a little sore, but I think we can try a few positons~"

Gillian snapped her fingers. "Kitchen. Coffee." She winked as the bathroom door closed, and Riley shrugged into a dress shirt as she opened the bedroom door. She took one step and nearly slammed into Priest.

"God! Damn it, Cait. Don't do that! Announce yourself or something."

"You were engaged~"

Riley waved her hands. "Just... stop." She saw that Priest had been crying. "What happened? What's going on?"

"We have to talk. Privately."

Riley was suddenly very cold. "Tell me now."

"No. You specifically said not to say anything where Gillian could hear."

Riley frowned. "What do you mean 'I said'?"

"Get dressed, Riley. We have to talk."

They were sitting in Riley's car outside the building, having left a hastily-scrawled note for Gillian explaining they had to do some 'case work' but she would be back in a few minutes. Once they were alone, Priest shared the story she'd heard from the other Riley. When she got to the part about what happened to Gillian, Riley opened the door and dry-heaved onto the street until she was capable of hearing the rest. She held the steering wheel in a vice grip, her knuckles whitening as Priest explained about Kenzie, Chelsea, the world gone mad. Finally, she got to the end of her story where Riley accessed the Ladder and was given the opportunity to make amends.

"That's who called Gillian this morning."

"I assume, yes."

Riley was cold, trembling, and she tried to calm herself. So close. So close to tragedy, to disaster, to utter devastation. She didn't want to move for fear of shattering something precious. Finally Priest broke the silence.

"There's something else."

"The price."

"Yes. How did you know?"

"Oh, there's always a fucking price with you people. What was it this time?"

Priest took a breath and let it out slowly. "You... the other you... changed fate today. Gillian didn't die as scheduled, and she will most likely live a very long time as a result. Balance had to be restored, so Riley, the other~"

"Otheriley," Riley said.

"Yes. Otheriley made a deal. If she succeeded in changing Gillian's scheduled death, then she offered to make hers concrete."

Riley frowned. "What does that mean?"

"In the other timeline, two years from now, Riley Parra stepped into the Ladder and vanished. She ended her timeline on that day. When she died this morning, she was thirty-eight years, seven months, three days and four hours old. Her agreement was that no matter what she changed by coming back, that would be permanent."

Riley stared out the windshield. "So what does that mean?"

Priest finally let her tears fall. "It means that in recompense for saving Gillian, you will only live to be thirty-eight years, seven months~"

"Two years from now," Riley interrupted.

"Yes," Priest said softly. "You have two years left."

Riley looked at her left hand, the ring there, and thought about Gillian's smile as the bathroom door had closed on her.

"Two years." Riley thought about it and then nodded. "Yes."

"Yes what?" Priest asked.

"Yes. Gillian was going to die this morning. If I stopped that, if I have to die in two years in order to keep that from happening then... yes." She smiled sadly. "It's worth it."

Priest covered Riley's hand with her own, and Riley linked their fingers. Two years.

She was going to have to make them count.

About the Author

Geonn Cannon is the author of over fifty novels, including the Riley Parra series which was adapted into an Emmy-nominated webseries by Tello Films. He's also written two tie-in novels for the television series Stargate SG-1. He was the first male author to win a Golden Crown Literary Society Award for his novel *Gemini*, and he won a second for *Dogs of War*. Information about his other works and an archive of free stories can be found online at geonncannon.com.

Prize Fighter

Six years ago, professional boxer Max "Wrecker" Reszke lost control in the ring. One moment of blind rage put her opponent into a coma from which she never woke. Though cleared of any criminal charges, Max hangs up her gloves and swears that she'll never risk losing control like that again.

Until one night, a chance encounter in an alley, a damsel in distress. Max leaps into action and saves the stranger. She soon learns that the woman she saved is actress Renee Lamar. Renee, anxious and paranoid about security, offers to reward Max's chivalry with a job as her bodyguard.

Max has nothing to lose by agreeing, but soon discovers Renee might be her own worst enemy. Half a decade after leaving the ring, Max faces a new fight that can't be won with fists.

Into the Furnace

Kelly Lake comes from a family of firefighters, but she still had to prove herself to her brothers and her father before they accepted her as one of their own. On her days off she tends bar at the firehouse hangout across the street and spends time trying to breathe life into a relationship she knows is doomed. Her life is cruising along just fine until the day her squad responds to a horrific arson that will cause her carefully-orchestrated balancing act to come falling down around her. The blaze claims the lives of eleven people, half of them children, and the fire department takes the blame.

Kelly soon finds herself at the center of a media firestorm when she inadvertently becomes the poster girl for the incident. The trauma of the fire is compounded by her personal house of cards collapsing. Her relationship begins showing its cracks at the same time long-buried family secrets rear their ugly heads. Attacked from all angles, Kelly starts thinking the only place she'll be safe is running headlong into the furnace.

"Easily one of the best samplings of queer fiction I've had the pleasure to read in a very long time. I could not recommend it more, and sincerely hope that upon its release in November Into the Furnace will light the same fire in each of your hearts that it has already lit in mine." - Tabitha Beth, The Rainbow Hub.